A MOMENT TO TREASURE

Thomas pulled off his shirt and sat bare shouldered on the garden bench, his back to her. Arianna saw the smooth, hard muscles of his back and shoulders. How can I do this? she wanted to say. How can I touch you, with you half-naked before me, and not put my arms around you and tell you how much I want you? Thomas, Thomas, my love.

She reached out and lifted a thick lock of golden hair off the back of his neck. As she did, her fingers brushed against the soft skin of his nape. She wanted to press her lips there. Instead, she opened the scissors and began to cut.

At last she was finished.

"You deserve a reward for such a fine job," Thomas said teasingly, and he leaned forward and kissed her lips, very quickly. He kissed her a second time, not so quickly, and Arianna felt all the longing she had locked away rising up.

He had not put his arms around her, he had made no move to touch her with more than his mouth, but that was enough. His bare shoulders were there, she could sense their sun-warmed strength, and she wanted to put her hands on them. Instead, she clenched her fingers tightly together in her lap. But her lips moved under his, wanting the richness of emotion he had to offer, accepting it fo⋯ ⋯ ⋯ his little moment . . .

CASTLE of the HEART

FLORA M. SPEER

PINNACLE BOOKS
WINDSOR PUBLISHING CORP.

PINNACLE BOOKS

are published by

Windsor Publishing Corp.
475 Park Avenue South
New York, NY 10016

First printing: November, 1990

Printed in the United States of America

For Beth and Kevin
and Mary and Anne
who know all
about love

"Moss grows on the castles of my heart as soon as they are built, but it takes some time for them to fall into ruin."

Gustave Flaubert

Author's Note:

Afoncaer, Tynant, and the Welsh lands immediately surrounding them are all completely imaginary, as are all the characters in this story except the following: King Henry I of England, Queen Matilda, their children William and Richard, Countess Matilda of Perche, the Earl of Chester, his wife, and his brother, Sir Ottuel.

In the early twelfth century, calendars had not yet been standardized, and there were various dates for the new year. In the interests of simplicity, I have used modern dates throughout, and have begun each new year on January 1.

The herbal remedies concocted and used by Meredith and Arianna reflect medieval knowledge and use of these plants as described in historical accounts and in herbal treatises of that period.

Prologue

Reynaud

I have returned to Afoncaer. When I left so many years ago, I thought I would never see it again, but here I am, once more installed in my old place in the tower keep. My room has become a library, lined with shelves to hold my books and scrolls, and fitted with a large table for writing and a thick-cushioned chair for my damaged body. I am comfortable here. My chamber is warmed by two charcoal braziers in the winter, and lit by all the fine wax candles I need. And I have friendship . . .

Of the accident which resulted in my crippling, and how I came to be here, I shall write more later, as I recount the vile intrigues which nearly led to the loss of this castle. I have questioned most of those involved, listening to several conflicting versions of the story, and I think I have come as close to the truth as any mortal man can. Lady Isabel was the instigator. I should have expected that, knowing her wicked character. And then the Welsh, working against us as always, did their best to destroy this Norman stronghold which stands so boldly within their border. I believe I have correctly unraveled the lies and half-truths of that time of peril. Selene, that beautiful, haunted creature, Isabel's tool, also did her part to betray Afoncaer. She avoided me, but I watched her, and it was not hard to guess what she had done. I think Guy suspected her, too, but, like myself, he kept silent for Thomas's sake.

It is a long and shocking story, but these volumes are a place for truth. I will tell all. And so I continue the work I began nearly a quarter of a century ago, the true and complete history of Afoncaer .

Part I

The Mothers
A.D. 1115

Chapter 1

Brittany
August, A.D. 1115

"Isabel, what joy it is to see you again after all these years." Lady Aloise stood in the great hall of her husband's castle, keeping her smile carefully in place while she greeted her old friend, and silently praising heaven that Sir Valaire was safely in England at the court of King Henry I. Not that that generous man would have grudged his wife the pleasure of a visit from Isabel, even though gossip still clung to Isabel's name after almost ten years. No, it was not the memory of the old scandalous story of passion and aborted ambition that narrowed Aloise's eyes as she regarded Isabel. It was rather Isabel's looks. Aloise ruefully acknowledged the contrast between them. Her own dark hair was heavily streaked with silver, there were lines about her eyes, and her waist had expanded over the years into a thickness inevitable for the mother of six children. Isabel, on the other hand, was as blonde, rosy-complexioned, and willowy as ever. Knowing her husband's wandering eye, Aloise was thankful Sir Valaire was absent. But how, she wondered, had Isabel done the nearly impossible and kept her beauty so long, and while in exile, too?

Isabel glided gracefully through the main portal and across the stone-flagged floor, her blue summer cloak floating out behind her in soft, elegant folds. She held out both hands, smiling the dazzling smile Aloise remembered so well.

"Aloise, my dear, it has been so very long. How good it was of you to invite me, how kind to a grieving widow." The sweet, musical voice was unchanged with time, the deep blue eyes as clear and innocent as they had been when Isabel was a girl of fourteen and a new bride, a stranger at the English court, with Aloise her only friend. Aloise sighed. A woman of thirty-nine should look, and sound, her age. Aloise, at forty-one, certainly did.

The two women embraced.

"I'm glad you have come," Aloise said, allowing only a slight note of insincerity to creep into her voice. The invitation had not been entirely her idea. Isabel had hinted in the letter announcing her widowhood, and when Aloise had not responded, Isabel had hinted again, more broadly, until Aloise, her curiosity piqued, had relented and asked Isabel to visit for one month. Life was boring when Sir Valaire was away. Any diversion was welcome, and while Isabel might sometimes be treacherous, she was never dull.

"We have so much to talk about, so much gossip to catch up on." Isabel's eyes sparkled. "I am eager to meet your daughter again. Selene, isn't that her name? I remember seeing her when she was only a few months old, and she was such a dear little thing. How long ago that seems. She must be fifteen now. You see, I have learned to count during my years in exile, so I know she's quite grown-up, and I expect she's a beauty, like her mother. You look startled. Did you think I had forgotten her?''

Isabel smiled again, and Aloise felt a little chill, the faintest breath of alarm. Isabel had never cared about babies or children. On the contrary, she had ignored Selene most pointedly when she had seen her as an infant. Nor had Isabel ever shown even the slightest concern for her own son Thomas. Indeed, she had willingly allowed him to be used as a hostage by his stepfather. What could she possibly want with Selene?

"Come to the solar," Aloise said, drawing Isabel's arm through hers. "It is sunny there, and much more quiet than this noisy great hall. We can talk. I'll have refreshments brought to us. You must tell me about your journey."

She led the way to the narrow stone steps and up their curving height, heading for the second-floor solar, and as she went, Aloise thought about Isabel's past, and her odd interest in Selene.

Isabel, Aloise recalled, had borne only one child, Thomas, to her first husband, Baron Lionel of Afoncaer, and no children at all to Walter fitz Alan, her second spouse. And that, Aloise thought irrelevantly, would explain Isabel's still-slim waistline. Constant childbearing quickly ruined a woman's figure, as she herself had experienced. With an effort of will unusual for her, Aloise made herself dismiss her frivolous concern with Isabel's appearance and think of more serious affairs.

It was just as well Isabel had had no other children, considering Walter fitz Alan's disgrace and subsequent exile. It had been a breathtaking piece of treachery, that attempt by Walter to secure the

Welsh border castle of Afoncaer for himself by using young Thomas as hostage. Aloise had always suspected that Isabel had had a hand in the plotting. But whoever had devised the plan, it had failed, and Baron Guy of Afoncaer, Isabel's former brother-in-law, had, with King Henry's permission, unknighted Walter and sent the two culprits away from Wales into permanent exile. They had lived in seclusion in Brittany ever since, existing on the charity of Walter's elder brother, Sir Baldwin. Now Walter was dead, and Isabel had come to see her old friend. Aloise wondered uneasily just what the real purpose of her visit might be.

It did not take Aloise long to discover why Isabel had come. Isabel was eager to tell her. She wanted a marriage arranged between her son Thomas and Aloise's daughter Selene, and she expected Aloise to cajole Sir Valaire into proposing it to Guy of Afoncaer.

"Do you think that if my daughter marries your son, you will be allowed to return to England?" Aloise asked. "I must speak truly, Isabel, and speaking truly, I tell you I do not believe that will ever happen. King Henry has a long memory. He has neither forgotten nor forgiven what you and Walter did on the Welsh border, and even if he should give you permission to go to England, you may be certain Baron Guy of Afoncaer would use all the weight of his friendship with the king to prevent your return. Lord Guy is a powerful man."

"Guy." Isabel's lip curled scornfully. "That cold-blooded, miserly man kept me a prisoner. Ah,

Aloise, you will know how mistreated I have been. I will tell you the story, all of it."

Which she did, and Aloise sat fascinated for an hour, listening intently to a version of those long-ago events at Afoncaer very different from the tale she had heard at court. Aloise knew and respected Lord Guy, and also knew Isabel well enough to be able to sift fact from invention and embroidery. By the time Isabel had finished speaking, Aloise had a very good idea as to how much Isabel herself had had to do with the treachery at Afoncaer, and she wished she had never invited Isabel to visit.

"Now you must admit," Isabel said at last, "that this idea of mine, that Thomas and Selene should wed, is a very good one. That Saxon peasant wench Guy married has given him only a daughter, so Thomas is still heir to Afoncaer, and to all of Guy's properties in England as well. It would be a fine match for Selene."

"It would appear to be," Aloise said cautiously, reminding herself that Thomas of Afoncaer was not tainted with any of the scandal that had surrounded his parents and his stepfather. The boy had spent his youth as a page in the household of that Henry who was now king of England, and then had been sent to Afoncaer, where he had remained. He must be close to an age for knighting by now. "How old is Thomas?"

"He will be twenty-three in June."

"And still not wed or betrothed?" Aloise's tone hinted at some defect in the proposed bridegroom.

"It is Thomas's own doing," Isabel said quickly. "I have been told he has spent the last two years at Llangwilym Abbey, near Afoncaer. It seems he seriously considered entering the Church, but later

17

realized his duty lay with Guy, as Guy's heir. So the sole result of his devotion is that he learned to read and write while at Llangwilym. He'll have small use for such skills when he's the baron! I have learned he will be knighted by the king himself this Christmastide. It would be a marvellous opportunity for a betrothal, to be announced immediately after the knighting."

"Hmm." Aloise was thinking hard. She decided to be blunt. "I know you well, Isabel, even after so many years' separation. You would never propose such an arrangement unless there was some prize for yourself in it. If you cannot hope to return to England, then what is your reward?"

"Why, simply the joy of knowing my beloved son is well-matched to a suitable girl."

"Isabel." Aloise's tone clearly conveyed how little she believed that statement.

"Oh, very well. You are my only friend, Aloise. I may as well tell you the truth."

"I wish you would."

"It's Baldwin, Walter's brother. He barely tolerated me while Walter was alive. He would not speak to me at all if he could possibly avoid it. It was only Baldwin's sense of family responsibility that made him allow us to live in that dreary little lodge tucked away in a desolate corner of his land—no society, no music, never a new gown, no one to talk to save Walter, and *he* was not the best of companions, no, all he could do was lament his ill fortune and the passion he once had for me that had led him to betray his honor, as though it were all my fault." Isabel paused for breath.

"Tell me about Baldwin," Aloise urged, feeling that there lay the answer to her question.

"Baldwin says he is tired of the burden of my

presence, and he wants me to retire to a convent. He says any widow of discretion and good will would have suggested this recourse herself as soon as her husband died. Since I now have no land or income of my own on which to live, I cannot long refuse to do his bidding."

"You do not want to go." Aloise could imagine nothing more unlikely than Isabel retired to a convent.

"What I want," Isabel said, "is to be granted a small establishment here in Brittany, and the income with which to maintain it. Once independent of that dreadful Baldwin I would live quietly and cause trouble to no one. It could be arranged as part of the marriage contract. Such grants to widowed parents are not unusual, and Sir Valaire would of course hold the property in his name. Oh, Aloise, please say you will speak to him. I'm sure he would agree if you begged him prettily. I remember how it was in the old days, how besotted with you he was. Surely you still have some influence over him."

Aloise momentarily forgot her mistrust of Isabel in the surge of youthful memories her presence had evoked and the pleasure of having an old confidante to talk to.

"Ah, Isabel, before we were wed," she cried, "Valaire loved my wildness and was the most exciting lover I ever had. But he chose to believe he was my only lover, and that I lay with him out of deep affection. I let him think it was so, for I did care for him. I still do. But once we were wed he expected, no, he *demanded*, complete fidelity. The times have changed since we were all at the court of King William Rufus. Then we could do whatever we pleased and no one would care, for the king himself was worse than any of us. Now we have a respectable king who is at least discreet about his affairs, and wives are expected to be faithful and chaste like the queen. It would not be so bad if Valaire were home more, and paid attention to me as he once did. But he is seldom here, and I know he has other women, and I am *bored*. How I long for some delightful intrigue to dispel the tedious propriety now expected of me." Suddenly Aloise was aware of the gleam in Isabel's eyes, that look she remembered all too well, and she shut her mouth firmly. But she had already said too much. She was caught, trapped by her own words. She knew it when Isabel smiled and took her hand. She ought to have been more cautious in her speaking.

"Dear Aloise," Isabel said, both hands folding over her friend's fingers in a comforting gesture that had the opposite effect on Aloise. "Don't you see how perfectly your discontent fits my need? Aid me in this plan of mine, and you will be invited to join Sir Valaire in England for your daughter's wedding. Indeed, you must accompany her on the journey to see to her safety and comfort. Think of it, months at the royal court. New gowns. Entertainments. Great feasts. Handsome young men to flirt with. How I wish I might go, too. But that cannot be," Isabel pronounced, heaving an exaggerated sigh. "You, my dearest friend, must be my emissary, and you will dictate letters to me, telling me all that passes and how my darling son Thomas is, how he has grown, if he resembles his father. Aloise." The slender fingers on Aloise's hand tightened. "Aloise, help me, for the sake of our friendship, and for the good it will do Sir Valaire to be joined with the Baron of Afoncaer in such a union. And for Selene's good, too, of course.''

The problem was, Isabel was right, Aloise realized later, while mulling over Isabel's suggestion in the privacy of her own chamber. A marriage between Selene and Thomas of Afoncaer made excellent sense. Sir Valaire would probably approve of the idea with very little coaxing from his wife, and if Aloise herself did not suggest it to him, she had little doubt that the resourceful Isabel would find a way to do so the next time he came home to Brittany. Aloise did not like one bit the thought of a still-beautiful Isabel teasing Sir Valaire into pleased acquiescence.

As for Baron Guy of Afoncaer, he was on good terms with Sir Valaire, and could have no objection to the offer of Sir Valaire's daughter as wife for his nephew. Selene's dowry was a large chest of gold coins, given to Sir Valaire for that express purpose by his father so the family lands could be passed on undivided to Sir Valaire's eldest son. Baron Guy had lands enough, he did not need more, but those golden coins would be most welcome to buy workmen and material to strengthen the defenses of Afoncaer. Furthermore, Selene would bring to her marriage bed an intangible value, her bloodline. Through her father, Selene was descended from the great Charlemagne himself. Any nobleman would be honored to know his future heirs would mingle that blood with his own. Yes, Baron Guy would almost certainly agree to Valaire's proposal, and Selene would have rank, wealth, and as much honor as any woman of that day might hope for. Better still, Aloise herself would be rid of the strange, difficult daughter she could neither understand nor love, whose pres-

21

ence always made Aloise feel vaguely guilty. Selene's marriage to Thomas of Afoncaer looked on the surface to be an ideal arrangement for all concerned. Why then did Aloise feel there was still more to this proposal than she had been told? Why did Isabel look to her skeptical eyes like a sleek cat poised to pounce upon a large bowl of rich, luscious cream?

"So you are Selene." Isabel's penetrating gaze took in the short, slender figure hovering uncertainly, fingers still on the door latch. Selene meekly bowed her head, and thick wings of straight black hair fell forward, obscuring her pale face, but not before Isabel had noted the delicate features and clear skin. The girl was lovely.

"Come in, child, and close the door. I would speak with you in private." Isabel had not moved from the stone window seat. She pulled the silk cushion at her back into a more comfortable position and then looked out the window with apparent indifference, waiting patiently for Selene to come to her across the lavender-strewn floor of the guest chamber.

The herbs on the floor rustled softly, sending up a faint fragrance, and Selene moved into view again. Out of the corner of one eye, Isabel could see her standing quietly in her plain dark blue woolen gown, hands folded before her. Isabel wanted to establish her own dominant position in this interview, so she let the girl wait a few moments before turning her head to look Selene full in the face. When she did, she met a pair of wide emerald eyes, challenging and scornful, before the girl dropped shadowed lids over their green fire.

22

Isabel, taken aback, said nothing, and Selene spoke first.

"The Lady Aloise has told me of your proposition, madame, that I should marry your son." The voice was surprisingly low-pitched to come out of so small a body, and it was charged with an anger most unsuitable to this occasion. Isabel noted that the girl had said "Lady Aloise," not "my mother."

"You sound as though you do not like the idea. But you must," Isabel said. "You have been raised, as all noble girls are, with the knowledge that one day you will be wed to a man chosen for you by your parents, and that you must obey them. I assure you, my son Thomas is young, handsome, kind-hearted, and in good health. He has a great future before him." Somewhere in the back of Isabel's mind rose the memory of her father saying something remarkably similar to her before her own marriage to Sir Lionel. How disastrously wrong her father had been. Isabel pushed that thought aside. This was different; this was Thomas she was speaking of, and all the information she had been able to garner about him indicated that what she had just told Selene was true.

Selene, though outwardly meek, apparently had a spark of defiance in her. Those remarkable emerald eyes glared at Isabel, and her low voice was husky with emotion when she spoke again.

"I do not wish to marry. I want to become a nun."

"You would be wasted in a convent." Isabel shivered a little, not wholly from the damp draft coming through the imperfectly fitted window beside her. Her own permanent incarceration in a convent was too near a threat for Isabel's comfort. No, this girl would do as Isabel wished. Selene,

23

and therefore Isabel, would remain outside conventual walls. "You are beautiful, and I suspect you are intelligent," Isabel added. "You would be much admired at the English court."

"Beauty is a snare," Selene replied loftily. "And a royal court is a place of deadly temptation to vanity and worldly ambition."

"Ah, yes, I had forgotten that Aloise foolishly sent you to a convent for schooling." Isabel had not forgotten a single piece of the information she had obtained about Selene before choosing her for Thomas's wife, but she wanted to hear what the girl would say next.

"I am not my mother's favorite child," Selene said, her low voice cold with self-control. "I know it, and it matters not at all to me. She was glad to be rid of me, and I happy to leave her domain, where I have never been welcome or at ease. A convent is the proper place for me, madame. I beg you, do not pursue this plan of marriage that you and my mother have concocted."

Isabel digested this a moment. Then she tried another approach. "I suppose you have learned to read and write while in the convent? Well, so can Thomas. He has been trained in an abbey. You two will have much to talk about."

"I do not expect that I will ever speak to your son at all, madame, for I do not intend to marry him—or anyone." Selene's voice held a note of desperation. She seemed to have realized that her plea had been dismissed by Isabel and would probably be equally disregarded by those others who were planning her life's course.

"Sit down, Selene." Isabel waved a hand toward the window seat opposite herself and tried not to laugh at this too-serious girl. Selene obeyed her, cloaking herself once more in the air of meekness with which she hid her frightened, yet still defiant, spirit. Isabel sat appraising her future daughter-in-law, amused and pleased with her. Selene would serve her purposes well.

"The marriage is not yet arranged," Selene said at last, apparently becoming impatient with the silence which Isabel had deliberately let go on and on. "When I see my father again, I will tell him I do not wish to marry. I pray he will listen to me if you and my mother will not."

Isabel shrugged, unconcerned by the threat. She had helped Aloise to dictate the letter to Sir Valaire which suggested that he raise the subject of Selene's marriage to Thomas of Afoncaer. The letter was well on its way to England. Once the arrangements had been made and the contracts drawn up, this child's wishes in the matter would count for nothing. Sir Valaire would never risk offending Baron Guy or his nephew by calling off the wedding arrangements. Meanwhile, she would use her charm on Selene to make her at least a little more agreeable to the idea. It would not do to have a violently opposed bride. From what she had learned of her, Isabel judged Selene capable of violence, or worse, if pushed too far.

"Would you like me to tell you about my son?" Isabel asked. "He was such a dear little boy, and such a handsome young man. Everyone loves him."

"Men." Selene gave a most expressive shudder. "The nuns have told me what men do to women. They told me on the first day I became a woman."

So that was it, and with all her information about the girl, Isabel had not previously guessed it. The

25

silly child was afraid of men. That could be put right easily enough. Isabel almost laughed aloud.

"It is not always unpleasant," Isabel said, recalling the early days of her marriage to Walter fitz Alan. She moved a little on the hard stone seat. Even now, after all these years, the memory could still stir her blood. Ah, Walter, Walter, what we once had, what we so foolishly lost in resentment and regrets. "The nuns have not told you everything, Selene. Sometimes it can be marvellously exciting. Delicious, like honey, or a rich, heady wine. It can be wonderful to be with a man."

Selene sat staring at her, lips parted. She had a small, pretty mouth, but rather thin lips. The girl is probably not passionate at all, Isabel thought, but I can fill her mind with Thomas, even try to think of something pleasant to say about Afoncaer, and she will come around. I have her interested now. Girls her age are always intrigued by talk of lovemaking, even if they pretend they are not, and she's still young enough to be impressed by an attractive adult who pays particular attention to her, especially if she doesn't get along with Aloise. How convenient for me.

"Shall I tell you about Thomas?" Isabel asked again.

"If you like," Selene said. "You are a guest in this house, and I must listen to you politely, madame, but I warn you, you will not change my mind about marriage."

Oh, but I will, Isabel thought as she began to talk. Her visit would last a month, longer if she could maneuver Aloise into a further invitation, and in that time she would make an ally of Selene. Before Isabel was done, the girl would love her as

26

though Isabel were her own mother, and at Isabel's bidding would willingly marry Thomas.

Isabel wanted to avoid entering a convent, as she had told Aloise, but there was more to her purpose, much more. Isabel wanted revenge on Baron Guy of Afoncaer. It was because of Guy that she had spent ten years in miserable exile. Now Isabel had a plan to pay him back, a long, slow, clever plan that need not depend upon a knife in his back or an army to unseat him from Afoncaer. Isabel was too clever, too patient, for such crude methods. And Selene, that cold, proud girl sitting stiffly across the window niche from her, listening intently to Isabel's words in spite of her feigned indifference, Selene would be her weapon.

By the time the castle chaplain had finished reading the letter from Sir Valaire to her, Aloise knew what she would do. It was not a sudden decision. She had lain awake many a night during the past two months wrestling with the problem, trying to find a solution to the fears that troubled her and unwilling to make the choice she had to make. But now she knew from her own husband's words on parchment that Isabel's desire had come to pass and Selene would wed Thomas of Afoncaer shortly after Christmas. Now that it was definite, Aloise's hesitation disappeared.

She dismissed the chaplain and went to seek the one person she could depend upon to render her the faithful service that would banish, or at least alleviate, her lingering fears. Aloise found her hard at work in the castle kitchen, lending aid to the temperamental cook by supervising the lesser kitchen help as in preparation for the midday meal they turned meat upon spits or chopped vegetables for stews. Aloise watched her fondly, a tall girl with a well-rounded figure swathed in a long apron, and a wealth of curling, dark brown hair shot through with red lights when she bent over into the fire's glow.

Aloise sighed. Her foster daughter had proven well worth taking in and nurturing. Aloise hated to send her away, indeed would miss her far more than she would miss Selene, but it must be done. She could see no other way.

"Arianna."

The girl turned, her golden skin flushed from the heat of the cooking fires.

"My lady." The wide, laughing mouth deflected one's attention from a nose that was just a little too long and hawklike for a feminine face. Her beautiful wide-set grey eyes, her best feature, were fringed with thick, dark lashes. Nothing about her individual features fitted the ideal of female loveliness, yet the impression Arianna gave was of strong, exotic beauty, lit by humor and quick intelligence.

Aloise beckoned to the girl, who left her post by the spit and followed the castle's mistress into a small pantry off one side of the busy kitchen. The servants, seeing their lady conferring with Arianna, thought nothing of it and went about their work, leaving the two in privacy.

"A message has come from Sir Valaire," Aloise said. "The marriage is agreed to, the contracts drawn up."

"Does Selene know?"

"Not yet. I want you to come with me when I tell her."

"My lady, she has seemed content these last weeks. The Lady Isabel has spent much time with her, and has apparently turned her mind toward Thomas of Afoncaer. I doubt Selene will be overly distressed, or even the least bit surprised, by this news."

"Arianna, I, too, have thought much of Thomas of Afoncaer. And of Lord Guy. I cannot let Selene go to Afoncaer unattended."

"But she will not, my lady. There will be servants, waiting women, pages, as large a company as she wishes. Sir Valaire will be generous with her."

"I must speak truly, Arianna," Lady Aloise said, using one of her favorite phrases, which Arianna had long ago noticed was usually followed by words she ought not to speak at all. But Arianna knew how to keep a confidence. She would repeat nothing Aloise said to her, and knew Aloise trusted her completely.

"I fear Selene will go to her marriage as a martyr," Aloise went on. "She will take as few folk from her father's household as she possibly can, and as soon as she is at Afoncaer she will send all those away. Once she is in a strange place, with unfamiliar people, who can tell what she might do? She could bring dishonor upon her father and me. I must try to prevent that."

"Surely her new husband will exert some control over her."

"I hope so. I don't understand her, Arianna. I never have. She is such a peculiar girl. I feel her hostility toward me, I've endured her terrible rages, and yet I don't know why she behaves as she does. She has been chastised, exhorted by the chaplain, whipped, prayed over, and nothing helps."

"She was content at the convent, my lady. Perhaps she should have stayed there. She may be better suited to the cloister than to marriage."

"She is too valuable to her father to be allowed that indulgence. Her marriage to Thomas of Afoncaer will seal the friendship between Lord Guy and Sir Valaire. Arianna, I want you to go to Afoncaer with Selene. She cannot send you away. She wouldn't want to—you are one of the few people she cares about. You know how to soothe her when she is distraught. Continue to be her friend, Arianna, as you have been in the past, stay close to her, care for her children when they are born, and be as faithful in your duty to Selene as you have always been to me." Here Aloise embraced her foster daughter with a warmth greater than anything she had ever extended to her own child. "You will have your reward in heaven, my dear, dear girl."

"Leave you, my lady? Leave this my home?" Arianna's surprised, initially reluctant expression lasted only a moment before her grey eyes began to shine. "I've heard the Welsh border is an exciting place. The Welsh refuse to be conquered. Sir Valaire told me that the last time he was home."

"You and Selene will be safe enough in Lord Guy's castle, Arianna."

"Oh, I'm not afraid of danger," Arianna laughed. "To travel so far, to see a new place, how wonderful it will be. I will miss you, my lady, for I love you dearly. You have been kind to me beyond anything I deserve. I owe you and Sir Valaire a great debt."

It was a debt Arianna knew she could never repay. Sir Valaire and his lady had taken her into their care when she was still a baby, orphaned and unwanted by her half-brothers, who had resented their father's second marriage to an unknown and untitled woman. Arianna had spent nearly all of her life in this household; it was home to her, and she would be sorry to leave it. But the blood of a crusader father and a daring mother who had defied her own parents to marry him mingled in Arianna's veins, and her spirits soared at the thought of crossing the Narrow Sea and living in a strange new land. Who knew what opportunities for usefulness might await her there? Selene would need her, of that she was certain.

"Yes, my lady, if Sir Valaire gives his permission, then send me," Arianna cried, her heart full of love and gratitude. "I'll do my best to watch over Selene, and her children, when she has them. It's little enough to repay you for all you have done for me. I will go to Afoncaer most willingly."

Part II

Selene
A.D. 1115–1116

Chapter 2

St. Albans, England
December, A.D. 1115

"I would have preferred," Thomas said, "to be knighted at Afoncaer, by Uncle Guy. I have dreamed of that since I was a boy."

The abbey church of St. Albans was to be consecrated this Christmastide, and King Henry had brought his court hither for the ceremonies. Thomas had come from Afoncaer with his family, unwillingly but dutifully, at his king's bidding, to be among the select group that would be knighted in the church by the king himself several days after the consecration. It was an honor and he knew it, but still he was unhappy about it.

"And," he went on with increasing irritation, "I wanted Geoffrey to be at my knighting. It's only right, I was his squire. He should be here." Thomas strode restlessly about the small guest chamber that had been allotted to the Baron of Afoncaer and his lady. A serving woman sat quietly in one corner mending the hem of a gown, but otherwise he and his aunt were alone.

"You know Guy felt it best for Geoffrey to re-

main at Afoncaer." Meredith spoke in a soothing tone, smiling up at the young man. She was
sure he had grown even taller in the last month.
He topped Guy by at least two inches, and he
looked so much like Guy it was uncanny. He had
the same golden hair and piercing blue eyes, and
the same square jaw. He was just like Guy when
she had first seen him and fallen in love with him.
Those old enough to remember said the late Baron
Lionel and his younger brother Guy had been as
much alike, but Meredith had never seen Lionel.
One of Meredith's hands came down on Thomas's
arm to stop his pacing and hold him before her so
he would listen carefully to what she said. "Geoffrey will keep the castle safe while we are away.
Guy feels there may be some trouble brewing
among the Welsh, and he wanted someone de-
pendable in charge. Captain John is not as young
as he once was. We will need a new captain of the
guard soon, I fear."

"The Welsh have no reason to dislike my uncle's rule. He has always been most fair with his
people, and that part of the border is more pros-
perous than it has ever been."

Meredith, who knew more of Welsh ways than
Thomas did and understood why they hated the
Normans so much, smiled at her nephew again
when he shook his head at the unpredictable
tenants of Afoncaer. Then she changed the subject.

"When you came in, you said you wanted to
speak about something very important. I think I
distracted you by mentioning your knighting."

"It's my marriage. It worries me. I've been
thinking about it constantly. I ought to be thinking
just as much about my knighting and all that that

36

means, but instead I lie awake half of every night wondering what will happen after I'm married."

"You don't object to the terms, do you? I thought Guy had made it all quite clear to you, every item in the contract, and all the arrangements for the ceremony, and you did agree."

"I still agree. I trust Uncle Guy, and Sir Valaire, and I know this is the way noble marriages are made, but, Meredith, I don't want a merely formal arrangement. I have seen you and Uncle Guy these past ten years, seen how you love and support each other, how you work together, and how good that is, for you two and my cousin Cristin, and for all of Afoncaer. My parents had the usual kind of marriage. They spent almost no time together—I scarcely remember my father—and I grew up feeling lonely and unloved, until I met you. I don't want my wife or children to live like that, in that cold, empty loneliness. I sometimes think that was why my mother did the terrible things she did. Because she was lonely, and afraid, and unloved."

"Walter loved her." Meredith's gentle voice was harsh whenever she spoke of Isabel.

"Perhaps Walter loved her too late. Or perhaps she loved him and he used her love for his own ambition."

It was the other way around, Meredith thought, but she did not say this aloud. Meredith believed Isabel had never loved anyone and had always known exactly what she was doing and why. Isabel had used her son and her second husband for her own ends, and had caused the deaths of people Meredith held dear.

"I would rather not remember that time," she said. "It is too sad."

37

"I'm sorry." Thomas responded quickly, touching her shoulder in mutual sympathy, for he had lost the same loved ones to Walter's and his mother's treachery. "I wouldn't have mentioned my mother, except that I wanted to explain to you how I feel. I know there are those who would call me soft and unmanly to care about such things as love, who would say I should be interested only in warfare and in consolidating our power on the border. I know I can speak freely to you, I always could, and you won't laugh at me. Meredith, I don't want my wife to end as my mother has, all alone, in exile, the object of hatred and scorn. That's why I want to meet Lady Selene. Now, today. I want time to know her a little before we marry. If we don't like each other, or if she doesn't want to marry me, I'll take a sacred oath at my knighting and make a pilgrimage to the Holy Land, never to return. Sir Valaire couldn't be insulted by that, nor could the Lady Selene, and it's better than marrying someone I shouldn't, or making someone else unhappy for a lifetime."

Meredith gulped back sudden tears. This was the earnest, thoughtful boy she had first met more than twelve years ago, the page determined to become an ideal knight and to be always fair and honest. How like him to be willing to give up his heritage and all he cared about in England to avoid hurting an unknown girl.

Meredith could not bear the thought of never seeing Thomas again. She loved him deeply—he was a substitute for the son she had never borne—but more importantly, he was the heir to Afoncaer. Guy, and Afoncaer, needed him. She had to see to it that Thomas carried out the plans Guy had made for him.

"Thomas, if you and your wife both come to the marriage with good will, and with the intent to make it a happy and fruitful union, then it will be a true marriage, and in time you will learn to love each other."

"You and Uncle Guy loved each other before you married."

"We were different. There were unusual circumstances."

"I want to be different, too. I want to love the woman I marry. Help me, Meredith. I know you can arrange for me to meet Lady Selene."

She put her arms around him, as she had done so many times when he had been a frightened, unhappy boy. Ignoring his size and strength, and the convention which said a man must be brave and unemotional, she pulled his head down onto her shoulder and held him close, promising to do whatever she could for him. And, she added silently, for Guy and Afoncaer.

"Lady Meredith is here," the serving woman said. "I heard her say she has come to see Lady Aloise. What do you suppose she wants?" Confronted by Selene's cold blank stare, the woman muttered a hasty apology and left the room.

"Perhaps they are going to cancel the marriage. Would that please you, silly girl?" The embroidered blue band around Arianna's head seldom kept the tumbling curls out of her eyes. Now she impatiently brushed a stray piece of dark brown hair off her face and grinned at Selene, her face full of mischief. But when she continued there was an annoyed note in her voice. "You have been uninterested in anything that has happened since we

39

left Brittany. The journey was so exciting. This abbey is beautiful. The new church is so glorious the good Lord Himself must be pleased with it. And the courtiers, how they dress! The jewels and furs! Look around you, Selene, open your eyes and your heart and admit how wonderful it all is."

Selene's only response to Arianna's plea was an indifferent shrug of her slender shoulders. The severe plain dark grey woolen gown she insisted on wearing drained all youthfulness and color from her face. She looked more like a condemned prisoner than a prospective bride. Arianna presented a striking contrast, with her russet-brown dress belted in blue to match the ribbon in her hair, her glowing complexion, and her bubbling vitality.

"If I had a chance of marrying a great lord," Arianna declared, "I would take it with rejoicing."

"He is not a great lord, he is only the heir to one," Selene replied coolly. She picked up her Book of Hours and sat down on a stool close to the brazier. The small room the two girls shared in the abbey guesthouse was well furnished, but it was cold, made more so by the drafts that blew through the shutters each time the wind gusted. Selene laid the book down on her lap and held out chilled fingers toward the heat. "I am reconciled to my fate. Only, I do wonder what they are talking about. Some change in the marriage contract, perhaps."

"Shall I go and find out what is happening?" Arianna laughed, her wide, humorous mouth opening to display flashing white teeth. "I know, I'll pretend I'm looking for my embroidery. I'll creep into the room and listen to what they say."

"Your embroidery is right there. I wish you

would not leave it in such a tangle.'' Selene gestured toward a rather untidy pile of silk and linen, carelessly tossed onto the heavily curtained bed. ''Pretending is lying.''

''Oh, Selene, I love you as though you were my sister, but you can be maddening,'' Arianna exclaimed. ''I think you are even more curious than I am, but you just won't admit it. It is your marriage, after all. I won't lie, I'll just ask a few questions. I'll be back as soon as I can.'' The bedchamber door closed behind her before she had finished the last sentence.

She thinks I hate lying, Selene thought, but she doesn't know, no one knows, what a liar I have become. Is there ever an excuse for such falseness? The nuns would say no, but Lady Isabel has said sometimes it is necessary to achieve great purposes. I believed her when she told me all those things, and what I must do, but now that I'm away from her, I wonder, and I'm afraid. What if they do cancel the marriage and I can't do what Lady Isabel expects? She would never forgive me if I were to fail, but I would be so relieved. What am I going to do?

Rising from the stool, she found her small hand mirror and gazed into it, seeing the blurred image of her thin, white face and her large, emerald eyes, and wondered how she had come, consenting, to the brink of marriage with a man she did not know, she, who four months ago had wanted only to enter a convent and live there forever.

And how, Selene thought, shuddering and turning away from her own reflection in disgust, how am I to lie in bed naked, with a naked man,

41

how to endure that terrible embrace? But I must, I must.

Arianna was back much sooner than Selene had expected. She shut the door carefully, then approached Selene as though she had a great secret to disclose.

"The Lady Aloise wants to see you at once," Arianna announced.

"Why?" Selene was wary.

"You will never guess." Arianna's grey eyes were dancing with the excitement she tried to hold inside.

"Then you had better tell me." There was no answering excitement in Selene.

"The Lady Meredith has come to make a request of your mother." Arianna could contain herself no longer. "Selene, she is beautiful, and I am sure she is kind. She will be your friend, I know she will. And she spoke of Thomas with such affection. Thomas wants to meet you before he signs the contract. Lady Aloise sent me to fetch you."

"What are you saying?" Selene looked, and sounded, distinctly frightened.

"Your future husband wants to meet you. We are to go at once, you and Lady Meredith and I. Lady Aloise was to go, too, but she must attend the queen, so I am to go in her place. Hurry, dunce, they want you now." Arianna grabbed Selene's hand and pulled her toward the door.

"I can't go like this. My dress, my hair."

"You always look beautiful. You are perfect. No, wait, you are too colorless." Arianna flung open a lidded basket and pulled out a brilliant red shawl. This she draped about Selene's shoulders with a flourish, and smoothed Selene's black hair over it.

"*Now* you are perfect. Men like bright colors. Lady Aloise told me so. Come on now, we mustn't keep Lady Meredith waiting." Arianna coaxed the unwilling Selene out the door and along a corridor, then through another door to Lady Aloise's chamber.

"Here she is," Arianna proclaimed, urging Selene toward a woman who stood alone in the middle of the room.

"Madame." Selene curtsied, then lifted her head and caught her breath. Arianna was right, this woman was beautiful. She was of medium height, perhaps twenty-eight or twenty-nine years old, but still bearing traces of the radiant freshness of youth. Soft, silver-grey eyes smiled into Selene's green ones with welcoming friendliness. Selene noticed a wisp of dark red hair, a curl escaping from the confines of the woman's fashionable coif. Meredith put out both hands to take Selene's.

"My dear child," Meredith said, "I hope you are not frightened by this sudden idea of Thomas's, but he thought it would be a good thing for you to learn to know each other. You may rest easy, you will not have to be alone with him. Arianna and I will be nearby."

"I am ready to do whatever you wish, my lady," Selene said, struggling to reconcile what Isabel had told her about this woman with Meredith's actual appearance. Despite what Isabel had said, this was no Saxon peasant wench, this was a noblewoman. Even Selene's limited experience recognized that. She let Meredith lead her from Aloise's chamber and through the abbey guesthouse until they came to a cloistered walk beside a garden that lay bleak and brown in the midwinter chill.

43

Arianna had brought cloaks for both girls, and now she wrapped Selene in hers, making certain the red shawl showed at the neck to lend a little color to Selene's pale face. Selene stood trembling, waiting. At the sound of a step behind her, she turned and beheld a tall young man. She moved back a pace, then looked up at him.

"Thomas," came Meredith's quiet voice, "this is Selene."

She was more beautiful than anything he had expected. Oddly, he had not really thought much of her possible appearance. He had hoped for a kind heart and an agreeable disposition and had thought he would be content with that, but this beauty before him, this enchanting, delicate creature who stood quivering like some timid bird who would fly away if he made one rough or hasty movement, this girl was more than he had ever dared dream of.

"Oh, Uncle Guy," Thomas whispered, "I thank you, and thank you again with all my heart."

"Thomas." That was Meredith again, dear Meredith, who had arranged this meeting for him, this very first moment to greet his love. His *love*. So Selene was, had been at the instant their eyes met, and so, he was sure, she would be for all his life. Thomas looked at his aunt and knew she saw the wonder on his face. "It is too cold to stand still, Thomas. Walk with Selene to keep warm, and Arianna and I will walk at this end of the cloister, so you may speak privately. Stay within sight of us. I promised Lady Aloise you would do so."

"Yes, I will. I mean, we will." Thomas stum-

44

bled over the words, grinning foolishly. He nodded at the tall girl with Meredith, scarcely noticing her in his astonished wonder at Selene. Selene. Selene. The name rang in his brain like a lovely silver bell. "Will you take my arm?" he asked.

"Yes, my lord." Her voice was husky, hardly more than a nervous whisper, and then Thomas felt the gentle pressure of her hand on his wrist. Together they walked away from Meredith and Arianna, along the length of the sheltered cloister.

Arianna watched them go, feeling as though a hot sword had pierced her bosom. She saw the blonde head bent toward Selene's smooth, dark one, heard the murmur of their voices. She wished she were at the other end of the world. No, she wished she were in Selene's place, with that handsome face bent toward hers. Thomas! Arianna shook herself, wondering what was wrong, why she who was usually so content with her lot should suddenly feel so alone and unhappy.

"We had better walk, too, or we'll take a chill," Meredith said, turning in the opposite direction from Thomas. She put an arm around Arianna's shoulders. "You are chilled already. Your eyes are weeping from the wind."

Arianna laughed and brushed the tears away as though they were nothing.

"Tell me about yourself," Meredith invited. "Lady Aloise said you are to accompany Selene to Afoncaer."

"Yes," Arianna said, trying to conceal the unaccustomed bitterness that surged into her throat. She glanced over her shoulder at the retreating couple. "I am an orphan, my lady, and seventeen,

45

two years older than Selene. My father was a landed knight of Anjou, a distant cousin of Sir Valaire, and they were close friends from their youth. My father went on crusade, and while in Byzantium he met my mother, who was the daughter of a Greek nobleman.

"Perhaps you do not know, my lady, but the Greeks are a different kind of Christian from us, and they are not too friendly toward the Frankish crusaders. My mother was cast out by her family when she married my father against their wishes, so he brought her back to Anjou, to his own lands, to have her child. She died when I was born, and he decided to return to the Holy Land. He left me with Sir Valaire and Lady Aloise for fostering. Unfortunately for me, he died soon after, and the eldest son of his first marriage, my half-brother, inherited all his lands, leaving the younger sons to seek their own fortunes in the church or as landless knights, and leaving me penniless, since my mother had had no dowry to pass on to me.

"I do not know what would have become of me had not Sir Valaire, out of charity and love for my father, kept me in his household. As I am undowered, I cannot hope to marry. I was useful to Lady Aloise, and now I am to go to Wales and be useful to Selene. I do not mind at all. I am eager to see Wales." Arianna had noticed Meredith's earlier close observation of Selene, so now she added, "You may think she is cold and unfriendly, my lady, but she is not always as you see her today. She has been kind to me. Selene is my dear friend."

Arianna saw no reason to mention Selene's rages. Perhaps, once she was married and far from the mother with whom she had never been on

46

good terms, that screaming anger would remain dormant.

They walked on. Meredith was silent a while, then said, "I think Selene may be afraid of all that awaits her. That is only natural, I suppose, especially for one educated in a convent as she has been, who has never been to court before, nor talked often to boys or men, and who now must marry and go to live in a strange place." Meredith paused in her walking to look appraisingly at the girl beside her. "I suspect you have a more adventurous spirit, Arianna. I am glad you are going to Afoncaer with us. We will help Selene, you and I, and perhaps the coldness I noticed in her will melt with love and time. You may tell her she need not be afraid of Thomas. He wants only to love her, if she will let him."

"I do not think you need to worry about that, madame." The note of bitterness was back in Arianna's voice, and she fought to disguise it. "I thought your nephew was stricken with lovesickness at his first sight of Selene."

Meredith smothered a chuckle and gave Arianna a sharp, sidelong glance which the girl found entirely too penetrating. They walked in silence to the end of the cloister, turned and began to retrace their steps. Arianna felt she did not want to talk about Thomas and Selene any more. Not now, not while that odd pain still burned at her heart. Adventurous spirit or no, she was afraid to examine its cause too closely.

"Tell me," Arianna said, resorting to the humor she often found effective when she was uncomfortable, "what life is like at Afoncaer. Is it true the Welsh are all naked barbarians who carry bows longer than a man is tall?"

Meredith laughed aloud. "The Welsh wear clothing, though it is not always like ours. They are content with just a shirt and mantle, and they usually leave their legs and feet bare. They don't mind the cold or the rain. They do not always think like us, either. That occasionally causes trouble. It's true about the bows."

"And are they all wizards?" Arianna asked impishly.

"Who has been talking to you? Well, there are some who can do strange things. I've known one or two."

"I've heard you can do magical things."

"I?" Meredith stopped walking and stared at her companion. "Who told you that?"

"Selene. Someone told her you enchanted Lord Guy to make him marry you."

"It would be fairer to say he enchanted me. We came to love each other. There was no wizardry, no magic involved, though I do have some knowledge of herbal lore."

"Really? They say my mother knew of such things. I would have liked to learn from her." Arianna paused before asking humbly, "I know a little, from helping Lady Aloise, but not enough. Would you teach me?"

Grey eyes met grey eyes, and Arianna felt that Meredith came to know her in that long moment. The older woman seemed to recognize and understand the deep pain Arianna was feeling, the cause of which she herself did not yet fully comprehend. Arianna felt a compelling urge to lay her head on Meredith's shoulder, to weep away old grief and future foreboding. Meredith put out her hand and gently brushed back one of Arianna's wayward curls, tucking it behind the girl's ear.

"Yes," Meredith said softly, "I will teach you whatever you are willing to learn. I think you will need something of your own, and I think Afoncaer can use you."

Thomas listened as Selene answered his eager questions by reciting the bare facts of her life, most of which he already knew: age fifteen, convent-schooled, the eldest child of six, the only daughter. Yes, it was true she could read and write. Yes, this first visit to a royal court was confusing and a little frightening.

"I hope," Thomas said, trying desperately to elicit some warmer response from the exquisite creature at his side, "I hope, Lady Selene, you will not be afraid of me."

The slim fingers resting on his wrist quivered, fluttering like a bird's wings, and he suppressed the urge to place his other hand on them, to hold them there.

"I will not be afraid if you do not want me to be, my lord."

"I want." Thomas stopped. He could not say, "I want you to love me as I already love you," for he sensed that would only make her more afraid. He realized he did not know what to do or say next. His experiences of women was limited to a few lusty, laughter-filled tumbles with willing serving wenches, occasions as natural and joyful as a refreshing shower during the summer's heat, and these had done nothing to prepare him for a terrified, completely innocent young girl. He wondered if Selene knew what would be expected of her on their wedding night. Surely someone would tell her.

They had reached the far end of the cloister. Thomas saw Meredith and her companion all the way at the other end, their backs toward him and Selene. There was no one else about; everyone was inside on this cold day, huddled at fireside. He stopped walking and looked down upon Selene's bent head, on the smooth, straight hair that lay sleekly across the delicate skull and poured down over her shoulders like some dark waterfall. The narrow line of the red shawl glowed at her throat like a barely extinguished fire that might blaze up at any moment. He wanted to stir fire in her, and watch her respond to his love. She had taken her fingers from his wrist and now stood with her hands folded before her. He could not see her face.

He was unable to resist the urge that overcame him then. He had to touch her, to assure himself she was real. His left hand stroked along her head and came to rest upon her shoulder, caught in the silken torrent of her hair.

Selene's face came up, her emerald eyes wide and startled, her lips parted. For an instant he thought she would scream, but she only stood very still, tense as a drawn bow, waiting. His right hand caught her chin, holding her face steady, as he lowered his lips toward hers. He paused a fraction of an inch away. He could see her parted lips trembling, then felt them beneath his own. There was no reaction from her at first, her softness simply lay against his mouth. But then the hand that had cupped her chin slid around her shoulders and drew her near. Even through her winter-heavy clothes and woolen cloak Thomas could feel the slender, haunting delicacy of her body, and he wished there was no clothing between them. He had to fight the need to grasp her hips and pull her toward the sudden hardness of his body that threatened to drive him mad with wanting her. Never before had he experienced this combination of reverent adoration and intense sexual desire.

Finally, very faintly, came a response, a slight movement of her lips under his, a returned pressure on his mouth. It was delicious, the taste of those lips, like honey-sweet mead, and he never wanted to let her go. But he did. Even in his aroused state, longing to continue what his body had started, he realized he must not push her too far. He must be gentle and patient. She would be his soon enough. His for the rest of their lives. The thought filled him with such joy he imagined he would die of it. He opened his eyes and looked at his love. She hung back upon his arm, lips still parted, eyes closed, and upon one curving lash lay a tear like a round, perfect pearl. Her hands were clasped together against his chest as though she were praying.

He could hear Meredith's footsteps pacing along the cloister, coming closer.

"Selene," he whispered, reassured by her brief return of his kiss, "I will love you, and you will love me. There is nothing for either of us to fear. We will be happy together just as my Uncle Guy and Meredith have been."

She opened her beautiful emerald eyes and looked directly at him. He saw in those eyes that the apprehension he had hoped to alleviate was still there, along with sorrow and—was it guilt? But what could this lovely, pure, half-child have to feel guilty about? As he watched her, grey-shadowed lids drooped over emerald fire, long, thick lashes lay against her perfect cheekbones.

"I will be whatever you want me to be, my lord," she whispered, just as Meredith and Arianna rejoined them.

Chapter 3

Arianna knocked at the chamber door, then waited impatiently for it to open. It was cold in the corridor. An icy draft blew along the stone floor. She shivered, pulling her shawl closer about her shoulders.

"Lady Meredith," she cried eagerly as the door swung inward, "I'm afraid I'm late. Oh, Thomas, I did not expect to find you here." She pressed one hand hard against her bosom, hoping to still the sudden, ridiculous pounding of her heart which began each time she saw him. It had been happening for days, and Arianna felt a surge of anger against herself. Selene's betrothed husband should not have such an effect upon her.

"Come in," Thomas invited, holding the door wider and motioning to her. "Uncle Guy and I were just leaving. We are going hunting with the king."

Arianna pulled dignity and self-control about her like a tattered garment and stepped into the room. It was no larger than the few other bedchambers she had seen in the abbey guesthouse, and like those others it was furnished with a curtained bed,

53

two wooden stools, and a small table, but still this room had a special atmosphere about it. Two richly carved wooden clothes chests were pushed against the wall and topped with green and blue wool-covered pillows to make comfortable seating. Arianna was certain the chests had travelled to St. Albans with the occupants of the room. She thought Meredith's hand must be behind the fresh rushes and sweet-scented branches of dried rue, hyssop, and woodruff which had been strewn on the floor. Also Meredith's doing must be the two large braziers that made the room more comfortably warm than the chamber of Lady Aloise, or the one Arianna shared with Selene.

Meredith had been talking with her husband, but now she came forward and presented Arianna to the Baron of Afoncaer. Arianna was so flustered at Thomas's presence that she did not even look at Lord Guy, only curtsied and stammered a few polite words.

"I've spoken to the infirmarer," Meredith said. "He will show us through the pharmacy before the noonday meal. I thought it would be well for your first lesson to come from him."

"It needn't be today, not if you are busy. I'll go now and come again another time." Intent upon making a hasty retreat, Arianna reached out behind herself for the door handle and caught Thomas's arm instead. Her hand closed over solid muscle beneath a smooth leather sleeve. She felt the heat of his body and his firm strength with a jolt that rocked her to the depths of her being. She had longed to touch him for days and had not dared. Gasping, she removed her hand from his arm and stood numb with confusion.

"Would you open me instead of the door, Lady

Arianna?'' Thomas teased. He laughed, and watching his eyes crinkle and his mouth curve with friendly good humor, she realized he had no idea of her feelings toward him. He saw only a girl who had come to speak to his aunt. She knew in the certainty of her aching heart that Thomas was incapable of seeing her as a woman. The only woman he could see was Selene.

''Oh, please, I must go.'' Arianna knew she was acting like a child who had been taught no manners. She could feel her cheeks flaming, and she was afraid she would burst into tears. She caught her breath in a sob when Thomas took her by the shoulders and gently pushed her forward into the room. She felt the touch of his hands even after he had let her go.

''Of course you will stay,'' Thomas told her.

''We really were leaving,'' Baron Guy said kindly. Arianna was so caught up in embarrassment at her ill-mannered behavior that she was aware only of twinkling blue eyes and a face rather like Thomas's before Guy picked up his mantle from the bed, kissed his wife on the cheek, and headed for the door, clapping his nephew on the shoulder as he went. ''Come along, Tom. These ladies have things to do that do not concern mere men.''

Thomas stood where he was a little longer, looking at Arianna, while his uncle waited by the door.

''Is my Lady Selene well?'' he asked anxiously. ''You two are usually together. She hasn't taken ill, has she?''

''No, my lord.'' By a great exercise of will Arianna forced herself to look directly into those devastating blue eyes of his while still making words come out of her mouth in some sensible

55

way. "Selene is with the seamstresses and Lady Aloise. They have no use for me—I'm not very clever with the needle—so I am free this morning."

"Well, Meredith," Guy said, laughing, "I can see you have a potential comrade of the heart in this lady. You never could use a needle, either." He gave a shout of laughter as a deep green pillow sailed through the air and hit him in the chest. He caught it, and still laughing, tossed it back at his wife, then ducked through the door before she could return his fire. Thomas followed him at once, and Arianna could hear their happy laughter echoing down the hallway, while Meredith, smiling to herself, plumped up the pillow and returned it to its rightful place on one of the wooden chests.

Arianna had followed this play between husband and wife with fascinated interest, but now the full meaning of their relaxed familiarity struck her. Thomas and Selene would be like that, laughing together in the same knowing way, shutting out everyone else, their eyes silently speaking intimate secrets.

Thomas. The pain stabbed at her heart again, threatening to crush her usually buoyant spirits. Arianna wrapped her arms around herself, clutching across her midriff and bending over, her eyes tightly closed to stop the tears she had for days refused to shed. But she could not hold back the anguished words that now tumbled from her lips. And somehow she knew, even in her pain, that of all the people she had met at court or in Sir Valaire's household, Meredith was the one person who would not condemn her inability to keep on pretending nothing was wrong.

"I can't do it," Arianna cried. "I can't go to Afoncaer. I dare not go."

She felt Meredith's strong hands on her, guiding her to one of the pillowed chests and easing her down upon it.

"Here," Meredith said. "Open your eyes, my dear, and drink this."

Arianna found a cup of herb-scented wine thrust into her hand. Obeying the gentle command, she sipped at it, while Meredith watched her closely. When the cup was empty, Meredith refilled it, then sat on the chest beside Arianna.

"We cannot help what our hearts tell us," Meredith began. "Never think you are to blame for what you feel, Arianna. We cannot determine the objects upon which our hearts fix. But our actions, what we do in response to our heart's urging, for that we are responsible. That we can control."

"I have never felt like this before." Now the soothing tears began to fall, she could not prevent them, and Arianna, all her defenses in ruins before Meredith's kindness, let them roll freely down her cheeks and made no effort to wipe them away. There, in that pleasant, peaceful chamber, she finally admitted what her deep affection for Selene had kept her from accepting until now. "It was only one look, the first time I met him, that's all it needed. I did nothing. I never intended—never—" She gulped back a fresh outburst of sobs and tears, struggling hard to regain some sort of composure.

"I know. I saw it happen." Meredith took her hand. "It was that way for me, too, the first time I saw Guy."

"But he," Arianna said bitterly, "was not betrothed to your kinswoman and dearest friend.

57

Lord Guy was not mad with passion for another woman.''

"That's true. I did not have to endure that pain.''

They sat quietly a while, Arianna alternately sniffling and sipping at the wine, until at last she leaned her head back against the wall.

"I can't even enter a convent,'' she said wearily. "I have no dowry, no title or great family to assure me a respectable place. No one would want me. What am I to do?''

"You had better come to Afoncaer as planned,'' Meredith told her. "I can think of no excuse you might offer to Lady Aloise, or to Selene, to prevent your going, that would not seem ungrateful and offend them deeply. The Lady Aloise has been most determined that you should accompany Selene.''

"I'm not strong enough,'' Arianna insisted. "I'm too honest, I couldn't hide my feelings, and I'd have to watch them every day and witness their happiness.''

"Or their unhappiness, which might be worse. That might prove a great temptation for you, so wish them happy. If you love them both, you must want them so.''

"I do. I pray for them each night. But, oh, it hurts me to see him look at her with shining eyes and know he will never look at me like that.''

"Will you trust me, Arianna?'' Meredith regarded her intently, as though making some grave decision, before continuing. "Long ago, when I was much younger than you are now, I began to learn about the Old Ways from a beloved aunt, and from a friend, an ancient Welsh Wise Man. I have no Welsh blood in me, so I was unable ever to match their proficiency, but sometimes I sense

58

things, and I have come to trust what my heart tells me at such times. I believe you were meant to be at Afoncaer. I have no reason to give you for my feelings, except to say it is time I had a pupil, so I can pass on the little I did learn from those dear people. I choose you, Arianna. If you will go with me to Afoncaer, I'll keep your secret, and help you live with it as best you can. I'll work you hard, and keep you too busy for sinful thoughts, and you can always talk freely to me, knowing it's in confidence. You will grow stronger, my dear, if you can meet this test and not run from it."

Arianna was silent.

"I need you at Afoncaer," Meredith said, "and I believe it is the best thing for you, too. However hard your going there may seem to you now, in time you will understand why you were called to Afoncaer."

"I will think about it." Arianna sighed.

"That's all I dare ask for now. We have another week before we leave, and you must decide finally whether to go or stay. Say nothing to anyone else about your doubts until you have decided. That way no one will require an explanation of you. Now, let us visit the infirmarer while we can. Come." Meredith put out her hand, and Arianna took it and went with her, and tried her best to appear interested in what the infirmarer had to say to them.

It was odd, but as the elderly brother talked with Meredith, answering her questions about his use of herbal preparations upon the sick who came under his care, and as Meredith gradually drew her into the conversation, Arianna found the pain at her heart lessening. She did not forget Thomas—she could never do that, he was in her heart to stay—but she did feel a growing sense of comradeship with Meredith, until, as the morning ended, she roused herself to ask about this or that ointment or tincture. She was genuinely sorry when Meredith's serving woman came to remind them it was time to dress for the midday feast. Perhaps, Arianna thought, Meredith was right and she would find peace and her own healing in learning to heal others. And, she reminded herself, in keeping her promise to Lady Aloise. But still she was afraid of the damage that would be done to her, both heart and soul, if she were to see Thomas constantly, and so she held back from final agreement.

"I like that girl. She reminds me of you," Guy said to Meredith later that night, when they were alone in their room. "It's her eyes, I think. You both have grey eyes, though hers are darker, but the look is the same. That searching look, so full of pain, like you when first we met."

"Let us hope, my love, that Arianna's pain can be relieved by hard work. I would not have her suffer more than she must, yet I feel certain I am doing the right thing by encouraging her to go with us. I pray she will agree."

"You have needed a pupil, and our Cristin is not interested, is she?"

"No," Meredith said ruefully. "Our daughter Cristin cares more for horses and for talking to the hawks in the mews than for learning about herbal cures and ancient wisdom."

"And," Guy added, laughing, "for teasing poor Geoffrey whenever he's about. She trails after him like an adoring puppy. He'll be half-mad with answering all her questions by the time we are home again."

"Home." She went into his welcoming arms. "How I miss Afoncaer. I will be glad to leave St. Albans."

"And I, my sweet. I'm fond of our king, but I've no real taste for court or courtiers. I'm thankful our position on the border leaves us free of the obligation to come to court every year."

And then his lips touched hers, and they both forgot everything else but the love that had sustained them for more than ten years.

"I have never been so near the king before," Arianna said softly. She was standing between Meredith and Guy, crowded amongst all the other courtiers who were gathered in the large abbey chamber which served as reception hall and throne room for the duration of Henry's stay at St. Albans. She looked the scarlet-clad royal figure over carefully, assessing his tall, powerful frame, noting the thick, black hair turning grey. "He's handsome, but older than I thought he would be. Sir Valaire says he's a good king, much better than the last one."

"He is that, though anyone would be better than William Rufus," Guy responded, smiling at her. She looked back at him with an answering smile. He had been more than kind to her on the few occasions she had seen him since their first meeting several days ago. When he had told her she would be welcome at Afoncaer, a bright ornament to his household, she had known that in his own way he was trying to convince her to accept his wife's offer. Arianna already thought of him as a friend, a male complement to Meredith's warm, feminine friendship.

Studying the Baron of Afoncaer, Arianna thought she could see how Thomas would look in another fifteen years, the gold hair threaded with silver at his temples, the lines radiating from his fine blue eyes, the stern lines from nose to mouth that relaxed into laughter when Meredith said something to him. She thought that Selene and Thomas would one day stand so, not touching each other but obviously in complete accord. The thought brought with it the pain which so often beset her soul these days, and Arianna, with an angry gesture of one hand, as if to brush aside the discomfort, tried to think of something else. She saw King Henry beckon to Guy, who promptly left the women and went to speak with his monarch.

Arianna looked around the room, her eyes lighting on Thomas. He stood near one wall, his golden head bent to Selene, who seemed to be staring intently at the floor. Arianna looked away, and caught Meredith watching her.

"I wish Selene would talk more," Arianna said nervously. "She always seems terrified of Thomas. And I wish she would listen to me and wear something other than black or grey."

Meredith started to say something, but before she could begin, Guy joined them, his face serious.

"I have had bad news from the king," he said.

"Is something wrong at Afoncaer?" Meredith asked quickly. "Cristin. I knew we shouldn't have left her there."

"No, not Afoncaer," Guy responded, taking her hand. "It's Reynaud. There has been an accident. He was badly hurt."

Arianna, seeing the stricken expression on Meredith's face, put one arm about her, and felt Guy's arm above her own, supporting his wife, who had gone white and was trembling.

"Would you like to sit down?" Arianna offered. "I see a bench over there."

They led Meredith to the bench, which was placed against the wall in an alcove between two stone pillars. Meredith sank onto the seat, holding fast to Guy's hand. Arianna went to find a goblet of wine. When she returned, Guy was sitting beside his wife, still holding her hand, and talking to her softly. Arianna was again struck by the closeness between these two. She had never seen anything like it between Sir Valaire and Lady Aloise. She handed the goblet to Meredith and then stood uncertainly, waiting to learn what Guy wanted her to do next.

"Thank you, Arianna." Meredith sipped the wine. "I am sorry to trouble you. I'm better now." She moved over on the bench to let Arianna sit down.

"Who is this Reynaud?" Arianna asked. "You must be very fond of him to be so distressed."

"He was the architect of Afoncaer," Guy answered, "and a good and true friend. He once helped to save Thomas's life."

"Then," said Arianna, "you must do whatever you can to help him now."

"And so we will," Guy replied. "We have been discussing that."

There was a rustle of movement before them. The throng of courtiers parted, and King Henry stood by the alcove. The three who had been sitting on the bench all rose, the women sweeping into deep curtsies, Guy bowing low.

"Are you ill, madame?" asked the king, watching Meredith's pained expression.

"No, my lord, only overcome with fear for my dear friend Reynaud. Can you tell me all that happened to him? When last I knew of him, he was in France, and in good health."

"He returned to England last July and went to Much Wenlock Priory, where they had need of an architect for the new buildings they plan there," King Henry said. "I'll not spare you, Lady Meredith. I know you are strong enough to hear the truth. A wall collapsed on him, and Reynaud was nearly killed by it. He has lost a leg, crushed beyond repair by falling stones, and it's believed he'll have no sight in one eye. They won't know for certain until the wounds are healed and the bandages come off. But he may die before that happens, for I am told his wounds have festered and he burns with fever. It is a great loss. He was a fine architect." King Henry shook his head sadly. "And now, if he lives, he will be an invalid."

Arianna was watching Meredith closely, concerned about her. Meredith was pale, and she swayed as King Henry recounted the brutal details of Reynaud's condition, but then she seemed to gather strength from some inner source. Meredith looked straight into Guy's eyes, and once more Arianna had the sensation that they understood each other's thoughts and were in complete agreement. She saw Guy give an almost imperceptible nod. Meredith nodded back and then spoke to the king.

"Is Reynaud yet at Much Wenlock, my lord?"

"The brothers there are caring for him," Henry replied.

"Is he still a lay cleric? I have not heard that he had taken final orders."

"That's true," Henry said. "Like so many other penniless young men, Reynaud entered clerical orders to acquire an education, and has taken only the minor vows. He's a reader, but not a priest. His true vocation is building, as you know. The Church, and you and I, Guy, have made good use of that talent of his. But what will become of him now, crippled as he is, I do not know. If he lives, he may never be well enough to become a priest, though he will always have shelter at Wenlock."

"I cannot forget all he did at Afoncaer," Meredith said. "We owe him a great debt for that, and now we will begin to repay it. Reynaud must come to Afoncaer, and I will try to heal his broken body."

"You cannot replace a lost leg," the king remarked dryly, looking at Guy for confirmation of Meredith's offer.

"I badly need a secretary," Guy said, "and there is still work to be done on Afoncaer. We need a stronger wall around the town, and a larger cistern. So long as he has even one eye, Reynaud could easily plan and direct such projects, given the right assistants."

"And you want my permission to employ him." King Henry looked pleased. "I trust this will be a permanent arrangement? You will keep Reynaud at Afoncaer, feed and clothe and house him for the rest of his life? Which, I greatly fear, will not be long."

"We will gladly accept Reynaud into our household once more," Guy promised.

"I am in complete accord with your idea, my friend," King Henry said. "I believe Reynaud would be content at Afoncaer."

"Sire," Meredith interrupted the men, "I can see a difficulty in this plan."

"What is that, my lady?"

"Reynaud's pride. We must present these arrangements to him as though we were asking for his help. Reynaud would not accept an offer made out of pity for a cripple. There is pity here for his condition, that is true, but there is much more of friendship and gratitude, though Reynaud may not see it so. We must be careful in dealing with him, or he may chose to remain at Wenlock and die."

"Lady Meredith," King Henry smiled upon her, "you are both wise and subtle. I would I had you among my councillors. Very well. After hearing prolonged entreaties from Baron Guy, which he continued to present to me at every opportunity during the entire period of your stay at St. Albans, I finally, to silence his pleas, and recognizing his dire need of a good architect, granted Guy written permission to take Reynaud from Much Wenlock Priory to Afoncaer. All of this, of course, took place before we learned of Reynaud's accident. Do you think that story will satisfy his pride when he hears of it?"

"I hope so, my lord," Meredith said demurely.

"It had better satisfy him," the king said sternly, but with a gleam of humor in his eyes that belied his hard tone. "If Reynaud raises any objections, I'll issue a royal decree commanding him to go with you. Stop at Much Wenlock on your way home to Afoncaer, and take that friend-blessed architect with you. I'll see to it he's duly informed of my will in this matter, and I'll explain the circumstances to the prior there."

"I thank you, my lord," Guy said, and Henry moved on to another group of courtiers.

66

Arianna had been watching and listening intently. Now she asked Meredith, "If this Reynaud is so badly injured, will he be able to travel? How can he be moved without it causing him great pain? Have you some herbal mixture to relieve his pain? What about his fever? And how will you treat such terrible injuries? You seem very confident of helping him."

"So interested?" Meredith eyed her speculatively. "Have you come to a decision then?"

Arianna's glance wandered to the opposite side of the reception room, where she could just see Thomas's head above the throng. It did not matter whether she was separated from him by the width of the whole world or in the same household with him; the anguish of loving him without hope would always be the same. But Meredith had offered her the opportunity to do something beneficial, and in that work she might find her salvation. In addition, she had still to keep the promise she had made to Lady Aloise, to whom she owed so much. Arianna took a deep breath and made her choice.

"I will go with you to Afoncaer," she said to Meredith. "I would learn all I can from you. Let me begin with Reynaud."

Chapter 4

Selene was terrified. Her wedding day had come, and she could not stop trembling. She and Thomas had met regularly after that first afternoon in the cloister, so he was no longer a complete stranger to her, though the presence of other people had prevented him from making any further advances toward her. She had thought several times that she had seen in his expression a desire to kiss her again, and that frightened her. She had been present at Thomas's knighting ceremony two days earlier, and at his request she had helped to arm him afterward. When they had sat together at King Henry's great feast the same night he had tried earnestly to make her unbend and show a little warmth toward him, but she could not. Her mother, and Arianna, and even her father, had all told her that Thomas was delighted with her and eagerly looked forward to their marriage. He had been teased about his obvious affection for her often enough by friends and courtiers, and once even by the king himself, Sir Valaire had said. It was clear to everyone who saw them together that Thomas had the deepest affection for his bride-to-be, and would treat her with great honor. None of that helped Selene now.

Her knees were shaking. She sank down on the edge of the bed, then immediately stood up again. The bed. She stared at it. She and Arianna had slept in it together since they had come to St. Albans, but tonight she and Thomas would sleep there. The fresh sheets had been laid on it earlier that morning, and Arianna had been banished to a trundle bed in the chamber Lady Aloise shared with Sir Valaire and their two younger sons. Tonight, only Thomas and Selene would occupy this room. A man. Doing *that* to her. Selene thought she would be sick.

If only she were not so confused. Her head whirled whenever she thought of the people she had met since coming to St. Albans and how different they seemed from Lady Isabel's descriptions of them. She could not understand it. They had been so kind to her it was difficult not to like the members of her future family. And Thomas. Isabel had not specifically warned her not to like him, but Selene had understood that it would be easier to do what Isabel wanted her to do if she could avoid caring for Thomas. She almost wished he were cold, or cruel, or brutal. She could have despised him then, and not felt so guilty at the betrayal of a husband's trust that would be necessary.

She wished she had never met Isabel. But she had, and every day for the three months of Isabel's twice-extended visit to Sir Valaire's castle the older woman had flattered the unhappy girl, charming her with kindness and professing complete understanding of her feelings, until finally, in the name of the friendship which had become precious to Selene, Isabel had made a request. And, unaccustomed to having so much fond attention paid her and overcome with love and pity for the woman she believed had been mistreated and betrayed and wrongly sent into exile, Selene had promised to do what Isabel wanted. No, it was more than a promise. With both her hands on the crucifix Isabel held before her, Selene had sworn a solemn oath. She had been well trained by the nuns who had taught her, and she knew that such an oath could not be forsworn without imperiling her very soul. Once the ritual was completed she had to do as she had vowed though it cost her life.

Now that she was at St. Albans and the Narrow Sea lay between her and Isabel, Selene had begun to regret the impulsive oath. But she had no one to talk to, no way to ease her troubled conscience. She could not speak of what she had done to the priest when she made confession because she feared that part of her penance would be to reveal all to Baron Guy and Thomas. She knew such a revelation would bring disgrace not only to herself but to her entire family. She could not do that to her honest father or her brothers. And now Arianna, her one-time confidante, had been acting strangely, avoiding her in favor of Lady Meredith's companionship. Having noted their growing friendship, Selene knew she dared say nothing of her pact with Isabel to Arianna. If she asked advice of Arianna, the girl might say something to Meredith, who would of course tell Baron Guy. It was plain to Selene that she had no one to trust or depend upon but herself.

The bedchamber door opened, and Lady Aloise

and Arianna appeared. Lady Aloise was garbed in her very finest blue silk gown and all her jewels. Arianna, in a deep green dress that brought out reddish highlights in her luxuriant dark brown curls, looked oddly solemn and subdued. Selene's glance only flickered over the two women before her thoughts turned inward once more, returning to her own problems. She paid little attention to what they were doing as they picked up the wedding garments spread out on the bed and began to dress her.

Her serving woman had helped Selene to bathe earlier, in water scented with dried rose petals and violet flowers, and had left her wrapped in a woolen robe, beneath which she wore knee-length stockings held up by blue ribbons and soft leather shoes trimmed with gold. Now Aloise slipped the robe off her daughter, and Arianna brought the thin linen shift and helped Selene to put it on.

"You have insulted the waiting women by refusing to have anyone but Arianna and myself dress you," Aloise told her. "They all expected to be here. It is the custom."

Selene did not respond. She heard her mother's words only as an irritating accompaniment to her own unhappy thoughts.

"You are cold, child," Aloise said, one hand resting on her daughter's shoulder.

"Then dress me and I shall be warm." Selene's voice was so flat and lifeless it startled the two women with her, and her mother looked at her with annoyance.

"This is a woman's lot," Aloise told her. "Your duty is to marry and bear children to your husband. Your father and I expect you to carry out that obligation humbly and with an agreeable

71

spirit. There will be no sulking, Selene, no cold withdrawal of your heart from your husband. You owe him total obedience. Curb any thought of defiance." Aloise snatched the fine cream wool underdress from Arianna's hands and pulled it over Selene's head, settling it on her rigid shoulders with a sharp tug. "I had hoped the nuns would teach you humility," Aloise grumbled. "But you remain a proud, stubborn, and ungrateful girl."

"I am like my mother in that," Selene said, staring into Aloise's shocked face. "But you may be certain I will never take as many lovers as my mother had. My sin may indeed be pride. At least I am not guilty of lust."

Aloise's hand slapped across Selene's cheek so hard the girl nearly fell. Selene regained her balance and stood straight and stiff, waiting for the next blow. It cracked upon her other cheek and Selene hardly moved. She fixed her eyes on the opposite wall, her chin high. Out of the corner of her eye she saw Aloise raise her hand again. Selene braced herself.

"My lady, please!" Arianna caught at Aloise's arm, stopping the forward motion that had already begun. "Don't beat Selene on her wedding day."

Aloise slowly lowered her arm. It was obvious she was fighting hard for self-control.

"You are right, Arianna. She deserves a good beating by her father, but we should not send her to her husband with bruises on her body. And I do hope," Aloise breathed, her rage not really cooled at all by Arianna's intervention, "I hope Sir Thomas has a strong arm and a large stick to keep you under control. You finish dressing her, Arianna. I cannot bear the sight of her another moment. Sir Valaire and I will return later to escort her to the church. And, praise to heaven, after today I need not see you again for a long, long time, Selene.''

"Thus you need not watch a young woman grow up while you grow too old for lovers,'' Selene hissed at her mother's departing back. Apparently Aloise had not heard her, for the bedchamber door closed with a smart click, and Selene's tense stance relaxed a little.

"Must you always antagonize her?'' Arianna asked. "You need not quarrel so much, if only your tongue were a little less sharp.''

"It doesn't matter any more. After today, I'll only see her to say a formal good-bye. That is the only happy thing about this marriage. I will no longer be under my mother's rule.''

"She is not so wicked as you would like to pretend, Selene.'' Arianna was struggling to separate the thick folds of the gown so she could lift it over Selene's head. Selene made no move to help her. "Your mother has always been kind to me.''

"That is because you are not her daughter.'' Selene raised her arms and waited for Arianna to put the dress on her. It took a while. The gown was made of a heavy silk brocade that had been brought from Byzantium at great cost and then worked into the latest style by Lady Aloise and her serving women. It was pale green, with a blue and yellow flower pattern woven into it, shimmering here and there with gold threads. The bodice was loosely fitted, with a wide, round neck. It had wide elbow-length sleeves, bordered in gold, which allowed the longer, tighter cream sleeves of the underdress to show. There was a belt of gold and green threads embroidered with jewels to wrap twice about Selene's slim hips. Below the belt a

73

hugely full circular skirt fell in stiff ripples to the floor, hanging long enough in back to trail after her when Selene walked. Arianna knelt to arrange the skirt.

"You look beautiful," she said, looking up at Selene. She rose, and taking up a wooden comb she used it to smooth and arrange Selene's hair until it fell straight down her back in gleaming, midnight-black splendor. A short veil of sheer white silk went on top of her hair, then a narrow gold circlet, symbol of Selene's rank.

"Will you wear the necklace?" Arianna asked.

"I suppose I must," Selene sighed, watching while Arianna lifted Thomas's wedding gift out of its silk pouch and held it up. It was of intricately worked swirls of gold—Welsh gold, Thomas had said—and it was set with emeralds. To match her eyes, he had told her when he had given it to her the day before. But jewels meant nothing to Selene, nor did all the festive preparations for the wedding. Because they would take place in an abbey, the celebrations would not be as boisterous as usual, and for that was Selene glad. She pulled her mind away from her own gloomy thoughts long enough to notice Arianna's subdued manner as she held the gold and emerald necklace, straightening it before placing it around Selene's neck.

"Are you jealous?" Selene asked, and watched Arianna's fingers grow perfectly still, holding the heavy gold. "Do you wish it were you, marrying some fine nobleman? I can tell you I am envious of you."

Arianna stepped behind Selene to fasten the necklace, and Selene could no longer see her face.

"Why should you envy me?" Arianna asked.

74

"Because you have no dowry, and therefore you will never be forced to marry. You will never have to bed with a man." Selene felt Arianna's hands on her shoulders, the fingers digging into her, and Arianna's voice sounded strangled.

"Thomas will be good to you, Selene, if only you will let him. He will love and honor you." Arianna's forehead rested on the back of Selene's shoulder for just an instant. "Please try to be happy in your marriage, Selene. Please, please, try to love him."

Selene moved away from her friend, caught up again in her own terror, not looking back at Arianna.

"Happiness and love," Selene said softly, "are not earthly things. You are speaking of lust. I hold myself above that."

"Don't hurt Thomas."

Selene turned around and looked at her. Arianna's eyes were bright with tears.

"He's a man. I can't hurt him," Selene said. She put out a hand and touched Arianna's cheek. "Don't worry about me, my dear friend. I know what I have to do, and I will do it. Oaths sworn must be fulfilled."

The wedding ceremony took place in the church porch, and then the wedding party went inside for a solemn mass to bless the vows just taken. Thomas walked first, with Selene's hand on his wrist, proudly showing off his new wife to the assembled guests. They were followed by Arianna and Sir Kenelm, who was Baron Guy's liege man and Thomas's close friend, and then by Guy and Meredith, and Selene's parents.

As she paced slowly down the aisle, Selene stared straight ahead, her eyes on the high altar. She felt her cheeks burning and knew they must be red. She could still feel the stinging blows of her mother's hand. She will never strike me again, Selene reminded herself. Never. She bowed her head as, in honor of the nuptial pair, the abbott himself began to conduct the mass.

Once the religious service was completed, the guests retired to the large reception room for a day-long feast. King Henry and Queen Matilda and their eldest son, William, called the Atheling in honor of his Saxon mother, sat at the table on the dais at one end of the long room, with the bride and groom beside them, along with Arianna and Kenelm, Guy and Meredith, Valaire and Aloise, and several other important guests.

The abbey cook had outdone himself, serving up fresh fish, roasted pigs, sides of beef, haunches of venison, all accompanied by complicated sauces, along with meat pies and vegetable stews, fine white bread, custards and sweetmeats, figs, raisins, and dates. The cellarer had ordered extra casks of wine for the occasion, the abbey's stores being nearly depleted after a month-long royal visit, and there was plenty of beer and ale, cider and perry. There were frequent toasts to the newly wedded couple.

Throughout it all, Selene sat quietly, eating little, willing herself to feel nothing, speaking only when someone spoke to her. She roused herself to make only the briefest responses to Thomas's attempts at conversation, knowing full well her withdrawn behavior would be taken as evidence of maidenly modesty.

The day passed rapidly with feasting and the entertainment of singers and jugglers and acrobats. Too soon for Selene, the time came for the bride to leave the table and be prepared for the wedding night. King Henry stood, slightly drunk, and toasted her on her way with words that brought a stinging blush to Selene's sore cheeks.

"Come," Meredith said, putting an arm around Selene's shoulders. "I have arranged that there will not be a crowd in your bedchamber. Aside from Lady Aloise and Arianna and me, we need only one or two more women."

Queen Matilda rose from her place beside the king. She had been a half-Saxon princess, daughter of the King of Scotland, and famous for her beauty and goodness. She was still lovely in middle age, with long gold braids, a sweet face, and the warmth of manner that derives from a kind and loving heart.

"I will go with you, Meredith," Queen Matilda said. She beckoned to an elderly woman at a nearby table. "I will bring with me Lady Constance, who would not frighten even the most timid bride. That will make five of us, and that's enough to bear witness to the bride's fitness, I think."

"And I," said King Henry, "will join Guy and Valaire, and Sir Kenelm here, and who else? Ah, William, my son, you come with us. It's time you learned of such matters. You are twelve years old now, and will have to marry yourself before long. The rest of you," Henry added, raising his voice, "remain here and continue the revels. We will see these two well bedded and then return to you for more feasting." A cheer went up at this, and again toasts were drunk.

Selene had time to notice with some scorn how

pleased Lady Aloise looked at these signs of royal favor, before Meredith and Queen Matilda urged her gently from the room and took her to her bed-chamber. There they quickly undressed her. The servants brought in a small tub of hot water. Selene stood in it while Arianna sponged her, letting the water run over her shoulders and down across her belly and back into the tub. It was more a ritual than a real washing, since she had bathed earlier.

Then, as required, she stood naked while the women examined her for obvious physical defects that might prevent her from bearing children. They were kind to her, and it was only a moment before Queen Matilda said, "Cover her, Meredith, the poor girl is shivering," and a woolen robe was draped over Selene's shoulders. Selene could hear laughter outside the door.

"The men are here with Thomas," Arianna said, looking white and shaken. She came to Selene and kissed her on both cheeks. "Be happy, my dear friend."

"Hurry, now." That was Constance, the queen's elderly lady. "Put her into bed."

The robe was pulled off Selene's shoulders and she was hustled between the sheets. Aloise plumped up the pillows and tugged a blanket to straighten it. Selene met her mother's eyes, then turned away, looking at the other faces surrounding her. She pulled up the linen sheet to cover her bare breasts just as the door burst open and the men spilled into the room. In their midst was Thomas, barefoot, chamber-robed, and blushing.

"The groom has been examined," the king announced, obviously enjoying himself very much, "and found fit to consummate the marriage."

78

While the ladies murmured their approval, Thomas was pushed toward the bed. Just as he reached it, he was stripped of his robe, and stood naked. Selene, averting her eyes from his body, saw Arianna turn her back on the scene.

Now Thomas was in bed beside her, his bare leg touching hers, while Lady Constance held back the covers so all could witness it. Selene wanted to pull away from that frightening contact with Thomas's body, but did not dare. Aloise and Meredith were on either side of the bed, drawing the blue woolen curtains closed. Selene saw Guy looking intently at her, and thought she saw sympathy in his face.

"Let us leave them," Guy said. "The work to be done here this night is best done in private."

"Come along, lads," King Henry said, shooing his son William Atheling and Sir Kenelm out the door. "We've witnessed them bedded together. The rest is up to Thomas."

Sir Valaire, who had said nothing during the bedding, came to Selene's side, just as Aloise was pulling the last curtain shut.

"Obey your husband in all things," Valaire said, and kissed his daughter on the forehead.

Selene caught a glimpse of Aloise, her face devoid of all expression, closing the curtain, and then she and Thomas were alone in the bed. It was dark. She pulled up the sheet, moved her leg away from the unwelcome contact with Thomas's leg, and sat very still.

"Do you think they've really gone?" Thomas asked. When she did not answer, he thrust the bed curtains partway open and looked out. A gleam of candlelight came through the opening, shining softly upon his golden hair and the strong muscles of his chest and shoulders.

"Good. We are alone." He was back inside the bed, but he left the curtains open. "I want to see you when I make you my wife," he said.

The two young people sat in the bed, side by side, looking at each other. Selene felt frozen, unable to move or speak or even close her eyes to shut out the sight of Thomas's handsome, serious face. The moment drew out, longer and longer, until Selene, had she been capable of sound, would have screamed. She saw Thomas swallow hard, and bend his face toward hers.

"I think I should kiss you," Thomas said. His mouth covered hers, gently at first, but then with growing warmth, and his arms went around her.

Selene continued to sit bolt upright, her arms braced behind her, eyes wide open, her lips unresponsive as she coldly fought back the feelings awakened by the touch of his warm, naked body against hers. After a while, the kiss ended.

"Selene," Thomas murmured, one hand caressing her cheek, "I know you are frightened. Any young girl would be. I'll be gentle, I'll try not to hurt you. Please trust me."

"My lord, I know I must allow you to consummate this marriage." Selene's low-pitched voice was husky with tension. "I have been told what will happen. I will be an obedient wife, and allow you to do what you wish. I ask only that you finish it quickly."

"Quickly? No, my sweet love, it will be slow, and tender, and you will find pleasure in it, too. I promise." His lips brushed hers again. "It is not only I who will consummate this marriage. We will do it together. With love."

"No, my lord," she choked, feeling she could not bear the awful waiting any longer. "Do it and be done with it. Please."

Thomas said nothing to this. He took Selene by each shoulder and gently pushed her down onto the pillows and held her there. Then he kissed her again, a firm, warm kiss that was entirely too pleasant. His mouth caressed hers, pressing harder, then withdrawing a little, only to return more firmly a moment later. His upper body lay half across hers, and the golden hair on his broad chest tickled her breasts as he moved closer. Selene twisted, trying to get away from the tantalizing prickling that was making her nipples tingle and harden, but she found she could not escape. His arms held her securely. Her breasts began to ache, and Selene, who had been determined that she would feel nothing at all during this encounter, knew the beginnings of panic.

She moved her hips and legs, trying to wriggle out from under him, but only succeeded in kicking off the bedcovers, and when she moved again, one of his bare legs slid between hers. Her startled outcry at the sensations this aroused was lost in his mouth. She managed another wriggle, and a hairy, muscular thigh surged upward between her own thighs. It felt wonderful. Selene gasped, and had to suppress an urge to move against him. Instead, she clamped her legs tightly around his, preventing further upward motion. Unfortunately, her movements only heightened her growing tension. Thoroughly frightened at her own reactions, she put her hands up to push frantically at his shoulders. Thomas broke off the kiss, but his lips remained only a breath away from hers.

81

"No!" Selene panted, struggling against him. "Let me go."

"I cannot. This is what we must do, Selene. Let me show you how sweet it can be."

"I don't want it to be sweet. This is lust, it's evil."

"This is love. I love you, Selene. We are married. There's no evil here, no harm to anyone. You are afraid now, but you won't be for long. Come, kiss me back."

"Please, my lord, no." She was close to tears.

"Do you suppose that you could possibly call me Thomas?" he asked.

He did not wait for her answer. His mouth was on hers again, moving slowly and tenderly. Selene reminded herself it was her duty to please him in all things. She stopped fighting him, and just for a moment she let herself begin to feel how pleasant was his nearness. Thomas was strong and clean, his youthful body hard muscled, and he smelled faintly of some unfamiliar, tangy spice that must have been tossed into his bathwater. His breath was warm and sweet. She told herself she was fortunate. He might have been old and fat and vile-smelling. She had seen one or two men like that at this court, men who swilled their wine and dribbled grease down their chins when they ate, and obviously never washed. She could not have endured the touch of one of those creatures. At least her new husband was attractive.

"Thomas," she whispered in obedience to his request, and was rewarded with a dazzling smile.

He held her face between his hands and played with her lips, placing soft, quick kisses across her mouth, then on her chin and nose. Selene lay quietly at first, her hands still on his shoulders, but no longer resisting him. He kissed her eyelids, and drew his mouth along one cheek and back to her lips. Selene's hands fluttered across his shoulders and into the thick, blonde hair at the back of his head. She felt his tongue brushing against her lips. She was so astonished at his action that she opened her mouth, and he thrust inside, his tongue moving against hers. Selene moaned, thrashing about on the bed, and felt the pressure of his thigh between hers again, pushing hard this time, until her legs fell apart completely and he was tight against her. She would have cried out and told him to stop, but now one of his hands was on her breast, teasing at a nipple. The motion sent flame into her belly, and then suddenly Selene herself was on fire.

She could not help it—it was utterly uncontrollable, some demon or devil had hold of her. This was not Selene behaving like this. Selene would never, never clutch at a man this way and pull his head to hers and push her tongue into his mouth to meet his tongue in a breathless, passionate duel. Selene would not rake her fingernails along his back until he cried out, caught at her hands and held them over her head so he could nibble and suck at her small, hard breasts while she screamed and then wrenched her hands out of his grasp and forced his head up so she could devour his lips again and again. She felt his hands playing across her abdomen and along her hips, felt her own body rising to meet his touch. But this was not, this could not be, Selene.

He knelt between her thighs and she saw his manhood, huge and stiff. She licked her swollen lips, feeling a surge of heat and moisture through her loins, and somewhere deep inside her another

Selene cried out in horror at the panting, heaving entity who reached out to touch that symbol of all that was lustful and evil, and stroked it with heavy desire.

"Ah, Thomas, I am afraid!"

It was a wild, hysterical sound, and Thomas paused for an instant, reining in his own almost uncontrollable desire, to kiss her trembling mouth and reassure her, but then he could not wait, not any longer. He wanted her so desperately, and the way she writhed on the bed, the sight of her heaving breasts in the dim candlelight, the movements of her small, strong hands on his body, all combined to drive him close to madness with urgent need.

"It must be now, Selene," he said, moving against her.

Her eyes widened as he sought entry to her most intimate place. With an almost superhuman effort, Thomas stopped his forward motion, giving her a little time to adjust to his presence. To his surprise, there was no more evidence of fear. Instead, she moved boldly onto his manhood, pushing herself upward, her lips parted and her expression rapturous. Her cry as he took her virginity was one of intense pleasure, not pain. She wrapped her arms and legs about him and bit at his shoulders and screamed again and again, like a madwoman, matching him thrust for thrust in a wild frenzy of hot, pounding desire. Thomas was consumed in her fire. He blazed brighter and brighter with white-hot, unquenchable heat, flaring into a final, nearly intolerable explosion of all his pent-up desire as his very essence poured into the avid, moaning creature of flame and ice who lay panting and throbbing beneath him, her emerald eyes staring sightlessly into his while she cried out her own passion over and over again in wordless sounds.

He thought he had killed her. He was still on top of her, his face tucked into the curve of her neck, and she lay so perfectly still and silent that he thought she was dead. Horrified, he lifted his head and looked at her. Her eyes were closed, the grey-shadowed lids shut tight, the thick, black lashes heavy against her cheeks. Her bruised and swollen lips were slightly parted.

"Selene." She did not respond. He tried again. "Selene, my love."

She drew a deep, shuddering breath, and Thomas uttered a wordless prayer of thanks. He kissed her lips. Her eyes flew open.

"What are you doing, my lord?" It was her usual low-pitched, throaty voice, and cold. So cold.

"I am loving my wife." Shaking off a twinge of fear at her tone and formal mode of address, Thomas rolled to one side, releasing her from his weight and pulling her into his arms to cuddle her against him. She came quietly, letting him arrange her body as he wanted. "I love you, Selene. You are wonderful."

His lips brushed her forehead. He sighed happily. She was silent.

"I did not hurt you too badly, did I? I tried to be gentle, but I have never felt such passion before." When she still did not answer, he added, "I thought you enjoyed our lovemaking, too. You seemed to."

"I will always do my duty, my lord," she said.

"It's no duty when it's love," he whispered, hugging her close.

85

Selene moved her head to a more comfortable position against his shoulder and lay quietly until his even breathing told her he was asleep. Then she carefully disengaged herself from his embrace and sat up in the bed, chin on knees, staring down at her husband. The single candle he had left burning by the bed so he could see her had guttered low, but still she could make out his form and his square-jawed face. She put out a tentative hand to brush back a lock of golden hair that had fallen over his forehead. But before she had made contact with his flesh she snatched her hand away.

"Thomas." It was barely a whisper, little more than a sigh. "How could you do that to me, make me turn into someone different? It wasn't Selene, you know. Selene would never do anything so disgusting. Selene is pure, and clean in spirit. Not at all like Aloise. Selene will never have a lover."

She saw then that there had been blood. It was smeared on her thighs and spattered upon the linen sheet beneath them. Blood. Selene's stomach heaved. She moved away from that part of the bed, removing herself from the evidence of her lost virginity.

Sensing the motion, the man beside her opened brilliant blue eyes. A large, strong hand reached across the space Selene had put between them and slid down along her arm, covering her slim fingers, then bringing her hand to his lips. She sat watching him coldly, seeing his smile falter and a shadow come into his eyes.

"Is anything amiss, Selene? You must be cold, all uncovered like that. Lie here beside me, and I'll warm you. We will love again. Come closer, my sweet."

Again? Selene glared at him, her chin tilting upward defiantly.

"Certainly not," she said. "I have done my duty for this night."

"Are you just going to sit there until dawn?"

"Perhaps."

"What is wrong? My love, you had pleasure, too, you know you had."

"I had to do it. I could not prevent it. I was only doing my duty."

"And will you do your duty to me again whenever I wish it?" he asked lightly, to cover his growing bewilderment.

"No!" Selene cried. Then, "Yes. I must. I have no choice."

"I think," Thomas said, only half-teasing, "that if you had a choice, you would still say no, and pretend to be unwilling, but then you would come into my arms with as much delight as the first time."

Selene said nothing. She seemed to be staring hard at the blue curtains that enclosed the foot of their bed, but she did not see them. She tried to blot out her husband's soft voice, and could not.

"My sweet, in time we will come to love each other as Uncle Guy and Meredith do. You'll see."

No, I will not, Selene thought as his arms encircled her tenderly and pulled her down next to him. I must not, I cannot, I dare not. I will not love you, Thomas.

But he began kissing her again, and soon she found the other Selene, who lived deep inside her, who could not resist him, taking over her senses once more. This time, with much of the strangeness of it gone, knowing exactly what he would do and how it would feel, thinking about it as he be-

87

gan to stroke and caress her, Selene felt the heat rising rapidly through her body. She reached for him, unable to stop herself or control the longing that filled her. She touched him, knowing it was shameful to do so, and watched him rise into life under her searching fingers. It was lust, no more, and lust was a sin. She knew it. But she was filled with a clamoring desire that spiraled into sweet bliss when he took her. The explosion, soft and quiet this time but earth-stopping, heart-searing nonetheless, made her bite her lips to keep from crying out, and then, when she could no longer hold back her ecstatic moans, made her curse the other Selene, the demon inside her, who made her do such revolting, degrading things, and enjoy them.

Arianna had not slept. She had gone to bed late after all the wedding feasting. Then she lay, open eyed through what remained of the night, listening to Sir Valaire's snores and the quieter breathing of his wife and two young sons, and trying not to think about what was happening two chambers down the corridor, where Thomas and Selene were. She failed miserably. She could think of nothing else. Toward dawn she rose and crept out of the bedchamber carrying her clothes. She fled barefoot and shivering to the lavatorium, where she quickly washed and dressed.

She was surprised that there was no one about. The king and most of his courtiers were planning to leave St. Albans today, so there ought to have been more activity. She found the reason for the unnatural stillness when she opened the guesthouse door and stepped outside. There had been a heavy snowfall during the night.

Arianna stood on the doorstep a moment. Breathing in the clean, icy air, so cold it made her lungs hurt, she let that cleanness dissolve all the unhappy thoughts the night had brought to her. It was still dark. Only the faintest grey light in the east pierced the heavy snowclouds to indicate the sun would soon rise. Torches had been lit on either side of the door, and by their light Arianna saw a stocky figure trudging toward her.

"Ye can get to the church easily enough now, my lady. I've shovelled ye a path," said the porter who usually guarded the door. He stopped before Arianna, shovel over his shoulder, his round face showing flushed and shiny with sweat in the torchlight. "There's another lady went before ye to the church. In a great hurry she was, anxious to say her prayers, and much she has to be thankful for, I'd say."

Arianna hurried through the cold to the church door. It was not much warmer inside. The monks were there, kneeling in their stalls, but few lay people attended this early mass. Arianna tiptoed forward. She nearly stumbled in surprise when she saw Selene kneeling on the stone floor. So that was who the porter had meant. Arianna knelt beside her, but Selene did not acknowledge her presence. When the service was over they walked silently out of the church together.

It was lighter now, but the wind had risen with the sun. It blew swirls of snow off the tops of high drifts and into the church porch. The path the porter had shovelled earlier was nearly drifted over.

Arianna shivered. Selene did not seem to notice

89

the cold. Her face was white and drawn, her lips pressed tightly together. Arianna took her arm.

"I was surprised to see you here," she said.

"Out of bed, do you mean?" Selene's voice was hard as ice. "Thomas did what had to be done, and now he's sleeping. I trust he will leave me alone for a while. Until then, I am free to pray for forgiveness of my many sins."

"Oh, Selene." Arianna did not know what to say. She could not believe Thomas had mistreated his wife in any way on their wedding night, yet Selene was obviously suffering. Arianna wanted to put her arms around her dearest friend and comfort her. But something told her Selene would not welcome the gesture.

"I never wanted to marry," Selene went on, half to herself and still in that cold little voice. "I warned my parents, but they would not listen to me. Now they have unleashed a demon. I changed into someone else. Not Selene. And there was blood." She began to moan softly, her eyes unfocused.

"Selene, stop this. Stop at once." Arianna shook Selene's arm, wondering if her friend had gone mad. But Selene regained her composure almost immediately.

"Let us go inside and break our fast," she said calmly.

Arianna, too startled by this sudden change to make any reply, followed Selene back to the guesthouse. There, bread and cheese and hot ale had been provided in the large reception room. Guy came in just as they were finishing their morning meal. Arianna saw his eyebrows go up at the sight of Selene. He came over to them, carrying a tankard of ale in one hand and a wedge of brown

90

bread in the other, and dropped onto the bench beside Selene.

"Where's Thomas?" he asked between bites of the bread.

"I do not know," Selene replied coldly, not looking at him.

"We two went to early mass," Arianna explained more warmly, feeling that Selene was being unnecessarily rude to a man she ought not offend. "Here comes Thomas now."

"Selene, my love," Thomas stood behind her, putting one hand on her shoulder in a possessive gesture. "You should have wakened me."

"I wanted to be alone," Selene replied, trying to shake off his hand. Thomas let go of her shoulder, caught her chin to tilt her face up, and planted a hearty kiss on her mouth.

"I thought you might have run away from me," he joked.

"I would not get very far," Selene retorted, leaving Arianna wondering if she actually had considered flight. "There is too much snow."

"She's right," Guy added, shooting a shrewdly appraising glance at Selene. "The roads are drifted too badly for travel. We all must postpone our leaving for another day at least."

He looked most unhappy about it. Arianna knew he was eager to be on his way to Afoncaer. She also suspected the good brothers of St. Albans, honored though they were by the king's visit, would be relieved to have their guests leave at last. No one would be pleased by the delay. With, it seemed, just one exception.

"I won't mind a bit. We will have more time together." Thomas beamed at Selene. She ignored him.

"I had better go and tell Meredith about the change in plans." Guy finished his ale and rose. "I've already told Kenelm and our men-at-arms, so you needn't bother about that, Thomas. Enjoy the day, my boy."

Guy left them, and Thomas, after a moment, held out his hand to Selene.

"Come, my love."

"Come where?" Selene's voice was still ice-cold and filled with distaste.

"To our chamber. Come." The warm look in Thomas's eyes left no doubt about his meaning. Unable to bear the sight of that look, or the haughty rejection on Selene's face, Arianna stared hard into her empty ale mug.

Her chin high, Selene sat very still for a while longer, letting Thomas stand and wait for her. Arianna stole a glance at her and saw two spots of color flaming in Selene's cheeks. At last she stood up with an oddly languid grace. There was a strange, wild look in her green eyes. Without a word to Arianna she followed Thomas from the room. And Arianna, who would gladly have changed places with Selene, could only gaze after them in appalled wonder at her friend's reluctance to bed with the husband who so obviously adored her.

Chapter 5

In that unusually severe winter of cold and snow, storms were all too frequent. The whirling blizzard which had begun the day after Thomas and Selene's wedding had kept the group from Afoncaer confined at St. Albans for three extra days, a circumstance which had finally made them all unhappy, each for his or her own reasons.

Thomas had at first been pleased to have more time in private with Selene before the journey began, but by the fourth day he, too, was eager to be on his way. Like Guy, he was always concerned about Afoncaer. They were both anxious to return to the restive Welsh border, where trouble might erupt at any time. They and the armed men who had accompanied them to St. Albans might be badly needed. Meredith longed to see her home and her nine-year-old daughter once more. All three worried about Reynaud and the difficulties of transporting a badly injured man from Wenlock Priory to Afoncaer in such weather.

Arianna chafed at the enforced inactivity of St. Albans. She had had more than enough of feasts and royal entertainments—and of watching

Thomas make all too plain his devotion to Selene. Arianna wanted to be gone from that place and ease her aching heart in the excitement of travel. Her deepest desire during those snowy days was to be at Afoncaer and to immerse herself in the new life and the opportunity Meredith had offered to her. While waiting for the storm to end she spent as much time as possible with Meredith. When she could not do that she went to the abbey church and knelt on the cold stone floor, praying that the unwanted, overwhelming, and totally hopeless love she felt for Thomas might before long be converted into something less painful. But at night, lying on the trundle bed in the room she still shared with Lady Aloise and Sir Valaire and their sons, she knew her love for Thomas was in her heart forever, and she must learn to endure the pain it caused.

As for Selene, she had her own variety of unhappiness to deal with as Thomas continued to make passionate love to her each night, and to drag her with him, all unwilling, into those realms of breathless, pulsating desire where she did not want to go. Now, on the fifth morning after her marriage, Selene was relieved to learn that immediately after mass the company bound for Afoncaer would set out upon the old Roman road, now called Watling Street, that led north and west from St. Albans. They could not be gone soon enough for her. She was heartily sick of bridal jokes and sly looks from the courtiers who were all also snowbound. They reminded her of the thing that happened at night when she was alone with Thomas, the thing she hated and tried to prevent, yet gave into repeatedly, unable to stop her body's response to him.

She had tried to appear indifferent to his love and to the amused comments of the sophisticated nobles and their ladies, maintaining her air of cold aloofness toward everyone about her. She had succeeded best with Thomas, who, she knew, was hurt and bewildered by the contrast between their wildly passionate nights together and the way she treated him in public.

"Could you not be a little kinder?" Arianna asked, following Selene into her bedchamber. "You insulted the poor man just now, and for no cause at all."

Selene shrugged and did not reply.

"Really," Arianna went on, "you are the most exasperating creature. Anyone else in your position would be happy, yet you do nothing but sulk all the time. You will drive Thomas away from you when he wants to honor and love you. Have some thought for him."

"I am not sulking, and my position is more miserable than you can imagine," Selene replied sharply. "I *loathe* marriage. And why should you be concerned for Thomas? He's nothing to you. Where are you going? I need you to help with packing the rest of these clothes. The serving women are all with Meredith. Arianna?" But Arianna had fled the room. Selene tossed the offending gowns upon the bed in frustration.

She wanted to be on the road to Afoncaer, and every delay irritated her. Lodging along the way, in abbey guesthouses or the occasional inn, would be crowded, the men and women in their group often separated. There would very likely be no opportunity at all for lovemaking until they arrived at Afoncaer. With more bad weather possible at any time, and the detour to Much Wenlock Priory to collect the mysterious architect Reynaud adding still more delay to the trip, Selene hoped for at least ten days of freedom from the romantic encounters that were a torment to her.

She heard the bedchamber door open and close.

"Arianna. So you have come back to help me after all. You should be ashamed of scolding me." She whirled angrily to face, not her friend, but a grim-visaged Thomas.

"So Arianna has been scolding you, has she? I'll add my voice to hers. I am most annoyed with you, my lady." Thomas stood, hands on hips, frowning at her in a manner very unlike his usual tender attitude.

"You have no reason to rebuke me, my lord," Selene said coldly.

"Have I not? How can you claim that when, less than an hour ago, instead of saying a proper farewell to your father, you insulted me before both him and Uncle Guy?"

"Will you beat me for it? My mother said you would if I did not always obey you."

"Selene, I would never beat you." Thomas sighed, running both hands through his hair and leaving it in complete disarray. "I only want to understand why you act as you do. At night, when we are alone together, you are the most passionate woman I have ever known, more than I ever hoped or dreamed a wife could be. I am mad with love for you. But before others you treat me as though you hate me, and that I will not allow, nor would any man with pride."

Selene stood quietly, her hands folded before her. She lowered her head, knowing that her silken veil would fall forward to obscure her face, as her maiden's loose hair had used to do when she wanted to hide her expression. If Thomas could not see her face, if he was unable to look into her eyes, he might not guess how frightened she was. If he knew the depths of blackness in her soul, he would cast her out. She told herself she did not care about Thomas, not really. But something—perhaps the secret, lustful Selene who lived inside her and only revealed herself in bed at night—made her want to stay with Thomas. Or perhaps it was just the recollection of what she had sworn to do for Thomas's mother that made her so meek when she spoke to him again.

"I am sorry if I have displeased you, my lord," she said. "I will try to be a better wife to you."

"Selene." He took her hands. "Tell me what is troubling you so sorely. I know something is. Let me help you."

She looked at her hands, nearly lost between his two larger, square ones, her wrists wrapped by his tapering fingers, the same fingers that caressed her unwilling flesh each night and made her desire him until she could not stop no matter how hard she tried. Just the touch of those hands was all that was needed to make the blood pound in her ears. She wanted him to pick her up in his strong arms and toss her onto the bed and take her. Right now. Without even undressing. She was wicked, lost in vile sin. She had to think of something else, something equally frightening, to take her thoughts away from his hard, strong body and the surging manhood that could fill her with unspeakably delicious, delirious passion.

"Selene?" He was looking at her strangely, and she wondered if he guessed at her thoughts. She hoped not. And then she thought of something that would distract him from the question she did not want to answer. She had planned to wait a while, but suddenly this seemed exactly the right time.

"Do you never write to your mother, my lord?"

"My mother?" Thomas dropped her hands and stared at her in astonishment. "Why do you mention her? She is forbidden to have any contact with me at all. I will not write to her and give her an opportunity to break her oath to Uncle Guy."

"What oath?" Selene was unsure what to say to this. Isabel had never told her of any stricture about contacting Thomas.

"It was part of the promise she made when she went into exile," Thomas said, "the promise that let her, and Walter fitz Alan, keep their heads upon their shoulders. I ask you again, Selene, why do you mention my mother?"

"She misses you. Each day of her life she longs to see you again. Walter fitz Alan is dead, and Lady Isabel is lonely."

"How do you know this?"

"She visited my mother this past summer." Selene saw the shock on his face at her words. Disregarding his obvious distaste for this conversation, she pressed on, saying what Isabel had wanted her to say to him. "She was most kind to me. I learned to know her well, and to know how much she loves you."

"Was it she who suggested we marry?" asked Thomas.

"Oh, no, my lord," Selene lied with every appearance of innocence. "It was my mother's idea; she had spoken to me about it long before Lady Isabel visited us. Though my mother did tell her what was planned, and Lady Isabel was greatly pleased that the children of two old friends should be joined. But the most important thing, of course, was my dowry, the chest of gold coins."

"Yes." Thomas gave her a searching look, which Selene bore as best she could, trying to look sweetly innocent. She understood in a flash of insight that Thomas believed her because he wanted to believe her, and in that moment she realized the power she might hold over him if she were very clever, power that would help her in her task for Isabel.

"Lady Isabel spoke to me often of her sorrow at losing you," Selene went on guilelessly, "and so I thought you might write to her, a letter now and then. You could tell her she need not break her vow by answering you, and your letters might relieve her grief by letting her know how you are faring."

"I will not do that. It's not wise, and it would upset Uncle Guy. My mother is a devious woman, Selene. She has earned her exile." Thomas looked at her shrewdly. "If you had any idea of writing to her yourself, you may forget it. I forbid you to have any contact with the Lady Isabel."

"Yes, my lord," Selene said meekly, her eyes downcast, apparently accepting her husband's will. "Please forgive me. I did not mean to make you angry. I only wanted to help you. I want you to be happy, Thomas, and content in our life together."

"Do you? It pleases me to hear you say that. Of course I forgive you, my love. You are so innocent you could have been no match for my mother when she tried to influence you to speak to me on her behalf. We'll think no more of it. It's over."

She did look directly at him then, and smiled with sweet artlessness when he kissed her tenderly and patted her on the shoulder, telling her to hurry her preparations for the journey. Thomas then went off to the stables to oversee the men-at-arms who were charged with transporting and guarding Selene's dowry. He left his wife well satisfied with the first steps she had taken in Isabel's plan.

Isabel had warned her what Thomas's reaction would probably be to the suggestion that he write directly to his mother, but they had agreed that Selene would try it before resorting to stealthier methods. Now Selene would begin to disobey her husband. She had a friend, a girl who had been at the convent school with her and who now was wed to a nobleman of Poitou, and this Lady Elvira loved secrets and intrigues. She would be delighted to receive an occasional letter from her friend Selene, and to pass along a second letter enclosed inside the first. It would be a long way from Afoncaer to Poitou to Dol in Brittany, and Selene could use the route only once or twice a year, but it would be enough to maintain contact. Isabel would have her revenge, and she would know about it, if not from Thomas, then from Selene.

In the meantime, Selene had deflected Thomas's anger from herself and turned aside his unwelcome questions, in the process discovering a way to manage her husband by using his love for her. She dismissed the serving woman who had arrived to help her, and humming a little tune as she worked, she finished packing her own gowns for the trip to Afoncaer.

That trip proceeded as Selene had assumed it would. As she had hoped, she was separated from

Thomas each night. Selene, Arianna, and Meredith regularly shared a bed, with their female servants rolled into blankets on the floor of whatever chamber the women were occupying, while the men all slept together elsewhere. The rigors of a journey over rough roads, the biting cold that whitened and numbed fingers and toes, noses and any uncovered ears, did not dismay Selene. She would sit patiently upon her palfrey, waiting while Guy's men forced their horses through the snowdrifts that so often blocked their way, and then, when her turn came, she would ride calmly through the trails they had made.

"How brave you are," Arianna said, shivering. "I'm wet and half-frozen, and my nose keeps running. You always look absolutely perfect. Your face isn't even chapped like everyone else's."

"I have a warm cloak," Selene replied. She patted her horse's neck, watching the steamy vapor flare from the beast's nostrils. There was a constant fog of expelled breath hanging about the travellers, and at night the smell of damp wool drying by a wood fire filled the air.

Selene loved it all. The frigid weather matched the cold in her soul, and Thomas could not touch her body to thaw her into lascivious need of him. She wished the journey could go on forever. But it could not, and despite a delay of two days when they were holed up in a miserably dirty inn by yet another snowstorm, they came eventually to Much Wenlock Priory.

The short winter day had ended and it was already dark when they arrived. Selene could see little in the dimness of the carefully husbanded oil lamps. She had only confused impressions of the priory's guestmaster handing the women over to a lesser monk who escorted them from the entrance gate to their chamber in the abbey guesthouse.

"It's not much different from St. Albans," Arianna said, looking around the room, "only smaller and more sparsely furnished. We women must still all sleep together. But it is clean, and we have our own fresh sheets and blankets."

Selene stood to one side of the chamber, watching the servants unpack what they would need for one night's stay, and secretly praying for a howling blizzard that would delay their trip even longer.

"Are you coming with us?" Arianna asked.

"Where?" Selene had not been following the conversation.

"To see Reynaud," Meredith answered. "He has been carried to one of the guest chambers within this building so we women may visit him while he's in bed, and so we can remove him from here in the early morning without disrupting the priory's usual routine. Guy wants to leave at dawn. We must travel more slowly with Reynaud than we did before, and Guy wants to reach Afoncaer before the weather turns bad again. Arianna and I are going to Reynaud now. Will you come with us?"

Selene was not at all interested in this injured architect who so concerned Meredith, but the two women were looking at her expectantly, so she followed them out of the room, along a short, dimly lit passage to a tiny chamber that was little more than a cubicle. It contained a stool, a small table cluttered with basin, ewer, drinking cup, and rolls of linen bandages, and a narrow bed, upon which rested a person Selene could not see because the room was so **full** of people. Or at least so it seemed to her at first, but it was not long before Selene realized it was not the number of people but the size of the room that made it seem so crowded. Besides the three women, Guy was there, and Thomas, and a tall, thin monk in a black robe who was explaining just how serious Reynaud's injuries were.

"I shall try not to die of this, my friend," came a weak, yet firm voice from the bed. "I will not be a burden to you. I pray I will soon be able to work again, and thus earn my bread."

The tall monk moved aside and Selene could see Reynaud. She gave a cry and started backward, hands pressed to her mouth, trying to control the sudden heaving of her stomach. Beside her, Arianna gave a soft moan of pity and moved forward, reaching both hands out to Reynaud, but Selene stood rooted, leaning backward, away from the sight. She had never been able to endure being in a sickroom. In her father's castle or in the convent she had stayed away from anyone who was injured or ill. Now she wanted to turn and run, but Thomas had seen her. He crossed the tiny room in a single step and put one arm around her shoulders, urging her forward.

"Come and meet my dear friend Reynaud," Thomas said. Selene knew he expected her to join Arianna, who was just being presented to the architect, and Meredith, who was sitting on the edge of the bed, holding a bandaged hand and talking to Reynaud while tears ran down her cheeks.

"This is my wife, Selene," Thomas said proudly. Reynaud tore his one visible eye away from

Meredith's face and looked at Selene. A pale blue warmth searched her face, growing steadily colder as he examined her expression and looked deep into her eyes. By the time he was done, Selene felt pierced by ice, and she thought Reynaud must have seen the cold evil lurking inside her, for he said nothing to her but only listened to Thomas's account of their wedding in the king's presence, and how happy he was with the wife his Uncle Guy had chosen for him.

Of Reynaud himself, not much could be seen but stained and dirty bandages. His head was almost completely swathed in linen strips, except for the one eye and his mouth and chin. His left arm was heavily bandaged, only his fingers showing, and these Meredith held. Reynaud was leaning rather awkwardly on his right elbow while Arianna adjusted pillows so he could sit up. Selene noticed below his hips, where his legs should be, a high mound beneath the thin blanket on the left side, a mound that reached only as far as his knee and then ended abruptly in a perfect flatness. Selene swallowed hard, imagining what the ugly mound contained.

The tall monk went out, followed by Guy.

"I'll join them," Thomas said to Selene. "There are some formalities to discuss with the prior, and I want to be there. From this time on, Reynaud is no longer a member of this particular religious community, but is a guest as we are. He's in our care now. Meredith will make him well. Help her as much as you can, my love." Thomas left her wondering what to do next.

"Come and help us, Selene." Meredith had wiped away her tears and had begun to unwind the bandages around Reynaud's head. "We'll

104

cleanse his wounds first. I've brought an ointment to put on them, to take away the pain and inflammation, and then we'll rebandage him with clean linen. That's all I can do until we reach Afoncaer and my other supplies. The medicines I brought with me were almost all used up on Guy's men-at-arms and their minor injuries during the trip. I'm afraid there is a hard journey ahead for you, Reynaud. Perhaps the infirmarer here has some poppy syrup that would ease the discomfort you are sure to feel."

"No," Reynaud said, his one eye on Meredith's intent face, his lips drawn tight with pain as she carefully eased the last of the linen off his nose and left cheek. "When I was first injured, Brother Infirmarer gave me that poppy syrup. It did help the pain, but it was all too tempting to ask for it again and again, so I could sink into the oblivion it offers. I'll not take that way. I can bear a few twinges and aches for the sake of reaching Afoncaer once more."

"I think you will have more than aches and twinges, Master Reynaud." That was Arianna, her face pale and set into severe lines of determination, her grey eyes dark with pity as she watched Meredith's hands slowly uncovering the architect's battered face. There was a wide gash extending from his right forehead across his nose and left cheekbone, and all the area around his left eye was hugely swollen.

"I can't open it," Reynaud said in answer to Meredith's question. "The swelling won't go down, and Brother Infirmarer thinks I will never recover use of that eye."

"I'm not sure," Meredith said, her fingers probing very gently. When Reynaud winced, she stopped her examination. "I can't tell for certain, Reynaud, but it may be that with the medicines I have at Afoncaer, I will be able to help your sight. Arianna, wash his face carefully while I get rid of this dirty linen. Selene, you may help with the ointment. You can learn, too."

"No. No, I can't." Selene stared at Reynaud's broken, discolored face and tried to choke back the bile that rose into her throat at the thought of touching that awful wound. "I can't. Don't ask me. I can't stay here." She fumbled for the door latch, found it, and tore it open. She nearly fell through the doorway in her haste to be gone from that room, with its heavy odor of sickness and infected flesh.

The drafty air of the passageway outside Reynaud's door fanned across her hot, perspiring face, cooling and calming her a little. Selene took a deep breath. She knew she was going to be sick. It was always that way whenever she had to look at something bloody or unpleasant. She hurried toward her room, hoping she would reach it in time. The passage was so dark and gloomy it was frightening.

Selene broke into a run, turned a corner she did not remember passing before, and flew straight into Thomas's arms. She did not recognize him at first. She gave a gasp of terror, reared back her head, and then saw who it was. His features were just discernible in the dim light. She clutched at him, catching his leather sleeves in fingers made strong by fear and horror.

"Thomas, don't make me stay there. Don't make me touch him. I can't do it. Please, please." Thomas's astonished face spun before her, the passageway blurred into total blackness, and Selene felt

106

her knees buckling. There was a great roaring in her ears that blocked out all sound.

Then strong arms lifted her, and her head rested on her husband's broad, leather-clad shoulder. She kept her eyes closed while he carried her back to the chamber door she had passed unknowing in her panic-stricken flight. Selene opened her eyes to candlelight as Thomas laid her down on the bed, then removed her veil and loosened the tight coils of her raven-black hair.

"You may go," Thomas said to the maidservants who had been unpacking and now stood about the room, staring at him. "My lady has fainted. I'll stay with her until she's herself again. Just give me some wine for her, and then go and eat. There's food set out for you in the guest hall."

Thomas held the wine cup to Selene's pale lips. When the maids had all left he latched the door and came to sit on the bed beside her once more. She was weeping, and he smoothed back her disordered hair and wiped away the tears.

"My dearest," he said softly, kissing her forehead and then her quivering lips.

"Thomas, please." She touched his face with a shaky hand. "Don't make me go back there."

"To Reynaud? Why should he frighten you?"

"It's not Reynaud. Not him alone. I can't stand the sight of blood, or of wounds. I never could. It makes me ill. Arianna is strong, she can help Meredith, but I can't."

Thomas gathered her into his arms, holding her and rocking her as though she were a hurt, frightened child. Indeed, she was so small and fragile that she might have been a child, and at first his feelings were an odd combination of paternal tenderness and disappointment. She had displayed a weakness most unbecoming in a woman who one day would be the mistress of a castle and who might, in the future, have to assume sole responsibility for the care of those wounded in defending that castle.

Ah, well, he told himself with a sigh, she was still young. She would have plenty of time to lose this peculiar fear of hers. Meredith would help in that. Meanwhile, they were alone together for the first time in too many days, and he had missed their nightly lovemaking. She was clinging to him and nestling her head beneath his chin while his one hand stroked her undone hair and his other arm and hand pressed her closer against him. Thomas felt the heat in his loins, felt his manhood growing in response to her nearness. His lips brushed across her cheek, and the hand that had been stroking her hair lifted her chin until their mouths met. Thomas tasted the salt of her tears on her lips, along with the sweetness that only Selene brought to him.

"Oh, my love," he breathed, and put his mouth on hers again and moved his hand downward to cup a small, firm breast. She moaned, and he felt the nipple harden beneath her fine woolen gown. His hand moved further, catching her hips and pushing them against his own as he pressed her down onto the bed and rolled on top of her, letting her feel his need, sensing her initial hesitation and then the sudden flare of her desire. She had been like that each time they made love. First refusal, then wild passion.

"Thomas, Thomas," she murmured, moving her head back on the pillows, her emerald eyes bright with yet unshed tears, her lips parted softly, her tongue poised to do battle with his own. "Thomas. You do love me, don't you?"

"More than my life."

Her hands pulled his head down toward hers, the small pink tongue reached out and captured his lips, playing with him, tormenting him until at last she ground her mouth against his and her tongue surged into him, attacking the hot moistness, demanding his response. He could not get enough of her mouth. He returned to it again and again, hungrily craving the excitement of that moist, welcoming warmth, until even that was not enough, and he knew her mounting passion was as great as his own.

He fumbled at his clothing, pulling up his leather tunic, tugging at the thongs that held his hose, Selene helping him eagerly, her fingers grasping, greedy, rubbing on him, bringing him to a point of intense, painful need. Then she let him go, and lifted her skirts, or tried to. Her dress had become tangled around her legs and she could not get free of it. She twisted and turned and lifted her hips, pulling at the fabric, her body brushing against his repeatedly during her struggles, further inflaming him, while Thomas tried to help her with clumsy, over-eager hands. Both of them were aware that someone might come to the chamber door at any moment, but they could not wait, they had to come together, they were desperate with wanting each other, and no matter what happened they could not stop now.

"Hurry, hurry," she moaned, finally dragging both skirt and underdress up to her waist. Thomas had a hasty glimpse of green leather shoes, of stockings held at the knee with blue ribbon garters, and above the stockings the smooth, creamy

109

skin of her thighs, opening to him, inviting him. "Thomas, please hurry. I burn. I burn. Ahhh, there, like that. I thought we'd never—never—oh, Thomas, Thomas."

She raised herself to meet his every stroke, taking him deeply within her, crying out in pleasure, and Thomas, his senses raised to feverish heat by her response, felt as though he were floating on the tide of her desire. He was lost in her, he loved her completely, he had never imagined a woman could be so exciting. She was everything he had ever wanted, and he gave himself to her totally, plunging into her sweet body again and again until she had had her fill of him and he was free to take his own pleasure, gasping out his love of her, his adoration, then at last coming to a peaceful rest across her now quiet form.

She was weeping again. She did that often after they had made love, and Thomas had by now given up the fear that he hurt her in some physical way. It puzzled him. He did not want her to be unhappy.

"It wasn't me," Selene whispered. "It was the other one, the demon. It wasn't me."

"My sweet love, what are you talking about?" Thomas raised himself on one elbow to look at her. She seemed to him more beautiful than ever, with her loosened hair tangled across the pillow and her lips bruised and softened by his passionate kisses. He wanted her again at that moment, as much as he had wanted her half an hour before, and he marvelled at her ability to stir his senses without even trying. He heard her whisper those strange words once more, and felt a chill down his spine.

"It's the demon," Selene murmured, her eyes

closed. "Selene would never do such a thing, in a priory, with other people about, pull up her skirts and take a man. Not Selene."

Terrified by those low, whispered words he could just barely hear, Thomas took his wife by the shoulders and shook her hard.

"Selene!"

The emerald eyes flew open, gazed blankly at him, then slowly focused on his face.

"Thomas," she said in her normal, husky tones. "Husband."

"Selene, what in heaven's name—" His words were interrupted by a knock at the door, followed by Meredith's voice.

"Selene, are you in there? Are you ill? Open the door, my dear. I need to speak with you."

"We are found out," Thomas said, forgetting his concern over Selene's strange behavior in the humor of the situation. "Caught in bed with my own wife, and before the evening meal, too." He scrambled to his feet, straightening his clothes hastily, then held out his hand to raise Selene from the bed.

"Selene, please open the door." That was Meredith again.

"My hair." Selene's hands were shaking as she tried to smooth the shining black mass now tumbling freely about her shoulders.

"Don't worry. Meredith will understand." Thomas grinned at her and pulled the door wide open.

Meredith looked at him in surprise, then at Selene, still in great disarray, attempting to straighten her skirts and her hair at the same time, and lastly Meredith looked at the rumpled bed behind them.

"I am sorry to disturb you," Meredith said,

111

warm laughter lighting her eyes, her smile matching Thomas's. "Shall we go away and leave you alone?"

"That won't be necessary." Thomas bent to kiss his wife. "I love you, Selene."

He went out, brushing past a white-faced Arianna. He scarcely noticed her holding on to the doorframe to keep herself upright as she realized what had just transpired within that room, upon the bed where she and Meredith and Selene would all sleep that same night.

It took three more days to reach Afoncaer. They travelled more slowly now, to ease the way for Reynaud, who lay rocking uncomfortably in a litter slung between two horses. On the morning of their departure from Wenlock Priory, Guy had picked Reynaud up in his arms and personally carried his old friend to the litter. There Reynaud was placed upon furs and blankets, his injured arm and what remained of his left leg eased upon pillows, and then he was covered with more furs until only the right side of his face was visible. He bore whatever pain this transfer caused him with great fortitude, nor did he complain during the journey.

"I fear for him," Guy said quietly to Meredith. "He was so light when I carried him. He's wasted away to bones and little else. And though he's brave, I think his spirit's badly damaged, too."

"Bring us safe to Afoncaer," Meredith said, both hands on her husband's arm, looking up at him with love and trust, "only get us home to Afoncaer and I'll do my best to make him well. And Arianna will help me." Here Meredith put

112

one arm around the girl who stood by her side, listening to their conversation with considerable interest.

"I've heard about your willing hands." Guy looked approvingly at Arianna. "Reynaud told me how gentle you were with him, and how you did not flinch at the sight of the stump of his leg. Others were not so strong as they should be." Guy's glance had fallen upon Selene and he frowned.

"We had best go if we're to reach Shrewsbury before dark," Meredith said, diverting Guy's attention from Selene. He took the reins of her mare from the groom who held them, and himself helped his wife to mount. Then he gave the signal to start the last part of their journey.

They stopped for that night at Shrewsbury Abbey. The next day they rode north, past Oswestry on their left, heading toward Chester. They rode with the great earthwork on their left, the dike that had been made centuries before to keep the wild Welsh tribesmen out of the more peaceful eastern farmlands. This border, often disputed, was no safe place for women or invalids. The men-at-arms Guy had brought with him rode close about them during this final part of the trip, especially after they had turned due west, onto the road that ran past Afoncaer and then into the very heart of yet unconquered Wales. They were fortunate and met no raiding parties but had only to fight the cold and the wind, and frequent flurries of snow interspersed with sudden, blinding sunlight.

They arrived at Afoncaer near sunset of the third day after leaving Wenlock. To Selene it looked huge and forbidding, a solid, white-washed stone bulk, forcibly impressed upon the landscape. It was much larger than her father's castle in Brittany, and much more strongly built.

Afoncaer lay on a high bluff between a deep river and a wild, rushing stream that met the river just beneath the tower keep. So fierce had been the Welsh opposition to Norman settlement here that the town which had grown up about the castle proper had been enclosed within its stout outer walls for safety's sake. But under Guy's rule there had been a period of relative peace, and the town had grown steadily until now houses crowded behind the wall and some even spilled outside it, squeezed between the far side of the wet moat and the plowed fields that lay beyond the town.

"We need another wall," Thomas said, seeing Selene's wondering look at the signs of burgeoning growth. "We have to clear more land for farming so we can feed all these newcomers. We will use Reynaud to plan it all, once he's well again."

The farmland laying outside the walls was relatively level, as was the area where the town had been built just inside the first wall. It was not until they had crossed the drawbridge over the wet moat and ridden along the main street of the town to approach the inner wall which surrounded the castle itself, that the land began to rise. Before this inner wall, there was a deep, dry moat with a sharply slanted drawbridge over it, and a strong, easily defended gatehouse. Once inside the bailey, Selene could see the steep upward rise of the bluff, and the great, square tower keep that stood on the highest point of Afoncaer. Next to the keep and connected to it was a large stone building that must be the great hall. There were other buildings in the bailey, but it was growing too dark to see very clearly, and Selene was too weary to look. She would find her way around the castle grounds another time. She slid off her horse and into Thomas's arms.

"Welcome home," he said, planting a kiss on each of her cheeks before swinging her to her feet. "I hope you and I live here long and happily, my love."

They stood aside, watching in the cold dusk while Reynaud was lifted out of his litter and carried up the stone steps into the keep, Meredith and Arianna following close behind him.

"Come," Thomas said, pulling Serene along with him to where Guy was talking with a man who had come out from the keep to greet him. "Geoffrey, well met." Thomas let go of Selene's hand to embrace the man.

"Sir Thomas! I can call you *Sir* Thomas at last!" Geoffrey pounded Thomas on the back. "For a year or so there, I doubted you would ever consent to knighting."

"Here is my wife, Selene," Thomas said, bringing her forward.

Geoffrey took her hand and bowed over it. He was shorter than Thomas and Guy, squarely built, with brown hair and eyes and an honest, open face that stood out clearly in the light of the flaring torches held by Guy's servants. Selene's first impression of Sir Geoffrey of Tynant was of his squareness and brownness, and of his open affection for Guy, whose squire he had been, and for Thomas, who had been his squire.

"Come inside," Geoffrey said. "You must be chilled, my lady."

The four of them moved up the narrow stone

stairway and into the keep, Geoffrey guiding Selene through a small forebuilding where a guard stood, then along a short, narrow passage, up a few more steps, and into the great hall. Fires burned brightly at either end of the long hall, and tables were being set up for a meal. Selene went at once to the nearest fire, holding out her cold hands to its warmth.

"You will want to go to your room," Guy said to Selene, "and you will want your women to attend you. Where is Joan?"

"Probably with Reynaud," Geoffrey replied. "She was always fond of him. She'll want to see him comfortably settled before anyone else is. Yes, *Sir* Thomas, go look for her, she'll want to greet you, too. We will stay here with your lady. My God, Guy," Geoffrey went on when Thomas had left them. "What happened to poor Reynaud? He looks as though you had brought him straight from the battlefield."

While Guy explained Reynaud's accident to Geoffrey, Selene looked about the great hall, noting its pleasing proportions and the tall, glazed windows that would let in light during the day. Rich tapestries of many colors hung upon the grey stone walls, while bright banners were draped from the rafters. Beautifully carved stone mantels surmounted the two enormous fireplaces that gave both light and heat. There were several finely made wooden chairs sitting upon the dais, and the high table was laid with a spotless white linen cloth and lit by wax tapers in ornate silver holders. Herbs were strewn upon the floor among the fresh rushes. There was little sign of the usual refuse from previous meals that had always littered the floor of Sir Valaire's hall. In place of the

116

stench of rotting food and more unmentionable filth, Selene breathed in the scent of rue and lavender and mellow woodruff. The servants who were arranging the trestle tables looked well dressed and well fed, and surprisingly clean. Obviously, Afoncaer was a wealthy, efficiently managed place.

"And there has been no trouble with the Welsh while I've been gone?" Selene heard Guy ask.

"One or two insignificant raids into Powys," Geoffrey replied, "before the weather turned bad. Even the Welsh don't care much for battle during a blizzard. I'll give you a full report tomorrow, and hear all your news, and then the next day I'll be off to Tynant. Afoncaer is a fine place, my friend, and I serve the time I owe to you gladly, but Tynant is home to me. I'll be happy to see it again, and to sleep in my own bed."

"Is there often warfare with the Welsh?" Selene asked.

"There was in the past, under Baron Lionel," Geoffrey told her. "But since Guy has been baron, it has been a quiet place. Sometimes I wish for a little battle, just for the excitement. We do have to stay on our guard always. You never know with the Welsh. You think all is calm and peaceful, and then suddenly they erupt into revolt, and you never know where it will be. Now, here is Joan, come to show you to your room."

Selene followed the sturdy, grey-haired woman out of the great hall and up a spiral staircase to the third level of the keep.

"Thomas chose this room for you before he went away to marry you," Joan said, "because he had been told your eyes were green. I hope you will be content here, my lady."

117

It was a richly furnished room, with a large bed curtained in green wool, and a deep window niche with stone seats on each side of the window, padded with green cushions. There was a bearskin rug on the floor, the walls were plastered and painted in green and gold, and two large braziers gave off welcome heat. Selene saw that the chests and baskets containing her personal belongings had been brought in and piled up against one wall.

"Your serving women are supervising the unloading of the rest of your things. They will be here shortly," Joan said. She stood still a moment, looking at Selene as though weighing the younger woman's merit, then added, "I hope you will make Thomas happy, my lady. I have known him since the day he was born, and I love him as though he were my own son. I wish you both joy of your marriage."

"If you have known him all his life," Selene said, "then you must have known his mother, too."

"Aye," Joan replied, her pleasant face closing in. "I was Lady Isabel's servant until she married Walter fitz Alan and moved to Tynant. Lord Guy asked that I remain here and act as his chatelaine. He wasn't married at that time, and he needed someone to manage the female part of his household."

"Then you can tell me about Lady Isabel."

"No, I cannot," Joan said firmly, "except that she was a vain, selfish woman, who never thought of anyone but herself."

"Perhaps you misjudged her. Surely she loved her son."

"I don't know whether she did or not," Joan said. "My lady, if you'll take my advice, you won't mention Lady Isabel to the folk of Afoncaer. Those who remember her did not love her." With that, Joan left her alone.

The woman was wrong, of course. Joan had misjudged Lady Isabel. Everyone had. Selene knew it, for Lady Isabel had told her so, during those friendly talks they had shared. Isabel had warned her that people would say harsh things about her and that Selene should pay no heed to their words, for they, poor souls, simply did not understand. Still, it was disturbing that no one seemed to have a kind word for Thomas's mother.

Selene was not left alone long. Thomas arrived to throw his arms around her and tell her how much he loved her.

"I have been to see Reynaud," Thomas said. "Meredith has given him an herbal drink to make him sleep, and Arianna is helping to change his bandages. I cannot help but admire that girl, Selene. I scarcely noticed her before, but now I see her working with Meredith and eager to learn all she can, and I am glad she has come to Afoncaer. She's a nice young woman, isn't she?"

"Yes," Selene said, not really paying attention to his words. She was wondering how to get out of the room before Thomas could coax her onto the bed and sweep her into that terrifying state where all she wanted was to come together with him until she lost her senses in wild, ecstatic lust. Feeling her heart begin to pound faster at the thought, she pushed him aside. "Yes, Arianna is a dear, good friend."

"Then she will be my friend, too," Thomas declared, attempting to take his wife into his arms again.

"Oh, Thomas, not now," she said hastily. "I'm so tired after that dreadful trip. Couldn't you be patient with me, and not insist on doing *that* to me until I'm more rested? Please?"

"Certainly, my love. I was thoughtless. I've no wish to force you, and we must very soon go down to the feast Joan has had prepared. Everyone at Afoncaer wants to meet you and to welcome you to your new home. We'll make love later. Until then, I'll take my pleasure in thinking about you." He tried to kiss her, but Selene pulled away from him again.

"No, Thomas, you said you wouldn't. Please leave me alone."

Thomas tried to put aside his aching need for her, but it was impossible. Selene presented such a tantalizing puzzle that no matter what he was doing, he could never get her completely out of his mind. He knew if he insisted, and kept kissing and touching her, there would come a moment—and it would not take very long, either—when she would suddenly flare into uncontrollable desire and grab at him, using him as though his body were an instrument created solely for her carnal pleasure. When it was over she would be cool and distant once more and murmur about someone else taking her place. It was frightening, but it was wildly exciting, too, and it had been that way since the very first time they had made love, when such violent passion in a virgin had surprised and delighted him, and then left him feeling oddly uneasy. But there had been no doubt that she had been a virgin.

He watched his lovely wife directing the maid-servants when they arrived, overseeing the unpacking of her belongings and then his, and he

120

thought he had never known a woman with such mysterious depths, so many secrets to be discovered. It would take a lifetime, a long, happy unfolding of their innermost selves to each other. Thomas, not half so experienced with women as he liked to think himself, looked forward to learning everything there was to know about Selene.

Chapter 6

Arianna's room was also on the third floor of the keep, but on the opposite side from Thomas's and Selene's. She had asked to be placed next to Reynaud in case he should need help at night. Meredith, who shared the large lord's chamber on the fourth floor with Guy, had readily agreed with this suggestion, and had ordered Arianna's choice of rooms prepared for her at once.

Reynaud had been bathed and rebandaged and fed, and had swallowed a cup of hot herbal brew before falling into an apparently peaceful sleep. Meredith had set a young serving girl to watch over him, warning the girl to call Arianna or her at once if Reynaud should waken, then had departed the sickroom for her own chamber.

Thus, in this interval before the evening meal began, Arianna was free to unpack her few belongings. Her room was small and simply furnished, and Arianna was well pleased with it. It was built into the thickness of the stone wall of the keep, and had only a single narrow window, now shuttered against the cold, with one stone seat in the niche. The bed was just big enough for one person, covered in a lovely shade of blue-green wool, with matching curtains to draw at night. Meredith had ordered a brazier for warmth, and had promised hot water for a bath would be sent soon.

Arianna folded away her good linen undershift and looked about contentedly. She had never had a room to herself before. She had always had to share with Selene, or, when Selene had gone away to the convent school, with several maidservants. Now she had her own private place, an almost unheard-of luxury in a crowded castle. She had useful work to look forward to, helping to nurse Reynaud back to health and, in the process, learning all she could from Meredith. She had friends in Guy and Meredith, in Selene, and in Thomas, too, if she could only control her unreasonable, foolish love for him and never let him see it. She was blessed beyond anything a penniless orphan ought to expect. She was grateful for what she had, and she knew she ought to ask for nothing more. And yet . . . and yet . . . some rebellious corner of her heart yearned for Thomas, forbidden to her, husband to her dear friend and kinswoman.

Arianna had bathed and washed her hair, and the tub and buckets of water had been carried out, when she heard a tap on the door.

"Come in," she called, assuming it was Meredith. The door opened to disclose, not the mistress of the castle, but a small, slender girl, nine or ten years old by the look of her.

"I pray your pardon for disturbing you, my lady," the girl said, all politeness and careful manners. "Are you the Lady Arianna?"

"I am." Arianna looked down into huge blue eyes and smiled at the child's serious face. Her copper-gold hair was in two thick braids which hung over her shoulders, glowing against her dark blue woolen dress. Curls had come loose from the braids, to make a halo about her head. Arianna noticed a sprinkling of freckles across the delicate nose.

"I am Cristin," the child said formally, "daughter of Lord Guy and Lady Meredith, and I am sent to escort you to the great hall for the evening meal, my lady."

"Cristin." Arianna considered the carefully composed demeanor and wondered what this girl was really like. "I'm not quite ready. Will you come in and wait? I won't be long."

"Yes, my lady." Cristin advanced a few steps into the room and stood primly, watching while Arianna picked up a comb and attacked her thick curls. They were still damp and thoroughly tangled after being washed, and as she tugged at them the comb caught on a snarl and flew out of her fingers. It clattered upon the floor and disappeared from sight.

In an instant the well-controlled Cristin was gone, changed into a young hoyden who dove to the floor to retrieve the comb, leaving Arianna staring at bare legs and tiny feet in leather slippers while the rest of the child was underneath the bed. She quickly came out again, dusting off her dress as she stood up.

"I have the same problem with my hair," Cristin said, handing Arianna the comb.

"I can see you have." Arianna could not help laughing. More hair had come loose from Cristin's braids and it stood up all over her small head in a mass of curls.

"Try braiding it," Cristin said wisely, hoisting

herself onto the bed and swinging her legs against the side.

"I have. It never stays. It doesn't seem to stay for you, either." Arianna went to work again, this time with more success. She finished the combing and picked up the blue ribbon with which she habitually tied back her hair.

"I like horses and hawks," Cristin announced, kicking her heels against the bed frame, "but not dresses and ribbons. My mother says I'll change when I grow up, but I don't think so."

"It will be a few years before you grow up, Cristin."

The swinging legs stilled, the childish face took on a solemn expression.

"Are you going to marry Geoffrey?" she asked, tilting her head to watch Arianna.

"You mean Sir Geoffrey? Why should you think that?"

"You're so pretty, I thought he might ask you. If he does, say no."

"I thank you for the compliment, Cristin, but I have no intention of marrying Sir Geoffrey."

"That's good," Cristin nodded approvingly, "because I am going to marry him myself. Later, when I'm old enough."

"Have your parents arranged it with him?" It was not at all unusual for a girl as young as Cristin to be contracted in marriage, but somehow it did not seem the sort of thing either Guy or Meredith would do. Cristin quickly relieved Arianna of this supposition.

"Of course not," she said scornfully. "They don't know about it. It's my own secret. I did tell Geoffrey. I had to, so he'd wait for me and not marry anyone else."

125

"I see," Arianna said weakly, not certain how to deal with these revelations. "What did Sir Geoffrey say to your plans?"

"He laughed at me at first, but after I kicked his shins he said when I grow up my father will arrange my marriage, and in the meantime I must behave circ—*circumspectly* and just be friends with him. Are you ready to go? I'm hungry. I'll die if I don't eat *right now.*" After this dazzling change of subject Cristin slid off the bed and headed for the door, a bewildered Arianna following her down to the great hall.

She watched Geoffrey of Tynant carefully during the evening meal, quickly concluding he had no interest in Cristin. His attitude was that of a tolerant adult toward an adoring child who followed him everywhere. Although he might not want to hurt Cristin's feelings, he clearly was not, as Arianna had at first feared he might be doing, planning to use Cristin to further his own ambitions. Arianna did not think Geoffrey was ambitious at all. He seemed devoted to Guy and quite content to rule Tynant as Guy's vassal. Arianna also decided that both Guy and Meredith were well aware of their daughter's feelings for Geoffrey, but aside from a gentle controlling word from Meredith now and then, were ignoring the situation.

"You've noticed," Meredith said, amused. "You could not avoid noticing. She's always under his feet, worshipping. We feel he's much too old for her, though otherwise quite suitable. Guy and I are hoping she will outgrow it, and Geoffrey does nothing to encourage her beyond ordinary friendliness. In another year or two, she'll be sent away for fostering, and perhaps that long separation will

126

end her adoration." Meredith dropped that subject and began to talk of her plans for Reynaud's treatment.

Now that she was relieved of any anxiety over Cristin, Arianna tried to keep her eyes from straying toward Thomas. She was not successful. Time and time again during that first night at Afoncaer, while Thomas, Guy, Geoffrey and young Sir Kenelm sat at table with their wine, talking together with Captain John, who headed Afoncaer's men-at-arms, Arianna found herself looking toward Thomas, until Meredith jokingly chided her for not paying attention.

"I'm overtired," Arianna apologized. "With your leave, my lady, I think I'll seek my bed."

"And because you are tired," Meredith said, leaning toward her and putting a hand on Arianna's arm to detain her, "you are also weak. You must find strength inside yourself, Arianna."

"Will I outgrow it, like Cristin?" Arianna whispered, desolate.

"Perhaps not, but you can overcome your desire for something forbidden to you. I'll help you all I can, but in the end you must do it yourself. I know you can. You are stronger than you think."

"She avoids him. Watch her." Arianna did not add that she would never have moved out of the reach of Thomas's arm as Selene had just done. Thomas's wife sat next to him, but separate, wrapped in cold dignity, apparently listening to the minstrel who sat nearby singing of ancient battles, and yet Arianna was certain Selene did not hear the singer. He was only an excuse to remove herself from Thomas.

"She's new to marriage," Meredith said, warning in her low voice. "It takes time for some

127

women to grow accustomed to a husband. Do not interfere, Arianna.''

"How could I," Arianna asked sadly, "when he is mad with love for her? He sees no one else. He hardly knows I'm here. There is nothing to fear from me.''

Later that night, when for the first time since Thomas's and Selene's wedding she was left to herself for more than a few moments, safe in the enclosed silence of her own small room, Arianna wept all the tears she had had to hide before others. Great, wrenching sobs shook her until she had to stop pacing back and forth across the room and lay upon the bed, knotting the blue-green coverlet in her fists, trying at first to stifle the sounds she made lest Reynaud, next door, should be disturbed by them.

There came an hour when she no longer cared if anyone could hear her. She recalled the first time she had seen Thomas, and her instant recognition of the one man she could love for all her life. Such things should not happen, it was beyond all reason, but happen it had, and each time she had seen Thomas since that first time, every encounter she had had with him, every action of his she had observed, had only confirmed and increased her feeling for him. And he could never love her. Never. His own heart was fixed on Selene and there it would remain. And she, Arianna, must learn to accept that and somehow live with the pain of it without destroying herself or hurting either of them.

Toward morning, her bitter grief spent, empty of all tears and weary of hopelessness, she found within herself the strength Meredith had said she had. Arianna prayed for forgiveness for the love she held toward another woman's husband, and then swore fervently to put that love aside, to lock it up tightly within her innermost heart, and be a true and honest friend to both Thomas and Selene.

It was a different Arianna who went to mass the following morning in the chapel built just off the second floor of the tower keep. She was pale and dark-eyed from lack of sleep, but she had herself well under control. She would weep no more for what could not be, and she would take full advantage of the opportunity Meredith had presented to her. She broke her fast with dark bread and a cup of ale, then went to Reynaud's room.

"He looks dreadful," she whispered to Meredith.

"He's bone-weary from the journey," Meredith said. "But it's more than that. He's in terrible pain and he has fever again. I wish the swelling around his eye would go down—that worries me most, but his leg is inflamed, too. Arianna, find Joan and tell her to choose the strongest wine we have and send me several pitchers of it. I'll be in the stillroom."

Arianna did her errand, and then herself took a large pitcher of the wine to the stillroom. She looked around at it, fascinated. Bunches of herbs were hung from the exposed rafters to dry, and baskets of dried flowers and leaves were lined up on narrow shelves, along with jars and vials of preparations Meredith had made. The room smelled marvellous, the pungent scent of lavender mingling with rose and mint, hyssop and sweet woodruff, tangy rue, and too many other fragrances for Arianna to separate and identify. She watched Meredith mix rue into the wine.

"And betony and rosemary," Meredith said, tossing them into the jug. "Here's Joan with more wine. You mix this next pitcher, Arianna, while I watch you. Then you may help me heat it, so the herbs will give up their healing qualities to the wine.''

"But if I make a mistake?" Arianna hesitated. "I don't want to harm Reynaud."

"You won't, I'll make certain of it. But this," Meredith told her, selecting a jar of ointment from the shelves, "this I will not let you make until years have passed."

"Trust my lady," Joan said, her complacent manner reassuring Arianna as much as Meredith's confidence had done. "Lady Meredith is the best physician I have ever known."

They heated the wine, stirring all the time, then strained the mixture back into the pitchers. When they were done they took the wine to the sickroom, along with the ointment and bunches of crackly dry rosemary and rue and hyssop to strew on the floor.

"These herbs will sweeten and cleanse the air, and their fragrance helps to stop inflammation in severed limbs," Meredith explained.

After she had sent Joan off to make an omelet for Reynaud, with rue and sweet marjoram and parsley in it, they removed his bandages and bathed his wounds with the wine they had prepared. Meredith gently applied the special ointment she had selected to Reynaud's battered eye, then wrapped his head in clean linen.

"At Wenlock they told me to rest and pray," Reynaud observed wryly. "They gave me poppy syrup when I was in pain, but not much else. I suspect they thought I would die whatever they did, and so they expended their greatest efforts on those who were less seriously injured."

"Whereas we know you will not die," Meredith said firmly. "We need you, Reynaud. Guy wants you well again by the time building season comes."

"I'll do my best to help you," Reynaud answered, his pale blue gaze on Arianna's bent head and her timid fingers as they removed the lamb's wool with which Meredith had packed the stump of his left leg. "Don't fear hurting me, girl, I can bear it. I've stood worse. This is healing pain. No, Meredith, I'm not going to die just yet. I foresee an interesting future for Afoncaer, and I wouldn't want to miss a thing."

Arianna was rapidly learning to watch her tongue and her expression before this clever patient. She secretly thought Reynaud might very well die of his injuries, but she realized it was important to make him believe he would live. Now, to distract him from the pain she was certain he would feel as she began to peel off the last of his bandages, she asked, "Are you a prophet, Master Reynaud? How can you see the future?"

"The introduction of one elderly cleric and two beautiful young women into an isolated outpost on a dangerous border must cause at least a few interesting changes." Reynaud smiled into Arianna's startled eyes. "You *are* beautiful, though I think you do not realize it. Now, lady, don't hesitate. You are far too gentle with me, and I'm braced for it. Pull off that linen and have it over with."

Meredith, finished with Reynaud's head wounds, stooped to see what Arianna was doing.

"Soak it with the wine first," she advised. "That way it won't hurt as much."

"You two will kill me with your kindness," Reynaud groaned as the acidic wine seeped into

131

his raw flesh and the last of the linen was removed. "I think I'd rather drink that wine than bathe in it."

Arianna tried to laugh at his brave joke, but could not. Reynaud's leg was much worse than it had been the day before, and she had to grit her teeth together and force herself to keep a blank face while she helped Meredith to clean and dress it.

Afterward, when Joan had arrived with the omelet and sat cajoling Reynaud into eating all of it, and the bread and ale she had brought along as well, they took the basket of soiled bandages to the laundry to boil them in water infused with cleansing herbs. This separate building near the kitchen was steamy and hot. There were washtubs, and boiling cauldrons, and a space fitted with wooden rods on which clean linens and clothing could be hung to dry. Meredith and Arianna stripped off their woolen outer dresses, tied huge aprons over their linen underdresses, and went to work.

"Do you really believe Reynaud will live?" Arianna asked.

"He must." Meredith gave the cauldron a stir with a long wooden paddle. "We need more fuel on this fire, Arianna. That's enough, thank you. I will not let Reynaud die. He is too important. We owe him too much. Now, these cloths are done. We'll rinse them in cold water and hang them over there, out of the way, until we need them again. It's better to dry old bandages in the sunlight, but that can't be done in winter, can it?"

They spent the better part of each day caring for Reynaud and preparing medicines either to feed to him or to put on his wounds. Arianna began to appreciate how extensive Meredith's knowledge was, and under Meredith's supervision she began to make the simplest preparations. It was tiring, exacting work. There was so much to remember each time she began to measure and stir the herbs, innumerable formulas for her to recite over and over again until they were memorized so well they could never be forgotten. Arianna was grateful when it was time to drop into her bed at night, and she slept deeply, with no repetition of her miserable first night at Afoncaer.

Except for the midday meal, when all the inhabitants of the castle gathered in the great hall, she seldom saw Thomas. He spent most of his time with Guy and the other men. Geoffrey had returned to Tynant, and Cristin had been ordered to spend her days with Joan, learning the womanly skills she would need to know when she married and had her own household.

"I hate cooking," she confided to Arianna. "I'd rather go riding."

"You can't do that when it's snowing all the time," Arianna said sensibly, "so you may as well learn something useful. The vegetable stew you made yesterday was, well, interesting."

"I'm glad Geoffrey wasn't here to taste it." And Cristin went off to try her hand at kneading bread.

Everyone who lived at Afoncaer had work to do, daily chores that were essential to the smooth running of the castle. All except Selene. She spent a great deal of her time alone in her chamber, or alone in the chapel, or sitting before one of the fires in the great hall.

"Meredith is so busy," Arianna said after a week had passed. "Couldn't you take some of her duties off her shoulders, help her just a little? You could see to the bedlinens, or check the food supplies, or at least do some mending or spinning."

"Joan can do all of that." Selene watched the flames devour a log.

"Joan is busy, too," Arianna cried. "We are all working hard. Only you sit idle."

"You were brought here," Selene said, "to be a companion to me, someone near my own age in a strange new place, yet I scarcely see you. You spend all your time with that disgusting invalid."

"You could visit him occasionally, Selene. You could read to him from your Book of Hours. He'd like that."

"Go into that room?" Selene shuddered. "I would probably faint from the smell and the awful sight of him. How can you bear it, every single day? Ugh." She shuddered again.

"I hate it here, Arianna. It rains or snows all the time. My bones ache from the dampness. And life is so rough here, so unlike court, or even Brittany. There is no suitable society for a gentlewoman," Selene went on. "There are only a few ladies married to Guy's household knights, and they are scarcely worth talking to. There are no noble ladies, or pages, not even another nobleman's daughter fostering here."

"Of course not," Arianna cried, stung to defence of her new home. "Wales is a dangerous place, and this is a fortress, not a royal court. You never used to care about such things! You wanted to become a nun and renounce all worldly pleasures."

"But then," Selene went on as though Arianna had never spoken, "after all, who would send an innocent girl-child to learn manners and the duties of a chatelaine from an ignorant Saxon peasant

134

wench? And what could she possibly teach a page?''

''Do not speak like that,'' Arianna exclaimed. ''Meredith has shown you nothing but kindness, and she has proven herself a worthy friend to me.''

''I,'' Selene declared, ''shall never make a friend of her.''

''How can you dislike someone you scarcely know?'' Arianna was becoming more and more upset. ''You have made no effort to be agreeable to Meredith, or to anyone else. She and Guy must be regretting they let Thomas marry you.'' Arianna shut her lips tightly together. She should not have said that. She did not want to quarrel with Selene. She had been sent to Afoncaer to be Selene's friend, not her enemy.

''They may regret the marriage as much as I do,'' Selene said calmly, ''but not my dowry. They are very happy to have those gold coins. You see, I know my worth to them.''

Arianna, afraid she would say something so sharp it would destroy their friendship, excused herself and went back to Reynaud. She could not understand Selene. She had everything any young woman might want. She should have been happy, or at least content, yet she drifted about Afoncaer like some sad wraith, doing nothing useful. Arianna thought there was something preying on Selene's mind, but she could not imagine what it might be.

Unknown to her, Thomas thought so, too. He had been patient for over a week since Selene had asked him to leave her alone. Each night she had had some new excuse, and it had been torture to

135

lie next to her in their marriage bed and not touch her.

"I'll do that no more," Thomas said on the eighth morning. "Tonight we will make love, Selene. And tomorrow you will begin to act as my wife should, and do some useful work instead of sitting about in this room so indifferent to everything that happens around you."

Selene glared at him, then stalked out of their room and went to the chapel without speaking a word. But that evening she sat looking at him over the rim of her wine goblet and there was a faint flush in her cheeks. Thomas was encouraged, believing that she had been thinking about his promise all day and that once they were alone in their bed she would accept him with the passion he knew she felt. Then he realized how much wine she had been drinking.

She staggered when she stood up at evening's end, and if he had not caught her, she would have fallen stepping down from the dais. He kept his arm around her until they reached the spiral stairs.

"Shall I carry you?" he asked.

"I can walk, my lord," she responded with pathetic dignity, reaching for the newel stone. She made it up the steps, slowly and none too steadily, Thomas following close behind her in case she should fall. When they reached their bedchamber at last, Selene grabbed at the bedpost to hold herself upright.

"You may leave me now," she said, dismissing him as though he were a servant.

"The only place I am going," Thomas declared, "is into that bed, with you. Take off your clothes, Selene."

"I won't."

136

"If you do not, I'll do it for you. I won't be gentle, either. You've tried my patience too far, woman. You are my wife, and tonight I'll lay with you."

"Please, no. Please, Thomas."

He ignored the plea, and the frightened look on her face. He pulled off the long, loose robe he wore indoors. In spite of the heat given off by the two braziers Selene kept burning at all times, the room was cold. The wind rattled the shutters. Thomas could see a fine sifting of snow on the floor beneath the narrow windows. Another heavy snowstorm had arrived, and howling winds echoed around the tower keep. Thomas shivered, wanting the warmth of the furs on his bed and the heat of his wife's passion.

Selene hadn't moved. She still clung to the bedpost. He saw her run her tongue across her lips as she stared at his naked body. She tightened her hands on the smooth, rounded wood she held, moving her fingers up and down on it, staring at him, and he knew what her emerald eyes had looked upon. She might deny it, but she wanted him, too. This reluctance was a game she played. It was stimulating, but it was over.

"I said undress, Selene."

"I can't," she whispered. "I'm drunk."

"You are that, but it's not as bad as you pretend. I know. I watched you in the hall. You have no excuses left, my lady. Take off your clothes."

She looked at him and saw in his face that he meant to have her tonight and every night for the rest of their lives if he wanted her. The delays were over. There was nothing else she could do. And now, tonight, the thing within her, the demon she had fought for so long, would gain ascendancy, would take over her life. From this night on, the Selene who stood before her husband trembling while she slowly, unwillingly, removed her clothing, that Selene would no longer exist, but would be gone forever. She stifled a sob. He would not see her cry. She still had her pride. While she was still Selene. For a moment or two more.

She laid down the last garment. She was naked. She did not feel the cold that was making her shiver.

"I am ready, my lord," she said, facing him bravely.

"Come here."

She made herself walk to him, until their bodies just touched, and then she stopped. He caught her face between his hands. He looked deep into her eyes, and Selene felt herself begin to vanish, and the other Selene begin to take her place. Her heart was beating wildly. That was always the first sign.

"My sweet love," Thomas whispered. "Put your arms around me."

She obeyed. She had no choice, and in that obeying she was lost, as she had been lost each time he had made love to her. She felt his hard body against hers, felt his need, sensed it as though she were a great distance away, standing outside herself and watching Selene and Thomas. She moaned, a soft, involuntary sound, one he did not hear as his mouth touched hers, but Selene heard it just as she vanished and the other one, the wicked creature inside her, took over her body.

She strained against him, digging her fingers into his back. His mouth was bruising hers, but she did not care. She opened her lips and took his thrusting tongue inside her, accepting him, needing him so desperately she thought she would die of it.

"I want you," she moaned. "I want you, Thomas."

With a cry of triumph, he swept her off her feet and carried her to the bed. He placed her there as though she were some great treasure, and then he lay down beside her. He buried his face in the soft curve of her throat, and gathered her close in his arms. He would have been gentle with her and restrained himself, though his need was great after two weeks of abstinence, broken only by the brief episode at Wenlock. He tried to hold back, but Selene would not have it. She hurried him, her searching hands stirring the fires he tried to keep banked, her kisses scalding his body, her mouth and tongue hot on his manhood, her ferocious passion driving him beyond all possibility of control. He felt her frantic motions, saw the look of pleasure on her lovely face as he possessed her, though at that moment he was not certain whether he had entered her or she him. They were one, that was all that mattered. He heard her cry out, felt the pulsing waves that wracked her body, and then he knew nothing but pleasure so intense it was painful.

"Not Selene. Not Selene."

Thomas dragged himself back from wherever he had been during the last few wild minutes, and tried to gather his wits together. She was doing it again, and he had to know what it meant.

"Selene did not. Would not. Selene is gone."

His wife lay beside him, her face colorless, one tear trickling from under closed lashes.

"Open your eyes," he commanded. "Selene, speak to me."

Slowly the thick, black lashes lifted. She looked lost and confused.

"Why do you say such things? You do it every time we make love."

"She's gone." The husky voice was just a little sad. "She has left me."

"Who is gone?" Thomas wanted to shake her, but he knew there was something very wrong here, and he feared hurting her.

"Selene." Her voice was so low he had to bend closer to hear it.

"You are Selene." Ice prickled up and down his spine. He did not know this woman. He possessed her body, that was all. They were still strangers, and the mysterious air about her that had so intrigued him was, on this icy, wind-howling night, more frightening than exciting.

Selene drew a deep breath, as though she had no air in her lungs at all, then let it out slowly. The blankness cleared from her eyes.

"Thomas. Well, you've had your way."

"You mean you have had yours. You very nearly attacked me, Selene. You were ravenous." An idea struck him, dispelling the puzzled fear he had felt. He looked at her more closely. "Why do you deny your feelings? Why do you pretend you don't want me when you so obviously do?"

She would have turned away from him and moved to the other side of the bed, but he caught a fistful of her shining hair and pulled her around so he could look into her eyes.

"Answer me," he growled. "What's wrong with you?"

Her expression was hostile, furious anger filling her eyes, but Thomas's determination more than matched her rage, and after a while she relented.

140

"Let me go and I'll tell you. It's only fair. You deserve that much. It's not your fault, Thomas. You have been very patient with me, though patience won't make any difference."

He removed his hand from her hair and lay watching her, ready to capture her again should she try to get away from him, but she only pulled a fur up to cover her shoulders.

"What do you know of my mother?" she asked.

"Lady Aloise? Not very much. I know more about Sir Valaire. I do remember Aloise was once married to a very old man. That was when I was page to King Henry. He wasn't king yet. His older brother was."

"King William Rufus," Selene said. "A wicked man. And so was my mother wicked, Thomas. She was wed at fourteen to Sir Stephen of Dol, who was nearly sixty and in his dotage. He let her do whatever she wanted. My mother led a scandalous life at court. She had numerous lovers."

"I do recall," Thomas said gently, "that she was very pretty. But how do you know this, Selene? Whatever happened during that time, it was before your mother married Sir Valaire, and long before you were born."

"I had the story from my father's mother," Selene said. "My grandmother detested my mother, but there was nothing she could do to stop her son from marrying his dear Lady Aloise."

"I have never heard a word of scandal about your mother since she wed Sir Valaire. How can you blame her for rumors about things that may or may not have happened before you were even born?"

"I do blame her," Selene replied heatedly. "I was born just one week too late for my grandmother to call me a bastard child, and I heard, throughout my childhood, how wicked my mother was, how tainted with the sin of lust. That's why I was schooled in a convent instead of being fostered at another noble home as most girls are. It was because my grandmother convinced my father I'd bring him bastard grandchildren if I had the chance. In a convent I would be safe, and he'd not have to worry about my causing a scandal. I was no sooner in that school than my grandmother died, but it was too late for me. I heard stories about my mother from the other girls, and from the nuns. I had to endure the shame of knowing that most of what my grandmother had told me was true."

"I knew you were not fond of your mother," Thomas said. "So this is why."

"I came to hate her. And to hate the lascivious nature I inherited from her. My grandmother's fears were justified. Aloise's tainted blood flows in my veins. As I grew older, I began to have sinful feelings. I thought about men. I have five brothers, I knew well enough what a man looks like, and sometimes I would imagine how it might be to be held in a man's arms, to have a man inside me."

"There is nothing sinful about that, Selene. Young men think about women, too, and about making love. It's perfectly natural."

"The priest to whom I confessed said it wasn't. He gave me a long and arduous penance. It was then I decided I had to become a nun. It was the only way I could think of to curb my lustful nature." Selene sighed and looked at him through her thick lashes. "I'm more drunk than you thought, Thomas, to tell you all this. I've never spoken of it before, not to anyone."

"I'm glad you didn't become a nun, Selene."

"That was my father's doing. He decided I ought to marry in a way that would be advantageous to him. I did not want to marry anyone," Selene went on. "I was afraid that once I had lain with a man I would never again be able to control my desires, that I would want dozens of lovers, just like my mother."

"And now that you have lain with a man, and found pleasure in it, do you want lovers?"

"No!" Her emerald eyes were wide with fear. "No."

"But you do want your husband, I think. Answer me truly, Selene."

"I try not to, but when you put your hands on me and begin to kiss me, then something happens inside me. There is another Selene who takes over my thoughts and makes me do those things, makes me touch you where I ought not to, and kiss you—oh, Thomas, there is a demon inside me, a wicked, lustful devil! The thing I have feared most all my life, that I would prove to be like my mother, is true. I am every bit as wicked as she was in her youth. That's why I have avoided you and refused you. I have to keep this demon locked up, lest it destroy me, and you."

"My love, my dearest love." Thomas pulled her against his chest, holding her tenderly. "It's no devil, it's your own divided heart."

"Lust is a sin," Selene insisted, her voice smothered as she clung to him, shaking with the relief of telling someone the terrible fears that had been bottled up inside her, and of finding that person did not turn from her in disgust.

"You are right," Thomas said. "It is a sin if you want someone else's husband or wife, or if you are not dealing honestly with someone. But that is not what we are discussing, Selene. Did you know I spent two years as a novice at Llangwilym Abbey? I seriously considered becoming a priest. I'll tell you what the abbott told me when I finally left, knowing I would have to marry some day. He said the good Lord meant His children to be happy, and therefore love between husband and wife that brings them pleasure is a joy to Him who made us."

"An abbott said that?" Selene sat up, moving away from him, her eyes wide. Thomas nodded, and she sat absorbing his words. "An abbott ought to be wiser about such things than a simple priest who comes to a convent to hear confessions."

"I'm certain of it," Thomas said.

"I'll have to think about this." Selene frowned. "But that other person inside me. It's as though Selene vanishes and the other person becomes Selene. Because she was so hungry for you I thought tonight that she would take over my being, and I would never find my way back. But when you told me to open my eyes and speak to you, I did come back. I wanted to be with you so much that I was able to overcome her."

"My dear love, don't you see how torn and divided you have been? Have you never heard a man say he is of two minds about something? After he has made his choice, then those two minds are one again. Isn't it possible that your two halves could become one? As you and I do when we make love? It might happen if you could stop hating what we do together, and learn to accept it as something good."

It seemed to Thomas there was a new light in

Selene's eyes, a gleam of hope he had never seen there before.

"I think it will take a very long time," she said after a while. "But I will try, if you will help me."

"I will, my love." She nestled in his arms, coming to him willingly, and for the first time relaxing against him in complete trust.

"Thomas, how are you so wise? How could you be so certain of how I feel, and of what I ought to do about it?"

"Because I have had similar feelings," he told her.

"You? About laying with me?"

"Never about you," Thomas said, tightening his arms about her for an instant, to reassure her. "I have loved you since the first moment I saw you. But like you, I was ashamed of one of my parents—my father—and like you, I tried to prevent myself from becoming what he was by withdrawing from the world. Do you know anything of him, Selene?"

"Baron Lionel? Only that he ruled Afoncaer, and that he was Lady Isabel's first husband."

"I think it may be his fault that my mother grew into the abominable person she is today. My father was too dear a friend to King William Rufus, and far too ambitious. He was a cruel baron to Afoncaer, until the Welsh rose against his oppression and killed him. I was afraid that in time I would grow to be like him."

"You could never be cruel," Selene said, recalling all the provocation she had offered him. Any other man would have beaten her many times over. "You have too kind a heart for cruelty, Thomas."

"That is just what Father Ambrose told me. My

145

friend, the abbott of Llangwilym, who helped me to better understand myself. He said I had no true calling for the Church, that I should go out into the world and do as much good there as I could, and be an honorable heir to Uncle Guy, who needs me."

"I think I would like to meet this Father Ambrose," Selene murmured.

"I'll see to it that you do. Now you know why I was two years late to my knighting, and how I understand your divided heart. We will make each other whole, you and I."

She was silent a long time, and he thought she had drifted off to sleep. At last she spoke again, very softly.

"Thomas? Would you—could we make love again, and this time I'll try not to be afraid?"

Thomas could have wept for joy. It was a sweet, slow surrender this time, filled with more tenderness than he had believed her capable of, and her hands on him were gentle, searching for ways to please him rather than to take from him, until near the end, when she suddenly became greedy again. She pulled him into her, demanding more, and still more, but by then it did not matter because Thomas was as avidly desirous as she, they were perfectly matched, and he had never, never been so completely satisfied.

"Thomas was singing," a laughing Guy told Meredith in the privacy of their own chamber. *Singing* to the falcons in the mews."

"Considering his voice, it's just as well he wasn't singing to his wife," Meredith said dryly. "Selene is better, too, much easier to deal with, and she is

146

beginning to assume at least a share of her rightful duties. That's a help to both Joan and me. Whatever was wrong between them, they've resolved it. She may even learn to love him in time."

Selene tried. She had a warm feeling in her heart each time she saw Thomas; she knew he was doing his best to help her reconcile her powerful and disputing emotions. It was only during the dark reaches of the night, when she lay beside him as he slept, that she remembered the vow she had made to Lady Isabel, and knew that one day it would have to be fulfilled. No opportunity had presented itself yet, but sooner or later, Isabel had said, a chance would come, and when it did, she must be ready to act. She had sworn a sacred oath to help Isabel. And when she did, Thomas would hate her for it.

Chapter 7

Early spring, A.D. 1116

"Who is Lady Elvira?" Arianna could not read very well yet, but she could make out the name on the packet Selene had just sealed with wax and her signet ring. "And what is this place where you are sending it?"

"Poitou. She lives there. Elvira is a friend from my days in the convent. We promised to write to each other at least twice a year."

"You have never mentioned her before."

Selene did not answer. She had gone white, and Arianna could see her forehead was damp.

"Help me." Selene gestured wildly. "I'm going to be sick."

Arianna looked around Selene's bedchamber, grabbing for the first vessel she could find, a wooden bowl. She gave it to Selene, who began to retch violently, and as it turned out, uselessly.

"My poor dear, you've nothing left in your stomach. Selene, have you been sick earlier today?"

"Yes." Selene leaned back in her chair, looking

exhausted. "It's worse when I don't eat, but I can't look at food, it makes me queasy."

"How long have you been like this?" Arianna felt Selene's forehead, which was cool and damp, tested her steady pulse, examined her clear eyes, and ended puzzled. Except for her extreme pallor, Selene had none of the signs of fever or illness for which Meredith had taught her to search. "Are you dizzy? Have you pain anywhere?"

"No." Selene shook her head. "Only the sickness, every morning for a week. I believe it's a punishment for my sins. I am going to die soon, Arianna."

Arianna was frightened by the statement, and even more by the perfectly calm manner in which Selene had made it. She was still very pale, and the retching had been real. Perhaps she was sick, and had been hiding it. That would explain her self-absorption. Poor Selene. She must have been afraid to tell anyone. Arianna felt a surge of pity.

"Stay in that chair, Selene. Don't try to stand. I'm going to get Meredith." Arianna left Selene's room, and made her way along the passage to the opposite side of the keep, knowing she would find Meredith with Reynaud.

"Have you come for another lesson?" Reynaud greeted her cheerfully. There was no longer any doubt that he would live, but he was still largely immobile, confined to his room by the severe weakness that kept him in bed or in the chair only a few steps away. Weak or no, his questing mind was clear and eager for work. Meredith had decreed, over his protests, that he must rest, postponing any possibility of his being carried out of doors to review the castle's defenses until the

149

weather was warmer and he was stronger. Thus prevented from returning to the work that had engrossed him his entire life, Reynaud had fretted his time away, the boredom of inactivity threatening to slow his healing, until Arianna had devised a plan to occupy his thoughts while allowing his body to recuperate.

She understood that Reynaud's pride had been injured, too, and that he would feel himself a useless burden to Guy and Meredith until he could work once more. She knew of something Reynaud could do that few others at Afoncaer could. He was, she informed him one snowy afternoon, going to teach her to read and write. She had always wanted to learn, but had never had the opportunity. Here she was with a learned cleric at her disposal, and she planned to make good use of him. Meredith had already given her approval.

Reynaud had had no qualms about educating a woman. He reasoned that women who could read, would read their psalters, which ought to please the Church. And a literate Arianna would be of greater help to Meredith. That would repay Meredith a little for all she had done, and was still doing, for Reynaud. An hour was appointed for each day's lessons, and Arianna, bolstered at first by curiosity and determination, and later by delight in learning, was progressing rapidly.

"Good morning, Master Reynaud," Arianna greeted him now. "It's not you I came to speak with, but Meredith. Selene is ill." Arianna described Selene's symptoms, and what her quick examination had found.

"I'll come as soon as I have finished with Reynaud," Meredith said. "Go back and stay with her."

"You don't seem very concerned."

"I'm not. I've been expecting this."

Meredith repeated those words half an hour later after her own examination of Selene and a few questions.

"You are with child, Selene. Haven't you guessed? I would say it will be born in October." Meredith counted quickly. "Early November at the latest."

"A child?" Selene looked frightened.

"Of course a child." Meredith laughed. "It's the usual consequence of marriage."

"And to think," a relieved Arianna said, trying to laugh along with Meredith at Selene's astonishment, though there was a catch at her heart at the knowledge that Selene would bear Thomas's child, "I never thought of the most obvious reason for your illness. I still have a lot to learn, Meredith."

"I didn't guess, either. I thought I had a wasting sickness," Selene said. "It mustn't be a girl. Not like me. I want a boy, just like Thomas." She brightened a little at the thought.

"Yes, hope for a son," Meredith told her, "an heir for Thomas. But should it be a girl, I know he will love it as Guy loves Cristin."

"You look as sick as I feel," Selene said to Arianna after Meredith had left them alone again.

"I was worried about you." Arianna put an arm about Selene's shoulders. "Thomas will be so pleased."

"It will be a son," Selene said. "It has to be."

It was not an easy pregnancy. Selene was violently ill every morning, her nausea eased only a little by the herbal tincture Meredith provided for her. But there finally came a day in late April when Selene was not sick, and then another. A week passed, and she began to eat heartily again. Her face lost its pinched look, and Selene took on a soft glow.

"You've cured her," Guy said to Meredith late one night.

"Not I. Time and nature. And there is still a long road for her to walk. She will be sick again, and most uncomfortable, before this is over."

"Whatever the reason, for the moment she is a much more pleasant woman than she was at first, and she certainly looks healthy. She is most insistent that the child should be a boy. An heir for Thomas, and for Afoncaer." Guy put his hands on his beautiful wife. "Somehow, I think I ought to feel older, with the next generation about to be born, but I don't. I still feel as though I were twenty-three."

"I know," Meredith laughed, caressing him. "You are still a young man, Guy. I can feel it. Come to me, my love. Come here."

Arianna tried her best to be happy for Thomas and Selene, and told herself she had succeeded. She could see Thomas's delight in his impending fatherhood, and his deepening affection for Selene was apparent every time he looked at her. As for Arianna, her days were full, she was needed and useful, and had it not been for that last little ache in her heart each time she encountered Thomas, she would have been completely happy.

Reynaud was up and out of his room at last. Every morning Arianna helped him down the stairs and into the great hall, where he sat by the fire for most of the day. The castle carpenter had made him a pair of beautifully carved crutches and had brought them to him while he was still very ill and confined to bed.

"I'll leave them here, propped against the wall where you can see them whenever your eyes are open, old friend," the carpenter had said. "Look on them, and tell yourself you will be using them come spring. We've missed you, Reynaud, in the years you have been gone. I'm glad you've come home to stay."

As soon as Meredith had allowed him to leave his bed, Reynaud had begun learning to use the crutches. They lay on the floor beside his chair, or next to his bed at night. So long as he did not have to climb the keep's narrow spiral staircase without help, Reynaud could get around well enough. Even that difficult climb, he insisted, he would be able to make alone, given enough time and practice.

The gash across his face had healed, leaving only a faint red scar. The swelling around his injured eye was long since gone, too, and he could open it, though he could see only light and dark from that eye, no more. Meredith continued to hope for a full return of his sight, and bathed it several times a day with a special herbal brew.

Guy wanted the outer wall, the one around the town, built higher and reinforced, and two new watchtowers added to it. Reynaud was well occupied in discussions with Guy and Thomas, and with drawing up the building plans. In his free time there were still Arianna's lessons. At her suggestion, Reynaud had begun to teach Cristin as well, and the murmur of his quiet voice, punctuated by Cristin's higher, girlish tones as she stumbled over her Latin grammar, were frequent sounds in the hall.

"It's satisfying to see him so content," Meredith told Arianna. "And you. I think you are at peace, are you not? You have done well, my dear."

"Like Reynaud, I am content," Arianna replied. It was only later that she wondered if contentment would be enough for the rest of her lifetime. She was almost eighteen. She ought to be thinking of husband and children—*would* have been had she a dowry. Perhaps if she had been fortunate enough to have a husband of her own she would not have had to endure this hopeless love for Thomas. But she quickly rejected such thoughts whenever they came. She refused to let impossible longings spoil the many good things she did have, or cast a blight upon the growing friendships she enjoyed with those who lived at Afoncaer.

Spring came in a sudden burst of greenery and flowers, releasing the castle's inhabitants from winter's long confinement. With the days now warm enough for mortaring, building could begin on the outer wall. A portion of the gold coins from Selene's dowry would be used to pay the wages of the stonecutters and masons who began to arrive from England for their seasonal work. Their presence swelled the town's population by half, and the womenfolk and children some of them brought along filled the few empty rooms and the new houses outside the village wall.

The women of both castle and village indulged in a frenzy of cleaning and laundry, while the villeins began tilling and planting the fields, and the lord of the castle and his knights went hunting for the fresh game that was so welcome after months

154

of salted and dried meats. The first delicate leaves of lettuce were ready for salads, and cress grew plentifully along the edges of the streams that wandered through the forest until they met the river.

"I know where to find the best cress," Cristin said one morning. "Come with me, Arianna, you haven't been in the forest yet. Reynaud is busy on the wall. He told me we won't have our lessons until evening, and my mother and Joan are counting the linens. We won't be needed for a while."

"I'd like to go with you." Arianna followed Cristin to the stables, where a slim, dark-haired lad of about fifteen or so leapt to his feet at their entrance and bowed to them, a clumsy effort that made Cristin laugh.

"Benet," Cristin commanded, "saddle us two horses."

"Yes, my lady." Benet flashed an engaging grin and hurried to do her bidding. "Have you a man-at-arms to go with you? Shall I saddle a horse for him, too?"

"We don't need anyone," Cristin replied haughtily. "The Welsh are calm just now. There's no danger."

"That depends on where you are going, my lady." Benet flung the words over his shoulder as he worked. "I'll go with you. You should never ride out alone."

Arianna had been admiring the horses while listening idly to the two youngsters. Benet led out a mare for her, and Arianna recognized the gentle animal on which she had ridden to Afoncaer. She patted the sleek head and spoke softly to it.

"That's right, my lady, introduce yourself to

155

her," Benet said approvingly. "I'll have your horse, and mine, ready in a moment, Lady Cristin."

"A stable boy for protection?" Cristin laughed.

"I ride well," Benet said quietly, "and I have a dagger I can use if need be."

Cristin's protest was cut off by Thomas's voice.

"The lad has good sense, Cristin." Thomas moved into the stable, frowning at his young cousin. "You should not go off without a guard."

"We are only going for cress," Cristin said. "Don't make a great pilgrimage out of it. Men-at-arms will only tramp around the stream in their heavy boots, and they'll squash all the greens while they pretend to look for Welshmen hiding in the bushes."

"Well, then," Thomas said, laughing at her, "why don't I go with you? I promise not to squash a thing."

"Would you?" Cristin's grin spread clear across her face. "That would be lovely. You've been too busy for me since you came home married. We haven't done a thing together for months. I've missed riding with you."

"Benet shall come, too," Thomas said, "in case I need reinforcements." Benet's delighted smile was nearly as broad as Cristin's.

The four of them rode out of the castle, down the main street of the town and through the outer gate, calling out and waving gaily to Reynaud as they went past the spot where he was directing the stonemasons. Once they were on the main road that ran between freshly plowed fields in the direction of England, Cristin impatiently urged her horse into a gallop, and Benet followed her. Thomas and Arianna rode more slowly.

"When I was Cristin's age I spent a lot of time wandering about that forest," Thomas remarked, nodding toward the trees they were approaching. "I used to know every path, and every rock and stream."

"Meredith has told me about your youth," Arianna said. "And hers. I find it hard to believe she actually lived in a cave for several years."

"Many of the Welsh live like that," Thomas replied. "Caves are all the shelter some of them have left since we Normans came. It was a nice cave, warm and dry. I used to imagine there was a guardian dragon in the inner chamber."

"A dragon?" Arianna wasn't quite certain whether he was joking or not.

"This is Wales, after all. The Welsh say there is magic in this land. Look around you." Thomas gestured with one arm.

They had reached the end of the cultivated fields, and leaving the main road, had ridden into the trees at the edge of the forest. Golden shafts of sunlight slanted through the early spring leaves, piercing the soft, drifting mist that swirled along the ground. The light was a fragile pale gold and green, and silvery where the mist lay. Shapes were indistinct except for the dark trunks of trees, oak and birch, rowan and alder, which stood out clearly. It was quiet, Cristin's laughter and Benet's lower voice floating back to them only faintly through the mist. Last year's dead leaves and this spring's green moss made a thick carpet to muffle the sound of their horses' hooves, yet there was no disguising the essentially rocky nature of the landscape. There were great boulders strewn about the forest as though by some giant's hand, some

157

of them sharp and rough-looking grey stone, others softened by moss or ivy, a few with bushes or small trees growing out of cracks. Off to her right, Arianna could hear water rushing over stones. Always water, Meredith had told her, everywhere you go in Wales. There was fragrance, too, the sweet smell of moss and early-season greenery heightened by the moisture in land and air.

Arianna breathed deeply, knowing she was foreign here, yet wanting to link herself to the place. She felt the mood of slumbering mystery that lay over the forest. It seemed to draw her into itself, alluring and always just a little out of her reach, incomprehensible to anyone not born there.

"You are right, Thomas," she said softly. "There is magic here."

They were riding side by side, making their way slowly along. Thomas put out a gloved hand and laid it on top of hers. She looked into his luminous deep blue eyes and thought she was drowning.

"I knew you would feel it, too," he told her. "Meredith said you have the gift."

"I?" She laughed and shook her head, dark hair curling tightly from the dampness, mist clinging to her eyelashes. She felt oddly free, here with Thomas. "What gift?"

"Of healing. Of learning. Meredith speaks highly of you, Arianna. Reynaud, too. You are a great asset to Afoncaer."

She felt herself blushing. She had almost never heard herself praised before coming to Afoncaer. When Meredith commended her work in the stillroom, or Reynaud told her she was a superior pupil, she had been able to accept their words, knowing she had earned them by her own efforts. But this admiration from Thomas was completely unexpected and unearned. She had thought he scarcely noticed her in his absorbed attention to Selene. Now she learned he had discussed her with both Meredith and Reynaud.

"I thank you, my lord," she stammered, not knowing what else to say to him. His glowing blue eyes still held hers, and Arianna felt as though they were suspended in time, there in the misty green of a Welsh spring, until Cristin's clear voice broke the spell that had held her in thrall to Thomas's gaze.

"I think she has found what she is looking for," Thomas said, laughing.

A moment later they caught up with Cristin and Benet, who had dismounted by the stream Arianna had heard earlier. Cristin's skirts were muddy as she knelt on the verge, gathering the cress that grew with its roots in the icy water.

"Look at it all," Cristin cried. "There's enough for a huge salad. Joan will be so pleased."

"Leave enough that it will grow back later," Benet advised, bending to help her.

"Of course I will, I know what I'm doing. Arianna, bring your basket, too."

Thomas helped Arianna to dismount, his eyes holding hers again as he did so, and she felt a sudden, nearly irresistible desire to melt into his arms. She quickly suppressed the urge. He let her go the moment her feet touched the ground, taking his hands off her waist abruptly and catching the reins of her horse, and his, to drape them around a sapling. Then the two of them went to do Cristin's imperious bidding, Thomas laughing and teasing his cousin until Cristin splashed him with water from the stream and it seemed a mock

159

battle would break out and they would all be drenched.

Arianna joined in the fun. Watching Thomas joking with Cristin and including Benet as though he were a friend and not just a stableboy, she told herself that the magic she had briefly felt, and had seen in Thomas's eyes, was only friendship, only his natural openheartedness. She was no more important to him than Benet the stableboy, and she would do well to remember it. But even that sobering thought could not dim her pleasure in the day, or stop her laughter at Cristin's impish jokes, and when at last they returned to the castle, baskets and saddlebags full of cress and a few delicate mushrooms Benet had found, Arianna rode between Thomas and Cristin, relaxed in the joy of easy friendship and refusing to let herself think of anything more than that.

Selene ate salads constantly. She came to the great hall eagerly, reaching with greedy anticipation for the bowl Joan always had ready for her, exclaiming with delight over each new green or vegetable or blossom that appeared in her salad as the spring progressed.

"I can't get enough," she said to Arianna. "I'm hungry all the time. I'm growing fat. But at least eating is some compensation for not being allowed to hunt. Thomas won't let me on a horse. He's afraid I'll be thrown and lose the babe."

"Thomas is right," Arianna said, and had Thomas's bright, flashing smile as reward for her support.

"Will you cut his hair?" Selene asked. "It hasn't been done since he was prepared for his knighting. You won't mind, will you, Thomas, if I don't do it?"

"No, my love," Thomas teased, kissing her cheek. "You'd rather eat a salad of lettuce and parsley and tiny violets or nasturtium buds, with Joan's wonderful dressing on it, wouldn't you? In fact, you'd rather eat than do anything else at all," he added ruefully.

"Naturally—" Selene said, the spoon piled high with chopped greens halfway to her mouth, the oily dressing running over the side and dripping back into the bowl, "naturally, I would not want to endanger the child. It's you who told me I must be careful, Thomas."

"I don't think it would hurt if we loved occasionally. You aren't sick any more." Thomas whispered the words into his wife's ear, but Arianna heard them nonetheless. She rose hastily from the table where the three of them had been sitting. Thomas leaned nearer. "Selene, I need you."

"I'll get the scissors," Arianna said in a strained voice. "I'll meet you in the kitchen garden, Thomas."

There was a bench there, near the wall, where the late April sun shone brilliantly. Arianna sat down on it, raising her face to the sun's warmth, trying to empty her mind, resolutely refusing to let herself think about the scene in the great hall and Thomas's whispered words to Selene. When he finally appeared in the garden she put on the most serious face she could, and made him straddle the bench at one end so she could walk around him as she worked. Thomas pulled off his shirt and sat bare shouldered, his back to her. Arianna saw the smooth, hard muscles of his back and shoulders and upper arms. As he had been working out of doors since the first warm day, he was already lightly tanned, and his golden body swam before Arianna's eyes.

"Aren't you going to start?" Thomas glanced back over one shoulder and laughed at her. "Don't look so frightened. If you hurt me, I'll scream and you can stop."

"How—" She wanted to say, how can I do this, how can I touch you, with you half-naked before me, and not put my arms around you and tell you how much I want you? Thomas, Thomas, my love. "How short do you want it?" she asked in a perfectly ordinary voice.

"Just below my ears. Go ahead, girl, it's not hard. Just cut."

She reached out and lifted a thick lock of golden hair off the back of his neck. As she did, her fingers brushed against the soft skin of his nape. She wanted to press her lips there. Instead, she opened the scissors and began to cut. They were the best and the sharpest in the castle, but like all scissors, the blades did not close together very well, so the cutting was an uncomfortable process of hacking, and sometimes sawing, at Thomas's hair. She did her best, concentrating on the job before her, trying not to pull too hard and hurt him, controlling her feelings, not letting herself think that this was Thomas she was handling so intimately. At last she was finished.

"There." She sat down on the bench, wiping the last few hairs off the scissors. Thomas stayed where he was, still straddling the bench, brushing clipped hair off his shoulders.

"Do I look like a courtier?" he asked, teasing her.

"The very finest in the land." She was amazed that she could sound so lighthearted when she was so intensely conscious of his nearness.

"You deserve a reward," Thomas said, and leaning forward he kissed her lips, very quickly. He kissed her a second time, not so quickly, and Arianna felt all the longing she had locked away rising up to threaten her new-found contentment.

He had not put his arms around her, he had made no move to touch her with more than his mouth, but that was enough. His bare shoulders were there, she could sense their sun-warmed strength, though her eyes were closed, and she wanted to put her hands on them. Instead, she clenched her fingers tightly together in her lap. But her lips moved under his, wanting the richness of emotion he had to offer, accepting it for just a while, for just this little moment.

When he finally took his mouth away from hers, Arianna looked down at the bench between them, too confused to think clearly. She saw the bulge at his groin and hastily lifted her eyes, to meet his amused, deep blue glance.

"You should only kiss your wife," Arianna said, trying hard to sound stern and failing miserably.

"I would," Thomas told her, "if only Selene would kiss me back, but she won't. She's afraid for the child."

"Then talk to Meredith. Tell her your problem, and have her speak to Selene. She may be able to help you. I can't." Her voice was sharper than she had meant it to be. His kiss, and the last hour of physical closeness, had too easily broken down the flimsy barriers she had erected about her heart over the last months. She was afraid of what she was feeling, and of what his need might do to her.

She started to rise from the bench, to flee from him to some safe spot until she could compose herself, but his hand on her elbow kept her in her place.

"Arianna, I did not mean to offend you. I would do no harm to you, and I would never betray Selene. The kiss was only a joke, like a forfeit during Christmas games, and this," he made a gesture, vaguely indicating the lower half of his body, "this is but the result of unwanted abstinence and the close presence of a lovely girl. You are a good friend to Selene, and I have begun to think of you as something like a sister. I don't want that to change. Please forgive what I could not help."

"I understand, Thomas." She did, all too well. His need was for Selene, not for her. She took a deep breath, sealed up her longing for him once more, and managed a smile. "Do talk to Meredith. I'm sure there's no need for you to be unhappy all the long months until October. Now I must go to Reynaud." She rose, and he let her leave. She glanced back when she had reached the garden gate. He was still sitting on the bench, bare shouldered, staring at the neat rows of vegetables, at lettuce and parsley and tiny new cabbages, those same green, sprouting things among which, to give him ease, she would gladly have thrown herself, pulling him with her, if only his need had been for her.

"I should leave Afoncaer," Arianna said. "Each time he speaks to me, or shows me a kindness, every time I am near to him, it grows harder. I have tried to fight what I feel, but I can't do it any more."

"You can." Meredith's hands were strong on her arms. For all she was a small woman, Meredith turned the taller Arianna around easily, the quick movement making the bunches of drying herbs swing above their heads. The medicine Meredith was making bubbled softly over a tiny brazier set on a stone table, sending forth a heavy, bitter scent. They had been in the middle of a lesson when Arianna had broken down at Meredith's mention of Thomas's name.

"Let me leave here," Arianna whispered. "There must be a convent somewhere that would take me if you would recommend me."

"A convent?" Selene stood at the stillroom door. "Why should you want to leave Afoncaer?"

"She's only feeling a little discouraged," Meredith said quickly. "What is it you want, Selene? I have never seen you in the stillroom before, though you are certainly welcome here." Both Meredith's face and voice expressed her surprise, effectively drawing Selene's attention from Arianna to herself.

"There is some trouble in the kitchen that needs your attention. I told Joan I would fetch you."

"Thank you, I'll go at once. Arianna, stay here and stir this," Meredith said, indicating the bubbling pot. "Don't let it simmer any faster than it has been. Are you coming with me, Selene?"

"No, you go on," Selene responded carelessly. "I want to speak with Arianna." When Meredith had left, Selene came a little further into the room, wrinkling her nose at the medicinal smell.

"What nasty stuff," Selene murmured. She looked sharply at Arianna. "Why did you say just now that you wanted to enter a convent?"

"How much did you hear?" Arianna asked cautiously.

"Just that. You must ask my permission if you want to go, not Meredith's. You were sent here with me. You may have forgotten that, but I have not. Why do you spend so much time in this tiny room?" Selene demanded. "Are you avoiding me?"

Arianna had indeed been avoiding Selene, and Thomas, too. She could not forget Thomas's kiss, and felt that by allowing it she had betrayed Selene's confidence and friendship.

"You would rather be with Meredith, wouldn't you?" Selene went on. "Or with that dreadful Reynaud. But you are supposed to be my companion. Mine, not theirs. I will not give you leave to go from Afoncaer, and I insist that you spend more of each day with me.

"Why don't you answer me?" Selene had been speaking in her most arrogant tones, but now a change came over her. Her eyes filled with tears and she began to plead. "Don't go, Arianna. You are my only friend. Don't leave me alone in this hateful place. I'm so afraid. What if I die when my child is born?"

Arianna put her arms around the small, stiff figure, comforting Selene and recalling her promise to Lady Aloise to look after this strange, difficult young woman. Selene was right to be frightened. The spectre of death in childbirth was real. Selene needed her. So did Meredith, and Reynaud. She was caught, held by her love for all of them. She would have to learn to bear the pain of the one love she did not want and put Thomas out of her heart and her thoughts. She would have to find a way to do that.

"I won't leave you," Arianna promised. "I'll stay with you, Selene, for as long as you want me to."

The lovely days of that warm spring degenerated into a cold, rainy summer. Crops rotted in the fields. Fruits and nuts fell from the trees before their time, and lay in sodden, stinking heaps across the landscape.

"There will be famine next winter," Guy said in late August. "There is little fodder for the animals. Even the hogs will starve—there will be nothing for them to root up. Everything is spoiling and decaying. Geoffrey has the same problem at Tynant."

"What about Kelsey or Adderbury?" Thomas suggested. Adderbury was Guy's desmesne in England, inherited from his father and his brother Lionel, while Kelsey had belonged to Meredith's late father, Lord Ranaulf. "Are conditions better at those places? Can we bring in supplies from either one to see us through the winter?"

"I had thought of sending someone to see how both are faring. I don't suppose you would care to go?"

"I would indeed. I'm not much use around here until my son is born."

"Son, is it? Still?" Guy grinned at the younger man, and Thomas smiled back, shaking his head.

"Selene is absolutely certain it's a boy. Uncle Guy, I need some activity, something to do, or I'll go mad."

"Yes." Guy was sympathetic. "I remember the weeks just before Cristin was born. Take Kenelm with you, and as many men-at-arms as you think you'll need.''

The day before he left Afoncaer, Thomas searched out Arianna, finding her just about to enter her own chamber.

"I need your help," he said. "It's about Selene." He looked around quickly when a footstep sounded on the nearby staircase. "I don't want anyone to overhear me."

"Then come inside." Arianna slipped into her room and Thomas followed her. He stood uncertainly, looking about at the bed and the chest that held her clothes.

"What is it, Thomas?"

"I don't know how long I'll be gone," he began. "Perhaps a month, possibly more. I don't know what Selene will do in my absence."

"Do? What do you mean?"

"She's grown so unpredictable," Thomas burst out. "Her moods are wildly changeable. And her rages. She flares into anger for no reason at all. She's the way she was just after we married, only worse."

"I've seen no sign of moods or rages recently," Arianna replied.

"No, you wouldn't have, it's always when we are alone. She's growing heavy and uncomfortable, and she blames me for it. Who knows what she will do when I'm not here for her to scream at?"

"I think all women in her condition are irritable," Arianna said, not knowing if her words were true or not. If only her experience as a midwife were not so limited. She had helped Meredith with only one birth. "It's quite natural for Selene to be afraid, and perhaps that causes the rages you spoke

168

of. But Meredith will take good care of her, and I'll help as much as I can. Once the baby is born, Selene will be herself again."

"Herself?" Thomas shook his head. "I love her with all my heart, but I see what she is, too. She's weak-spirited, Arianna. I'd say that to no one but you. You love her, too, and I think you understand her better than I ever will. As you are her friend, and mine, watch over her while I am away. Help her to grow stronger, to be more like you and Meredith. She will be lady of this castle one day. That needs a strong woman. And I need a woman to wife, not a weeping little girl."

Arianna felt the full irony of her situation. But she loved them both, and she wanted Thomas to leave on his journey without misgivings. She put out her hand, and he took it in both of his and held it as she promised to watch over Selene in his absence. After he had left her, she was uncertain whether to laugh or to weep.

Selene was not sorry to see Thomas go. She had grown surprisingly fond of him, and out of that fondness she had tried to satisfy him once Meredith had assured her lovemaking would cause no harm to herself or the child she carried. But as she had grown heavier and more ungainly, and as she felt increasingly unwell, she had given up the effort, and he had said he understood. She was not sure he really did, any more than he could comprehend why she was so angry with him all the time. But it was his fault that she was so miserable. He had done this awful thing to her. Her ever-larger girth made it nearly impossible to get comfortable, and her hands and feet were swollen by each day's end. Meredith dosed her with various herbal preparations to ease the swelling, but they only helped a little.

"I'm glad Thomas is gone," Selene said to no one in particular, coming into the great hall at noon. "I don't like him to see me looking this way. My face is so puffy."

"You should not have eaten so much last spring," Joan told her. "It will be harder for you when the birth time comes if you have grown a big baby."

"Well, there's not much chance of that now, is there? The child must be a poor, famished thing," Selene snapped, considering the meager display of food the servants were laying out for the midday meal. "I'm half-starving all the time. I could eat twice as much as my share, and still I swell larger and larger." She burst into tears. "I'm hungry! I want a nice green salad, and there's nothing in the garden but wilted, slug-chewed leaves even the hogs won't eat. I want bread, and Meredith tells me to eat nothing with rye in it, because all the rye flour is moldy and rye mold will make the babe come before its time. I want apples, and they are all on the ground with worms in them. We will all starve to death this winter, and I shall have a starved, dead baby."

Arianna put her arms around the distraught woman and led her to a chair.

"Be patient, Selene. Thomas will bring more food when he returns, and if I know him, he'll have some special gift for you. He loves you so much. Be brave, and endure this deprivation for him, and for your child."

"Yes. My son." Selene put a protective arm across her belly.

"And here," Arianna added, "Joan has made an omelet just for you, with herbs in it."

"The slugs are eating the herbs," Selene sniffed, refusing to look at the omelet. "I detest slugs. They leave slimy trails. I can't eat slimy things. Take it away."

"There are no slugs in this," Joan declared, plunking the wooden plate down in front of Selene. "These are all good dried herbs from Lady Meredith's stillroom. Ask Cristin, I sent her to fetch them. If you don't want this omelet, tell me before it's too cold to eat, and I'll give it to Master Reynaud. He can use the strength in those eggs—and eggs are precious. The hens aren't laying well."

"Eat it for the baby's sake," Arianna urged, and Selene relented.

"She's a baby herself," Joan said later, when Selene had gone to her room to rest. "Why, even Cristin is more grown-up than that. Cristin wastes not a morsel of food, she's been helping me to make cheeses—at least the cows are still producing milk—and now look at her, learning her letters from Master Reynaud." Joan nodded toward the place across the hall, where Cristin's curly copper-gold head was bent over Reynaud's shoulder to see the book he held open on his lap. "Cristin is a good girl, if a bit wild, but my Lady Selene will not make a worthy mistress for this castle."

"It's the baby," Arianna said, surprised at this outburst from the usually mild-mannered Joan. The bad weather was getting on everyone's nerves. "Selene will be better after the baby comes."

"I doubt it. She's weak, I see it in her eyes. There's something about her, something I don't trust." Joan picked up a tray and stalked off to the kitchen, calling to Cristin to come and help her.

"She's right, you know." Reynaud laid aside the book he had been reading to Cristin and shifted about in his big wooden chair, resettling his body more comfortably on the cushions. Arianna knew the constant dampness made his injured joints ache. She could tell by the tight look to his mouth that he was in pain. She wondered if the tingling and discomfort he had once told her about, which made him think his lost leg was still there, still attached to his knee, was bothering him again. "Joan is right about Selene. I've looked into her eyes, and I've seen terror there, and something else. It's as though she's keeping some deep and terrible secret."

"The baby," Arianna began, but he would not let her finish the excuse.

"She had that look before she got with child. I've tried to befriend her, but she avoids me. Perhaps she thinks I see too much."

"Reynaud, forgive me if I hurt your pride, but what you saw may have been Selene's response to your injuries."

"No." He interrupted her again, his manner more intense than she had ever seen it before. "Arianna, I tell you, that young woman is not to be trusted. I've known men with that look who later committed some terrible deed. Sometimes I see her watching Thomas, and I fear for him."

"Stop!" Arianna put out one hand as though she would forcibly silence the cleric. "I've known Selene all my life, she's like a sister to me, and I believe, no, I am *certain*, that she cares for Thomas. If she were capable of violence, which she is not, she still would not harm Thomas. I tell

172

you, once her baby is born, this strangeness you and Joan think you see in her will cease."

"I pray, my dear, that you are right and I wrong." Reynaud's pale blue eyes held Arianna's grey ones. "Unfortunately, I know too well that violence, and bloodshed, are not always necessary for treachery. And," he added, his soft voice sinking to a whisper, "I will continue to watch Selene."

Part III

Gwenefer
A.D. 1116–1117

Chapter 8

Autumn, A.D. 1116

In his secret stronghold hidden deep within the Welsh forest, Emrys the rebel leader sat drinking and plotting with his most trusted aide.

"It's Afoncaer we must destroy," Emrys said. "I did not agree with those few raids last winter, the way Gwion took his men into Powys so openly. It was unnecessary, the loss of so many good *Cymry*, and for what? We only killed a few Normans, and we were lucky to escape with our lives."

"Gwion was a fool," his friend agreed. "Brave enough, but too hot-tempered. He never stopped to think before he loosed his arrows, and see what has become of him. He and his men are all dead, and therefore of no further use in our fight against these cursed Normans, who always have more men to send against us."

"Aye, Cynan, you are right about that. The Normans are too strong for us to meet them in open battle. Treachery is the way to best them. What we need is a clever, devious plan, and the patience to wait until the time is right. A plan like mine. Have you found a girl for me?"

"I have. She's a distant cousin by marriage of my wife's brother. Her father—"

Emrys cut off the flow of his friend's words. The family histories his fellow countrymen loved to recite were not only interesting, they were often useful, revealing relationships among those who fought the Normans that Emrys could depend upon for his own advantage, but this time the listing of relatives could wait until he had decided whether or not to use the girl.

"Where is she?" Emrys asked.

"Waiting out there." Cynan tilted his head toward the closed door of the rough stone cottage that served the rebels as headquarters.

"What, all this time in the rain? You could have brought her inside at once."

"Since when has a little rain bothered anyone who's true *Cymraes?* Besides, you said you wanted someone patient. I was testing her."

"Well, if you think she's been tested enough," Emrys said, refilling his cup with ale, "bring her in."

Cynan flung open the door and called into the wet night. After a pause a figure entered the cottage. Cynan slammed the door shut on the rain and came back to sit by Emrys. They waited, watching her, both tense and alert. They were very alike: short, dark, wiry men whose sharp-featured faces bespoke their blood relationship. They were similar, too, in the almost religious fervor with which they hated the Normans.

The girl pushed off her hood and threw the edges of her grey cloak back over her shoulders, then walked to the firepit in the middle of the cottage floor and held her hands out to the flames. She was small, as many *Cymraes,* Welsh women, were,

178

and from what Emrys could see of her she had a softly rounded figure. She did not wear the usual white headcovering, though her hair was cut short in the Welsh fashion, and black curls clustered damply around her face. Dark eyes under thick dark eyebrows met Emrys's look with no evasion. She had a good face, not pretty, but with strong Welsh bones and pale clear skin. Emrys thought she was the kind of woman who could make a man believe she was beautiful, even though she was not.

"What's your name?" Emrys asked.

"Gwenefer." Her voice was rich and full, and Emrys imagined she was one of those who would rather sing than speak.

"Are you a virgin, Gwenefer?"

"I am." She did not appear at all shocked by the question, she simply answered it.

"Can you prove it?"

"How shall I do that?" A flicker of amusement crossed the strong young face, and the rich, musical voice was filled with mocking laughter. "Shall I bring you all the men who have offered for me, with whom I have not lain, or shall I swear it before a priest?"

"It is very important," Emrys said.

"I know who you are, Emrys, and I have told you truth." Her dark eyes did not waver. The momentary laughter was gone from her voice and she was perfectly serious again.

"Do you hate the Normans, Gwenefer?"

"It is *galanas*, blood feud, between me and them."

"Why, Gwenefer?"

"The Normans raped my mother until she died. They made my father watch what they did to her,

179

and then they took him to Afoncaer and hanged him."

"And why did they not rape you, too?"

"That was seventeen years ago. I was but a babe at the time. My mother hid me in a clothes chest before the Normans broke into our home, and that is where my uncle found me later, sound asleep, with my mother's blood all around and my father gone. They held a mock trial for him at Afoncaer before they hanged him, and he said publicly what the Normans had done. There are still men and women alive who remember it."

Emrys sat very still, watching her.

"Name your parents, Gwenefer," he said at last.

"My father was Cadwallon ap Rhodri, my mother Angharad."

"It's all true," Cynan assured his leader.

"I know it's true. It was in the time of Baron Lionel. I knew your father, Gwenefer. I was only a lad then, but I was in that group of angry *Cymry* who tore down the half-built walls of Afoncaer and overran the place and killed Baron Lionel. I had the pleasure of loosing one of my arrows into that bloated pig as he stood on the inner wall directing the defense."

"I thank you for that," Gwenefer said, her voice low.

"And now," Emrys went on, "Baron Lionel's younger brother Guy rules at Afoncaer and tempts his Welsh subjects with the safety of his walls, and Norman justice equal to that dealt to the Saxons he has settled on his lands, and with more of their own harvest than the Normans elsewhere think is due to villeins. Oh, he is a monstrous kind and fair ruler, this Baron Guy, and his is the same blood

180

that spilled your parents' blood. Will you join with me to destroy Afoncaer?''

There was a third stool by the table, and Gwenefer sat down on it, placing her strong, well-shaped hands flat on the table's surface. She faced Emrys with no diffidence but rather with the straightforward gaze of one who meets an equal.

''Lord Guy has rebuilt Afoncaer until it is so strong no mere raid will have any effect on it,'' she said. ''You must know that. I think instead of direct attack, you have some treacherous plan in mind. Tell it to me.''

''There is a man, Sir Geoffrey, who is Lord Guy's former squire, and now his liege man. This Geoffrey is the Lord of Tynant Manor, half a day's fast ride from Afoncaer, which he holds in fief to Lord Guy.''

''And how will he help us bring down Afoncaer?''

''Whenever Lord Guy leaves Afoncaer, taking with him a goodly number of his armed men, he calls Sir Geoffrey to that service he owes his liege, and puts Afoncaer into Geoffrey's charge.''

''This Geoffrey must bring his own men with him to Afoncaer as reinforcements,'' Gwenefer said.

''Not so many as you might think, for he must leave most at Tynant to guard that place, which is not so well fortified as Afoncaer. Our best chance to take the castle is to do it while Lord Guy is absent.''

''I think you will never take it. But if you should, Lord Guy will bring an army back to Afoncaer and seize it from you, and kill us all. How will that give us the revenge we want?''

''First, you will help us to get inside the castle.

181

More of that later. Once inside, we will kill everyone there. My spies tell me there's a new bride come to Afoncaer, and she's with child. If we wait long enough, we may have the chance to kill two heirs to Lord Guy, young Sir Thomas, and Thomas's child." Emrys grinned, enjoying the thought. "When Lord Guy returns, all unsuspecting, we will have bowmen waiting along his route to pick off as many of his troops as we can before they reach Afoncaer. When they arrive at the castle we will open the gates and let them inside and slaughter them there. All of them. Once Afoncaer is ours, enough of our fellow-countrymen will join us there to hold off the English king's armies until we have destroyed it. When we are done, not one stone of that castle will remain standing on another, and all its people will be dead. Thus will our revenge be complete."

"And what is it you want me to do?" Gwenefer asked.

"I warn you, you will need patience," Emrys said. "We must move slowly and cautiously. It may take a year or more to do this. You are to become Geoffrey's mistress. You are to charm him so completely that wherever he goes, he will take you with him. Sooner or later, he will take you to Afoncaer while Lord Guy is away, and when that happens, you will open the postern gate to us and let us inside the castle. In the meantime, you will send us whatever information you can about those pestilential Normans and their plans, so we can be well prepared for our day of justice."

"I am to be a spy," Gwenefer said, and Emrys nodded.

"Since you are a virgin," Cynan spoke up, "and Sir Geoffrey will be your first lover and have proof of that, he will trust you the more. You might even give him a child."

"No," Gwenefer said firmly. "I will bear no child to a Norman. I'll go to an old woman I know of who will give me some herbs to prevent that. I will give up my virginity to him, for I see it's the best way to do this thing and make him trust me. It will be my sacrifice to my fellow-countrymen. That, and my life, if I'm caught. Now, Emrys, tell me how I am to meet this Sir Geoffrey and how to enter his service."

"There is an elderly woman who manages his household."

"He's not married?" When Emrys shook his head, Gwenefer smiled and looked pleased. "Good. With no wife to be jealous of me, my task will be easier. What of this old woman?"

"You will go to this Rohaise and ask for employment. Tell her some sad story. Cynan has said you are capable of taking her heavier duties off the woman's shoulders."

"I am. My aunt trained me well. I could manage Afoncaer itself if I had to."

"So you shall, when the time comes, for as long as the castle stands. You will endear yourself to Rohaise, and make yourself valuable to her. Next, very slowly and reluctantly, for you are, after all, a sensitive, pure virgin who would prefer to save herself for her future husband, but slowly as I say, you will let yourself be enticed into Geoffrey's bed. Do not hurry this part of our plan. The longer you delay your consent, the more he will value your surrender when it finally comes. He must be bursting with desire for you before you go to his bed. Tease him a little. Make him suffer. You should enjoy that. A first, small revenge."

"And what," Gwenefer asked coldly, "am I to do when this brutal Norman lord simply rapes me before I am ready to say yes to him?"

"From what I have been able to learn of Sir Geoffrey, I do not think that will happen. He has a few serving girls he enjoys, and he treats them well. They will satisfy his physical urges while you entangle his heart and his thoughts. Make him love you if you can."

"Very well. What then?"

"You are cool, Gwenefer. I hope you will be warmer in Sir Geoffrey's bed."

"I do not know what I will feel when that time comes, but I promise you I will act my part well. What shall I do once I am Geoffrey's mistress?"

"You will go on as you did at first, being kind to Rohaise, helping her in every aspect of managing Tynant, and passing to us all the information you can about Tynant, Afoncaer, and the Normans who inhabit both places. I want to know all their weaknesses."

"How shall I send this information to you?"

"I will tell you," Emrys said, "after you have made your promise to us."

The three of them, Emrys, Cynan, and Gwenefer, clasped hands and swore an oath never to betray each other or their goal. Gwenefer swore on the blood of her Norman-dead parents. Then they sat through the night, planning.

Chapter 9

Selene's labor began on All Hallows' Eve and continued into the next day. Meredith and Arianna had prepared a small room for the birth, cleaning it well and strewing cleansing herbs about the floor. To it they brought Selene after it had become clear that this was no false beginning, and there they made her walk back and forth across the room until she could no longer stand without help and her linen shift was damp and bedraggled.

Arianna's heart was wrung with pity for her friend. Over the last ten days Selene's hands and feet and face had all swollen so much that Arianna could barely recognize her. Meredith's medicines had not helped.

"It's all water," Meredith had told Arianna several days before, "and I do not know why it won't pass out of her body. I've tried everything I can think of. I know this will frighten you, Arianna, but you need to be told everything, so when the time comes you can help me. I have seen this happen to only one woman before, many years ago. When the hour for her hardest labor came, she was seized with a great convulsion and she and the baby both died. We must do everything we can to prevent that from happening to Selene. When the labor is far enough along, I will give her a medicine I am making from rotted rye seeds. It will make her body expel the baby faster. It's dangerous, but I think it is the only chance she has of living through this. We will not," Meredith added, "tell anyone about my medicine, Arianna. The men would not understand, and Thomas, out of fear for Selene, might forbid it."

Arianna had agreed, promising her silence. So here, in the tiny, candlelit room, Arianna steeled her heart against Selene's piteous moans, and held her upright, and made her keep walking.

"Meredith says it is easier this way." Arianna tried to sound encouraging. "If you walk, the babe will move downward naturally. If you lie down, it will take longer and be more painful."

"It's painful enough now." Selene paused in her walking, her fingers gripping Arianna's shoulders until the present spasm had passed. "How could Thomas do this to me? I'll never forgive him for this. Never."

"Come along, Selene, keep walking," Arianna urged, telling herself Selene really was in pain, and would quickly forget her anger at Thomas once she held her child in her arms.

"Drink this." Meredith brought a wooden cup to Selene.

"No." Selene turned her face aside as another pain caught at her. "I hate you, Thomas! You never loved me. Ohh—ohh!" She let go of Arianna's arm and bent over, clutching her belly.

"Stop that nonsense and stand up and drink this!" Arianna had never seen Meredith angry before. Silver-grey fire shot from her eyes, and her

186

face was hard as stone when she spoke. "I will not hear another word against Thomas. This is your duty to him, you silly child. Stop thinking of yourself all the time. Swallow this drink, I say. It will hasten the pains, but end them sooner." She pushed the cup at Selene. "Drink now, before the next pain comes."

"Do as she says, Selene." Arianna had realized that Meredith was badly frightened for Selene's sake, and that her fear was being expressed in anger. "Drink it all, my dear, it's for your benefit."

Confronted by that combination of pale-eyed fury and concerned friendship, Selene obeyed. The brew began to work almost at once, the pains coming harder and faster, until Selene's shrieks rang through the tower keep, nearly deafening the two women with her, and bringing Joan to the chamber door.

"Thomas has nearly lost his wits for worry," Joan said, surveying the scene before her. "What shall I tell him, my lady?"

"Tell him I hate him!" Selene screamed.

Joan nodded understandingly.

"It will soon be over," she observed calmly. "D'you need my help?"

"Yes." Meredith pushed a bright red strand of hair off her forehead. She and Arianna had stripped down to their long-sleeved linen shifts, and both were wet with perspiration. "Go down and tell Thomas all is well, then bring us water to wash her with. You can take care of the baby when it is born. Arianna and I will be busy with Selene."

By the time Joan reappeared with a bucket of hot water, Selene was past walking, and Meredith had her kneeling on a straw pallet on the floor.

"I'll hold her," Joan said. She knelt behind Selene, supporting her while catching her around the waist with strong arms and pressing down hard on her heavy belly. Meredith knelt in front of Selene, holding her hands and encouraging her.

Arianna crouched beside her frightened friend, mopping her damp face with a cool cloth and urging her to obey Meredith's instructions so the child would be born quickly. She thought Selene did not hear her, for her emerald eyes were wide with terror and she was panting like some trapped animal. When the next pain began Selene shrieked wildly, turning into a madwoman, struggling against Joan and trying to break free from her restraining arms, refusing to follow Meredith's orders, pulling her hands out of Meredith's grasp. Arianna tried to recapture Selene's flailing arms and called to her over that rasping, screaming voice. Selene's resistance did not last long. Nature had its way, her body took over its natural function, and she could not help pushing as she was supposed to do, until at last, in a great gush of blood and water, the baby was born, crying almost as loudly as its mother.

"Blood," Selene gasped, her voice hoarse from all the screaming. "I can't stand blood." Her eyes rolled back and closed, and her head lolled against Joan's shoulder as her body went limp.

"No! Selene, come back," Arianna cried, chafing Selene's cold hands. "She's dying! Meredith, help her."

"She's not dying, only exhausted by foolish resistance. Lay her down, Joan," Meredith advised. "Arianna and I will care for her. Here, you take the baby. She looks healthy enough."

Selene lay in a stupor, unable to move or speak.

Meredith and Arianna worked until they had her bathed and in a fresh, dry shift. With Joan's help they lifted Selene into the narrow bed they had prepared for her at one side of the room, and then Joan went to call Thomas.

"Arianna?" Selene's eyes had opened, but her voice was no more than a whisper and her hand moved weakly on the blanket. Arianna took the hand and held it tightly.

"You have a beautiful daughter, Selene."

"No," the weak voice said. "No, a son."

"It's a girl, Selene." Meredith brought a swaddled bundle to the bed. "Would you like to hold her?"

"Too tired." Selene's eyes closed.

There was a tap at the door and Thomas appeared, followed closely by Guy. Thomas bent over his wife and kissed her cheek tenderly.

"I failed," Selene murmured huskily, her eyes still closed.

"Never say that, my love. We can have sons later."

"No more," Selene whispered weakly. "I'm punished enough. No more children."

Thomas looked at Meredith, a fearful question in his eyes.

"She's worn out," Meredith said. "It was a hard birth and you know how much she wanted a son. Take nothing she says seriously until she's stronger. She can have more children, Thomas. She only needs time to recover."

With a sigh of relief, Thomas turned back to Selene. He hadn't even looked at the baby, but now Guy poked a finger at the bundle in Meredith's arms, moving the wrappings aside to see the little face. Arianna, watching Guy in preference to the

189

sight of Thomas adoring Selene, saw the older man's eyes fill with tears.

"My first gr—" Guy said softly, then stopped suddenly, and he and Meredith exchanged a look of deep meaning. Meredith laid the baby in his arms.

"How beautiful she is," Guy said in wonder. "Thomas, see your daughter."

Thomas left his wife's bedside and took the baby from Guy, holding it awkwardly, staring at the infant's features with an expression similar to Guy's.

"You need practice," Guy said, laughing, and reached to adjust the bundle. "Knights are taught to hold swords, not babies, but you will learn if you want to. I did. It's not unmanly to love your own child."

The smile on Thomas's face lit up the room, and Meredith brushed a few happy tears off her cheeks, but Arianna wondered what it was that Meredith and Guy understood and the rest of them did not.

Selene was still terribly weak the next day, and she showed no interest in the baby.

"You are going to feed this child yourself," Meredith told her sternly. "You are still bleeding, Selene, and if you nurse it will help to stop the bleeding and you will return to a healthy state sooner. You are to drink red wine, and milk, and eat everything Joan or Arianna or I bring to you." Seeing a tear roll down Selene's pale cheek, Meredith relented in her scolding and went on in a gentler voice. "You nearly died during that terrible labor. I was so afraid for you. But the risk is not over. I'm sure you know there are women who die days or even weeks after giving birth. I don't want that to happen to you. Let me help you. Please do as I instruct you."

Selene burst into uncontrolled weeping, and Meredith, dismayed, took Selene into her arms and held her as though she were an injured child.

"This sadness afterward often happens, too," Meredith soothed, "and I promise you it will pass. You will be well again, and the day is not far away, either."

"After all that pain," Selene wept, "and all those months of feeling sick every day, all I have for it is a girl. Thomas must hate me."

"He doesn't, I assure you. You haven't even seen your daughter, Selene. She is beautiful, she looks just like her father."

"Not like me?" Meredith was surprised to see that Selene looked almost hopeful as she brushed away her tears with both hands. "Like Thomas?"

"She has golden hair and big blue eyes, and I think she has Thomas's disposition, for she seems quite happy, though she must be hungry by now. Would you like to hold her?" Meredith did not wait for an answer, but simply went to the cradle, took up the baby and placed it in Selene's arms. As she straightened up she saw her own daughter hovering in the doorway. "Did you want to see the baby, Cristin?"

"Could I?" Cristin tiptoed across the room. She had stayed well away from Selene during the last few weeks, not wanting to feel the lash of her erratic temper, and now she was more than a little hesitant.

She need not have worried. Selene had just fallen in love with the tiny creature she held, and in the unexpected upwelling of joy and deep affec-

191

tion she felt, she was ready, for a time at least, to embrace the whole world. She pushed back the baby's wrappings so Cristin could see better, and even let her hold one tiny hand.

"When she's big enough," Cristin said solemnly, "I'll make Geoffrey teach her to ride." Selene burst into laughter.

"What are you going to name her?" Cristin asked. "She's part Welsh, isn't she, since she was born here? She ought to have a Welsh name."

Selene was about to reply sharply that her baby was most definitely not Welsh, when it occurred to her that Cristin had just shown her a way out of an unpleasant dilemma. She did not want to name her child after Lady Aloise, which she was afraid Thomas would suggest, or Meredith, as she feared Guy would want. Both men might consider a Welsh name to be a gracious gesture toward Guy's subjects, and would thus not raise objections to her wishes.

"Tell me some Welsh names, Cristin."

The girl began reciting a long list, until Selene, laughing again, told her to stop.

"Where did you ever learn all of those? Deirdre," she said, "I like that one. My baby is Deirdre."

"If Thomas approves," Meredith cautioned her.

"He will," Selene said, determined to have her own way on this. "I'll make him agree."

When Thomas came to see her later, bringing with him an exquisitely wrought gold and amethyst bracelet as reward for the safe birth of his first child, Selene thanked him so prettily, and kissed him so tenderly, seeming to promise future delights as soon as she was well enough, that he

192

readily consented to her choice of a name for their daughter.

It was often hard to keep a fall-born baby alive during its first winter, but Meredith did everything she could to see that Selene was well fed and cared for, so she could pass her strength on to the child. Still, with all her concern for the new mother, it was a full two weeks before Selene felt well enough to go to the great hall to eat, and she adamantly refused to return to the room she had shared with Thomas. She spent all of her time with the baby, allowing only Cristin to help her, and she avoided as much of the Christmas celebrations as she decently could.

"Don't worry," Meredith said to Thomas, trying to make light of a situation that had begun to worry her. "Selene still tires easily, and as for Cristin, this is fine training for her. I'm glad to see her out of the stables for a while. Selene is exerting a good influence on her. Cristin has asked for a new gown. As for the other, she'll come to your bed again soon. Give her a little more time." She watched his unhappy face and wished she dared tell him to find himself a serving girl to occupy his nights until that happened. She did not. She knew Thomas well enough to guess he would only be satisfied with Selene.

Selene herself fought a daily battle within her own heart. She loved her baby, and she was fond of her husband, but she feared his desire lest he get her with child again. She was torn between the two of them and fear for her own life. She could not have another child. It was too terrible a process, and Meredith had said she had nearly died bearing Deirdre. She knew it was her duty to give her husband a son, but that duty she would shirk entirely. Guy had been content with only a daughter; Thomas must be, too.

As for the promise she had made to Isabel more than a year ago, which also preyed on her thoughts, that, too, she would avoid fulfilling if only she could, and Selene had thought of a way. If Isabel were to come to Afoncaer, she could do whatever needed to be done herself, and Selene need do nothing. If she were the instrument of Isabel's coming, she would be free of her promise without actually betraying Thomas. She approached Guy that very night, while they all sat at table.

"It would be lovely if my baby's birth were the impetus for peacemaking," Selene said to him. "I thought of asking Lady Isabel to visit and meet Deirdre. Will you write to her, my lord, and ask her to come to Afoncaer? Will you tell her she is forgiven, and invite her home?"

Guy choked on his wine. A silence fell over the table, and all eyes turned to Selene. She saw Reynaud staring at her with his cold, pale blue eyes, watching her as he always did. She tried to ignore him. It was harder to pretend not to see Meredith's hurt face or Arianna's astonishment.

"Are you mad?" Guy gasped when he could speak.

"Selene, what can you be thinking of?" Thomas cried. "You never spoke to me of this."

"There wasn't time. I only thought of it this afternoon," she told him sweetly.

"King Henry exiled Lady Isabel for the rest of her life," Guy declared.

"You mean you did," Selene replied. "Thomas told me it was you. My lord, you are a near-

194

independent ruler here. You could allow her to return if only you would."

"Selene, stop this at once!" Thomas commanded.

"I will forgive your suggestion," Guy told her, his face pale with anger, "only because you were not here at the time to know everything that woman did."

"But she is Thomas's mother," Selene persisted, disregarding Thomas's continued efforts to make her be still. "It's most unkind not to let her see her grandchild."

"If it had been left to Isabel," Meredith put in, her voice shaking with outrage, "Thomas would not be alive to father a grandchild for her."

"Meredith is right. Isabel," Guy said with a snort of derisive laughter, "never cared for any child, not even her own. No, Selene, Isabel will not return to Afoncaer, not while I'm alive. And you will never speak of her to me again."

His dark blue eyes, devoid of all warmth, locked with Selene's, and in her guilt it seemed to her that Guy saw into her heart, knew what she was doing and why, and felt nothing but revulsion and disgust for her.

"With your permission, my lord," Selene said, rising, "I will retire to my bedchamber. I am very tired."

"A good idea," Guy said coldly.

Thomas burst into her room half an hour later.

"How could you do such a thing?" he demanded. "I have told you what happened here when I was a boy."

"Your mother said he was a cold-hearted, spiteful man," Selene declared. "I see now that it's true."

"You will never find a more warm-hearted, more generous man than Uncle Guy," Thomas sputtered. "How dare you speak of him that way?"

Selene wasn't listening to him. She did not care that she was at odds with Guy and Meredith. She had never really liked them, having judged them by Isabel's opinions, and she dismissed the thought of them easily. It was Thomas who concerned her. She knew she still had power over him so long as he wanted her. Perhaps if she let him make love to her just once he would then be agreeable to the plan that had suddenly come into her mind. It was a risk, but only yesterday she had overheard Joan say that a nursing mother could not get with child. A glance at the cradle assured her that Deirdre was fast asleep. She decided to chance it.

"I am sorry I suggested Isabel come here. I was only thinking of you and our child," she said softly, moving closer to him. "I never imagined Guy would be so angry."

"I think you did know. You have heard enough about my mother to guess what his reaction would be."

"Don't be angry with me, too." She pouted a little, her right hand moving lightly along his sleeve.

"I am angry, Selene." But he did not pull away from her stroking fingers.

"I think you are just unhappy that we have been apart so long." Her hand, continuing its soft rubbing motions, reached his warm fingers and slipped around them.

"That is your doing," Thomas said, "not mine. It's more than two months since Deirdre was born, and still you refuse me. Were it not for Meredith

196

counselling patience, I would have ordered you back into my bed weeks ago."

"I am not refusing you now." She took his hand and put it on her breast. "I want to lay with you, Thomas."

He looked at her as though he did not believe her, but when he moved his palm across her breast, she knew with certainty that she did want him, had wanted him for days. He must have seen the open desire in her face, for he caught her against him. His mouth came down hard on hers, and she lost her fears, even forgot her hasty plan for a moment, in the pleasure his nearness brought her. She led him to the narrow bed where she had slept for two months, and he looked at it doubtfully while she removed her headdress and shook out her hair.

"There's not much space there," he said.

"Then we shall be that much closer together." She reached down to the hem of her gown and pulled it up and over her head in one graceful motion. Her underdress followed, then linen shift, shoes, and stockings, and when she was completely unclothed she lay down upon the bed and smiled at him.

"Come, Thomas," she said. "Come and love me."

"You are so beautiful, even lovelier than you were before." He knelt beside the bed, and slowly ran his hands along her body, thrilling her with his touch as he moved from throat and shoulders to richly full breasts, lingering there to tease at her sensitive nipples and watch her writhe sensuously under his attentions, before continuing to the curve of her waist and her still-slender hips. Her abdomen was slightly rounded now, and he buried

197

his face in its soft smoothness, while his hands moved further down along her flanks until she cried out and moved against them.

"Undress," she moaned. "Why don't you undress?"

"Shall I?" he teased, straining upward to nibble at her lower lip, and keeping his hands where they were.

"Yes. Yes. Please," she panted. "Please."

His tongue flickered across her lips, then plunged into her mouth, while below, down *there*, his fingers probed gently. Her hips arched upward, her body opening to him, and suddenly Selene burst into wild, pulsating pleasure. It happened so fast, and therefore so unexpectedly, that she could do nothing but give in to it. It was over quickly, and when he moved away from her she was close to tears.

"Why didn't you undress? I wanted to feel you inside me."

"So you shall, my love." Now, at last, Thomas began to pull off his indoor robe. "I've been apart from you too long, Selene, and I've had no other woman. I want you so badly I was afraid I'd lose my wits and attack you. I wanted you to feel the joy of it first, so you would remember how wonderful it was. And now," he said, lying down beside her, "now it is my turn."

He took her hand and placed it on his engorged manhood, and Selene felt the fire between her thighs begin to burn once more.

"I want you again," she whispered in amazement, pulling him toward her.

"I hoped you would." He entered her slowly, carefully, as though he feared he might hurt her. She sighed, pressing herself against him, feeling

198

his warm flesh on hers, imagining she was slowly absorbing him into herself. She did not even remember her earlier fears about this act, all she knew now was Thomas, holding her close, bringing ever-increasing warmth to the very center of her being. She lost all sense of time or place. She was an empty vessel waiting to be filled, and Thomas filled her, made her whole, and then broke her into a thousand tiny fragments of intense joy, before he molded her softly back together again. She lifted heavy eyelids and saw him looking at her with love.

They made love again and again that night, while across the room Deirdre slept peacefully. Selene was so drugged with Thomas's loving that she forgot her purpose for a while, but in the grey dawn, with his head pillowed on her bosom, she recalled it. He had just told her he adored her and would do anything for her. Anything.

"Will you take me to Brittany?" Selene asked. "I would like to show Deirdre to my parents." She felt him tense within her arms, and knew she had better not remind him Isabel was in Brittany, living in the house Sir Valaire had provided. Once they were in Brittany, she would convince him to visit his mother.

"You have told me repeatedly that you do not like your mother," Thomas said. "Why should you want to see her now?"

"It's for my father," Selene replied. "I would like to take his granddaughter to him."

"We can't leave Afoncaer. Uncle Guy needs me. In any case, I think your father will have other concerns for a while. King Henry is going to Normandy after the new year. There will be war with

France again. I won't take you, or our daughter, into danger.''

Selene could have cried with frustration at the failure of her plan. She knew there was no way to change Thomas's mind, and in her heart she agreed with him about crossing the Narrow Sea during a war. Isabel would have to wait. Selene would discharge her obligation to Thomas's mother at some other time.

Meanwhile, Selene discovered she had opened a door she could not easily close again. After their romantic night together Thomas expected her to move back into their shared bedroom, and he wanted to make love to her regularly. That could only lead to one thing: another child.

Selene worried constantly, her nerves strung to acute tenseness, her temper exploding at the slightest irritation. Cristin began to avoid her again after being slapped for picking up the baby without permission. Arianna was screamed at when she tried to help Selene with Deirdre's laundry. They did not speak for two days, until Selene, at Thomas's express order, apologized to her friend, and the two reconciled with tears and promises not to quarrel again. The next day Selene ordered Meredith away from the baby. She could not seem to control herself. Everything that happened within her sight or hearing annoyed her, everyone who spoke to her was blasted with harsh words. Reynaud bothered her most, watching her, always watching.

Deirdre became fretful. Selene's milk dried up, making her nearly hysterical. Meredith, who thought her concern was all for the baby's sake, assured her the wetnurse she had found was clean and healthy and had more than enough milk for both her own and Selene's child. Having lost the protection nursing offered against another pregnancy, Selene worried even more. She used every excuse she could to avoid Thomas's lovemaking, until he threatened to take her by force.

Relations between them deteriorated still further. To keep Thomas away from her, Selene quarrelled with him frequently, always over trifles. Too often the quarrels degenerated into rages so intense that afterward she could not recall what she had said or done, though the evidence lay all about her in broken dishes or torn clothing or dismantled bedlinens.

"I have tried not to strike you," Thomas told her after one such episode. "But I warn you, Selene, if this goes on much longer, I will lose my temper, and when I do, I will surely beat you."

"I don't care," Selene raged at him, her anger flaring again. If she made peace with him he would want to make love to her, and the inevitable result of that terrified her. She could not stop herself, she began screaming senseless threats and scratching at his eyes and face.

Thomas, barely avoiding her sharp nails, slung her over his shoulder, dumped her onto the bed, and held her down until her shrieks of rage and fear had subsided into helpless sobs, then tearful quiet. Finally, her fury spent, Selene slipped into exhausted slumber.

Thomas sat there still, upon the bed they shared, shaking with his own reaction to her unmanageable frenzy, and wishing he could weep. He had wanted to make love to her. He no longer did. He touched her beautiful, pale face, but she did not move. Her silky hair had come loose during their struggle. It lay tangled across the bedcover. He

201

lifted a strand and twisted it about his fingers, then sighed and let it go.

He sat a moment longer, watching her and admitting to himself for the first time that the passionate affection he had once felt for her was weakening. He loved her still, with a sad, hopeless love coupled with deep regret for her inability to love him in return. Despite her constant denials of his need, he still desired her lovely body. But he had had to make too many excuses for her, first for her lack of charity and industriousness, then for the bad temper and self-absorption that had characterized her pregnancy, and now for the cruelty and indifference with which she treated everyone she met. He needed a woman who would face life's inevitable problems and tragedies with reasonable, calm, and fortitude, who would gain the respect and loyalty of the rest of her household.

Selene was not reasonable. There were doubtless those who would say she was half mad. Pity rose in Thomas, blocking out his anger and frustrated desire.

"Poor child," he whispered. "We are linked together whether you want it or not. I can only try to help you grow into what you should be, and into what I need."

Days passed, and Selene's temper grew worse instead of better. Thomas was close to complete despair. It was Guy who offered a suggestion that might provide some relief.

"Selene is destroying the peace of everyone in the castle," Guy said. "She has become intolerable. I think it might help if the two of you went away for a while. Leave Deirdre with us, and take Selene to Tynant. If she refuses, you must insist upon it. There's good reason for you to go. Reynaud has completed his plans to make Tynant safer from Welsh attack. Take the plans and go help Geoffrey build the new defenses. Geoffrey can use you, and Selene will be the only woman there, apart from the servants. She will have no interference with anything she wants to do, no woman who ranks above her. Perhaps that will pacify her. Settle your differences there."

Thomas recognized that Selene could not go on as she had been doing. He agreed readily to Guy's suggestion, knowing Geoffrey's placid character would accept Selene calmly whatever she said or did, and offer no provocation to her uncertain temper.

Neither Guy nor Thomas knew then of the most recent addition to Geoffrey's household. It was at Tynant that Selene met Gwenefer.

Chapter 10

Tynant Manor
January, A.D. 1117

"I can hardly believe it," Thomas said. "Geoffrey and a woman."

"Hasn't he had women before?" Selene asked.

"Of course, but not like this. Just unimportant girls. This is different. I think he loves her. Do you mind that she sits at meals with us? I can tell Geoffrey to take her off the dais and send her to one of the lower tables while we are here."

"I don't mind," Selene said. "I'm so tired of seeing the same people all the time at Afoncaer, and they always talk about the same things. Gwenefer is different, and very amusing with those songs she sings, and all those funny stories. She has a lovely voice. She can provide our entertainment each night. I would never have guessed a Welsh woman could be so delightful a companion. I thought they were all half-naked barbarians." Selene did not think it necessary to add that Thomas's mother had told her that.

"I am glad to see," Thomas said complacently, "that here as well as at Afoncaer, fairness and a mild hand have pacified the Welsh who live directly under Uncle Guy and Geoffrey. It is only the Welsh who live outside their direct rule, or those who live under less gentle Norman lords, who cause trouble now.''

Thomas had reason to feel pleased, not only with the peaceful Welsh, but with the improving condition of his marriage. Selene had readily agreed to come to Tynant, wanting only to bring Deirdre with her. Meredith had quashed that plan by pointing out how much safer Afoncaer was, and how it might upset Deirdre to be moved from her familiar surroundings. Selene had relented with unusual graciousness. Now that they were at Tynant she was calmer than she had been at Afoncaer. There had been no quarrelling at all and no outburst of temper for these first two days. She had even allowed Thomas to kiss and fondle her at night, though her reluctance to do more was obvious. Not wanting to disturb the new-found peace between them, Thomas had not persisted, hoping she would come to him willingly if he were patient a little longer.

Selene was content enough to be at Tynant. She rather liked Geoffrey's new mistress. Gwenefer exerted herself to be agreeable to Selene, who recognized what Gwenefer was doing and took it as a compliment. In the afternoons they sat together in the second-floor solar, Selene with her embroidery, Gwenefer spinning wool. Their conversation was light-hearted and easy, yet Gwenefer always made it plain that they were not equals. Selene was a great lady, Gwenefer only a servant, deferring always to one set far above her. They discussed housekeeping concerns whenever Geoffrey's aging chatelaine Rohaise joined them, turning to more intimate subjects when Rohaise had gone off to kitchen or cellars.

"She doesn't resent your presence here?" Selene asked one afternoon when Rohaise had just left them.

"Not at all. We are fast friends, and I am a great help to her. She depends on me."

"I thought she might disapprove of your friendship with Sir Geoffrey."

"He is the master here and we are all bound to obey him. Rohaise will never object to anything Geoffrey wants."

"I have wondered, Gwenefer," Selene hesitated.

"What is it, my lady? About what do you wonder?" Dark, compelling eyes looked deep into Selene's.

"I do not condemn you. I understand the situation of a young woman in a household where she is subject to her lord and master's wishes, and his desires. It is not so very different from my own condition, after all. I know that you share Geoffrey's bed."

A peculiar look passed over Gwenefer's face, then cleared. Her voice was without emotion when she answered.

"I do, my lady. What is it you wish to know?"

"You lay with him, yet you are not with child."

"No. Nor will I be." There was mockery in Gwenefer's dark eyes. "I know ways to prevent it."

"You do?" Selene could not hide her interest. She laid down her embroidery and stared at Gwenefer. "What ways?"

"Do you really want to know, my lady?" Now the mockery had reached Gwenefer's lilting voice.

"Surely you would never use such methods yourself."

"I recently had a very difficult birth," Selene confided. "I don't want to go through that again. Just for a little while, you understand, until I've had time to recover completely. It was so painful." Selene closed her eyes, remembering the pain, and the blood, and the weakness afterward, and thus she missed the gleam in Gwenefer's sharp gaze, a flare of triumph, quickly extinguished.

"I can sympathize with your feelings, my lady. But you must understand, the ways of which I know are ancient, and forbidden to outsiders. I doubt if your husband would be pleased if he knew what you are considering. He's Norman, after all. He must believe you owe him a son and heir as soon as possible."

"Thomas loves me. He would not begrudge me a little time to recover myself before another child begins."

"Then tell him what you want, and refuse him your bed. That's the safest way."

"I've tried that, but he won't listen to me any more." Selene's voice had taken on a desperate note. "He wants to lay with me every night, Gwenefer, and I have no more excuses to make to him. I really don't want to refuse him. I—I—" She stopped, near tears.

"You want him, too," Gwenefer said softly. "He touches you, and your blood runs hot, and all you can think of is his body on yours, and the pleasure you give each other, and so you willingly say yes to him, and afterward you hate yourself. And always you live in fear of the future."

"You do understand," Selene breathed. "Is it the same for you with Geoffrey?"

"Unfortunately, yes. I never thought it would be, not with a Norman, but it is."

"Then be my good friend, Gwenefer, and tell me what you do so I may do it, too, and not have to deny Thomas, or myself, any longer."

"I cannot do that, my lady."

"Please." Selene caught at Gwenefer's hand. "I beg you. It's so important."

"I can see it is."

"I'll pay you, Gwenefer."

"No, not money." Gwenefer relented. "Lady Selene, you have been kind to me. Despite the difference in our rank, we are becoming friends, are we not? I would like to do something for you. I dare not tell you where I obtain the medicine I take, but I'll give it to you myself, out of my own supply. And I'll tell no one you have it. You must promise to keep the secret, too."

"I promise. And I thank you with all my heart. How will I ever repay you?"

"Perhaps some day," Gwenefer said lightly, "I'll want to sit on the dais at Afoncaer, and I'll be refused, but you will say I'm your friend and invite me to sit by you. Or you will help me in some other way. Don't worry about it now, it's not important. What we must do is make it possible for you to lay with your husband without fear, and thus keep him happy and devoted to you."

Selene knew she could trust Gwenefer. This was a woman's pact, something neither would ever reveal, for the Church had strong teachings about it. Woman's duty was to bear her husband's children, that he might have heirs. Selene had heard it whispered that any woman who attempted to avoid that duty would die young. If such a wife had already borne children they, too, would die young, and without heirs, so that, for the wife's sin, both husband and children would suffer. Knowing this, she had never dared approach Meredith for help. With all her herbal knowledge, Meredith must know of such medications, but Selene thought she could imagine what Meredith's response would be to any request for them, especially since Meredith felt deeply her own failure to give Guy a son. Meredith would never be able to understand Selene's revulsion at the thought of enduring another pregnancy and childbirth. How fortunate that Gwenefer could help her. No one else need ever know what she was doing.

Gwenefer brought the medicine to Selene later, in an earthenware vial stoppered with wood, and told her how many drops to take each day.

"Remember your promise," Gwenefer said. "Speak to no one about this. 'Tis you who'll feel your husband's wrath if he discovers what you are doing. Though I've no doubt I'd be punished, too, for helping you. This is a secret between friends."

"I won't tell a soul."

That night, when Thomas came to their bed, expecting nothing more than one or two reluctant kisses from Selene, she turned to him with such warmth and tenderness that he was astonished.

"Uncle Guy was right," Thomas remarked afterward. "He said we would resolve our differences if we were alone at Tynant."

"Hardly alone," Selene murmured, reaching for him again. "You spend most of your time with Geoffrey."

"We have been busy, I'll admit that," he whispered into her ear, pausing to nibble at the lobe.

"But if you promise to greet me this way every night, I'll leave my work with Geoffrey and come early to bed."

For the next few weeks, Thomas was a happy man. Selene welcomed him into her arms each night. She did her share of household work, and had begun to act more as a nobleman's wife should. Perhaps, he thought, she had only needed time and patience.

They stayed at Tynant from just after Twelfth Night until mid-April, and by the time Thomas was ready to return to Afoncaer the wooden palisade around the manor was being extended and made higher, a new watchtower was being built, and there were more well-trained men-at-arms to keep Geoffrey's domain secure. Everyone at the manor was interested in what was being done to protect them from attack, especially Gwenefer, who encouraged both Geoffrey and Thomas to talk freely about their work on the defenses.

Selene and Gwenefer had become close friends in those three months. Or at least Selene thought so, until the day they walked through the meadow beside the stream for which Tynant was named, strolling idly through the pleasant spring afternoon.

"We are returning to Afoncaer the day after tomorrow," Selene said, not telling Gwenefer anything that resourceful young woman did not already know. "Gwenefer, I will need a goodly supply of our medicine to take with me."

"What?" laughed Gwenefer. "Are you not ready yet to give your dear husband the son he wants and needs?"

"No! I can't do it. Not yet, that is. Not for a

while. Just a little longer, a few months, a year perhaps. Or two years."

"So long? That's a great deal of medicine, Lady Selene. How would you hide so many vials? If I could get them for you, which I cannot." Gwenefer, quite unconcerned, bent to pick a tiny blue flower and stood sniffing its delicate fragrance.

"But you must. I need it. You promised."

"I promised nothing, my lady," Gwenefer said, "but to keep the secret that you are taking it. I have done so."

"Oh, Gwenefer, please, as you are my friend, I beg you, get me more of that liquid."

"Well," Gwenefer looked over Selene's shoulder, smiling into the dim, mysterious greenness of the Welsh forest, "I might think of something to help you. It will take a while."

"I need more medicine before we leave Tynant. I've just enough for tonight and tomorrow."

"And after that, it's a big belly for you, isn't it?"

"Gwenefer, don't laugh at me. I'm desperate."

"Yes," Gwenefer said, "I believe you are."

"Please, Gwenefer."

"I never thought," Gwenefer said, tossing the blue flower away with careless grace, "that I'd hear a Norman lady begging me for anything."

Selene stopped walking and stood staring at Gwenefer's triumphant face, while understanding dawned on her.

"What do you want of me?" she asked.

"I believe I can provide you with one more vial," Gwenefer said. "I'll give it to you tomorrow. Just one vial. For friendship's sake."

"And after that is finished? How will I get more when I am at Afoncaer?"

"Why, then someone will have to take it to you.

211

A cousin of mine. And you will have to pay for it."

"Pay what?"

"Information. There is a lot my cousin would like to know about Afoncaer."

"I won't do it."

"Of course you will," Gwenefer said pleasantly. "If you don't, I'll tell Sir Thomas what you have been doing with my help."

"If you do, then Geoffrey will know you have been doing the same thing."

"Do you really think Geoffrey will care that I've taken steps to avoid giving him bastard children?"

"How could you?" Selene cried. "I thought we were friends."

"There can be no friendship between Welsh and Norman."

"You tricked me!"

"You are easy to trick. You think only of yourself. Now, I think we should walk back to the house, don't you? Your eager husband will be waiting for you. Tomorrow we will talk again, and I'll tell you where and how you are to meet my cousin Cynan. There must be a suitable place near Afoncaer. You do ride out frequently to hunt, or for pleasure, don't you? It shouldn't be too hard."

It was not until much later that night, when she lay wide awake beside Thomas, that Selene realized Gwenefer had put into her hands the opportunity Lady Isabel had said would come to her. The Welsh wanted to use her, but perhaps she could use them to accomplish the vengeance Isabel wanted. If she were very clever about it, Thomas need never know. She met Gwenefer confidently the next morning.

"I make a condition to my help, and that is that

whatever you are planning, I will not be harmed, nor my daughter, nor Sir Thomas.''

"What reason could we have to harm you or your child?'' Gwenefer said easily. "As for your husband, well, he is a fighting man, and if he takes up weapons against us, who's to say what will happen? He'd expect a fair fight, you know.''

"I suppose you're right. But Deirdre and I, do you promise that we will be safe?''

"Of course.''

"Then I'll do what you want.''

"I knew you would,'' Gwenefer said. But after they had arranged the exchange of information for the secret medicine Selene wanted so badly and Selene had left her, Gwenefer smiled to herself. "Promises made to Normans mean nothing,'' she said.

Chapter 11

Life at Afoncaer was considerably more pleasant once the unpredictable Selene had gone to Tynant with Thomas. Even Arianna, though still loyal to her friend and distant kinswoman, rejoiced at the absence of quarrels over the smallest concerns, tears, reproaches, and thrown dishes, and Selene's periodic refusals to let anyone else touch Deirdre.

Arianna had been put in charge of the nursery. As she had helped to care for the younger sons of Lady Aloise and Sir Valaire when they were babies, she had had plenty of experience. Meredith had also assigned a former kitchen girl, Linnet, to help with Deirdre, and this gave Arianna enough free time to continue her reading and writing lessons with Reynaud, or to work with Meredith in the stillroom.

Arianna was also able to ride with Cristin frequently. She noticed that Benet the stableboy always appeared at the right time and place so that he was the one who accompanied them. She regarded the dark, intelligent lad with a combination of amusement for his eagerness and pity for the look in his eyes whenever Cristin was near. Arianna could sympathize with what Benet must be feeling, caring for one who was unattainable to him. She knew that pain herself.

And yet, she was fully aware that she was happier than Selene would ever be. Selene had complained bitterly about the roughness of life and the remoteness of Afoncaer, situated as it was on the Welsh side of the border, and she had managed to quarrel with nearly everyone in the castle at some time or other. In contrast, Arianna had felt completely at home from the very first day. She knew in some deep, inner part of herself that Meredith had been right to insist she come here. She belonged in, and to, Afoncaer.

So peaceful were the days that early spring, so gentle the sun or the soft, misty-grey days of rain, that in mid-April Arianna was almost sorry to hear that Thomas and Selene would return in a few days.

"I hope Selene will let me continue to care for Deirdre," Arianna said to Reynaud.

Over the last few months he had been teaching her to play chess. They sat at a small table before one of the fireplaces in the great hall, the board between them. It had been a rainy day, and Arianna knew Reynaud's joints ached. She had suggested the game, hoping it would distract him. He certainly seemed to be concentrating. He made no comment on her remark, and did not look up when Guy came to stand between them, looking down at the carved ivory pieces. Arianna saw Guy's fingers twitching and laughed.

"I think you see the move I should make," she said.

"For a beginner," Guy responded, "and a

woman besides, you are a fair player, Arianna. You have patience and the ability to look beyond the present moment. I've known men who had neither."

"Perhaps I'll challenge you to a game when I'm more skilled," she teased, and Guy laughed back at her, then sobered, frowning.

"I heard what you said about Selene," he told her. "You will remain in charge of the nursery. That is Meredith's wish, and I stand behind her. Selene will not be allowed to disrupt Meredith's domestic arrangements. There will be no repetition of this past winter's rages, or the Lady Selene will find herself confined to her bedchamber. I will have peace in my household." He moved on to speak to Sir Kenelm.

"Peace." Reynaud's pale blue eyes met Arianna's. "We shall see."

"She doesn't mean to be so difficult," Arianna said.

"Then why is she? Well, perhaps she has changed. Yesterday I read a letter to Guy that Thomas had written. He says Selene is quite happy, and that all is well between them."

Selene, when Arianna saw her again, did not look happy. She was pale and quiet and withdrawn into herself. She went to the nursery as soon as she had greeted Guy and Meredith. Arianna had been waiting for her there, not trusting herself to meet Thomas after so long without revealing to him or to others how much she had missed him. When Selene appeared in the nursery, Arianna gave Deirdre to her mother. The baby, not recognizing the mother she had not seen for more than three months, began to cry.

"Here." Selene handed Deirdre back with a

sigh. "You take her. She will have to learn to know me all over again, I suppose."

"Are you well, Selene?" Arianna watched her friend with sharp eyes, trying to think what could be the cause of the change in her.

"Yes." Selene headed for the door.

"Have you nothing to tell me?"

"What should I tell you?" Selene looked almost frightened.

"I thought," Arianna said, patting and soothing Deirdre out of her tears, "I thought you might tell me we need to begin sewing for a new baby. I thought you might be with child again."

There was a flare of something in Selene's eyes, a glimmer of the uncontrollable anger that had surfaced after Deirdre's birth. Arianna wondered for a moment if Selene would throw something, but whatever it was, it died away, and Selene stood serenely by the door, shaking her head, a half-smile curving her lips.

"No," she said firmly. "I am not with child."

Selene slipped back into the daily routine of the castle, making no real change in the order of each day, and not disputing Arianna's control of the nursery. She did ride more frequently than she had before, either with hunting parties or with Arianna, Cristin, and Benet. When she did, she almost always wandered off by herself for a time, saying afterward that she had gotten lost, or hadn't been paying attention, or just that she had wanted to be alone for a while.

"Be more careful, my love," Thomas scolded her gently. "Don't go too far afield without an escort. There are always a few untamed Welshmen who are not our villeins lurking about the fringes of Uncle Guy's lands. You must have better protection when you ride out. I don't want any harm to come to you."

"I'll watch where I go and not get lost again," Selene said meekly.

She began to attend the weekly market that was held in an open field on the far side of the outer wall and wet moat. Each week she brought home some little trinket for Deirdre or Cristin.

"You always buy from the same man," Arianna observed, as they walked across the bailey after one such excursion. "That little dark fellow. He talked to you for quite a long time, while I was at the next booth."

"He's amusing," Selene responded, giving her friend a bright red ribbon. "This is for your hair. Next week I'll try to find a green one for Cristin."

"Are you ill, Selene? You are so pale, and you are always so quiet these days."

"Am I? I suppose I'm just growing older, and perhaps more settled into this borderland life." Selene turned to leave Arianna, and bumped into the man who had limped up behind her. "What are you doing, Reynaud? Are you spying on me?"

"I only thought to join you and Arianna, my lady. You are going to the hall, aren't you?"

"Stop watching me! Stop staring at me!" With a visible effort, Selene regained control of herself. "You frightened me, Reynaud. I did not hear you behind me. I'm sorry I shouted at you. Excuse me, please, I had better go to Deirdre." She hurried on before them, running up the steep steps to the forebuilding and disappearing into the keep.

"Now, what do you suppose ails her?" Reynaud wondered. "She has never apologized to me before."

Spring slipped into summer, with the border so

peaceful that Guy decided it was time to visit his English properties.

"We are going to Adderbury and then on to Kelsey," Thomas told Selene. "Uncle Guy and Meredith, you and I. There is a great deal to be done at both places, we haven't been to either for so long. We will be gone at least two months."

"Two months?" Selene exclaimed. "We only just returned from Tynant."

"Nearly three months ago," Thomas laughed. "I had no idea you were so fond of Afoncaer."

"I don't want to leave Deirdre. She has just gotten to know me again after our last separation."

"Then we'll take her with us, and Arianna, too. We'll all go."

"Not in the summer heat, Thomas. The poor child will be sick from all that travelling. No, you and Guy and Meredith go, and I will stay here. I'll manage very nicely with Arianna and Joan to help me, and Captain John to guard us."

"Geoffrey will come to Afoncaer when we leave. He always does."

"Geoffrey?"

"I suppose he will want to bring Gwenefer with him. Joan won't like that much."

"Gwenefer, too? Well," Selene said brightly, "you must see that I cannot possibly leave. I'll have to mediate between Joan and Gwenefer. That old woman is certain to be scandalized when Geoffrey brings his mistress here and expects a private room for them both."

Thomas burst into laughter.

"Selene, I have never heard so many silly excuses, not even from you. I know you have no interest in any other man, so you can't want to stay behind to meet a lover. Tell me the truth. Why don't you want to go with me?"

Selene thought rapidly, seeking one more excuse, a story that would satisfy him. She found it in the possibility that frightened her so badly every time it came into her mind.

"I didn't want to tell you until I was certain," she said, "but you force me to it. I may be with child again, Thomas, and I'm afraid to travel for fear I'll miscarry."

"Do you think so?" Thomas's face came alive with such joy that Selene felt drowned in shame for the lie. She was not with child, but she feared she soon would be if she left Afoncaer without a supply of her medicine, and Cynan never brought her much. She had to meet him far too often to get more vials of the stuff, and he frightened her. And now she had had to lie to Thomas again. She felt as though she were a fly caught in a spider's web, unable to get free.

"Please don't tell anyone," she urged. "Wait until you return. I'll know for certain by then." When he did return, she would tell him she had been mistaken, and then she would blot out his disappointment with her body, in the way that pleased him best.

"You look frightened," Thomas said.

"I was remembering how difficult it was the last time, all that pain, and the blood. Will you come to bed with me now, Thomas? I forget everything when I'm in your arms. I don't want to be afraid any more."

Geoffrey and a few men from Tynant arrived on the first day of August, and the following morning

Thomas, Guy, and Meredith rode off to attend to their English properties. Sir Kenelm went with them. He had spent his childhood at Adderbury, until coming to Afoncaer ten years before, and he was betrothed to the daughter of Guy's seneschal there. They would be married at Adderbury, and Kenelm would bring his new wife back with him in October.

"They have taken more men than we can rightly spare," Geoffrey said to Reynaud. "I will sorely miss Kenelm. But it has been quiet all summer in this part of the border. Perhaps it won't matter that we are short-handed."

Gwenefer had not come with Geoffrey. She waited until the day after the Baron of Afoncaer and his party had left before she appeared. She rode in at the gate in a brilliant red dress, trailing behind her two serving girls and a packhorse loaded down with boxes and baskets of clothing.

"I don't like that woman," Cristin observed jealously. She was in the kitchen with Arianna and Joan, helping to arrange the midday meal. "Why did she have to come here and spoil everything? I was so looking forward to riding with Geoffrey every day, and now he won't pay any attention to me at all."

"What Sir Geoffrey needs," Joan said to Arianna, not troubling to hide her disgust, "is a good wife, not a strumpet like that. And she's one of those awful Welsh, too, and not even from Geoffrey's own lands. He ought to be ashamed of himself. He would never have dared bring her here if Meredith were at home."

"What's a strumpet?" Cristin asked.

"Avoid her as much as you can," Arianna advised, trying to ignore Cristin's question and wishing Joan would be silent in front of the child. "And for Geoffrey's sake treat her politely when you must deal with her."

"I'll set her place at the foot of the lowest table in the hall," Joan grumbled. "She doesn't belong here. She ought to be in the town, in that disreputable house by the gate."

"What house?" Cristin followed Arianna out of the kitchen, along the passageway, and into the great hall. "What were you and Joan talking about? Geoffrey isn't going to marry Gwenefer, is he?"

"I doubt it," Arianna said truthfully.

"He had better not," Cristin said. "I won't allow it. What do you think of this Gwenefer, Master Reynaud?"

The architect stood leaning on his crutches, waiting for the trestle tables to be set up before he made his way to his customary chair.

"I think, my dear, that you had better remember your manners. Do not forget you are the daughter of this castle, and your parents' representative in their absence."

They were all shocked when not Geoffrey, but Selene, insisted Gwenefer must sit on the dais, next to her.

"We became friends at Tynant," Selene said to Arianna, while Geoffrey looked embarrassed. "Gwenefer is most entertaining." But Selene looked white and tense, and Arianna noticed she did not speak to Gwenefer at all during the meal. Nor did Selene appear to be listening when Gwenefer sang for them afterward.

"I wish Selene had not done that," Geoffrey remarked later to Arianna and Reynaud. "Gwenefer had agreed to eat with the common folk while we are here, but I could not oppose Selene's wishes.

She is the ranking lady at Afoncaer while Meredith is gone, and I am bound to obey her in domestic matters."

"It is very unlike Selene," Arianna said. "She is usually so proud of her rank. Too proud, in fact. She keeps her distance from the common folk."

"Yes," Reynaud agreed, his pale eyes on Selene. "It is odd. Most curious."

"I should never have allowed Gwenefer to come here." Geoffrey looked uncomfortable, and Arianna realized he was trying to apologize. "She said she could not bear to be parted from me for so long, and I wanted her near me. I fear I've let affection cloud my judgement, and I regret it already. I suppose I ought to send her back to Tynant."

Captain John, the grizzled old leader of Guy's men-at-arms, called to him, and Geoffrey left them to attend to some problem in the barracks.

"Now, Arianna, you see the value of a celibate life," Reynaud remarked dryly, making Arianna smile in spite of her distaste for the situation Geoffrey had inflicted upon them. "He won't send her away either, I'll wager, though it would be the wisest thing to do."

"Cristin is heartbroken over Geoffrey's new love," Arianna said, sobering at the sight of the girl's stricken eleven-year-old face across the hall.

"Cristin will recover," Reynaud predicted. "She's young and there will be many young men she will sigh over before she's done. It's Selene who worries me. I see terror in her eyes. She reminds me of a rabbit trapped in a snare. If she does not find her way free soon, I don't know what will happen to her."

"She has become oddly quiet," Arianna agreed.

223

"We are not as close as we once were, and it's not just because she is married and I am not. It's as though some secret door in her heart has been shut to me, and she will not open it again."

Summer heat descended on Afoncaer, and bright, sunny days followed each other in golden profusion, unusual and welcomed after the wet devastation of the previous year. Afoncaer lay basking peacefully in the sun while its people labored at their summer chores. The crops were good. The villeins worked cheerfully in the fields, knowing there would be no hunger for humans or animals when winter finally came. Arianna carried baskets of herbs to the stillroom to hang them so she and Meredith could use them later when they were dried. Joan put Cristin in charge of the kitchen garden. She was to weed and water the vegetables, while at the same time chasing birds and insects away from the fruits drying on racks. More fruits were preserved in honey, laid down in large earthenware crocks. The cool storerooms beneath the great hall and the keep began to fill with baskets of grain and root vegetables. The new cistern was finished, and with the castle's expanded water supply assured Reynaud was free to turn his full attention to reinforcement of the gatehouse at the outer entrance to the village. He spent long days there directing the carpenters and masons.

In the third week of August rumors began. They spread among the villagers first, but it was not long before the whispers reached the castle. Flickering lights had been seen in the forest at night. Odd noises had been heard. Some said witches or other supernatural beings were causing the commotion. More practical minds suggested an earthly explanation when Reynaud, Geoffrey, and Captain John conferred together.

"Could it be the Welsh?" Reynaud suggested. "They have been too quiet lately. Perhaps they are preparing an attack."

"It's always possible," Geoffrey agreed. "I'll send a couple of men to Tynant to be sure all is well there, and I think a thorough inspection of the castle's defenses is in order."

"I'll see to it at once," Captain John said. He had every inch of the walls examined, both castle and town. The towers were secure, and so were the gatehouses, and they would be even safer when Reynaud's improvements were completed.

"Another few days, that's all we need," Reynaud said. "But the present arrangement is strong enough to hold should an attack come. Post extra guards if you are worried." Geoffrey did.

Lastly, the postern gate was checked. The way to it was a narrow, steep stairway that zigzagged through the foundations of the castle wall. The entrance to the stair was at one side of the inner bailey, near the tower keep. The door was thick and strong, secured with a bar and a heavy lock. It could only be opened from inside the castle wall. At the bottom of the long stairway lay a second door, even stronger than the first, and it, too, opened only from inside. There was no sign of tampering.

"All's well," Geoffrey said, coming back to the inner bailey a little out of breath. "That's a difficult staircase to climb, and the steps cut into the cliff below the gate down there are even worse. It would take a very agile goat to climb up here from the river. You built well, Reynaud. Heavily armed men could never get in that way."

"It was planned for escape," Reynaud said, "not for easy entrance."

The postern doors were barred and locked again, and Geoffrey went on to the corner towers and the wall by the keep.

"All is secure," he finally reported. "Just the same, I have ordered extra guards and we will stay alert. I think we can rest easy, though. Nothing seems amiss. This castle is too strong for anything but the heaviest siege engines to breach the walls, and we know the Welsh have no such equipment."

"But you are not easy, are you?" Arianna said to Reynaud when he spoke to her later of Geoffrey's efforts.

"I feel," he told her, "the way I do when a thunderstorm is about to break, or a blizzard in winter. My bones ache. Something is going to happen. And soon."

"What can we do?"

"Wait." He smiled at her, the deep lines in his face crinkling. "And plan."

He looked around Meredith's herb garden. He liked to sit there in the sun while Arianna worked cutting herbs or trimming off dead blossoms. It was a quiet, private place, though only a few steps away from the bustling inner bailey. Nothing that was said here, behind its enclosing stone walls, could be overheard outside.

"Tonight," Reynaud said, "I will write to Guy, in secret, and tell him of my ominous fears. I've seen this sort of thing before. This is the way the Welsh work, Arianna. They cause false alarms and give us reason to post extra guards, and then they do nothing until we are so wearied by sentry duty and sleepless nights that we finally begin to relax.

That is when they move, and it is usually something sudden and totally unexpected. I have confidence in Geoffrey's military skills, and I know he sends regular reports to Guy, but he will put a good face on events so Guy won't worry while he's far from home. I believe Guy should know exactly what is happening here. I'll send the letter off tomorrow, disguised in the normal coming and going through the outer gate, and you and I and the courier will be the only ones who know of it. Can you tell me of some clever lad who could get from here to Adderbury quickly but without being noticed?''

"Yes," Arianna said, after a moment's thought. "Benet, one of the stableboys. He's a friend of Cristin's. He would like to be a great knight and throw all his honors at her feet."

"Tell him he will be honored for this," Reynaud said gravely. "Come to my room at first light. I'll give you the letter to pass to him. You must be my intermediary in this, Arianna. Since I can't ride, I never go to the stables. It would look strange for me to do so now, and I do not want to arouse anyone's suspicion. Warn this Benet that speed and secrecy are essential. If Guy is not at Adderbury, Benet is to insist on an armed escort to take him to Kelsey or wherever else Guy has gone. I will also write to the seneschal at Adderbury and tell him to provide Benet with whatever aid he needs."

No one commented on Arianna's visit to the stables later that day, nor on her quiet talk with Benet, since she often conferred with him about plans for her and Cristin to ride.

She had not misjudged Benet. He had felt the tenseness and the undercurrent of fear that had gripped Afoncaer for weeks, and he was eager for action, especially for something that would bring credit to himself. He promptly suggested a plausible excuse for his absence.

"I had word last week," Benet said, "that my uncle, who lives near Shrewsbury, is sick. Several people know of it, so it won't seem strange if I ask leave to go and visit him. There are enough other stableboys to do my chores for a week or two. Just give me the letter when we meet in the hall early tomorrow morning, and tell Master Reynaud I'll do my very best for him."

Arianna approved of this plan, and so the letter was sent. After Benet had left Afoncaer, the strange noises and lights continued. Another inspection of the castle and village walls was made, and again nothing unusual was found.

"Although," Reynaud said thoughtfully, "it's hard to tell along the cliff. It's so steep we can only look down from the top of the walls, or up from across the river. The side next to the stream is even worse, with all those slippery boulders."

"Which is why it's safe," Geoffrey told him. "You built it that way." And then he sent men over the side on ropes to inspect wall and foundations, just to be certain, and ordered a detachment of men into the forest to search for anything out of the ordinary. Nothing was found. The noises and lights stopped for a week. Everyone waited to learn what would happen next.

Within the castle itself, tension grew daily beneath the outward calm. Selene became more and more withdrawn, keeping to her room most of each day. Though nominally in charge of domestic affairs during Meredith's absence, she did little, leaving Arianna and Joan to plan meals and direct the female servants.

A fire began in the village one night. It spread, and Geoffrey ordered men from the castle to help fight it. Selene came out of her room to see what the excitement was. Having satisfied herself it was nothing serious, and that Deirdre was safe, she started back to her room.

"It is a fine night, is it not? A lovely night for starting fires," said Gwenefer behind her. Selene stood still, held by the compelling note in that silky, quiet voice, as Gwenefer continued. "I think, my friend, it is time for you to repay me for all I have done for you."

"What do you expect of me now?" Selene hissed over her shoulder. "I've fed your cousin Cynan all the information I could get. You have been sitting on the dais at every meal for more than three weeks. Isn't that what you wanted? Isn't it enough?" Selene was filled with loathing for Gwenefer, and for herself. She was consumed with guilt every time she looked at the Welsh woman, and yet she knew when Thomas returned she would take Gwenefer's medicine again, and keep taking it, doing whatever Gwenefer demanded in payment. She would never bear another child in blood and pain if she could possibly avoid it.

"You have only paid part of the cost," Gwenefer said pleasantly.

"What more can I do for you?"

"How generous you are to offer, Lady Selene," the mocking voice behind her said.

"Just tell me what you want and then leave me in peace."

"I want the keys to the postern gate."

"Why?" Selene knew perfectly well that there

was only one reason Gwenefer could have for making such a demand, but she needed time to think. This was horrible. She had never imagined anything like this would be expected of her. How had she become so entrapped?

"Perhaps I want to escape," Gwenefer said, joking into the silence between them.

"Then walk out the main gate. I won't help you any more."

"But you will. You have already betrayed Afoncaer, Selene. You betrayed your husband, and his need for an heir, the day you decided to take my medicine, and you have betrayed him, and the castle, each time you met Cynan and exchanged information for more medicine. You would go on doing it forever, if you could. What are two small keys against all of that?"

"I didn't think—I never meant—oh, Isabel, did you mean this to happen?" Selene's voice broke on a sob.

"Be quiet, someone will hear us. Who is Isabel?"

"Someone who should be here now, to do this for herself."

"I don't know what you're talking about. Listen to me, you silly fool." Gwenefer caught Selene's shoulders and shook her hard. "Stop crying! You are chatelaine of this castle in Lady Meredith's absence, you can go anywhere. Get me those keys."

"You promised," Selene wept. "You gave me your word that Deirdre and I would not be harmed."

"If I said it, it must be so," Gwenefer said lightly. "Will you stop crying, or shall I slap you?"

"I can't take the keys," Selene whispered, trying to regain some self-control. "They are in a locked box in the wardroom, just inside the entrance to the keep, and there are always men in there.''

"Tomorrow night," Gwenefer said, "there will be another fire, a larger one this time, and more men will be sent out to fight it. You can easily distract the attention of any men-at-arms in the wardroom by calling to them to come and see what is happening. They will never suspect you. Slip into the wardroom and take the keys, then return to your own bedchamber. I'll be waiting outside your door. You need not even speak to me. Simply hand me the keys, then go to your room and stay there. Do you understand me, woman?''

"Yes, I understand. You promised—Deirdre and I—''

"I've heard what you have said, Selene." There was a movement in the darkness.

"Wait, don't go. Why a second fire? What are you planning?''

"Why, my Lady Weakling, you can't think I'd tell you Welsh secrets. You'd only think of a way to betray us while trying to save yourself. Do as I've told you, and ask me no more questions." Another motion and Gwenefer was gone, leaving Selene to stumble into her bedchamber, where she huddled in terrified anticipation for the rest of that night.

The following day passed in deceptive calm. Selene kept to her room, but that had become so usual for her that no one remarked on it.

At sunset Cynan and a friend of his slipped out of the forest and mingled with the folk who were returning to the village. It had been a market day, and a larger crowd than usual was pressing through the entrance, all hurrying to get inside the

231

gates before they should be shut for the night. Cynan and his companion were used to making themselves inconspicuous, and thus got into the village with no trouble, walking innocently by the alert but overworked guards.

Just after dark, at the hour previously arranged with their leader Emrys, the Welshmen set several fires. While the attention of the guards on the wall and at the gate was thus distracted, they hastily climbed the stairway against the wall and overpowered the two men who were standing watch in the corner tower nearest the stream. Then Cynan let down the rope he had carried wrapped around his waist, and after the men hidden among the boulders below had secured it, they used it to haul up a heavy rope netting. They had barely finished fastening it to the tower before Welshmen were swarming up the net, pouring over its top edge, and fanning out along the wall.

They were soon seen; not all the guards on the wall had forgotten their duty in watching the fire, and the alarm was given just as a rain of arrows soared over the wet moat and the wall. A good Welsh bowman could loose twelve arrows a minute and hit a target two hundred and forty yards away, and the men Cynan led had been practicing for years. They picked off the guards along the front wall within minutes, then aimed the next flight of arrows into the village. Meanwhile, the Welsh who had made it over the wall and lived to reach the ground fought their way through the village toward the gatehouse in the outer wall, their goal to open the gate and let their comrades in.

Inside the castle proper, in the great hall, Arianna heard the shouting and saw Geoffrey rush out.

"What is it?" she cried. Then, "It's the attack we feared, isn't it, Reynaud? Come, I'll help you into the keep. Where's Joan, where are the kitchen maids?"

"More importantly," Reynaud said calmly, "where is Selene?"

"She must be in her chamber. No, there she goes, past the door to the wardroom. She must have been outside. She's probably going to Deirdre."

"Listen to me carefully, Arianna. Find Selene, and the two of you take Deirdre and Cristin and barricade yourselves in Lord Guy's private chamber. It's the last place of defense, and it will take a great deal to break down that door."

"Come with me, Reynaud. I'll help you up the steps."

"Go now, Arianna. Obey me. We must allow no valuable hostages to be taken. Stop in the wardroom and find yourself a dagger. Be quick about it now. And do not hesitate to use your weapon on anyone who threatens you or the children. Anyone at all." The urgency in his voice propelled Arianna out of the great hall.

"Joan!" Reynaud shouted. "Ah, there you are. Collect all the female servants and get them into the keep. Lock all the doors behind you."

"I will." Joan ran for the kitchen, calling orders to the women as she went.

Reynaud hobbled to the wardroom. It was filled with men busily arming themselves. He scanned the room quickly, then demanded, "Where are the keys to the postern gate?"

"They should be in this box," came the answer. "No, the box is broken open, and the keys are gone!"

"Where is Geoffrey?" Reynaud asked.

"On the wall," one fellow answered, "directing the men-at-arms."

"Go tell him the keys are gone," Reynaud ordered, and the man ran across the bailey toward the inner gates. "The rest of you go secure the postern gate on this side."

They understood the danger and would have obeyed him for all he was no soldier, but it was already too late. The small door in the inner bailey wall flew open. A single line of men issued from it and headed toward the inner gatehouse.

"Seal up the keep," Reynaud ordered. "Let no one in save Geoffrey and his men."

Seeing there was no more he could do and that he would only be in the way of any fighting might develop, Reynaud left the wardroom and made his way slowly and clumsily up the spiral stairs, clinging to the stone newel post, winding around and around on one leg and his crutches. It took him too long to reach the third floor and his own chamber. When he did get there, and looked out the narrow window, he saw by the light of fires and flaming torches that the inner gate was open.

"They could never have fought their way through those defenses," he muttered. "It was treachery. Only treachery could bring Afoncaer down."

He barred the stout door to his room and pushed his writing table against it by the simple means of leaning hard on the table and letting himself fall to the floor as it moved. Then he found his crutches again and pulled himself upright. His precious books were in this room, and all the castle records, along with the history of Afoncaer upon which he had worked so long. He would not let

234

those Welsh barbarians destroy them. He heard voices outside the door. Someone banged on it, then went away. He was certain the Welsh were inside the keep. They would go to the lord's chamber.

The only things more precious than his books were the souls in that chamber, just above his, the two children and Arianna. He could hear shouts coming from the spiral stairs and knew he could never get to them that way. But there was another route, one he and Guy had built with their own hands some twelve years ago. Only the two of them and Meredith knew of it. Reynaud made his way to the wooden shelves that lined one wall. He pushed a heavy parchment scroll aside and his fingers searched for the spring. It worked as easily as it had the last time he and Guy had tested it, and the hidden door opened. The wooden steps concealed behind the shelves went straight up to the lord's chamber. Slowly, painfully, and as quietly as he could manage on one leg and two crutches, Reynaud began to climb.

Chapter 12

On the fourth floor of the keep, Selene stood backed against the closed door of the lord's chamber, her arms outstretched protectively, holding on to the frame at either side in fearful yet determined defiance of the two who faced her.

"You promised," she cried, panting in wide-eyed terror. "Gwenefer, you said Deirdre would be safe. And I."

"Tell them to open the door, Selene," Gwenefer demanded. "They will open it for you."

"You can't have my baby as hostage. I did what you wanted, now go away."

"I," Emrys said, his dagger pointed at Selene's throat, "would like very much to kill you. And I will if you do not order that door opened at once."

"No," Selene whimpered, shrinking against the door in her effort to get away from the menacing man before her. Every bolt on the strengthening iron bands that crossed the solid wood pressed hard into her back, hurting her. She thought she would be impaled upon that door, held there forever by Emry's knife and her own guilt.

"Now," Emrys threatened softly, moving one step closer. "Call to them now."

Suddenly, Selene's resistance crumbled. She did not want to die. Not yet. Not yet.

"Arianna." Her voice cracked with fear. "Arianna, open the door."

"Are you alone?" Arianna called through the heavy wood. "It's not a trick, is it?"

"Open the door," Selene sobbed. "Please. I'm so afraid."

The bar slid back with a grating sound that rumbled through the wood behind Selene's ear, and the door opened a little. Gwenefer caught at Selene, turning her and pushing her toward the opening. Arianna, seeing only Selene, moved the door further to let her in. Emrys reached over Selene's shoulder and thrust the door wide. Arianna stood firmly, weapon in hand, blocking the entrance to the room.

"Deirdre. Don't let them take her." Selene got no further. Emrys pushed her from behind and, overcome by terror, she fainted, leaving the Welshman open to frontal attack as she collapsed toward the floor. At once Arianna slashed at him with the dagger she held.

"Have a care, wench," Emrys growled. As he spoke he cracked her smartly across the wrist, knocking the blade from her grasp before she realized what was happening. She had never seen anyone move so fast. "Get out of my way," he snarled at her.

"Never." Arianna refused to move. The entrance to this chamber was constructed so that one defender could block entry, and this Arianna was determined to do for as long as she could.

"Move or die," Emrys said, lifting his dagger. "I

want those hostages, and I will have them, but you are all going to die in a very short time, so it may as well be now for you.''

Arianna looked him straight in the eye and stayed where she was. She saw his blade coming closer and knew he would kill her, but the danger to herself seemed unimportant. She had to protect Cristin and Deirdre and hope that help would come in time to save them. She uttered a quick, silent prayer and stood her ground.

She heard a sound behind her, and her startled senses noted an object flying past her ear. There was a loud, cracking thud. Emrys crashed to the floor. Stupefied at what had happened so quickly, amazed to find herself still alive, Arianna looked down and saw a gash along one side of Emrys's face, and one of Reynaud's carved crutches on top of his inert body.

''I never thought,'' came Reynaud's calm voice behind her, ''when my friend the carpenter made those crutches for me, that either would ever serve as a weapon. Luckily, my arms are strong from using them every day.''

She whirled around to stare at him. He was hanging on to his remaining crutch and one post of the bed where Cristin cowered with Deirdre in her arms, and he was grinning at her like a young boy.

''How did you get here?'' she cried.

''It's a secret. Will you hand me my crutch, please? Was he alone?''

''Gwenefer was with him, but she's not here now.''

''Ah, yes, the traitor within our walls. No doubt she has gone for reinforcements. Is Selene hurt?''

''I think she has only fainted.'' Arianna felt

rather like fainting herself, but she held herself upright by a great effort of will and handed Reynaud his crutch.

"Cristin," Reynaud ordered, "put the baby down and help Arianna to drag Selene into the room. Then push that murderous Welshman out and bolt the door again, and this time open it for no one."

"Listen!" Cristin scrambled off the bed and ran for the window niche in the eastern wall.

"Get away from there, girl," Reynaud called. "There are arrows flying. Keep those shutters fastened."

"Don't you hear it?" Cristin's face was all alight. "A trumpet. It's my father, I know it is. He's come to rescue us."

"That may be," Reynaud told her, "but in the meantime, the Welsh are still within the bailey, and we need to close the chamber door. Now, stop dancing around and help Arianna."

It was no great task to remove Emrys. He was not very large, and he had been knocked backward by the force of the blow that had felled him. They needed only to twist his legs around and roll him over in order to heave him into the corridor.

Selene was another matter. At first she was unconscious, a dead weight, and Arianna would never have believed anyone so small could be so heavy. Arianna herself was trembling and weak-kneed in reaction to her brush with death. She tugged and pulled at Selene, and Cristin tried to help her, but it was a difficult job. Just when she thought they were succeeding, Selene awoke from her faint and began to scream and cry and thrash about on the floor, her wild movements further impeding them.

"Stop kicking me," Cristin cried, still tugging at Selene's ankles. "We're trying to help you."

"Slap her hard, Arianna," Reynaud called over Selene's wailing. "That will silence her."

Arianna knew he was right. It was the only thing to do, and it had better be done at once before Gwenefer returned with more men. She drew back her right arm, put all her strength behind it, and hit Selene as hard as she could. She was surprised by how good it felt. She had to restrain herself from doing it again, and at that impulse realized she was close to the same kind of collapse Selene had suffered.

Selene fell completely silent.

"Get up," Reynaud ordered coldly. "Walk over to that chair and sit in it. And keep quiet."

Selene obeyed him meekly, while behind her Arianna finally closed and bolted the door.

"And now, Master Reynaud?" Arianna had retrieved her dagger and stood before him holding it, pale but composed, having forced herself back from the edge of hysteria. Reynaud nodded approvingly.

"Now we wait," he said, "and hope Cristin is right that Lord Guy has come. Sit down, my dear, before you fall, and tell me why Selene was in the corridor with that Welsh woman, and not in here with you and the children."

"She was behind us on the stairs, and when she shouted for us to close the door, I did."

"The mother, protecting her child."

"Why, yes," Arianna said, puzzled at his sarcastic tone. She saw Selene sitting quietly on the chair where Reynaud had ordered her, tears running down her cheeks. Arianna wanted to go to her and offer comfort, but her own legs would no longer

240

hold her weight. She climbed onto the huge bed and huddled there, shaking.

"This same protective mother," Reynaud went on, "then told you to open the door to certain murderers."

"I suppose they forced her. I could not see, Reynaud, I only heard her voice."

"Reynaud, it is my father," Cristin called from the window niche. "Look at all the torches! And how many men he has with him! They are in the inner bailey. Come see, there's Thomas."

"Thomas?" Selene started up from her chair. "Thomas is here? I must go to him, I must tell him what happened. I have to explain." When she ran toward the door, Arianna jumped off the bed to pursue her, stumbling and nearly falling on still-shaky knees.

"Stay here, Lady Selene!" Reynaud exclaimed. "It is dangerous to leave this room. The Welsh may still be within the keep. Wait until Thomas comes for you."

Arianna put her arms around Selene, brought her back to the chair, and gave her Deirdre to hold. And then they waited for hours, their vigil punctuated by Cristin's eager descriptions as the rising sun revealed the results of the previous night's attack. Cristin would not be kept away from the windows. She ran from one side of the room to the other, peering through chinks in the shutters to see whatever she could.

"There are a lot of people lying on the ground. There's blood all over," Cristin reported with childish excitement. Selene moaned and closed her eyes and looked ill, but Cristin went on relentlessly. "Those must be the prisoners the guards are surrounding. There aren't very many of them.

241

Oh, Geoffrey is hurt, look at his arm. Why don't they hurry and come for us, so I can go to help him? What is Benet doing with my father?" Cristin turned from the window, her face so pale the freckles across her nose stood out boldly. "My father is hurt, he's limping and leaning on Benet. Reynaud, please let us go out now. My father needs me."

"Stay here, child. It won't be long, I promise."

It was only a moment or two later that they heard Sir Kenelm's familiar voice on the stairs, and at Reynaud's nod Arianna threw open the door.

"Guy sent me," Kenelm said, his quick soldier's glance noting the condition of all the occupants of that room. "It's safe to go to the great hall now."

Cristin ran past him and down the steps, calling out for her father and for Geoffrey. Selene, the still peacefully sleeping Deirdre in her arms, was not far behind.

Arianna went more slowly, glad to hang back and help Reynaud down the stairs and thus miss Selene's reunion with Thomas. Kenelm also lent his brawny strength to support the tired architect. The three of them walked into the great hall together.

The first thing Arianna saw was Thomas, with his arms around Selene and Deirdre snuggled between them. Arianna left that tender scene, and found Guy in his big wooden chair with young Benet beside him pressing a bloodstained rag to his thigh. Geoffrey sat nearby, his left sleeve soaked in blood. Cristin fluttered anxiously between the two men.

"Are there many wounded?" Arianna asked Kenelm, already going over in her mind the list of supplies she would need.

"Not many," Kenelm answered. "We surprised them with all the gates opened, and we were armored. There wasn't much of a fight."

There were in fact twenty wounded men, including Guy and Geoffrey. Arianna had them all brought into the hall so she could tend to them more easily. Only a few were seriously hurt. Geoffrey had only flesh wounds to his left arm and side, which would heal quickly. Guy also had a flesh wound in his right thigh, caused by a Welsh arrow. It was painful, but clean, and his chief concern over it seemed to be that his chain mail hauberk had been damaged and would have to be repaired.

"You are fortunate the links weren't embedded in the wound," Arianna told him, wrapping a linen bandage around his leg. "Let the blacksmith have the extra work and rejoice that you will be healed within a week or two."

"The blacksmith is dead," Guy said sadly. "We'll have to find another. It won't be easy. He was a good man."

There were others dead, some dear friends. Captain John had fallen defending the inner gate, along with several young men Arianna knew well. Worst of all was the loss of Joan. Arianna found her face-down in the kitchen, along with two of the serving girls, and she and Cristin wept together over her before going back into the hall to mend the wounded as best they could. Cristin worked by Arianna's side through the rest of that day, never once flinching at what was required of her.

"I've helped in the stables with the horses from time to time," Cristin said. "I'll just pretend that's what I'm doing now. I'm not afraid of blood."

The one who did fear blood, Selene, had gone

to her bedchamber, taking Thomas with her. He reappeared an hour or so later, looking flushed and happy, but of Selene there was no further sign that day.

Some of Guy's household knights were married, and their wives, who had sheltered in their own rooms inside the keep, now made their way to the hall to look for their husbands and to offer what help they could among the wounded.

In Selene's absence Arianna took charge of the domestic side of the castle, so smoothly that she herself hardly realized what she was doing. She simply saw what was needful and made arrangements to supply it. She called the carpenter and ordered coffins made for the dead, spoke to the village priest and arranged for the bodies to be washed and prepared for burial. She had the kitchen cleaned and restored to its usual neat condition and put the most intelligent of the serving girls in charge of the evening meal. She sent Linnet to help Selene with Deirdre. She told the glazier to come the next day to measure the broken windowpanes for replacement, and the carpenter's assistants to repair damaged shutters and doors as soon as possible. The inner bailey must be cleaned, and fresh sand sprinkled on the dreadful stains that had soaked the ground and the floor of the great hall and corridors. The village folk needed help in setting their disturbed lives to rights once more. And all the time, while issuing orders and seeing more and more that must be done, she tended the wounded. It was not until she at last sat down to eat something, long after nightfall of that endless day, that Arianna remembered the Welsh prisoners someone had told her about, and ordered food taken to them.

"Small need," Kenelm said. "They won't live long enough to starve. Guy, I wish you would let me try to get more information out of them. They are all most unwilling to talk." Guy had that afternoon appointed Kenelm Captain of the Guard to replace Captain John, and Kenelm seemed prepared to take his new post seriously.

"There will be no torture," Guy said. "They will all hang for what they've done, but I want each of them able to walk to the gibbet, so their fellow countrymen can see that what I am meting out here is justice, not brutal vengeance. I want to discourage further attacks, not make more enemies."

"Is Gwenefer among the prisoners?" Arianna asked.

"She is," Guy said, "and more guilty than most of the others. You already know, I think, that she was the spy who gave the rebels the information about our defenses, and she is the one who opened the postern gate. Selene told Thomas the woman befriended her and tricked her into revealing a few unimportant facts, but mostly Gwenefer employed her wits and her charms on men most effectively, to learn what she wanted to know."

"And I chief among those men," Geoffrey said. "Guy, I am heartily ashamed of my part in this. I'll never trust a woman again, and I'll give up Tynant, turn it back to you at once. I don't deserve your confidence in me, or your trust any more."

"By that speech you've proven your fitness to keep it," Guy responded, reaching across the table to clasp Geoffrey's hand. "You've learned a hard lesson, old friend, and you will be the wiser for it. Tynant remains yours."

"Thank you." Geoffrey was perilously close to unmanly tears. Seeking distraction from his overflowing emotions, he nodded toward the dark young man standing behind Guy's chair. "Have you taken a new squire? He looks familiar to me."

"This is Benet," Guy told him. "He has well earned his position. I'll tell you all about it later. At the moment, I badly need a few hours' sleep."

"When will my mother come home?" Cristin asked. "I wish she were here now."

"I told her to remain at Kelsey until I sent word it was safe to return to Afoncaer," Guy replied, rising from his seat, "but I know my Meredith, and I expect the messenger to meet her on the road. I'd not be at all surprised to see her ride through the gate in a day or two. Now go to your bed, my brave girl." Guy left the great hall with one arm across Benet's shoulders for support, and the other around his daughter.

When Arianna stood up to leave, too, Thomas came to her.

"Reynaud told me how you faced down the Welsh leader."

"It was Reynaud who struck the necessary blow," Arianna said. "Did he tell you how?"

"He did." Thomas's blue eyes laughed down into hers. "You were very brave, and very foolish, Arianna. I am so proud of you. Meredith will be, too, when she hears of it." He took her hand and kissed it, and reached out to brush a stray curl off her forehead, then he bent and kissed her cheek. When he went away, to the bedchamber he shared with Selene, Arianna stood looking after him for a long time.

The prisoners' cells at Afoncaer were carved out of the solid rock beneath the storerooms, at the

246

very lowest underground level of the tower keep. Gwenefer, being the only woman among the captured Welsh, had been given the smallest cell to herself, and there she sat, or paced the few steps from one side to the other, not knowing in that windowless, airless place, whether it was day or night. Sir Kenelm, the Captain of the Guard, had come to question her, full of his new dignity. When she had refused to tell him anything more than he already knew about her part in the raid, he had gone away again, leaving her surprised that he had used neither rape nor torture to make her speak. Surely torture would come later, before a painful death. Gwenefer was glad she knew nothing of her countrymen's intentions beyond the immediate plans Emrys had had for Afoncaer. What she did not know, she could not be made to tell.

She heard her cell door open and tensed, believing pain was imminent. A guard came in, the torch he carried adding to the light of the tallow dip they had given her earlier. The guard stuck the torch into a wall bracket.

"You have a visitor." He moved aside to let Geoffrey enter the cell. "I'll be at the top of the stairs, my lord. Call out when you are ready to leave, and I'll come down and lock her in again."

Gwenefer studied her former lover, seeing the deep new lines in his kind, honest face and the pain in the brown eyes that had once looked at her so tenderly.

"Have you come to punish me in person, my lord?" she taunted him. "Shall I bare my bosom for your blade?"

"I want you to tell me," Geoffrey said, "why you betrayed me. You let me believe you cared for me, Gwenefer."

247

"So I did. It was a *Cymreig* trick, my lord, in order to gain access to Afoncaer. You know how sly we *Cymry*, we Welsh, are, how untrustworthy. You should have been more careful."

"There must have been some good reason for what you did. Tell it to me, and I'll explain to Guy. He's not a cruel man, and I know he hates the thought of hanging a woman. He'd revoke your sentence for just cause, I'm certain he would."

"Hanging? Every one of us? That's all?" When Geoffrey nodded, Gwenefer's hands flew to her slender throat. "I had thought he'd want to give us some long and painful ending. When is it to be?"

"At noon tomorrow." Geoffrey caught her hands and held them against his chest. "Gwenefer, it need not happen. Just give me a reason, some extenuating circumstance for what you did, and I'll arrange for you to be sent to some secure convent where you may live out your days in prayerful peace."

She pulled her hands out of his with a harsh laugh. She would tell him the truth, but not all of it. She did not want her parents' names on Norman lips. She herself was no longer worthy to speak their names.

"I doubt there is a convent anywhere that could make use of my talents, my lord. You, who were the recipient of my skills, must appreciate that. So you want a reason, do you? I'll give you one." She fairly spat the next words at him. "You Normans have invaded my homeland. You build your castles wherever you can wrest enough land from us, and then you try to turn my fellow countrymen into your serfs. Normans do not belong in *Cymru*.

248

We will fight you however we can until we drive you out again."

"Gwenefer, please. Tell me something I can use to help you."

"I'll tell you this, Norman. If you save me from the noose and send me to a convent, I'll find a way to escape, and I'll join the next band of *Cymry* planning to attack Afoncaer. I'll be back to do as much harm as I can, so you had better kill me while you have the chance."

She saw by his face that he believed her. She had deliberately left him no opening through which he could help her. It was what she wanted. She had never swerved for a moment from the path she and Emrys had agreed she would take, but the tenderness she had come to feel for Geoffrey was a betrayal of the Welsh cause and of her parents, whom the Normans had killed. For that dual betrayal she deserved to die.

"Will you kiss me?" Geoffrey asked.

"Why?" She made herself laugh at him, wanting his mouth on hers one last time, and denying herself the thing she yearned for. It was part of her punishment. That, and watching him while she coldly destroyed his love for her. Considering what she had done to him, it was only right to set him free of her, but the pain of doing it was worse than that which the hangman's noose would inflict on her tomorrow. "I never wanted to kiss you, Geoffrey. I certainly do not want to now."

He looked at her with eyes gone cold and blank, and then he went out, calling to the guard to come and lock her door.

"A priest will come to you later tonight, Gwenefer," he said from outside her cell. "None of you need die unshriven, and you will all be left unharmed until tomorrow."

Gwenefer made no reply. She stood still, listening to his footsteps on the stone stairway until a heavy door slammed and all was silent once more. Then she sank onto the damp stone floor, weeping quietly, loving him and deeply ashamed of her love. *Cymreig,* Welsh, could not love Norman. But she did, and would until she died. She choked back hysterical laughter. Until she died. That would not be so very long. Less than a day. She could bear it until then.

It began to rain during the night, a drifting, misty rain to end the unusual stretch of sun and heat. The cool greyness settled over Afoncaer, matching the subdued atmosphere of the day. In the morning, those who had been killed in the Welsh attack were buried. The prisoners would be executed at noon. The entire population of Afoncaer, both castle and village, everyone above the age of twelve, was expected to attend both events.

Selene had existed for the last two days in a state of barely suppressed hysteria. She was certain Reynaud sensed that she had had more to do with recent events than she had admitted. Hoping to divert any blame that might be placed upon her, she had given Thomas a highly colored, truncated version of her brief friendship with Gwenefer. She believed he had accepted what she had told him and would defend her against whatever suspicions anyone might hold toward her for that ill-fated association. She had confirmed her husband's trust and devotion by flinging herself upon him in a wild paroxysm of sexual abandon. She had successfully convinced him that she had missed him terribly in his absence, and that she was as disappointed as he to learn she was not with child after all. Selene knew he imagined she was trying to conceive now, to make up for that disappointment, and so he co-operated willingly whenever she approached him, pleased and flattered by her frequent invitations.

But what Selene was really doing was drugging herself with Thomas's body as she sought to forget her fear that Gwenefer, or Cynan, or Emrys, their leader, would speak her name in connection with what had happened at the castle and thus confirm Reynaud's impressions. She was afraid to ask any questions aimed at discovering whether she had been implicated in the Welsh plot. Questions could arouse more suspicions.

She put on a black gown and dragged herself to the funeral service in the village church, pale and shaken at what she had helped to bring about. There she prayed sincerely for the souls of those whose deaths were partly her fault.

"I can't go to the hanging, Thomas," she said afterward. "I can't."

"We all have to go, Selene. Arianna will be there, and I'll be right next to you."

She could not tell him she feared one of the Welsh, or all of them, would stand on the scaffold and point her out and say she belonged with them, that she, too, should have a noose about her neck.

Guy had decided not to hang the Welshmen from the battlements, which was the usual punishment for prisoners taken in such an attack. Instead, in an effort to display solemn, measured Norman justice, a scaffold had been erected outside the village walls, in a narrow, unfarmable field that ran along the river. They all rode out to the spot, Guy leading them, followed by Thomas and Geoffrey, Benet and the other squires, Selene and Arianna, Kenelm and his men-at-arms, and lastly, on foot, the household staff. Reynaud had come in a horse-drawn litter. They all stood together, and behind them the villagers gathered in a crescent. Only Guy remained mounted. The wound in his thigh pained him badly, and he had not wanted to appear weak in public by needing help to get off and on his horse, so now he sat high above them on his huge black stallion, his face set in grim lines, watching the village gate, waiting.

The six prisoners came last of all, riding in a wooden cart and accompanied by the village priest, Guy's sheriff, and a few armed guards. One or two wore bandages over wounds they had taken in the fighting, but it was perfectly clear that they had been fed and well cared for, and that no one had been tortured. The crowd fell silent as the prisoners were led to the scaffold.

It began to rain harder. Selene, forced by the press of people to move forward until she stood much too close to the wooden platform, saw Gwenefer lift her face to the sky, to the last Welsh rain she would ever know.

The sheriff read the execution order he and Guy had stamped with their seals the day before.

"Have you anything to say?" the sheriff asked, and Selene swayed, holding her breath. Just a few moments more and either she, too, would stand condemned, or no one would ever know what she had done. Her fate depended upon the five men and one woman standing before her.

Emrys began a short, impassioned speech, declaring that the Normans would soon be driven out of Wales forever. While he spoke, Gwenefer looked straight at Selene, who thought her heart had stopped in fear. Emrys ended his speech. Selene knew Gwenefer would speak next and condemn her. She knew it.

"Does anyone else have aught to say?" called the sheriff.

Selene waited, transfixed by Gwenefer's dark eyes. There was a long, long silence. Or so it seemed to Selene, but when she blinked the nooses had been placed about six necks and Guy sat sternly on his horse, his right hand raised.

Gwenefer never took her eyes off Selene's face and it seemed to Selene that she could read the Welsh woman's thoughts. Gwenefer had decided not to speak. She would leave Selene to the guilt so plainly written in her expression, and to the possibility of further betrayal in the future. For how could Selene ever be certain Gwenefer had not told someone else what Selene had done, someone who might use that information as Gwenefer had used it, to make her help the Welsh? That, Gwenefer's dark eyes seemed to say, would be Selene's lifelong punishment.

Gwenefer smiled at Selene with a deep, secret amusement. The smile lasted only a moment before Gwenefer sought out Geoffrey, and there her gaze remained.

Guy's raised hand began to fall, and when it came down, the six Welsh rebels were no more, and Selene hung limply between Thomas and Arianna, supported only by their entwined arms.

Part IV

Arianna
A.D. 1117–1121

Chapter 13

Just as Guy had anticipated, Meredith came home the day after the executions, in time to help Arianna nurse Selene through a month-long illness.

Selene had spoken to no one since she had fainted in front of the scaffold, and she showed no interest in anything except Deirdre. Every morning either Arianna or Linnet brought the child, now ten months old, to Selene's bedchamber. Selene would touch her daughter, as though reassuring herself Deirdre was safe, perhaps smile at her, then sigh and close her eyes and push the little girl away and ignore her until someone took her back to the nursery.

"Selene has no fever," Arianna said, "no rash or pain, no signs of any bodily ill. What is wrong with her?"

"I don't know," Meredith admitted. "Perhaps the shock of all she witnessed during the raid has affected her. You said she was terrified for Deirdre's sake."

They could think of nothing else to cause such an illness, and nothing that might cure it save the passage of time. Each day they fed and washed Selene and combed her hair, talking to her on pleasant subjects all the while, trying to lift her spirits. Beyond that, they could only pray she would recover soon.

"It was the hanging," Thomas said to Arianna. "I should not have forced her to go to it. She was unwilling, she begged me to let her stay behind, and I refused. The fault for this is mine."

"It pains me to see you so unhappy." Arianna put one hand on his arm. They stood in the great hall, where he had come after one of the visits he daily made to Selene's bedside. "Thomas, if you continue to grieve so over Selene's condition, and to blame yourself, you will only make yourself ill, too. Then what will Selene do when she is well again and you are ill?"

"Do you really believe that she will ever be well?" Thomas asked. "I've nearly lost hope."

"I have not," Arianna declared firmly. "And when she is recovered, she will need you, Thomas. Please, for her sake, and your own, don't give up."

"She's right, you know." Guy had come into the hall with Reynaud, and now he joined Arianna and Thomas. Reynaud, who walked more slowly, lagged a step or two behind him.

"Support me in this, Guy," Arianna urged. "I think Thomas should go hunting with Kenelm. Take Cristin and those two goshawks she's been helping the falconer to train. Ride a bit, and come back tired and hungry, and eat a hearty meal for once."

"And tomorrow," Guy added, "come with Reynaud and me. We are going to mark out a new town wall to enclose all those houses that are springing up on the other side of the moat. They are brave folk to build there after what has just happened, and they deserve better protection from their lord."

Reynaud had joined them. He stood next to Arianna and spoke to her under his breath.

"I'll take Thomas's mind away from his wife's condition. I know how to catch his interest." Raising his voice, the architect added, "I thought a high wall with several watch towers. As for the gatehouse, something clever, to stop would-be invaders at several places before they can get inside. Your uncle has told me, Thomas, about a castle he saw once in the Holy Land, and I've made a sketch from his description."

"May I see it?" Thomas was plainly interested, and Arianna sent Reynaud a grateful look. She did not have time to thank him in words until later, for her attention was claimed by one of the new serving girls who needed her advice.

There were more people housed in the castle these days. Guy had added to the number of his knights and squires while visiting his English properties, and some of the knights had brought their ladies and children to live at Afoncaer. Meredith had made still more additions to the household staff, bringing with her from Kelsey and Adderbury half a dozen serving women and several pages, young lads away from home for the first time, nervous and needing both reassurance and instruction in their duties to the ladies of the castle.

Kenelm's new wife had come with Meredith, too. A plump, pale blonde, aptly named Blanche, this daughter of Adderbury's seneschal had brought along four female attendants of her own.

She and Kenelm had been given two rooms on the third floor of the keep, granted so much space because of Kenelm's rank as Captain of the Guard.

The castle was fairly bursting with the crowd, and the presence of all these new and attractive young people enlivened life in great hall and kitchen. Arianna, observing various pairings-off with an amused eye, suspected several of Guy's currently unwed knights and men-at-arms would take wives before winter was over.

By early October the necessary repairs had been made to damage done during the Welsh raid, both in castle and village. The harvest was well under way. And Selene was finally showing signs of recovery. She had begun to speak again, and she was out of her bed, though she still kept to her room. One morning she surprised Arianna by asking for parchment and quill pen. Once she had the writing supplies, she sent everyone away and spent the rest of the day locked in her chamber. She emerged at day's end with a thick sealed packet and a second, thinner letter. More importantly, she had dressed herself and appeared ready to join the evening meal for the first time since her collapse.

"Could you next courier to King Henry's court in Normandy take these also?" she asked Guy, handing him the letters. "My father will see they are given to my mother, and she will have the packet sent on to Lady Elvira in Poitou."

"Only a small note to your mother, and such a long letter to a friend?" Guy joked, turning the two folded parchments over as though weighing them.

"I haven't written to Elvira for a long time," Selene countered.

"But you have," Reynaud said, fixing Selene with his pale blue gaze. "If I remember correctly, you sent her a letter just after you and Thomas returned from Tynant last spring."

"What could you possibly know, Reynaud—" Selene's voice was louder and sharper than she intended, but the man irritated her so, watching her closely when she came into the hall just now, as if he knew something about her and was waiting for her to make a mistake. "What could you know of the things dear girlhood friends write to each other? So much has happened recently. I wanted to tell Elvira all of it, and the telling has helped to make me well again. I've put it all behind me." It was in fact Isabel to whom Selene had told all, in sentences carefully phrased lest someone else should read the letter. But Isabel would understand and approve what Selene had done. Now, if only the too-curious Reynaud would turn his attention elsewhere and forget his suspicions of her, she could begin to feel safe.

"Indeed," he said, still watching her closely, "you do look much improved, Lady Selene."

"It is no concern of yours how I look," Selene snapped. Ignoring Reynaud's expression of surprise and Guy's raised eyebrows, she went on, "Have I no right to send a letter to a friend if I chose? It will be no inconvenience to you, Guy. You told Thomas yesterday you had a letter to go to my father."

"I did, and there is no difficulty in adding these to the packet," Guy assured her.

"There, you see?" she said triumphantly to Reynaud. He did not respond, but later, after the meal was over, Arianna took her aside.

"Selene, treat Reynaud more kindly," she advised. "He would be your friend if you would let him."

"I don't need him for a friend. I can't bear to look at him with his crutches and that missing leg. He's a dreadful sight."

"Selene, he's not at all disfigured, thanks to Meredith's good care. However he appears to you, never forget that he saved your life, and Deirdre's, by using one of those crutches you so disdain."

"And now he stares at me all the time, as though I had done something wrong. Why doesn't he leave me alone?"

"You are imagining it," Arianna said. She watched sadly when Selene turned her back on the assembled company and left the hall, murmuring, "You are not recovered yet, my friend. What ails you?"

Thomas soon had cause to ask the same question, for Selene, once roused from her month-long torpor, flung herself into frantic activity. She joined every hunting party that set out from Afoncaer, riding as though the devil himself sat behind her, and when no hunting was planned she rode alone with only a servant or two and a squire, despite Thomas's reservations.

"Remember the Welsh," he said. "It's not safe to go too far from Afoncaer until we are certain there will be no revenge for those we hung."

"I'm not afraid of the Welsh." Her voice was strained, as though she were trying to convince herself.

"Stay at the castle, Selene. You never see Deirdre any more. Days go by—"

"Deirdre has Arianna."

"I don't understand. First you cling to the child, then you ignore her."

"She doesn't need me." She could not explain to him her fear that Deirdre, the one creature she loved more than herself, might be contaminated by her evil. Better to stay away from the child altogether and thus keep her safe. Selene fled from Thomas to the chapel, the other place where she spent her time.

If her days were divided between horseback and fervent prayers that her traitorous deeds might never be discovered, Selene's nights were devoted to passionate encounters with Thomas. They had slept apart during her long illness, but no longer. She began to ration most carefully the tiny remaining portion of Gwenefer's medicine. Before it ran out she had to bind Thomas to her so thoroughly that he would love and defend her no matter what anyone might discover about her part in the Welsh attack. She diluted the medicine with wine, swishing it around the small earthenware vial to mix in every available drop of the stuff, then peered into the vial. So little was left. What would she do when it was gone? Selene considered the long years ahead of her, nights spent with Thomas, and shuddered at the thought of childbirth. She had to make the liquid in the jar last as long as possible. Gwenefer had warned her it was very strong, that more than the recommended amount would harm her. Perhaps she could use less of it, to make it last longer. Selene began to take the medicine every other day.

Through the autumn Arianna watched and wondered at Selene's odd, secretive manner, and did not know if she felt greater pity for her or for Thomas. The old friendship between herself and Selene was broken, their relationship held together only by the tenuous ties of distant kinship. Selene had shut Arianna out of her heart along with everyone else, and seemed now to live in some strange, tightly enclosed world of her own making, where Arianna could not follow.

"Leave me alone," Selene said to every suggestion Arianna made for joint activity. Selene was not interested in making a new perfume in the stillroom, although she had once enjoyed that, nor did she want to help Arianna count the linens and decide which needed mending, or cut out a new gown for the seamstress to sew for her, or do anything at all in the kitchen. "I have my own concerns, Arianna. Leave me alone."

Into the lonely void Selene's withdrawal left came Blanche, Kenelm's new wife, who was Arianna's own age. She was shy at first, making tremulous overtures toward friendship as though afraid to overstep her position. But she was always there to help when help was needed in that busy harvest season, not too proud to roll up the linen sleeves of her underdress and tie on an apron and lay down fruits in honey or baste the side of beef turning on the spit. Before Blanche had been at Afoncaer a month, she had quietly assumed most of Joan's old duties, freeing Meredith from long hours in kitchen and laundry.

"What a well-trained housekeeper she is," Meredith said. "What a relief to me."

"And funny," Arianna added. "She makes everyone laugh. She says good humor improves good food."

"So it does." Reynaud had overheard them and looked up from the parchments he had spread across the high table. "Her food is marvellous, a delight to the tongue and palate. I notice Sir Kenelm growing plump and contented. It must be the gingerbread."

The two women laughed, for Blanche had brought with her the recipe for the new delicacy, flavored with spices carried to England from the distant east beyond the Holy Land. Kenelm relished the tasty treat, and Arianna thought he doted upon the pretty wife who saw to it he had his fill of his favorite food.

"Blanche is a fine needlewoman, too," Meredith said, putting an arm around Arianna as they walked toward the stillroom. "A good thing, that, considering our joint lack of talent."

"I wish Selene were only half as agreeable as Blanche. For Thomas's sake."

"She's not and never will be." Meredith glanced at her companion, a shrewd look, seeing much that Arianna would have kept hidden. "Thomas must make his own accommodation with his wife, and we must stand aside and leave him be. You have done well, Arianna. You've not given in to the temptation his difficulties with Selene, or her illness, have offered to you. I'm proud of you."

Arianna, considering the striking contrast between the two couples, could only worry about Thomas.

There came Kenelm to the great hall each midday, sleek and well fed, his short black hair smooth and shiny, easy laughter on his lips. And there was Blanche, dimpled and bright-eyed, directing the serving girls with the trays of food. They were both

265

discreet, no sign of affection ever passed between them before others, yet contentment lay upon Kenelm and Blanche for all to see.

Meanwhile, in her place at the high table Selene sat cold and withdrawn, Thomas, overly thin and grim of mouth, beside her. And between them lay the suggestion of half-slumbering passion that drew Thomas's eyes to Selene's beautiful, indifferent face again and again, made him touch her hand where it lay on the table, made everyone around them uncomfortably aware of Thomas's desire for her. Arianna wondered how anyone could endure the pain in Thomas's eyes, and wished she could do something to help him.

No sooner was the harvest gathered in than the storms began. Weeks of heavy rain and sleet, and an early snowfall, put a temporary end to hunting and to Selene's daily rides.

"It's just as well," Meredith said when they were snowed in just before Christmastide. "Selene won't sit a horse again until next summer is nearly done. Thomas won't allow her to ride."

"She's with child?" Arianna felt a cold chill at the pit of her stomach, remembering how difficult had been Selene's last pregnancy, how dangerous her childbirth.

"Look at her," Meredith replied, "pale, with shadows under her eyes, and not eating in the mornings. I'm not sure she realizes it yet, but yes, Selene is with child again."

Selene refused to believe her own body's message. Gwenefer's medicine, diluted, taken only every other day, was long gone, but how could it happen so soon? So quickly her appetite vanished, her breasts ached, her waistline thickened. And Selene knew, she was absolutely certain, that she would die in childbirth. It would be heaven's punishment for the terrible things she had done. She lived each day in terror, and under that pressure her temper flared dangerously, as she searched for some outlet in place of the confession she dared not make.

"You did this to me," she raged at Thomas shortly after the new year began. She could hide her pregnancy from him no longer, and when he came to their bedchamber and put his arms around her she drew back, hating the tenderness she saw in his eyes, resenting his obvious delight at the renewed possibility of a son. "Look at me. Are you pleased with yourself, my lord? Are you proud of your manhood?"

"I am happy to know our love has had this result," he replied mildly, trying to placate her. "You should be, too."

"Do you expect me to be pleased that I'll be sick again for so many months, and swollen out of all recognition, and then at the end of it have to face that terrible pain and very likely die? I nearly died when Deirdre was born; it is a certainty this time. And all for your lust."

"I love you, Selene. I still love you in spite of your bad temper," he teased, trying to gentle her as though she were a nervous colt, but she broke away from him, and picked up a wooden cup that stood beside a pitcher of wine, threatening to throw it at him.

"You will not touch me, my lord. Not until long after this child is born. If then. If I live." Her voice broke in panic.

Thomas reached out and caught her wrist, took

the cup out of her hand and set it down again. He kept tight hold on her wrist, drawing her closer to him, all gentleness gone from his manner.

"I am your ruler, madame. You will do as I say at all times." At the cool anger in Thomas's voice, defiance flamed brighter in Selene's green eyes, and her own voice dripped contempt for her husband and his needs.

"Will you deliberately harm your unborn child, my lord? If you lay with me, and I miscarry, it will be your fault. Go and find yourself a serving maid."

She would not listen to anything he might say, and she struggled, weeping, when he tried to embrace her again. The few words she would speak to him were reproaches about her uncomfortable condition, until Thomas, unwilling to take by force what was rightfully his and thus chance hurting her and the baby she carried, gave up. He lay rigid with anger and utterly defeated on his side of their huge bed, while Selene curled into a ball as far away from him as she could get.

It was the first of many such nights. Selene would have nothing to do with him except to berate him for what he had done to her.

"Consider," he said to her one morning, forestalling yet another tongue lashing, "that you may bear a male child, the heir to Afoncaer and all the rest of Uncle Guy's lands. The thought of the honor due to you in that case should rejoice even your proud heart."

"It is the only thing," Selene told him, "that keeps me from throwing myself off the castle wall and into the river."

"Selene!"

"Why not?" she asked, laughing wildly. "Such

a death would be quicker, and much less painful than this long, drawn-out torment, and what awaits me at the end of it."

"You know the church's teaching on suicide," Thomas said, horrified, and watched Selene shrug her shoulders.

"I am beyond redemption," she whispered, very low.

"What did you say? I couldn't hear you. Speak to me, Selene, tell me you did not mean that terrible threat."

"Of course I didn't mean it. I'm too much a coward to take such action. You needn't fear for your precious son-to-be. Now leave me." She picked up parchment and ink bottle, preparing to write one of her long letters.

Dismissed like the lowliest of servants, Thomas went searching for Meredith. He found her alone in the stillroom, busy with mortar and pestle, compounding some herbal mixture. Perching on a stool, feeling like the lost little boy he had been when he had first met her so many years ago, he poured out his problems to this dearest and most discreet of friends.

"She's mad," he concluded. "There is no other explanation for the things she says and does. She was difficult before Deirdre was born, but this is worse. And this time she's not even sick, Meredith. She was only a little queasy for a few mornings."

"Where is she now?"

"Shut up in our chamber, writing to her friend Elvira."

"What, again?"

"I don't understand it. She almost never writes to Lady Aloise. Why to this Elvira, and twice since

269

last summer?'' Thomas ran his hands through his golden hair, disarranging it into a thick, boyish tangle. ''I don't understand anything about her, Meredith. When we were first married, I believed that in time we would learn to be happy together. Now I think Selene doesn't want to be happy. She fights every opportunity for happiness as though it were a mortal sin.''

''I'll talk to her,'' Meredith promised, ''and see if I can reconcile her to this new child.''

Whatever Meredith said to Selene had little effect, and that was quickly lost in the excitement of the announcement that came in mid-February. Meredith, too, was with child, and it would be born a month after Selene's.

''I can hardly believe it,'' Meredith said to Arianna. ''After all these years, and so many false hopes.''

''You must be very happy to have another chance to give your husband a son,'' Arianna replied.

''Yes, I am.'' Meredith's radiant face confirmed her words. ''But Selene is not pleased.''

Selene was in fact jealous, spiteful to Meredith, and cold to both Thomas and Arianna. Worst of all, she continued to ignore the daughter to whom she had once been so devoted, and Deirdre's care was left completely to Arianna and her helper, Linnet.

Cristin had used to help in the nursery from time to time, but in March, Cristin was sent to another noble family for fostering. She would be gone for at least two years, until it was time to arrange a suitable marriage for her. Arianna missed her cheerful prattle about horses, and hawking, and most of all, about her adored Geoffrey, who had

270

by now been forgiven his passion for Gwenefer and restored to his rightful place in Cristin's affections.

"She'll forget him once she meets a few handsome squires," Thomas said on one of his frequent visits to the nursery. "Geoffrey would not make a good husband for Cristin. He's grown morose and says he distrusts all women. He's holed up at Tynant, feeding his dislike of the Welsh. No, Geoffrey is not for Cristin, whatever she thinks. It's best not to indulge in such youthful passions. They only bring sorrow." His face was closed and somber as he regarded his sixteen-month-old daughter toddling about the room, followed by Linnet.

"Cristin could always marry Benet," Arianna said, teasing and hoping to rouse him from painful thoughts. "He's a good lad, and bright, too."

"But not well born. Uncle Guy will want to arrange a better marriage than that for his daughter." Thomas scowled and reached forward to take a wooden doll from Deirdre's mouth. "She could fall and hurt herself on this, Arianna."

"Nonsense. It's perfectly safe." Arianna removed the doll from Thomas's hand and gave it back to Deirdre, thus forestalling the child's threatened tears. "I think it's time to feed her, Linnet. Would you go to the kitchen and get her food?" After Linnet had left, Arianna turned back to Thomas.

"Benet could rise in the world," she said. "Determined men have done so before. He loves Cristin. That's plain for anyone to see, and with that inspiration, who knows what he may do?"

"Love is a dream," Thomas said. "It has nothing to do with marriage. What matters is the

271

strength of a man's arm when he takes sword in hand, his position in the world, and most of all, his honor. Nothing else.'' The deep blue eyes now meeting Arianna's were full of pain.

''Surely not,'' she faltered, knowing only too well what had caused that pain. ''There is friendship. You have so many friends, Thomas, and we all care deeply for you.'' There was no point in pretending she did not know how it was between him and Selene these days. The entire household knew, probably the whole town, too. Life in a castle allowed little privacy. The only real secrets were the ones people kept locked up in their own hearts.

''Friendship.'' Thomas's hand touched her shoulder. ''You have been a friend. Since the first day I met you, you have been nearby, to ease pain and offer comfort. How good you are. How true.'' He put his arms around her and held her, and Arianna, realizing there was no passion in it, but only the need for human contact, put her arms around him, too, and held him close in tenderness and the friendship she had spoken of. They stood that way for a long time, while Deirdre played at their feet, and Thomas drew strength from the peaceful atmosphere of that room. After a while he let her go, smiling, holding on to her hands, bending toward her again to kiss her forehead.

It was at just that moment that Linnet reappeared with Deirdre's meal on a tray. Thomas, still smiling, picked his daughter up, tossing her over his head until she squealed with laughter, then gave her to Arianna. His hand lingered along Arianna's cheek.

"I thank you, dear friend," he said, and was gone.

Linnet, returning Deirdre's empty porridge bowl to the kitchen a while later, told the cook what she had seen. It took less than half the day for Selene to hear of it. She came to the evening meal hard eyed and icy tongued.

"I hear you are sleeping with my husband," she hissed, stalking past Arianna on her way to the high table. "Have a care that he doesn't get you with child, too."

"You misunderstood," Arianna cried, knowing well what the latest gossip was, for Blanche had warned her. "We are friends, no more."

"So were we friends, you and I. Once." Selene took in Reynaud, standing close behind Arianna. "First a cripple, then another woman's husband. You are rising in the world with each lover, Arianna. Will it be Guy next, while Meredith's belly is big?" Selene swept toward the dais and her chair, leaving Arianna too shocked to make any response.

"The woman is filled with poison," Reynaud said. "Everyone here has felt it, even Guy. No one will believe that accusation, Arianna. Come, let's eat. Pretend she never said a word. That's the best way to pay her back. Don't let her see it if she's hurt you."

But someone carried the tale of Selene's cruel attack on Arianna to Thomas, who had come to the hall too late to hear it for himself.

"She will not speak so to you again," he promised Arianna after the meal was done and the lower tables were being folded up and put away. "I'll beat her if I must, or lock her in her room till her temper improves. And she shall apologize to you before everyone who was here when she spoke those slanderous words." He took a purposeful step toward the place where Selene still sat on the dais.

"Don't make her do that, it will only upset her more," Arianna exclaimed, catching at his arm to hold him back. "Can't you see she's not well? Treat her gently. She will be better once the child is born."

"You are far more generous than she." His attention suddenly caught by a burst of laughter in the center of the hall, Thomas glanced at a group of younger knights and ladies gathered there. "What, are they going to dance? Good, you shall dance with me."

"I don't think that's wise, Thomas."

"It is an excellent idea." He smiled down at her, his anger gone, dazzling her with unexpected laughter. "We shall dance, together first, and then with other partners, and all shall see we are but friends. I shall flirt with Blanche, and with Sir Lambert's wife, and you do the same with the husbands. That way no one will imagine it's only each other we care about."

"But I do care." The words slipped out before she had given them thought. She saw something in his eyes that answered her, a quick glimmer of understanding, as quickly extinguished in favor of merry laughter.

"Don't," he said. "Never give your heart lest it be broken. Come." He took her hand and led her to the dancing, and she did as he had bidden her. She laughed and flirted with every young man who asked her, and some not so young, and even danced once with Guy as her partner, after Thomas had pulled him onto the floor.

Selene, prevented by her condition from joining in the fun, sat in her chair at the high table, watching, pretending she did not notice Meredith and Reynaud talking quietly two seats away from her, refusing to join them when they spoke to her. When she finally slipped away and went to her chamber, no one missed her at all.

Arianna was well liked and much respected. There were few in the castle who had believed the gossip about her, so the talk ended as quickly as it had begun. To assure that tongues did not begin to wag anew, Thomas saw to it that he and Arianna were never alone together again.

Spring and summer dragged on, Selene growing more sharp of tongue each day, until Guy swore he would have her confined to the dungeon were she not carrying Thomas's child. At dawn on the second day of August, with Meredith, Arianna and Blanche in attendance, she produced a son with remarkable ease.

"It was dreadful, an endless torture," she said to Thomas, exaggerating her discomfort when he came to see her and the baby. She was in fact feeling quite well, and was much relieved that she had lived through it, believing heaven had granted her a reprieve, but she would not have Thomas know how easy it had been. "You cannot expect me to give you any more children, not in such unbearable pain. You have your heir. Be content with him."

Thomas said nothing. He listened with apparent meekness to all Selene's complaints, but Arianna, standing at one side of the room holding the baby, sensed deep anger in him at this shrewish attack

275

during what should have been a tender moment between husband and wife. There was in his eyes a cool emptiness in place of the love that had once filled them each time he looked upon Selene, and Arianna saw this if Selene did not. Selene took his gift to her, a pair of heavy gold bracelets set with precious stones in many colors, and tossed them carelessly upon the bed.

Arianna, fearing Selene in her present defiant mood would provoke him into open warfare, came forward and gave Thomas his squalling, robust son to hold. He regarded the red-faced baby with a serious expression.

"I'd like to name him Jocelyn," Thomas said. "I had a friend once, when I was page to King Henry. Joce died of a fever before he was old enough to become a squire. I'd like to remember him."

"Whatever you want." Selene turned her head away from the sight of her husband and son. "I don't care. Just stay away from me."

Thomas clasped his son to his bosom and bent to kiss the baby's forehead, and Arianna bit her lip to keep from crying out at the look on his face, half proud over the child, half desolate at his wife's rejection.

She found him in the chapel an hour or two later, prostrate before the altar. So deep was her concern for him that she did not wait until he had finished his prayers.

"Thomas, don't, you'll catch a chill," she cried, bending over him. "That stone is so cold."

"How would you know that," Thomas asked, rising, "unless you have lain on it yourself?"

"I have, once or twice," Arianna admitted.

He stood staring down at the cold stone floor, and when he spoke again it was as though he was continuing a conversation with her, and expected her to understand his thoughts.

"I tried to help her, to be patient with her. I hoped she would change if we had a son," Thomas whispered. The blue and red of the stained glass windows shone on his head when he moved into the light, facing her. "I see now that won't happen. It will always be like this, for the rest of our lives. How can I bear it? How can she?"

Arianna could think of nothing to do but take his hand and hold it tightly. She was reassured by the answering pressure of his strong fingers before he went on.

"I, who wanted to love my wife as Uncle Guy loves Meredith, no longer feel anything for her at all, except irritation, and contempt when she is cruel to others. As she has been to you these last months, though you have always been her staunchest friend. And Reynaud. She treats him as if he were a leper. Everyone I love she has harmed in some way. Nor am I so blind as she thinks. I suspect there's more, some secret she keeps, some great guilt. I may never know the truth of that, but it's there, between us." He turned aside, hiding his face, dark red light splashing across his golden hair, outlining his head in a fiery halo, and Arianna ached for his torment.

"I shall go away," he said. "I'll go to Normandy and join the king in his war with France. I should have done it long ago, but Uncle Guy said he needed me here."

"He does. Don't leave us, Thomas. You could be killed."

"Better if I were."

"Don't say that."

He turned quickly at that frightened sound, and

277

saw the look on her face before she could compose her features. They stood in the glow of stained glass and sunlight, their faces patterned with vibrant color, looking at each other, looking for an eternity, while full comprehension grew in Thomas.

"I should have known," he whispered. He opened his arms and she went into them. His mouth found hers, taking her freely offered lips with tenderness and warmth, finding in this dearest and most steadfast of friends all that he had once hoped to find in his wife. Their embrace lasted only a moment, before Arianna was pushing against his chest, fighting to free herself from his arms.

"No," she cried, "not in this place. Not here. What we do, what we are thinking of, is a sin."

"Arianna," he whispered hoarsely, his discretion overcome by deep emotion, "Selene doesn't want me. I've lived like a monk all these months. If you and I chose to enjoy each other, where's the harm?"

"It is adultery, that's the harm. Selene is my kinswoman. She has just borne your son. How can you say such a thing? Perhaps you had better go to Normandy after all."

She was gone. She had run out of the chapel in tears, taking the light with her, leaving him more alone than he had ever been in his life. Thomas was wracked with shame. There was no excuse for what he had just tried to do to Arianna.

It was not at all unusual for men of rank to lay with the women in their households, whether servants or noblewomen, but Thomas, inspired by his faithful uncle, had tried to be content with his own wife. Until today he had honestly imagined his feelings for Arianna were those of friendship and no more. But in those few magical moments when they had looked at each other without pretense, he had finally seen what ought to have been apparent to him long before.

Arianna loved him. Worse, what he felt for her was much more than friendship. It was something deep and true and enduring, richer by far than the wild, erotic passion he had once known for Selene and in his youthful inexperience had mistaken for love. He did not love Selene. He might have grown to love her had she been a different kind of woman. But after years of an impossibly difficult marriage he saw his wife clearly for what she was—a tormented, half-mad creature, unable to control her emotions and incapable of loving him.

And he was bound to her for the rest of their lives. He could not set her aside as some men did with wives they no longer wanted. He and Selene were in no way related by blood; Guy had made certain of that before agreeing to the match. And she had given him children. These were the only two acceptable reasons for ending a marriage: a too-close blood relationship or a wife's barrenness. Selene was his wife forever, and Arianna was lost to him. He knew Arianna's strength and firmly believed she would never consent to adultery.

Thomas moaned aloud and sank to his knees, acknowledging bitter truth. Grief and despair overcame him. He fell onto the stone floor of the chapel, lying as Arianna had found him earlier, struggling with his sorrow and his shame.

He did not know how long he stayed there.

279

When he rose at last he was in no way comforted about the future of his marriage, but he knew two things. First, because he loved her, he could never do anything that in any way might hurt Arianna. Second, after Meredith's child was born and his own present tasks for Guy were completed, by early spring at the latest, he had to leave Afoncaer.

On the first day of September, after a brief labor, Meredith brought forth a daughter, and then, half an hour later, surprised everyone by giving birth to a twin, a tiny, but completely healthy son. Casks of wine were sent to the village so everyone might celebrate, and the entire household gathered in the great hall to drink to the health of the castle's lord and lady and their children.

"It's wonderful," Thomas rejoiced, refilling his cup for another toast. "Uncle Guy is so happy. He won't leave Meredith's bedside. I'm to lead the celebrations here."

"It is *not* wonderful." Selene glared at him. "Don't you see what this means? You are displaced as Guy's heir. Your son, *my* son, will be shunted aside and replaced by this new baby."

"It doesn't matter, Selene. I am still to have Adderbury. It was my grandfather's estate, and then my father's. Uncle Guy has said it will be mine in time. Kelsey will be Cristin's dowry, and Adderbury will come to me. We will never lack for lands or a home."

"Adderbury is not the same as Afoncaer," Selene snarled. She saw Reynaud watching her again.

Wherever she was, his eyes followed her. "What are you staring at, Reynaud?" she demanded.

"At a young man whose heart is great enough to rejoice at another's good fortune," Reynaud replied smoothly. "A man whose uncle loves him and will never forget him."

But Selene was not satisfied. Reynaud knew something about her, she was sure of it. She had to get away from Afoncaer, and the sooner the better. She began that very evening to work on Thomas. Not using her body, as she had in the past. It was too soon after Jocelyn's birth for that, and she was not certain Thomas would be amenable to that kind of coaxing after her long denial of him. But she had a tongue, and she employed it well.

"Adderbury may be a fine place," she began, "but would you not like to have more to leave to your son? And what of a dowry for Deirdre? You cannot expect your Uncle Guy to provide one. He has two daughters of his own now. Thomas, the time has come for you to go to court and make your fortune. The king is fond of you; I've seen that for myself. Who knows what honors you might earn by employing your sword in his service during this war with France?"

"I had thought of it," Thomas admitted cautiously. He had not told her of his earlier decision to leave Afoncaer. Now it occurred to him that it would be wise to take Selene with him when he went, for the sake of everyone's peace, except his own. But he would leave her soon enough, to go to war.

"Isn't the king's son to be married in the spring?" Selene went on. "The one who was at our wedding?"

"William Atheling, yes, to the Count of Anjou's daughter."

"We should be at the wedding, Thomas, to represent Afoncaer. Guy won't want to leave—who knows what the Welsh might do during such a long absence—but we could go in his place."

"What about the children?" He would miss them both, but he did not want them with Selene. Her ready answer relieved his concern about them.

"We will leave the children here with Arianna," Selene said blithely. "She can take care of them."

"I'll speak to Uncle Guy in a day or two. You are right, Selene. There will be honors and lands to be won in King Henry's war."

It was not very difficult to convince Guy. He understood far more than Thomas had realized, and agreed it would be best for Thomas and Selene to leave. He asked only that they wait until after the new year had begun. Then he would entrust Thomas with despatches for the king's secretaries, and private information about activities on the border which Thomas was to deliver to the king's ears only.

Selene was making her own plans. While Thomas was away from court with the army, she would visit her parents' castle in Brittany, and from there she could easily contact Isabel. Perhaps if she could meet Isabel face to face that lady would relieve Selene's guilt over all she had done and then would finally discharge Selene from her oath. Selene might even be able to arrange for Thomas to meet his mother. That would further please Isabel. Whatever happened, she would be far from Reynaud and his penetrating eyes. Selene began to feel a little hope.

For Arianna, caught between relief that Thomas was going away, thus removing her great temptation to sin, and fear each time she remembered that he was going into danger, for Arianna, there was heart-rending anguish such as she had never known before. It had been easier for her when he had not known she loved him, before she had seen that he loved her. Now all pretense was gone between them, and their every meeting was an agony of trying to hide their feelings from others, and of trying not to give way to the need to touch each other or to embrace. They scrupulously avoided being alone together. How she got through the days and the long, sleepless nights Arianna did not know. She moved like a sleepwalker, discharging her duties competently enough, though often she could not remember later whether she had done a thing or not.

He came to her on his last night at Afoncaer, tapping lightly at her chamber door after midnight, and Arianna, imagining Linnet had knocked to tell her one of the children was sick, opened her door wide and stood blinking at him in surprise, shivering in her flimsy nightgown. He stepped inside before she could make a sound, and closed the door.

She stared at him, reading in his blue eyes the desire that answered her deepest hunger. She could not prevent herself, she went into his arms and clung to him, letting him kiss her, opening her mouth to him, feeling his hard body pressed tightly to her own. Her mind gave up thought and whirled into sweet, passionate feeling, her heart throbbed eagerly against his. But when he lifted her into his arms, and would have carried her to her bed, she still had sense enough to stop him.

"Put me down," she demanded, "and leave me. I will not consent to do this thing, however much I want you."

He set her down slowly, letting her body slide along the length of his, and at that touch desire flamed in her, she who had never known a man, and she thought she would swoon from it. He knelt before her, his head bowed.

"Forgive me," he murmured. "I vowed I'd never do you harm, yet I would have broken that vow out of love and passion. I only came to say farewell to you in private, and to ask for one kiss, since we may never meet again. But when I had it, one kiss was not enough. Arianna, forgive me."

"I am as guilty as you," she whispered. "I let you into my room, and I let you kiss me. I wanted you to. There's naught for me to forgive."

His arms were wrapped around her knees, his head pressed against her thighs, and she wanted to bend to him and take him into her arms once more. Her hands lightly caressed his smooth, golden hair, and through the linen of her night-gown she felt his burning lips pressed upon one knee and then her thigh. Her stroking hands were stilled by powerful emotion. She was unable to stop him, she welcomed that hot, sensual touch, and she wanted more.

"I love you," he whispered hoarsely. "I love you so."

"Never say those words to me." She did not know where she found the strength. She caught his head and pulled it backward, stopping those fevered motions that set her thighs atremble, making him stand. "You must go, Thomas."

"I love you, whether you want me to or not."

"Please go, you will break my heart," she wept.

He went to the door and opened it, then stood a moment looking at her, and it seemed to Arianna he was drinking in every line of her face and form, absorbing her into his heart and his memory.

"When I die," he said, "my last thought will be of you."

Chapter 14

Thomas was a good correspondent. He regularly sent couriers with letters to Guy, which Reynaud read aloud to him and to Meredith and Arianna as well. Thus they all heard of the splendid wedding ceremonies for Henry's heir William Atheling, and how Count Fulk of Anjou had given his daughter Alice and her new husband the entire county of Maine for a wedding gift. They learned of King Henry's campaign against King Louis of France, of Thomas's growing friendship with William Atheling, how the two young men had ridden into battle together at Brémule on August twentieth and covered themselves with glory. William emerged unscathed, while Thomas had a slight wound in one arm. It was nothing to worry about, it was healing well because he had used the herbal salve Meredith had given him. Selene was visiting her mother in Brittany, and would stay there until the war was over. He did not add that they had agreed to live apart more or less permanently, but that was easily inferred from the words he had carefully chosen.

The day after this last letter arrived, the Welsh

made a brief, lightning-fast strike. Reynaud watched it all in horror from the safety of the gatehouse, and he later told Meredith and Arianna what had happened. He, Reynaud, had been standing nearly all day at the outer edge of town where the new wall was being built. In late afternoon he crossed the drawbridge over the wet moat to the gatehouse to sit a while and rest his aching leg. He had just sat down upon a bench, his back against the wall and a flagon of cool ale in one hand, when he saw that Guy had ridden in after a day's hunting and had paused to check upon the building. He had waved his hunting companions on to the castle, else there would have been more dead and wounded. Guy remained with Kenelm, Benet, and another squire, a friend of Benet's. They walked their horses along the wall, stopping here and there to see the latest work on it.

Guy had turned in his saddle to speak to Kenelm when the Welsh longbowmen loosed their arrows. It was turning that saved him, for the arrow did not take him squarely in the chest, and he was well protected by his chain mail hauberk and the padded gambeson beneath. At Guy's orders after the last year's raid, all who rode outside the castle walls went fully armored, and now his own command benefitted him. But Welsh arrows were deadly, and this one tore through chain mail and padding to embed itself deep in Guy's left shoulder, too near his heart, and the force with which it struck him was so great he was knocked backward half out of his saddle. He struggled to stay upright, clinging to reins and saddle pommel with his right hand while the left dangled uselessly. His frightened horse reared, further unbalancing him. His right foot slipped out of the stirrup, but his left foot caught, entangled as he fell, and his body twisted underneath the horse.

Then Benet was beside him, that squire who had once been a stableboy and knew every animal in Afoncaer's stables. How Benet had moved so quickly Reynaud, telling the story later, could never say, but he had flung himself off his own horse and leapt to catch the reins of Guy's mount. He pulled with all his strength, holding the reins tight and talking to the horse, calling it by name, while blood streamed down his own arm from a bad flesh wound. When Guy's rearing stallion came down, its sharp hooves landed a scant inch from Guy's head, missing it only thanks to Benet's efforts.

"His leg," Benet shouted. "Someone free his leg. I can't hold on much longer."

One of the stonemasons, braver than his fellows, left the cover of the new-laid wall where they had all huddled fearing for their lives, and ran to untangle Guy's ankle from the stirrup while Benet held the horse and tried to calm it.

Reynaud heaved himself to his foot and crutches within the gatehouse, and ordered the alarm bell rung at the same time that Kenelm shouted the same command. And then, disregarding his own safety, Reynaud crossed the drawbridge and hurried as fast as he could toward Guy.

"Get back!" Kenelm shouted, wheeling his horse. "They will loose more arrows. Get back to safety, Reynaud."

Kenelm was unharmed, but the second squire, Benet's friend, lay face down over a freshly cut stone intended for the wall, a Welsh arrow in his back. His horse lay thrashing on its side nearby, felled by two arrows, and Benet's horse was wounded, too, both so badly hurt they had to be dispatched later by the village butcher. Benet and the dust-covered mason knelt on either side of Guy, shielding him with their bodies.

Reynaud saw that Kenelm was right. He could be no help but only a target in the open, and a problem to Kenelm, so he hobbled back into the gatehouse, past armed men now streaming forth.

"Bring that table," Reynaud called to two of the men. "You will have to carry your lord home on it." They took the top of the trestle table out of the common room in the gatehouse and ran with it to where Guy lay unconscious. They lifted him upon it and raced with it through another storm of Welsh arrows, the men-at-arms making a wall of shields around them, and brought their master into the gatehouse. The men-at-arms then went out again and brought the masons, four of them dead, six wounded, and the fallen squire inside the wall by the same method, using their shields for protection. Lastly Kenelm came in, still untouched though a fine target on his huge stallion. Perhaps the Welsh had thought him too brave to kill, Benet suggested later, since the Welsh were said to greatly admire personal courage.

The wounded were carried, or walked if they could, through the village and back to the castle for treatment, and the dead were taken to the village church.

Arianna had heard the shouting and the alarm bell. She ran out of the herb garden into the inner bailey, heading for the keep, and so quickly had it all happened that before she had reached the steps Guy was being carried senseless across the bailey, the long arrow still protruding from his left shoulder. Behind him came Reynaud, moving faster than she had ever seen him, and Benet, drenched in blood.

Arianna rushed up the steps and past the wardroom, calling out for Meredith. Meredith came from the stillroom, white-faced but calm in her manner, and ordered Guy taken to the special room she used for nursing the sick or injured. Blanche appeared, ready to help as always, to provide aid for those whose wounds were less dangerous and stanch the blood of those badly wounded until Meredith or Arianna could tend to them.

They had the armorer in, to cut the chain mail away from the arrow in Guy's shoulder. When he had finished, Meredith and Arianna pulled carefully at Guy's silk undershirt, the tightly woven garment nearest his skin, each pulling at a side with both hands, lifting out with the strong silk the broken metal links and fragments of padding from the gambeson. Then they cut out the arrowhead, cleaned the wound, and sewed it up, Meredith, who claimed no skill with a needle, doing a neat job of it, never once flinching as she worked on the body of the man she loved so dearly.

But Arianna, looking at Guy's white and unconscious face, so like his nephew's, had a swift and terrifying vision of Thomas lying so, wounded on some foreign field, and with no one half as skilled as Meredith to tend him. Arianna swayed, her sight blurring, a great ringing in her ears, so that Meredith had to ask her twice for the herbal salve to spread over the now-closed wound. This was no time for tears or fainting, Arianna told herself, they had to save Guy. Upon his life so much depended.

Blanche came into the room as they were finishing, and looked down at Guy, nodding approval.

"There is no bloody foam on his lips," she said. "I saw a man like that once at Adderbury, and the priest said when that happens, wounded men will surely die. Guy has not that sign, so he will live."

Arianna had recovered from her faintness enough to notice that Meredith seemed cheered by Blanche's optimism, and she silently thanked Blanche for those words. At Meredith's nod Arianna went with Blanche to sew up the wounds of the other men. She assured Benet that the gash in his arm would heal cleanly and he would soon ride again. She tried to console him for the loss of his friend, then moved on to tend the others.

Guy was most seriously wounded of all, and Kenelm and Reynaud were of the opinion that he had been the intended target of the attack. On the second day after, he developed a high fever. That, and the blow to his head when he fell from his horse, kept his wits addled for days.

"Kenelm," Meredith said on the third night, "in Guy's name I appoint you seneschal of Afoncaer. You are under my orders until Guy is better, but I leave the day-to-day defenses in your hands."

At the end of a week, Guy was enough improved to be moved to his own bedchamber. Meredith never left his side, sleeping on a straw pallet by his bed each night. Arianna tended the other wounded and the children, and Blanche managed the castle's domestic affairs.

After another week it was evident that Meredith's skill had saved Guy. He would live, for the time being at least, but it would be many months, if ever, before he would be well enough to resume all of his duties.

"Kenelm is a good captain," Reynaud told Meredith and Arianna, "but he needs a strong commander over him. He dislikes the Welsh, so his decisions concerning them are too often harsh and stir up the very trouble they are meant to quell."

"We can't ask Geoffrey to come here," Meredith said thoughtfully. "There have been several attacks on Tynant recently. He's needed there."

"What of you, Reynaud?" Arianna asked. "Could you not carry Guy's orders to the men? They all know you, and know the confidence Guy has in you."

"I could, if Guy were well enough to give them, and the men who know me well might obey me on a peaceful day, but in time of battle, I doubt it. And there are some who would never listen to a cleric, not even if their lives depended on it. They need a knight, a soldier, to lead them."

"I won't have Guy troubled by these problems while he's ill," Meredith said firmly. "Afoncaer needs a healthy lord. Write to Thomas, Reynaud, and tell him he must come home at once. Write to the king, too. Tell him what has happened. He knows how important it is to keep this fortress strong. He will give Thomas leave to come here. Until Thomas arrives, I will rule Afoncaer, with Kenelm to back me."

The letter was sent, and in mid-October, ten months after leaving Afoncaer, Thomas returned.

Arianna was in the nursery. She and Linnet had just finished feeding their four young charges when she glanced out the window and saw a band of armored men riding up the river road toward the castle. Above them floated the personal banner of their leader, azure with three silver rings interlaced.

"Thomas." Arianna's hand flew to her throat. There he was, a tall, broad-shouldered figure riding in the lead, his azure mantle billowing out behind him, chain mail hauberk and helm gleaming in the misty autumn sunlight. She could not see his face. She did not need to. Her heart knew him. She knew she ought to go down to the great hall to join Meredith and the rest of the household in greeting him. It would be the wise thing to do, it would stop any gossipers before they recalled last year's whispers. Let everyone see at once that they met as friends, no more.

She gave Linnet quick instructions to wash Deirdre's face and hands, and prepare her and Jocelyn to meet their father. Leaving the nursery, she flew to her room to tidy her simple blue dress and adjust the blue ribbon holding her curls off her face. She ran down the spiral stairs to the bottom and into the great hall to stand next to Meredith and Reynaud. She could hardly breathe. Her heart was pounding so hard she was certain everyone else must hear it, too. She knew her cheeks were flaming.

She heard voices coming from the wardroom, Kenelm's, then someone else's, then at last the deep, clear tones her heart recognized. Thomas. Thomas.

He was there, filling the hall with strength and vitality. She saw the silver chain armor, helm thrown back, the azure mantle swinging as he walked, his thick, golden hair, his deep blue eyes looking right into hers.

Thomas, her heart sang, Thomas, my love, and she saw the answering greeting in his eyes. He looked older, thinner, his cheeks hollow as he bent to kiss Meredith. Arianna watched the older

293

woman cling to him a moment in a rare display of weakness that must have told Thomas just how much she had endured since the attack on Guy. She heard Thomas's quick questions about Guy, and Meredith's soft, reassuring answers. Then Thomas stood before her. He took her hand and kissed her cheek as though they were no more than friends, but she saw in his eyes that he loved her still.

"The children?" he asked. "I'm sure you've cared for them well."

"Did Selene not come with you?" she murmured, all the while feeling nothing but his warm hand clasping hers as she fought the urge to throw herself into his arms.

"Visiting her mother still," she heard him say. "She sends her love to you and the children."

Love. Love. Thomas, my love.

He let go of her hand and embraced Reynaud. Kenelm reappeared. Arianna heard the three of them talking in the clipped, rapid speech men used when discussing military matters.

"More later," Thomas said after a while. "First a hot bath. My every muscle aches from the long ride. Next I'll see Uncle Guy, then my children."

Arianna stared after him, wishing she might go with him, forcing her feet toward the nursery instead. He came there later, and spent half an hour with his children before taking her arm to lead her toward the great hall and the meal now being prepared.

"Uncle Guy looks terrible," Thomas said as they went along the corridors. "So frail, as though he could vanish at any moment."

"Be glad you weren't here to see him a month ago," Arianna answered. "I don't know how Meredith kept him alive. She must have been dying inside herself, fearing to lose him, yet she never wavered, and she never left his side. He has improved since we told him you were coming."

"Meredith says you did as much for Uncle Guy as she did." Thomas stopped walking, his hand still on her arm. "I would have stayed away in Normandy, Arianna, had this not happened. I've no wish to torment you, or myself, yet it seems I'll be here a long time."

"I understand. We will be friends, Thomas. That is what we were at first. We can be so again."

"Can we?" His hand moved on her arm, sending warmth from her elbow to her heart. She knew she should pull away from him but she could not.

"For Guy's sake we can," she said, "and for Meredith's, yes. Friends and no more. For your soul's sake. And mine."

"My dearest—"

"We will never meet alone, Thomas, never speak in private."

"Only say you love me. Let me hear that if I can have nothing else."

"The words themselves would be a betrayal. I will not say them."

"Never mind, I see them in your eyes." He took a step, coming closer, and she caught the clean, washed scent of him, smelled the orris root and lavender in which his fresh clothes had been stored during his absence. "One kiss, Arianna, that's all I ask, and then we'll not meet like this again. I have dreamed of your delicious mouth every day I've been apart from you."

"If we kiss, we'll never stop," she cried, trembling, aching for him until she thought her heart would break with want and denial. "It would be wrong, Thomas. I'll not let you besmirch the good friendship we had—and will have again."

"You are stronger than I, my love. Go then." He dropped his hand and moved away from her. "I'll not stop you, and I'll do as you wish. I would not hurt you, nor would I create a scandal that would only place greater burdens on Guy and Meredith, and break their hearts for our pain."

Arianna tore herself away from him, running up the stairs to her room. She went down late to the meal that welcomed Thomas home, and so happy were those gathered at the tables to have their young lord back that no one remarked on Arianna's pale face or her red-rimmed eyes.

Thomas took control of Afoncaer with a sure hand, and Guy, relieved of worry, began to mend more rapidly. By Christmastide he was spending most of each day in the great hall, seated in his well-cushioned chair by the fire. But when he spoke of resuming his daily rides around his lands right after the new year, Meredith scolded him roundly.

"You will stay indoors until the weather is warmer," she said. "Your wound weakened your lungs. I'll not have you exposed to cold air until you are completely healed."

"You would make a baby of me," Guy grumbled.

"If you would only pretend to be sicker than you are," Reynaud advised wisely, "not only would Meredith continue to coddle you most delightfully—and I think you enjoy that however much you protest, my friend—but Thomas would stay here longer."

"That's true," Guy laughed. "And a welcome thought." His laugh changed quickly into a cough that would not stop. Meredith sent Arianna running for his medicine. When she returned to the great hall Thomas was there, brushing snow off his shoulders and shooting worried glances at Guy. Meredith's concoction of rosemary, honey, and several other herbs worked quickly. A short time later Guy sat back in his chair, the coughing eased, though he looked worn out after the spasm. Arianna noticed Thomas watching his uncle closely over the next day or two. Thomas looked worried.

It was several days later that Thomas followed her into the stillroom and shut the door firmly.

"My lord," she began, backing against a table, afraid he would attempt to take her into his arms, and knowing that if he did she would not be able to resist him, that all her good intentions would vanish at his touch. "My lord, we agreed we'd not be alone together."

"I must talk with you without anyone overhearing. Arianna, I have to know the truth, and I trust you to tell it to me. Will Uncle Guy ever recover his health? Or will he always be an invalid like this?"

"It's not for me to say that, Thomas. I am still only Meredith's pupil, and nowhere near as wise as she is about illnesses or wounds. You should ask her that question."

"I have tried, but for the first time since I've known her, she evades me. I begin to fear she is only hoping he will get well, because she loves him so much, not because she really can heal him."

"She cannot let herself think he might die," Ar-

297

ianna said. "She wants him to believe he will live, so she has to believe it herself."

"And will he die?" Thomas asked, quietly but relentlessly.

"I don't know." To her chagrin, Arianna began to cry. "I love him, too, Thomas. He's such a good man, and he has been my friend since the day I met him. I can only tell you that he has improved since you returned." This last remark ended on a sob, and Arianna tried to wipe away the tears that would not stop coming.

"If he remains an invalid," Thomas said, thinking aloud, "he cannot continue as baron of Afoncaer. This castle needs a strong ruler."

"He could continue here if you would stay."

"Yes." Thomas sighed. "I had hoped he would heal quickly enough for me to rejoin King Henry by spring. But I owe Uncle Guy too much to leave if he still needs me. And it is for Henry's benefit, too, that I stay here, to help keep peace on his border."

Arianna could not stop crying. She brushed the tears aside with both hands, but they kept overflowing. She had held in too much feeling for too long, her fears for Guy's life, concern for Meredith, and most of all, her hopeless love for Thomas and her fear for him, fighting in a far-away war.

"Don't leave again, please," she begged, trying to say and do the right and honorable thing, though it broke her heart in two. "Stay here. Afoncaer needs you. If it comes to that, if it makes you too unhappy to have me here, I'll go away. I'll find a convent somewhere that will accept me, I'll leave and never come back to trouble you again."

He took her into his arms, and, forgetting all her vows to keep her distance from him, she nestled there, trying to regain control of herself, knowing she should not be where she was.

"I couldn't let you do that," he murmured, his lips on her forehead. "You are a part of all that makes Afoncaer dear to me."

"Oh, Thomas, what are we going to do?"

He did not answer that despairing cry with words, but with his mouth. His lips were warm and firm, and Arianna, in answer to that most-desired kiss, let her arms creep around his neck, and pressed herself against him. The kiss deepened, Thomas's tongue sought entrance to her mouth and she accepted him gladly, giving herself up to the embrace she had dreamed of for so long. His arms tightened around her until Arianna felt she was becoming part of him. It was what she wanted, to be one with him and never let him go. They strained together in that herb-hung, sweet-scented room, tasting love without fear or reserve.

Too soon the kiss ended. They both drew back, staring at each other breathlessly, wanting to kiss again, knowing they could not, for if they did, they would never stop until they had done the thing that would condemn them both as adulterers.

"We promised we wouldn't," Thomas said.

"I should never have allowed this," Arianna breathed.

They stepped apart slowly, backing away from each other, fingers sliding off shoulders and down arms until only hands touched, then fingertips. Then they were separate.

"Upon my honor, I will not do this again, my love," Thomas vowed.

"Nor I, my love."

"My love," he repeated softly. They smiled at each other, tears glistening on their cheeks.

He was gone from the room. Arianna knew he would not break that vow. They would see each other every day, speak to each other as friends. She would care for his children, help to mend his wounds, if he were injured, but he would never, after that oath, embrace her again. Never.

Chapter 15

Spring came, and with it news that King Henry had resolved his differences with King Louis VI of France. With the war's end William Atheling had been made Duke of Normandy.

"Peace at last," Guy said. "Will you be content to stay at Afoncaer now, Thomas, or are you still determined to seek your fortune elsewhere? King Henry and his son are both your friends. You could have a brilliant future at court."

Guy's health had improved steadily but more slowly than he would have liked. He had begun walking about the inner bailey, using a cane to support himself when he grew weary, but he could not sit a horse yet, and climbing stairs left him breathless. Thomas watched him, standing in the sunlight with the keep behind him, and thought how old and gaunt he looked. There were heavy streaks of silver in the thick hair that had once been as golden as Thomas's own. Deep lines etched his eyes, deeper creases ran from nose to mouth. The old battle scar on the left side of his jaw showed white against his sun-flushed skin. Guy was forty-three years old, and looked it, and

Thomas, who had always thought of his uncle as young and strong and indestructible, was suddenly filled with frustration by the unstoppable passage of time.

"I think," Thomas said, "that you need me here."

"That I do, but what do you want, lad? What's in your heart?"

"Lad?" Thomas laughed. "Hardly that any more." His eyes swept along the castle wall, scanned the solid bulk of the tower keep and the great hall next to it, and came to rest on the gate to Meredith's herb garden, where she and Arianna were working, Deirdre babbling happily beside them. "Afoncaer is home to me. It always has been."

"A man may feel he should leave his home." Guy's glance had followed Thomas's. It rested now on Arianna's slender back and bent head as she patiently explained something about an herb to Deirdre. "Sometimes he leaves for good cause."

"I have been thinking," Thomas said slowly. "The reports we've had lately all say King Henry plans to bring his court back to England in autumn. I'll stay here through the summer, Uncle Guy, in case the Welsh attack again, and I'll see the harvest safely gathered in. Then I'll travel to Normandy. I'll carry any messages you have for King Henry, and when he sails for England, Selene and I will be with him. I'll let her have Christmas at court. That will please her. Kenelm can manage well enough here until the new year; the Welsh seldom attack in winter. After Twelfth Night, Selene and I will return to Afoncaer, and we will stay here permanently, except for the times when Henry requires our presence at court."

302

"I do not think Selene will be pleased with your decision." Guy was still watching Arianna. "Are you sure you want to bring her here again?"

"She is my wife. I have been too gentle with her. It's time she resumed her duties. All of them." Thomas's face was grim. He had lain a few times with serving women, driven by a purely physical urge, and he had found himself much changed from the days of his casual youth, for there had been no pleasure in the dalliance. He wanted Arianna, but knowing he could not have her, he would force himself to lay with Selene. It was his duty as her husband, and his right. He would expend his manly desires upon his lawful wife, and if he got her with child again, well, he would see to it that her ill temper did not disturb those he loved. Selene would have to learn to control her emotional outbursts, as he was learning to control his desire for Arianna.

"I had a letter from Sir Valaire in the last packet from court," Thomas went on. "He made it quite clear he is unhappy at Selene's long stay in his household. She and her mother quarrel constantly. Valaire wants her removed. He will join me in insisting that his daughter obey me."

"We will try to make Selene welcome here," Guy said.

"I'll see to it she causes no trouble. Not to anyone."

It seemed to Thomas that his decision had lifted a burden from Guy. The older man's step grew almost springy as summer progressed. His health was noticeably improved, and that made Meredith happier. Thomas felt certain he had made the right choice.

There were no Welsh raids that summer. Geoffrey rode in from Tynant several times, looking more cheerful than he had done for a long while. One of his men told Guy and Thomas that Geoffrey had recently taken a pretty Saxon mistress, a placid girl who adored him. The deep wound to his esteem inflicted by Gwenefer's betrayal seemed to be healing.

Thomas and Arianna had kept their oath to treat each other as friends. They met daily, maintaining rigid control over their feelings, though Arianna could not hide the sadness that filled her eyes when Thomas told her he would bring Selene back to live at Afoncaer.

"It is the best thing for Jocelyn and Deirdre," was all she said. "And you need a lady by your side."

"You won't leave, will you, Arianna?"

"No. You and Selene and I need not be thrown together constantly. Linnet is well enough trained by now to care for the children, so I am not in the nursery as often as I once was. I am spending more time with Meredith in the infirmary she has set up in the village. I still have a great deal to learn from her. And Reynaud has agreed to begin teaching me Greek this winter. At least I'll be able to speak my mother's tongue. I shall be well occupied, Thomas. There is nothing to prevent me from being friendly with Selene again, if she wishes it, too." She gave him a bright smile that fooled him not at all.

Because of the constant unrest along the Welsh border, Guy was exempt from sending fighting men to the king's service for the usual forty days each year. When Thomas left Afoncaer he took with him only a dozen men-at-arms for protection, and, at Guy's suggestion, Benet as one of his squires.

"He has little to do until I'm fully recovered," Guy said, "and he deserves a reward for his faithful service. Let him see something of the world beyond Afoncaer. Let him see a royal court." Thomas, who liked Benet, readily agreed.

Their crossing of the Narrow Sea was delayed by bad weather. It was not until mid-November that Thomas and a properly impressed Benet knelt before King Henry.

"You have come here only to turn around and go back to England," Henry said. "Still, I'm glad to see you, and William will be, too. Come sit here and tell me all the news of Wales before you leave to find your lady wife."

It was his father-in-law Thomas found later. He learned from him that Selene had not come to court but was still in Brittany with Lady Aloise.

"They will join us next week," Sir Valaire said, "since they are both to sail to England with us."

"I want to see Selene before that," Thomas told him. "I have made my report to King Henry, and I visited with William, so I'm free to join her. My men and I will ride to Brittany and escort the ladies to Barfleur in time to meet the ships on sailing day."

"I'll send a message to Aloise that you are coming," Valaire said. "A word of advice, Thomas. Use a firm hand with Selene. She has done as she pleases for too long, and you leave yourself open to gossip and mockery by letting her have her own way. She's had naught to do with other men while you were living apart, I can vouch for that, but I am ashamed to say my daughter is willful and stubborn, and entirely too bad tempered."

"I intend that she will change greatly," Thomas assured him.

Selene was not waiting in the great hall of Sir Valaire's castle to greet him as a wife should. It was left to his mother-in-law to do that honor.

"She's in the solar," Lady Aloise told him apologetically. "She asks that you join her there after you have bathed and refreshed yourself from the journey."

"Does she indeed?" Thomas's eyes narrowed. Lady Aloise looked distracted. Thomas suspected she had had a difficult time with her daughter. "Is she very angry that I expect her to return to Afoncaer with me?"

"She was." Aloise produced a bitter smile. "I spent two extremely unpleasant days trying to convince her, Thomas. For a while I feared you would have to take her back by force. She is more reasonable now. If she opposes you, beat her as a good husband should. You have been too lenient with her. Her stubborn pride must bend to your will, and would have done so long ago had you not always been so foolishly gentle with her."

Thomas almost asked if Sir Valaire had ever beaten his wife, but seeing Aloise's expression, he bit back the irritated words. He doubted Aloise would understand his desire to have a wife who looked upon him with affection rather than fear.

"I'll not wait. I'll see her now if you will show me the way," he said.

"But I've ordered bathwater taken to your room at once."

"Good," Thomas responded. "Selene can help

306

me bathe. She can begin her wifely submission in that way." Aloise nodded in grim agreement.

Thomas paused in the hall just long enough for Benet to remove his heavy chain mail hauberk, before following his mother-in-law up the staircase to the castle's second floor.

Selene sat on a stool in the solar, close to a window, her head bent over bright-colored embroidery. A few silken strands of thread glowed smoothly across the knee of her dark green woolen gown, placed there until she should need them for the next stitches. The light fell softly upon her face and set her crisp white linen coif aglow. Her profile was perfect. Thomas concentrated his thoughts on her beautiful face and body and the pleasure he had once found in both, trying to dredge up some faint stirring of desire for her.

She heard his step and looked up. Thomas saw her emerald eyes grow almost black as the pupils dilated and a look of fear crossed her face. It was swiftly erased into smooth blankness, but her eyes still glowed bright and dark. Gathering up her embroidery, she rose from the stool and knelt to him.

"My lord," she said, her husky voice trembling just a little. "Welcome, sir."

"In the future," Thomas said coolly, "when I return to a place where you are, you will greet me at the door."

"Yes, my lord." Grey-shadowed lids were lowered over her eyes so Thomas could no longer see the expression in them. He wondered if it was hatred.

"Get up," he said, "and come and bathe me."

"Surely one of the serving women can do that."

"It is you I want to serve me, Selene." He put out his hand and she took it, rising and following him meekly along the corridor to the room Lady Aloise had shown him.

A tub of steaming water waited by the blazing hearth. Two serving women stood next to it, one with a bowl of soap and linen towels, the other with a large pitcher of hot water for rinsing.

"You may go," Thomas told them. "My lady will wait on me."

When they had left he bolted the door after them. Selene stood with hands folded before her, in the posture he remembered so well, looking at the floor with apparent great interest, so that her face was hidden from him.

"You may undress me now," Thomas said.

She did not look directly at him while she removed his travel-stained garments, his padded gambeson and hose, and his silk undershirt. Thomas thought she was trying not to see his body, which had begun to react to the touch of her slender fingers as she handled his clothing. He encouraged his own response, trying to recall how much he had wanted her in the early days of their marriage, making himself remember the feel of her smooth flesh beneath his hands and the way she had always moaned in pleasure as he took her. When at last he was naked and shivering slightly in the drafty chamber, longing for the muscle-easing warmth of the inviting tub of water, she walked across the room and picked up the soap bowl and a small linen cloth.

"If you will get in, my lord, I will soap you," she said, still not looking at him.

"Not yet, Selene. You will stain that lovely gown. Take it off. Your headdress, too."

"Please, my lord, no." The delicate hand holding the soap bowl was shaking.

"God's Holy Teeth, woman!" Thomas exploded. "I've had enough of this nonsense. You are my wife, Selene, not some terrified virgin about to be raped. I want you bare-headed, in your undershift, kneeling before me."

"Yes, my lord."

He watched her undress. When she bent to remove her shoes and stockings, Thomas, satisfied that she would not run away, stepped into his bath. He sat in the linen-draped wooden tub, with knees drawn nearly to his chin, and felt his tense muscles begin to relax in the pleasant heat.

Selene knelt beside the tub wearing only a long-sleeved linen shift. Its wide, rounded neck left the beautiful line of her throat exposed. She had partially released her hair so that it hung down her back in a single thick braid. Still she did not lift her eyes, and her small mouth was pressed into a firm line, but Thomas could see her lips were trembling a little.

"Shall I soap your back, my lord?"

"Yes," he said, and moved forward a little to make room for her to reach between his back and the side of the tub.

She worked silently, efficiently, her eyes never meeting his, and Thomas marvelled how she held herself in check. The Selene he had once known would have drowned him in a flood of angry words. He sensed the churning emotions beneath her serene exterior, and found they gave an exciting edge to the physical need that at last had begun to rise in him as she handled his body. Selene, however angry and determined to avoid laying with him, had always turned into a wanton, wildly passionate woman as soon as she realized he would have her no matter how she protested. He chuckled aloud at his body's sudden, urgent reaction when her hands, lathering soap across his chest and abdomen, met the stiffly raised banner of his manhood and stopped. Her eyes flew wide open, no longer shielded from him. Thomas saw anger, fear, and pain mingled in their emerald green depths, and something more, the flaring, passionate look they always held just before she accepted his lovemaking, and he knew she would offer him no great resistance. He wanted to rise dripping and soapy from the tub and fling her onto the floor and have her there. He could almost feel her hot flesh pulsating beneath him. Somehow he controlled himself, knowing that if he waited, and lured her cleverly, she would come to him, and it would be all the better for his patience.

When she had finished soaping him and had poured most of the pitcher of fresh water over his head and shoulders, he stood up so she could finish rinsing him. He stepped out of the tub and stood on the wet floor, letting her dry him.

"My legs, too," he said when she had finished his back. He felt the linen cloth along the backs of his legs, felt it linger across his buttocks. "The front, too, Selene."

He reached around and grabbed one arm to pull her forward, disregarding her sudden yelp of pain.

"Kneel," he commanded, pressing downward on her arm. She went to her knees, face to face with his rising desire for her.

"Thomas. Ohh—Thomas." A dry whisper, wrenched out of a constricted throat. She touched him, with her fingers first and then her mouth, and pleasure and heat and throbbing physical need surged up in him, mingling in sensation so intense he thought he would burst with it.

He bent down and took her by each arm, raising her to her feet. She was weeping. Her rosy lips were slightly parted, and with a surprised start he remembered he had not kissed her yet. He would, in a moment.

He lifted her into his arms and carried her across the room to lay her on the bed. She cried out, wincing, as he moved his hands across her back, then lay still, watching him. He stretched out beside her, and with one hand turned her face to his. That beautiful face, pure and delicate, and without blemish.

"Selene," he murmured, "wife, this is our duty. We've neglected it too long."

"Yes, my lord."

She was still wearing her damp linen shift. It clung to her body. He could see beneath its sheerness the pointed contours of her small breasts, the soft mound of her belly, and below that, the patch of smooth black hair, into which, in a few moments, he would plunge as they slaked their violent passion on each other. But first, he wanted to see her entire body without covering. She was his possession, he owned her, and if he must live with her, he would look at her whenever he wanted. He tugged the shift upward.

"Take this off," he ordered. When she hesitated, he tugged harder, pulling the linen up to her waist, exposing slim legs and thighs, softly rounded hips, and that place—that place into which he wanted to dissolve himself. Now. This instant. "Hurry, Selene."

She sat up and twisted away from him, affording him a tormenting glimpse of inner thigh and creamy buttocks. Thomas licked his dry lips as another surge of heat swept over him. This, he knew,

311

was the lust Selene had always feared, unsoftened now by any thought of love. She belonged to him, was his chattel. He wanted a woman. He would take her. It was remarkably simple.

"Will you hurry, woman? Get that thing off!" He sat up, glaring at her, unwilling to wait any longer to ease the purely physical desire that surged through his body.

With a sob Selene pulled the shift over her shoulders and head and threw it on the floor. Thomas could not pause for kissing or tender caresses. His arm caught her across her chest to push her down and take her without further delay. She cried out, wincing again when her shoulders hit the bed. He was on top of her, one leg thrusting upward between her thighs, his fingers digging into her shoulders. Her scream of pain cut through his blurring, pounding senses. He drew back a little, wondering why Selene was not accepting him as she always had when it came to the moment, why there was no desire in her at all, only pain in her face and her continuing moans.

And then he saw the marks on her upper arms. At that sight, all passion drained out of him, leaving him suddenly weak, his manhood limp and shrivelled. Tears were streaming down her cheeks as he turned her over and stared at her back, seeing what the linen shift had hidden.

"Who did this?" he demanded, horrified.

"My mother, with a stick. Because I said I would not receive you back as my husband," Selene told him. "She meant well. It is a parent's privilege to chastise an errant child."

"Dear God." Thomas's fingers traced the pattern of welts and broken skin that ranged across Selene's back and shoulders and upper arms.

"Why are you disturbed, my lord? It was for your benefit. You have your wife back in your bed."

"Where you do not want to be."

"No, my lord."

Thomas sat up and swung his legs over the side of the bed. He reached for the linen towel Selene had used on him, and draped it around his hips slowly, giving himself time to think.

"Do you hate me so much?" he wondered.

"I do not hate you. If I could love anyone, I would love you. I do hate childbearing, and because of that I fear your lovemaking. Women pay heavily for whatever pleasures they find in bed."

"And also I think you still fear you will become like your mother. But you are not like her, Selene."

"No," she said. "I have no taste for lovers, and I have never beaten my daughter. But I have done other things to be ashamed of."

Thomas was overcome with pity. He got back into bed, and sitting up against the pillows, pulled Selene into his arms, gentling her when she went rigid at his touch.

"Don't fight me, my dear," he murmured. "I promise I won't attack you again. It was an attack, God help me. I wanted to humble you, teach you who your master is."

"My mother taught me that, my lord."

And now he did kiss her at last, gently, with no trace of desire. Her lips were soft and unresponsive under his.

"I cannot seem to make myself into the tyrant husband I wanted to be," he observed ruefully.

"It's not in your nature. You are too kind

hearted." He felt her hesitation before she began to speak again, plunging onward in a sudden spate of fearful words. "Thomas, I have much to confess to you, and I will tell you everything, I swear I will, all in time, but for now there is one very important thing. It must be said today, since we are to leave on the morrow for Barfleur and then England."

"Well, what is it?"

"In the year and a half since I came from court to stay here after we parted from each other, I have seen Lady Isabel often. We are close friends."

"You have been seeing my mother?" In his voice was all the disapproval he felt.

"She has a small manor house nearby. The provision was part of our marriage contract."

"I remember. That is your confession? I'm not happy you have renewed your old friendship with her, but since you are not likely to see her again, we will forget it." Thomas relaxed a little against the pillows. Poor Selene, with her exaggerated emotions and her tendency to feel terrible guilt over unimportant matters. Her next words jolted him out of his growing drowsiness.

"Thomas, she loves you and longs to see you. Would you visit her before we leave?"

"No." His tone should have quelled her, but still she persisted.

"Please, she's growing old. She says she hasn't long to live. She wants so much to see you again."

"I said no."

"It would be a Christian kindness. Honor thy mother."

"My mother," Thomas responded harshly, "has no honor. I will not see her." He told himself it was weakness in him to want to be with his

314

mother again after the terrible things she had done. It would be disloyal to Guy, and to the dear friends whose deaths Isabel had caused, if he were to go to her now. He forcibly stilled the childish longing in his heart.

"Then, if you will not go to her," Selene said, capitulating as gracefully as she could, "will you give me permission to say good-bye to her? When last I saw her, we parted on my promise to take you to her. Let me make a proper farewell, and I can tell her that you are well. I could carry her a message if you would only send one."

"There will be no message from me," Thomas said firmly, in control of his emotions once more. "But since you have made a promise to her, you may go. Make it clear to her that when you have parted today, there can be no further contact between you."

"I will, my lord. I will go now, if you have no further need of me."

Thomas assented, sighing. He doubted he would ever feel need of her again. Pity, yes—he would pity this hapless creature forced into a marriage she did not want, forced into being wife and mother when she would have been better off by far in some convent—but not need. He watched her dress, noting every line and curve of her exquisite body, and knew not the slightest craving to possess her. He briefly considered leaving her in Brittany, but decided against it. She would be safer at Afoncaer, away from her mother. At least he would not beat her. And there she would be far from Isabel's pernicious influence.

Selene, fully dressed, came and curtsied to him as he sat in bed, then took up her cloak and went out to see Isabel. And still he sat, wondering what his future could possibly be like, living in the same castle with an unwilling wife he did not want, and a beloved friend he could not have.

be there possibly be like Isabel in the castle with an earring, why he did not want and

Chapter 16

"Thomas will not come here? You are a poor friend, Selene, if you could not manage him better than that. I depended upon you."

"Isabel, I'm sorry, truly I am, but he absolutely refuses. I have promised him I'll not meet you again or write to you. This is farewell."

"Promised *him?* What of your oath to me?"

"I fulfilled that when I betrayed Afoncaer. And when I wrote to you repeatedly from Wales, knowing I should not."

"I see. You think you are quit of me."

"I plan to tell Thomas everything I have done. After we reach Afoncaer I'll tell him. After I've seen my children again. Then I will accept whatever punishment he decides upon."

"To ease your guilty conscience?" Isabel looked amused. "Confession and penance. How appropriate for one who once wanted to be a nun."

"I wish I had been." Selene swallowed hard, trying not to cry. "Thomas deserves a better wife than I have been."

"I suppose he does."

"At least I can be honest with him now."

"You poor fool." Isabel began to laugh. "You will never tell him anything. You are too cowardly."

"I will! I swear I will!" Selene's tearful protests were drowned out by Isabel's continuing laughter.

"Tell him or not, whichever you want," Isabel said, wiping her eyes, still laughing. "It doesn't matter to me. Either way, you have accomplished my purpose. You were the weapon, Selene. I recognized you at once for what you are. I knew you would never love any man, not even Thomas. I felt certain you would make him unhappy, and bring strife and dissension to Afoncaer, and thus make Guy miserable, too. When you let that Welsh woman trick you into outright betrayal I was delighted, though sorry the attempt failed. And now, if you can bring yourself to confess, what a marvellous finish to my little plan. Knowing what you have done will hurt them all deeply, I've no doubt of that. Guy, and his dear Meredith, will suffer as much as Thomas. Their hearts will break over his distress."

The mockery in Isabel's voice stunned Selene as much as the revelation of how blind she had been. Isabel had used her in much the same way Gwenefer had. Selene was consumed by self-hatred and guilt.

"You were never my friend," Selene cried. "It was pretense, a lie. And I, fool that I am, believed you all these years."

"Five years, yes," Isabel said calmly. "I've been in exile fifteen years now, sent away from England by that cruel man."

"Guy is not cruel, he's kind and good. He would have been my friend if I had let him. He and Meredith. They tried, but I always repulsed them. Because of you. And you used me as though I were some common spy you had hired."

"Have you no blame for yourself, Selene? You, with all your prattling about sin, and your long hours at prayer? You hypocrite!"

"You took a foolish, innocent girl and perverted her mind and heart. But you are right, I am to blame, too. I knew what I did was wrong, even as I did it. I have committed deeds that betrayed Thomas, but I'll do them no more." Selene looked at her mother-in-law, a long, hard look that finally saw the vanity and coldness and the hatred beneath the elegant exterior. Isabel was laughing at her again.

Selene lifted her head high and without another word walked out of Isabel's house. The groom who had accompanied her stood waiting with their horses. It was not a long ride back to her father's castle, but Selene had ample time to think over her meeting with Isabel.

She found Thomas sitting before the fire in the bedchamber they would share. She threw off her cloak and fell on her knees beside him.

"My lord, I have been a very bad wife to you," she cried. "But I will improve, I promise. I will learn to love you as you want, I will even bear you more children if God wills it. Take me to bed now, let me show you what a good wife I can be. Please, Thomas, let me begin to repair the damage I have done to you."

"Is this my mother's doing?" Thomas asked. "One of her schemes?"

"Isabel? No, why should you think that?"

"You have just come from her. My mother always has an intrigue a-plotting."

"We said good-bye. I will never see her or write to her again, I promise. I swear it."

"Write? Again?" Thomas's eyebrows went up in surprise, and Selene realized what she had just revealed.

"My dear lord," she began, but he stopped her.

"It doesn't matter," he said.

"Will you come to bed now?" she pleaded. "Come and love me."

"I loved you once," he mused, "until you destroyed everything I felt for you."

He knew he would never lay with her again, but he would let her learn it gradually. When this odd mood that was on her tonight had gone, she would recall how much she hated everything about childbearing and be grateful to him. He stood up with a sigh.

"Come to bed, Selene. You on your side, I on mine."

Selene began to undress, as slowly and provocatively as she could. Thomas avoided looking at her, but she believed that would not last long. She knew she was still lovely, and he had never been able to resist her before. In time, if she were patient, he would come back to her, and she would make it up to him, all the things she had done that he need never know about.

For, now that she thought about it more calmly, she was forced to admit to herself that Isabel was right. She was a coward. The very thought of telling Thomas the entire truth of the last five years made her quake with fear. But perhaps he need not know after all. There would be no further contact with Isabel, and no one else knew what had been done. She remembered Reynaud's constant scrutiny and dismissed it. She had been away from Afoncaer for so long that Reynaud must have forgotten his suspicions of her by now. No one would tell Thomas what she had done if she did not, and if she could live with her own guilty conscience and keep quiet, she would be entirely safe. She would have her children, and Thomas would soon begin to care for her again. If she were forced to bear more children, she would consider it penance and endure the pain as cheerfully as she could.

No, she decided, lying beside him in the dark, there was no reason at all to disturb Thomas with a truth that he would not enjoy hearing, and that could only hurt herself. All she had to do was keep silent, and soon Thomas would be content with her, and she with him. And they would forget that Lady Isabel had ever existed.

Chapter 17

Barfleur
November 25, 1120

"Are you coming on the king's ship, or will you cross with young William Atheling?" Sir Valaire asked Thomas.

"William has invited us, and Selene seems delighted at the prospect of the entertainment he is planning. We will both sail on the *The White Ship*," Thomas replied.

"I thought you would. It will be a merry voyage. The entire court is sailing to England, save for the Atheling's wife and a few of her ladies." Sir Valaire clasped Thomas's hand in farewell. "If we are granted a fair wind, Aloise and I will meet you and Selene in England tomorrow. A safe passage, Thomas."

"And to you and your lady." Lady Aloise had already boarded the king's ship. Thomas could see her on the deck, in animated conversation with several other women of about her own age.

The younger courtiers were to embark in William's company, but King Henry's heir was late. The king's ship had sailed and night had fallen before William arrived at the harbor. In the meantime, the magnificent new vessel, *The White Ship,* had been heavily stocked with casks of wine and great hampers of food. The musicians had just boarded when William appeared, accompanied by his younger brother Richard, his halfsister Matilda, Countess of Perche, the earl of Chester with his new bride and his brother Sir Ottuel, and a crowd of other nobles and their ladies.

"Thomas," cried the young earl of Chester, "well met but late, my friend. We've missed you. Where have you been?"

"Gathering up my wife," Thomas replied. "She's aboard already. May I introduce her to your lady?" He bowed over the extended hand of the countess of Chester.

"Certainly. I've heard you will be staying at court for a while. We must go hunting together one day. We should become better friends, Thomas. You and I can be of use to each other on the Welsh border." The earl clapped Thomas on the shoulder. "Here comes Captain Fitz Stephen. Are we ready to sail?"

"We might better wait for the morning, my lord." Captain Thomas Fitz Stephen frowned as he surveyed the noisy troop of nobles crowding toward the gangplank. He had had *The White Ship* built by his own shipwrights to his special design, as a gift for King Henry. He was proud of her and had no desire to risk his beautiful creation to the dangers of the night sea. "Where is William Atheling?"

"I am here, Sir Captain, and I'm ready to sail," replied King Henry's eldest son. He had been drinking and his cheerful face was flushed, his eyes bright, as he walked a little unsteadily toward the gangplank.

"But my lord, we should wait until daylight," Captain Fitz Stephen urged. "It would be safer."

"Nonsense. We are all gathered together at last. It has taken us the entire day to reach the dock," William exclaimed merrily. "Who knows if we would get here at all tomorrow? I would not even vouch for myself. Where is my father the king?"

"Sailed before you, my lord. He grew impatient with waiting," Captain Fitz Stephen responded, casting a doubtful look at the Atheling's companions.

"What, gone? Then we'll go after him." William laughed. "I am seized by a delightful idea, good captain. You have boasted this new ship of yours can outsail any other. We will test it, and you. Let's see if we can overtake my father. A purse of golden coins for you, and all the wine your crew can drink, if we are in England to greet King Henry when he steps ashore."

A cheer went up from William's companions at this challenge.

"My lord, I am at your service." Captain Fitz Stephen knew well enough not to argue too long with royalty.

"Follow me," William called to his friends. "Board the ship!"

In the near stampede that followed, Thomas rescued the countess of Perche just as she was teetering on the edge of the gangplank. As more young men and women crowded toward the ship, he found the countess of Chester clinging to his other arm. Realizing that while he was completely sober, they were not, he politely guided them both aboard and then toward the center of *The White Ship*'s deck, where Selene awaited him.

Thomas, himself serious of mind and abstemious in eating and drinking, was amused by the carnival atmosphere surrounding these young courtiers. He knew if the need came again, the men would once more ride into battle with the same high spirits they had shown in the war with France. If they must, they would die for King Henry's cause. Why not, then, enjoy the sweetness of their lives while they could? As for the women, they faced arranged marriages with unknown men, death in childbirth, and incurable diseases with a bravery equal to that of the men. Though most of them appeared frivolous on the surface, their underlying courage in the face of life's dangers touched his tolerant heart. Thomas could not find it in himself to condemn their sometimes childish or licentious revelries. No one among them had ever condemned him for not participating in them. He had found good friends at King Henry's court and in his army, among them the husbands of the two women he led across the crowded deck toward his own wife. Selene already knew the countess of Perche, and was pleased to meet Chester's wife. The earl and his brother joined them soon after.

"Food," laughed Chester, plucking a roasted capon off one of the tables set up nearby. "Let us eat while we may. Who knows what will befall our stomachs once we reach the rough waters outside the harbor?" He tore the bird apart in his hands, distributing pieces of the meat to those standing near him. "Sweet, white breast for you, my lady wife, in honor of your own, a juicy thigh for my lady of Perche, a wing for you, Lady Selene, that you may fly ever higher in this world, and for you, sir," turning to a rather effeminate young knight, "for you, the back, a most appropriate piece of flesh."

Raucous laughter greeted this comment and was joined in by the knight himself, who instead of being offended threw one arm across the earl's shoulders, raised his winecup and toasted his friend in a long, confused speech.

"More wine here." That was William Atheling, moving about the deck and courteously seeing to the needs of friends and guests. "Let us have music and dancing. And you there, open a few casks for the crew. They'll row the faster for a bit of wine in their bellies. Tell them, good Captain Fitz Stephen, there will be more wine for them in England. And for God's sake, cast off. Let's be on our way. We'll never overtake the king if we stay all night at dockside."

"It will be nearly another hour before we can leave, my lord," Captain Fitz Stephen replied. "There is a new load of baggage yet to come aboard, and a few stragglers from your own party. But have no fear, sir, we'll crack on all the sail we've got, and with the rowers working besides, we'll easily outrace the king."

"I'm depending on you," William said. "Come, Lady Selene, will you dance with me? I trust I have your permission, Thomas?"

At Thomas's nod, Selene curtsied, blushing prettily at the honor, and went off with the earl and countess of Chester, leaving Thomas standing alone next to the earl of Chester's brother.

"By heaven, I nearly forgot in all this confusion," Sir Ottuel cried, striking his forehead with one hand. "Thomas, forgive me, I am truly a dunce. There's a man on the dock who wants to speak with you. He says it's important."

"I thought my people were all aboard," Thomas said. "Did he give his name?"

"I don't think it's one of your men. I've seen your servants, and his clothing is not like theirs. He gave me no name, but said it had to do with Afoncaer."

"Did he mention my Uncle Guy, or Lady Meredith?" All Thomas could think of was the horrible possibility that Guy, or one of the others he loved at Afoncaer, was sick or dead. What if Guy's wounds had reopened and felled him all these months later? Or might the Welsh have made another attack? "I should never have left them," he muttered.

"The man mentioned no names," Ottuel said, "but he's still there, see, in the grey cloak standing by those casks. You have plenty of time to speak to him before we sail, and if aught is amiss at Afoncaer, you could have no faster transport back to England than this ship. We've a little room left, I think. If he's from Afoncaer, bring him aboard with you. William won't mind."

"I wonder he did not come aboard himself to find me. I see my wife is still dancing. Should she ask for me, will you tell her I'll rejoin her as soon as I can?"

"Gladly. I'll ask her to dance myself, if William will give her up."

The man waiting on the dock was a smooth, black-haired fellow with eyes that did not look directly at the person he spoke to, and Thomas knew at once he was not from Afoncaer.

"What is your business with me?" Thomas demanded, one hand on his sword hilt, prepared for treacherous attack.

"There's no need for that, my lord," the dark man said, shifty eyes following the motion of Thomas's hand. "I've not come to take your life, only to plead for your presence. Your lady mother is desperately ill and like to die this night. She charged me to beg you, on my knees before all the Atheling's court if I must, to let me take you to her. She would ask your forgiveness for her sins against you before she dies."

"I cannot go to her," Thomas said. "She is bound by the documents she sealed on the day she left Afoncaer. She may not contact me or see me."

"That can scarcely matter once she's dead, can it?" the man asked. "Would you deny the last wish of your dying mother? Will you not give her the forgiveness she so desperately wants, and send her peacefully into the next life?"

"She is truly contrite?" Thomas did not know what to think. Selene had said days ago that Isabel wanted to see him, and he had refused, though in his heart he had wanted to go to her. Had she perhaps been ill even then? It was possible she had changed after so many years, and really was sorry for what she had done in the past. He believed she had always loved him. He hesitated, torn and uncertain what to do. The messenger saw his confusion.

"My lord, she is desperate for your presence," the man insisted, adding, "I came here alone, but I have brought extra horses with me in case you wish to take your own men with you. We need only mount and ride."

Thomas still hesitated, but he discounted the

328

idea of treachery, since he would indeed take several of his own men along. They would be well armed and alert.

"She is at her house near Dol?" he asked.

"Yes, my lord," the messenger said.

"Too far for me to ride there and back and still sail with William as I should. And yet, if she is really dying, I may regret all my life that I did not take this last chance to see her."

"Just so, my lord. Lady Isabel was certain you would feel that way, and confident you would not fail her. Consider that the Atheling would not be angry with you for leaving him under such circumstances."

"Wait here for me," Thomas said, making his choice.

He hurried back aboard *The White Ship*. He met Selene by the gangplank, her face flushed with wine and dancing, her eyes shining. She wore a deep wine-red gown belted in gold, a gold net on her hair, and she was exquisitely beautiful. She took his hand to pull him into the throng on deck.

"I thought you had deserted me," she cried. "We are ready to sail. We are going to a new life, Thomas, where I will do all I can to make you happy. I swear it. Come and dance with me."

When he told her what the messenger had said, all the glow went out of her face, and she stood before him, white and haggard.

"No, Thomas, you can't go to her. Stay here with me."

"How could I do that, laugh and dance and drink my way across the Narrow Sea while my mother lies dying? I must go to her. I'm surprised at you, Selene. Only a few days ago you were urging me to visit her."

"She's evil. I saw it at that last visit with her. Stay away from her, Thomas, I beg you."

"She has repented of her evil and wants my forgiveness. The messenger said so. You will come with me, Selene."

"*No!* No, she doesn't want to see me again. It's you she wants to speak with."

Thomas, although surprised at Selene's vehemence, agreed with her after only a moment's reflection. He knew from what the messenger had said that he should make haste. He did not want to tarry long enough to have all their belongings and the servants disembarked and to make provisions for them to stay at Barfleur until he returned, and if he insisted that Selene go with him she would only delay him. He could ride much faster without her.

"There is no time to discuss this," he said. "I must leave at once if I'm to reach Dol while my mother still lives. Perhaps it's just as well that you do stay on board. I'll take Benet for squire and two men-at-arms for guards. The rest of our people and our baggage I leave in your charge. When you reach England, go to court as we had planned and remain there until I join you. I'll see to my mother's last wishes and attend to her funeral, and when it's over I'll sail to England. From what the messenger said, it won't be very long, a day or two at most. I pray she lives until I get there."

"Thomas, don't leave me." Selene put her arms around his waist, laying her head on his chest. "Please stay with me. I love you, dear husband."

He held her briefly, thinking how sad it was that she should say she loved him after he had ceased to love her at all, and wondering if she really meant it. Then he took her slender shoulders in his hands and set her gently aside.

"If you love me, do as I wish," he said. "Tell William what has happened. I don't have time to search him out in this crowd. See to all my belongings, my goods and my people, and especially to yourself, Selene, and I will join you at court as soon as I can."

She reached toward him once more, clutching at his sleeve.

"I will obey, my lord. Will you kiss me before you go? Just one last kiss."

He bent his head and her arms crept around his neck. She pressed her body against him, but he did not embrace her. His mouth was on hers, and he felt her lips open under his, her tongue searching across his lips. Thomas did not, could not, respond to her. He reached up and caught her wrists, unlocking them from the back of his neck and holding her away from him.

"I trust you to carry out my orders," he said, and turned to leave the ship.

Selene watched him go, feeling fear beyond anything she had known before. What good were all her intentions of winning back Thomas's affections and making herself into a perfect nobleman's wife if Isabel ruined everything by confessing to Thomas all the things she and Selene had done? Was Isabel really sick? She had appeared to be in perfect health a few days ago. Perhaps the message was a ruse. If it was, its purpose could only be to lead Thomas face to face with his mother, where she would betray Selene and tell all. Dying or healthy, Isabel would surely do Selene irreparable harm. And there was no way she could stop whatever Isabel planned, for after much delay, the lines had finally been cast off and *The White Ship* had begun to move out into the harbor.

The night was ink-black except where torches and oil lamps flared to light the wild scene on deck. Most of the participants had had entirely too much to drink. A few particularly rowdy young nobles leaned over the railing hurling pieces of food and open taunts at the elderly priest who had come to harborside to pronounce a benediction upon the ship and all who sailed in her. Selene, shocked at their behavior, crossed herself and turned aside.

"There you are, my lady." Sir Ottuel of Chester stood before her. "Come and dance with me again, I beg you."

Selene resolutely forced her tortured thoughts into the back of her mind. There was nothing she could do now save follow Thomas's instructions. After she was in England she would find some quiet place, and there think on what means she might use to win her husband back to her should his mother tell him of their mutual treachery. But not here, not in this laughing, noisy throng. Selene put on her best court smile. At least Sir Ottuel was reasonably sober, unlike most of the others.

"I shall be happy to dance with you, Sir Ottuel, but first I must find my lord William. I have a message for him from my husband." She moved off across the crowded deck, searching for the Atheling, Sir Ottuel trailing happily in her wake.

Isabel was not dying. She did not even look the slightest bit sick. Pale, yes, but that might have been from emotion at seeing her son again after so many years. Garbed in her favorite shade of brilliant blue, she sat in a high-backed chair next to the hearth, leaning her head against its carved wood, her long, tapering fingers resting lightly on the arms. Thomas had noted the rich appointments of the house as he was led from the entrance through the great hall and up a flight of steps to this private bedchamber. Sir Valaire, whose generosity had provided the house, had played fair by Isabel.

"Your messenger told me you were ill," Thomas said, looking at her keenly. "Dying, in fact."

"So I was told two days ago," Isabel replied. "But as you see, I've tricked the doctors."

"And tricked me, too, I've no doubt." Thomas sat down across the fire from her. He had to sit, for suddenly his knees were trembling and he was embarrassed by the powerful emotion he felt. Mother or no, after all she had done at Afoncaer to him and to Guy, this woman should mean nothing to him. He thought he had torn her out of his heart, but that was not so. He took refuge in anger, and it was not mock anger, either. "This meeting breaks your solemn oath to Uncle Guy. You had better have some deep reason for calling me here, madame. Why did you want to see me?"

"Why not, after so long? Selene told me you were both returning to England. I'm growing older. Who knows if I will live until you come to these shores again? I thought I had better take my chance, while you were still here." Isabel smiled at him. "You have grown into a fine, handsome man, Thomas. Like your father and your uncle. You resemble them both."

333

"When Selene came to me after her last visit with you she was sorely distressed. What happened between you?"

"She didn't tell you? Then I shall have to. But not now, not tonight. It's late and you have ridden hard. I've ordered a room prepared for you."

"I'm not staying," Thomas declared.

"What, still so hot to be with your fish-blooded wife?" Isabel laughed at him. "But if my messenger plucked you from the very deck of the royal ship, then your dear Selene must be halfway to England by now. Sleep, Thomas, and tomorrow we will talk. I will open my heart to you. And after you know all, you may return to Selene, and to Afoncaer. If you still want to."

"What do you mean by that?" Thomas rose to stand over her with a menacing look. Isabel remained totally unafraid of him.

"What could I mean, my dear son, but that I will put no impediment in your way once you know the truth?"

Isabel rose, too, gracefully slender and tall for a woman, and Thomas suddenly recalled how he had always had to look up at her when he was a boy, bending his head far back to see her face. She had seemed like a queen to him then, far away and incredibly lovely, a distant, perfect ideal of womanhood. And almost always irritated or angry with him. Always pushing him away lest his childish hands soil her lovely gowns. He had worshipped Isabel, but he had never had a true mother until he had found Meredith. And now he was taller than she, he looked down at her, not up, and he saw the lines about her eyes and the grey hair just visible at the edge of her coif. She was growing older, as she had said, and in spite of all she had done—and he knew most of it, Guy had told him the full story of her treachery and Walter's those long years ago—in spite of it all, he loved her still. It was that love that had brought him here today, against his better judgment. He decided he would hear whatever she had to say, and forgive whatever she wanted forgiven. He could do that much for her.

"Very well," he said. "Since I am here, I will stay the night."

"I am so glad." Her hand moved up to touch his cheek, an odd, wistful gesture. "Dear Thomas."

The servants came to lead him to his bedchamber, where, after eating a little, he slipped between fresh linen sheets. He fell asleep at once, his dreams untroubled by any premonition about the morrow.

Selene had tried, but she could not banish the tormenting thoughts that plagued her. She ought to have gone with Thomas. Then she would have been able to counter at once whatever Isabel said about her. Thomas would hate her. How could he do otherwise? She thought of all the possible punishments an outraged husband might inflict upon his wife and shivered. Whatever happened when they met again, no matter what she said to him, how many excuses she made, one thing was certain: she had lost him forever.

In addition to her emotional distress, Selene was feeling a bit seasick. She knew she had drunk too much wine in her efforts to calm herself, and she had eaten more rich food than she really wanted. Whirling about in so many dances had further disturbed her stomach, so that the ship's slightest motion made her queasy. It might not have been so bad had they not been travelling so fast, but William Atheling had insisted they must catch up to King Henry's ship. Additional sails were hoisted, and the rowers below deck were urged to greater efforts. A double row of long oars, fifty of them altogether, rose and dipped into the sea and rose again. The ship strained forward, into the rough open water of the Narrow Sea.

Selene felt the first slapping surge of the choppy waves and her stomach heaved. She would not give into it, would not suffer the indignity of hanging over the side and casting the contents of her stomach into the sea. She found a coil of rope and sat down on it, heedless of the damage dirt and tar might do to her gown. Pressing her lips firmly together she concentrated on taking deep breaths through her nose until she felt a little better. Sitting as she was, she did not see the white foam breaking over the reef called *Le Ras de Catte.*

No one else saw the reef, either. *The White Ship,* hurtling through the darkness with all sails full and all rowers laboring to the limits of their strength, crashed headlong upon the rocks, then slewed off to one side, the jagged rocks tearing open a long gash below the waterline.

Selene was thrown forward by the impact, sprawling onto the sharply slanting deck. Shrieks of panic and cries for help sounded all about her. Selene crawled to the rail and pulled herself upright. Sir Ottuel appeared beside her, dragging the weeping countess of Chester with him.

"Stay here," he cried, putting her hands on the rail next to Selene's. "Hold on. Lady Selene, make her stay with you. She is hysterical. We can't find my brother."

"The ship is sinking," Selene gasped, looking over the edge into sucking black water.

"Yes, and there are not enough lifeboats," Ottuel told her. "At least that fool Fitz Stephen has put the Atheling into one of them. He will be safe enough, we aren't far from shore. Help will come soon. Stay here, both of you. I'll come back for you." He was gone, sliding across the tilting deck into the night.

They were lower in the water now. One of the sails, billowing loose from its lines, had blown against a torch and caught fire. Its brilliant glare lit up a nightmarish scene of broken bodies on the ship and people in heavy court dress trying desperately to stay afloat in the water. Selene saw Sir Ottuel reach for a rope, miss it, and plunge headlong into the sea. She uttered a silent prayer for him. Beside her, the earl of Chester's wife sobbed softly.

"William, William, don't leave me!" That was Matilda of Perche, the Atheling's favorite sister, leaning over the side and stretching out her arms toward a boat Selene's straining eyes could just make out at the edge of the firelit scene. There was a great shout from the sea, and the small boat seemed to be returning. Selene watched with odd detachment as Countess Matilda flung herself over the side and into the water.

The ship settled deeper. Water lapped at their feet. Selene watched it coming closer. The cries of pain and shouts for help receded into a distant clamor. She scarcely felt the shuddering of the ship as it ground upon the rocks, breaking up and sinking toward the bottom of the harbor. The flaming sail was nearly burnt out. It hung on the yard a moment more, then fell into the sea in a shower

337

of sparks, and all was dark. The cries and the ship's movement and creakings receded even further from Selene's consciousness. She was only dimly aware that the weeping woman beside her had loosed her hold on the rail and fallen across the deck and into the sea.

This is the way, Selene thought calmly, the best way to end it. I'll never have to listen to Thomas's reproaches or know his hatred, never have to face Guy and Meredith, or see the pity in Arianna's eyes when I am brought to punishment. Reynaud, that constant watcher, will never look at me in triumph and know his suspicions have all been confirmed at last. When I am gone, Thomas won't have to tell anyone what I've done, my children won't have to be ashamed of me. It will all be forgotten because I am dead. Whatever Isabel says to Thomas won't matter at all, and I know him, he won't repeat it. The truth would hurt too many people.

She felt no fear at all, only a sense of relief that Thomas was safe on shore. In a moment it would all be over, the pain and fear, and the hot, desperate wanting.

The ship settled a little lower, the motion nearly jerking her hands off the railing to which she still clung. Selene pulled herself up onto the rail and perched there, hearing the last remaining cries of the drowning like the calls of faraway seabirds.

She closed her eyes, breathed a quick prayer, and let herself fall into the blackness. The water was cold, like black ice all around her, numbing her body. Her heavy gown pulled her down, down, and Selene sank gratefully, willingly, giving herself up to the sea without a struggle. She kept her eyes closed, and in that all-encompassing blackness, in the silence of the sea's cold embrace, Selene found the peace she had searched for all her life.

Chapter 18

Isabel had put Thomas off all morning, remaining in her private chamber and refusing to meet him until it was time for the midday meal. Thomas seriously considered leaving without seeing her again, but he did not. He was held in her house by an intense curiosity about what she might have to say to him. Still, he decided to let her know that he was angry with her for making him wait so long. They finally came together in the hall, where food was being placed upon the tables and his men had joined Isabel's household, all of them hungrily awaiting her arrival so they could begin.

"I know what you are attempting by this delay, madame," he stormed at her. "You think to keep me here another night, but, by heaven, I tell you I will leave the moment this meal is finished, whether you have said what you have to say or not."

"Very well, Thomas, but let us at least sit down and begin to eat. You are frightening my servants with your quarrelsome ways. My household is usually more peaceful than this." Isabel glided past him, heading for her chair on the dais. Thomas followed her so closely that he nearly bumped into her when she whirled about at the sound of loud voices at the door. Isabel exclaimed in irritated surprise as the same messenger who had accompanied Thomas from Barfleur burst into the hall. "Alain, what do you mean by this rude intrusion?"

"My lady." The messenger made a hasty bow and began to speak, his words tumbling out on top of each other, yet for all his hurried, confused manner, what he said made dreadful sense. "News from Barfleur . . . a great tragedy . . . *The White Ship* sunk . . . William Atheling . . . tried to save his sister . . . dead, all dead."

"What are you saying?" Isabel demanded impatiently. "Who is dead?"

But Thomas had grasped the import of Alain's story at once, and had turned deathly white.

"They are all gone?" he gasped, catching at Alain's arm. "Selene? All?"

"All save one, my lord, and that a butcher from Rouen, on his way to the English court to serve in King Henry's kitchens. He alone lived to tell the tale. I am sorry, my lord," Alain added sympathetically.

"Selene." Thomas sank into the nearest chair, hearing the loud murmuring among Isabel's servants as they, too, began to comprehend the magnitude of the disaster Alain had described.

"Here. Swallow every drop." Isabel thrust a goblet of wine at him, and he drank in stunned, childlike obedience to her command. He was sharply aware of Isabel ordering everyone else out of the hall, of Benet and his other men leaving with many concerned backward glances, and of servants picking up trenchers and platters and disappearing behind the screens passage toward the kitchen. He took another deep gulp of the wine, wishing it would numb the pain and blur the unnatural clarity with which he saw and heard everything.

"I should have been with her," he said, his voice just above a whisper. "I might have saved her."

"Had you been there, you would have drowned, too," Isabel told him. "Count yourself fortunate that you came to me instead. Well, this changes everything."

He gaped at her wordlessly, shaken by her coolness, and then he began to weep. It was unmanly, he knew, but he could not help it.

"She needed me," he cried, "and I wasn't there. She was my responsibility, my charge. She must have been terrified. She was afraid of the sea."

"Selene was afraid of everything," Isabel said scornfully. "She was afraid of life itself. Don't weep for her, she wasn't worth a single tear."

"This is your doing," Thomas accused her. He slammed down the wine goblet and rose to stride back and forth across the hall as if he did not know what to do next. "I would have been with her but for your lying message." He ran his fingers through his hair in a gesture of frustration and despair.

"I had nothing to do with the ship sinking. You can't blame me for this accident," Isabel exclaimed.

"I need not. There is enough else to blame you for. I'm no fool, madame, whatever you may think. I suspect much of the unhappiness at Afoncaer in recent years can be laid to your charge. I believe you had something to do with Selene's inability to love me, and her coldness toward Guy and Meredith."

Isabel laughed, a spiteful sound he remembered well from his unhappy childhood. Her voice, after a moment's pause, fell on his ears like ice.

"It is true, Thomas. It was I who first suggested the marriage, and I who convinced Selene to marry you when she was most unwilling to wed anyone. Were it not for me, your marriage to Selene would not have come about at all, and that dowry of hers, that chest of gold coins Guy wanted so badly, would never have been his for the benefit of Afoncaer."

"You did that? You? And let us believe it was Lady Aloise's idea?"

"Of course. And you never guessed the truth. You were too concerned about Afoncaer to ask many questions about the proposed bride's character, and too trustingly certain that Guy and Valaire, those honest fathers, would make an agreement beneficial to everyone involved. Poor Thomas." Isabel laughed again. "Not so clever after all. No wonder Selene never loved you. You are just like your father. Doing the right and honorable thing is all he ever thinks of, too. He could have been so much more than a mere border baron were he only willing to bend a little and fit his conscience to circumstances. The king is his friend, he could have had power at court, and wealth beyond his wildest dreams, but all he will do is stay at Afoncaer with his precious Meredith and worry about the welfare of his people. His people? The Welsh care nothing for him. They've shown that well enough recently, haven't they? And you are as foolishly wrapped up in Afoncaer as he is."

Thomas stared at her, the blood running cold in his veins. At first he thought she had gone mad, but then he realized that Isabel was in full possession of her senses. She was irritated with him, as she had ever been, but she was quite cool and sensible, and she was deliberately telling him something she wanted him to know. Thomas staggered as the full impact of her words struck him. He could hardly breathe. He struggled to form chaotic thought into words and force them out of his mouth.

"Lady," he said, taking a purposeful step toward her, "are you saying that Sir Lionel fitz Lionel was not my father? That you committed adultery with Uncle Guy? That is a damnable lie! I could believe it of you, madame, but not of him. Uncle Guy would never betray his brother in such a foul way. So, if my father is other than Sir Lionel, you had better tell me his name. I have no right to inherit anything from Uncle—from Sir Guy, if this is true."

Isabel said nothing, but only smiled, watching him, taking in his horror and his building anger.

"Speak, madame!" Thomas exploded. "This cruel claim is too much after Selene's death. I want the truth of this. Answer me now, before I do you violence."

Isabel continued to smile upon her son, her voice sweet and caressing as she sent her words like arrows into his already hurt and bleeding heart.

"Sir Lionel did not love women," Isabel said. "He only lay with me once, to consummate the marriage, then would have nothing more to do with me. I needed to produce an heir. One night Guy was on guard in the anteroom outside our chamber. I went to him in the dark and lay with him. He called me by some other woman's name;

344

he thought I was she. Then I got into bed with Sir Lionel, and the next morning I told him he had made love to me. He had been very drunk the night before and could not remember what had happened. He always believed you were his son. My reputation was so spotless he had no reason to doubt it."

"How could you do such a thing?"

"I had little choice if I wanted to safeguard my position. It only happened the once, Thomas. There was never any love lost between Guy and me, but don't you see what a good idea it was? The bloodlines are the same. The inheritance that passed from your grandfather to Lionel, and from Lionel to Guy, will pass from Guy to you, as it should. You are the old man's grandson. It's not as though I lay with a stranger."

Thomas knew, without further question or thought, he simply *knew* that Isabel was telling him the truth.

"Does Uncle Guy—does my father know of this?"

"He knows. I told him just before I left Afoncaer forever. The day I went into exile at his command."

"I remember that day," Thomas said. "You would not even bid me good-bye. You rode out of the gates without looking at me."

"I could not trust myself to speak," Isabel told him.

"No, not to me. But into his ear you could pour your poison. My mother. You wicked, deceitful, adulterous bitch! I have many times excused you," Thomas went on, "to those who criticized your deeds, telling them it was your unhappy marriage to Sir Lionel that molded you into what you are.

345

But now I think you would have been the same abominable creature if all your life you had had all you wanted. In fact, had you never been restricted by Sir Lionel, or Uncle—my father, you might well have been worse than you are now. It's in your nature, isn't it? Vain, shallow, calculating, caring for no one but yourself. I am ashamed to call you mother.''

Isabel did not answer him for a moment, and when she did her voice was low and weary.

''You have no idea what it was like to live at court and give no heir to my husband. People whispered about what he was, about his love for King William Rufus, and everyone laughed behind my back. With one act I silenced them all.''

''An act of adultery.''

''Only one. And for it I was sent from court by a jealous king as soon as my pregnancy was obvious. I do deeply regret my abstinence for all those lonely years afterward, until I married Walter. I have not had a happy life, Thomas.''

''That is in large part your own fault. I have done with you, woman,'' Thomas declared. ''I will never see you again, unless you devise some new scheme against Afoncaer or those souls I hold dear. In that case, I will come to you, and, by heaven, I swear I will kill you with my own hands.''

''And you will go home to Afoncaer and tell Guy all I have told you, will you not?''

''We will settle the matter between the two of us. You and I have nothing more to do with each other.'' The look Thomas gave her was one of pure hatred. Then he was gone from the hall, calling to Benet to saddle his horse and bring his armor.

Isabel sat down in her chair on the dais, staring straight ahead, not moving until the sounds of

Thomas's departure had ceased. On her face was a smile of triumph, for her revenge against Guy was completed, or would be when an angry, unforgiving Thomas confronted him, but at the same time, unchecked tears poured down her cheeks in recognition of what that triumph had cost her.

Chapter 19

Thomas rode in frantic haste from Isabel's house outside Dol to Barfleur, hoping vainly that the reports of shipwreck were false. He prayed he would find Selene and all the other passengers were safe, either delayed in Barfleur or transported to England. He discovered on his arrival at the harbor that the story was true. One hundred forty noblemen and women, in addition to servants, squires, pages, musicians, and the crew of *The White Ship* had perished on that terrible night, and all that was left of Captain Fitz Stephen's beautiful new ship was the top of one mast poking above the waves just outside the harbor.

"I should have been with Selene," Thomas repeated over and over. He had not loved her, but still, she had been his wife, she had borne his children. He wept for her. "I failed to help her so many times, and at the last, when she needed me most, I had abandoned her."

"You could not have known what would happen. It was not your fault, my lord." Benet's attempt at comfort only reminded Thomas just whose fault it really was that he had not been present to help Selene. He might have cursed Isabel then, had he not been so stunned by the suddenness of the tragedy. He could not even begin to think just yet of the grief of those others who had also lost relatives and friends, or of what the loss of the heir to the throne would mean to King Henry and to the future of England.

In his despondent state Thomas hardly knew what he was doing. It was Benet who saw to what was needful, who found lodgings for the two of them and the men-at-arms, who made Thomas eat regularly though he had no appetite, and who each day went with Thomas to the docks and then to the local church so they could check on the bodies that had been recovered.

" 'Tis only a squire's duty," Benet said when Thomas roused himself enough to thank his faithful companion.

"It is more than that." There was the faint hint of a smile on Thomas's somber face, the first indication that he was beginning to recover some of his usual spirit. "These are acts of friendship, Benet, and I'll not forget them."

It was six days before Selene's body was found. Thomas could identify her only by her waterlogged gown and her long black hair, and the pitiful ruin of what had once been so lovely haunted his nightmares for weeks. She was buried in the local cemetery along with the other victims, including Thomas's dozen servants and men-at-arms, who had been recovered from the sea. When it was done, and he had made arrangement for masses to be said for her troubled soul, he found a ship to take him and his remaining men back to England.

Instead of going directly to Afoncaer as he would have preferred, Thomas sent a messenger there

349

with word of the tragedy and rode to Brampton, where Henry was holding court. He thought he ought to see Sir Valaire and Lady Aloise, and to offer his condolences to the king.

Henry was much changed, sunk in grief, an old man no longer interested in governing. His clothes were rumpled and stained, looking as though he regularly slept in them, and his eyes were dazed and haunted.

"I lost my dear Matilda only a year and a half ago," Henry wept when Thomas was admitted to private audience with him, "and now this. Oh, William, my son, my son, all I did was for you, that you should rule securely after me. And Richard, dear lad, too young to die. How can they both be gone at once?"

Thomas was shocked by Henry's appearance and his manner. This was not the vigorous, resilient man to whom he had once been page. Putting aside his own sorrow at the loss of Henry's sons, who had both been his friends, Thomas tried to think of something to catch the king's attention and recall him to his duties as ruler.

"Sire, I assure you, Baron Guy and I will do all we can to keep your peace along the border," Thomas promised him. "And further, we will freely offer whatever assistance is needed by the late earl of Chester's people, with no thought for our own advancement in his territories."

"What do I care for border disputes now?" Henry cried. "All my pride and ambition lies at the bottom of the sea with my sons. There is nothing left for me."

"You are a brave and strong man, sire," Thomas insisted. "You are bowed down now, but you will recover from this loss. You must, for your people

350

need you, and when you do, remember that my Lord of Afoncaer and I are your loyal servants, and that you have but to command us."

Sir Valaire and his wife were in slightly better condition than the king. But then, Thomas reminded himself, they had not had so many hopes riding on their child's life.

"Henry has lost two sons," Valaire said, "while I still have all of mine. I grieve for Selene, and always will, but Henry's loss is greater, for it is England's loss, too."

"He did nothing but weep while I was with him," Thomas said.

"It's all he does all day. Bishop Roger of Salisbury, his treasurer, holds the reins of government now, and there are many who do not like that. There's a plot afoot to try to convince Henry to marry again, in the hope of getting another heir." Valaire had a speculative look. "Will you stay at court, Thomas? With so many nobles lost to us, there is easier preferment for a capable man with ambition. You could go far. I'll be happy to speak in your behalf to Salisbury."

"I thank you for that, sir, but the only place I want to go is Afoncaer. It's where I belong. I'm not overfond of court life. I much prefer the freedom of the borderlands. And until we are certain what will happen next in this realm, or who will rule it after Henry, we must keep a strong guard at Afoncaer. The Welsh may take advantage of this situation to try to drive us out."

"I understand." Valaire accepted Thomas's decision with good grace. "Don't let our friendship languish, Thomas. Our families are still connected by affection."

"And by Jocelyn and Deirdre," Thomas added.

"You must come to Afoncaer to see your grand-children."

"Will you send Arianna back to us?" asked Lady Aloise, who after a first tearful embrace had sat quietly during Thomas's conversation with her husband.

"She's part of Afoncaer now," Thomas replied, warmth welling up in him at the mention of her name. He tried to control it. He would not allow himself to think of Arianna. Not yet. It was too soon after Selene's death, and he owed his wife a suitable period of mourning. But he could not let Arianna leave Afoncaer—not unless she wanted to, and he did not think that was likely. "Arianna has charge of my children. She is dear to my Aunt Meredith and also to Uncle Guy. I don't think they would want her to leave."

"Then let her stay where she is," Aloise said. "There's no real place at court for a penniless orphan. Let her be useful to you and Meredith."

Thomas had planned to question Aloise about the way his marriage to her daughter had been arranged. He had wanted to know if she had been aware of Isabel's plotting. But watching the plump, self-satisfied court lady who had been his mother-in-law, he decided to say nothing. Isabel had probably used Aloise as heartlessly as she had used Selene. It was over and done now. No need to cause unnecessary grief or trouble. He took his leave of Aloise and Valaire most courteously.

And then it seemed to Thomas that there was no more reason to stay at court. He wanted to be with those he loved, to feel their comforting presence. Royal permission to leave court was easy to obtain; in his present mood Henry did not care what anyone did. On a cold, grey morning in December, Thomas, with Benet and the men-at-arms who had been at his back since Barfleur, set out on the long journey to Afoncaer.

The closer they came to the border, the harder they pushed their horses and themselves, wanting to reach home with a mutual yearning that urged all of them toward the northwestern horizon, where storm clouds had been steadily gathering for days.

"There will be a blizzard," Benet predicted, "a bad one."

They pressed on toward the warmth and safety of Afoncaer, until, just before the early dark of that Christmas Eve, they thundered across the drawbridge to shouts of welcome from the guards who recognized Thomas's blue and silver banner. Up the main street of the village they rode, over the sharply slanted wooden bridge that spanned the dry moat, through the main castle gate, and into the inner bailey, just as the snow began to fall. Thomas leapt from his horse. He ran right up the stairs of the keep and through the door, startling Kenelm out of the wardroom to see what the noise was. At last he came into the great hall, showering drops of moisture and unmelted snowflakes on anyone near him.

Guy was standing in front of the nearest fireplace, warming himself at the roaring blaze. He spun around at the sound of boots on the stone floor.

"Thomas!" His arms opened and Thomas went into them, knowing Guy for his father. He could not speak of it yet, but he would, in time. For now it was enough to feel the strength in Guy's arms and know he was well recovered from his wounds of the previous year.

Thank God, Thomas thought, he was not lost to me before I knew who he truly is. We've so much to say to each other.

Over Guy's shoulder Thomas saw Reynaud smiling at him in greeting, and then Meredith came hurrying into the hall, and behind her Arianna, with his son Jocelyn in her arms and Deirdre clinging to her skirts. Bewildered as he was by a rush of conflicting emotions over Selene's death, his feelings for Arianna, and his newly discovered relationship to Guy, Thomas could think of nothing to say to Arianna. He was uncomfortably aware of a large portion of the castle's population crowding into the great hall to welcome him, and he wanted to do nothing before others that might embarrass her or make her the subject of gossip.

She seemed to understand. She smiled bravely at him, tears welling in her eyes when Selene's name was mentioned.

"Welcome home, Thomas," she said quietly. "Here is your son," she said, handing Jocelyn to him.

It was not at all like a meeting of would-be lovers, and yet in the expression of their eyes and the quick touch of their hands as he took the boy from her there was something that soothed his aching spirit. She had not changed, she loved him still. She would wait. He knew it. And knew something more: Arianna genuinely grieved for Selene.

"I will forget the unhappy times when she was not herself. She was my playmate when we were small," Arianna said. "She was kin, though distant, and I loved her."

While he tried to think of a suitable reply, cursing the slow wit and wooden tongue that left Arianna to carry the burden of this too-public moment, Jocelyn broke the mood. Wriggling and squirming like any other two-year-old, young Joce demanded to be put down at once. Thomas complied, laughing, and Joce, once his small feet were on the ground, made for the nearest dog he could find and began to pull its tail.

"He never stops," Arianna said. "He wearies us all. But Deirdre is quiet and well behaved." Deirdre had hidden herself behind Arianna's skirt and now peeped out, her blue eyes wide and round as she regarded her father.

Before Thomas could speak to the child, he was surrounded by men. Guy had questions for him, Kenelm had the latest news to tell, and others crowded about him, separating him from Arianna. He looked for her and saw her leading his children out of the hall. She was taking them back to the nursery, he supposed. He had no chance to be alone with her that night, nor, as it turned out, for some time to come, and that was his own doing.

After all the greeting was done, after those gathered had wept again over Selene's death, after Christmas mass and a very subdued feast for the holy day, and visits with the survivors of those others who had died, Thomas found, on the day after Christmas, that he had no desire to rise from his bed.

Meredith came to see him.

"Your spirit is weary," she said. "Too much has befallen you. You need to rest." She gave him one of her hot herbal brews to drink, and after taking it he fell asleep and did not wake completely for two days. Then she fed him until he felt like a stuffed pheasant before roasting, and made him stay in bed for days longer, until he snarled at her in unaccustomed irritation at the restrictions she had put on him.

"I've been waiting for that sign," she laughed. "You are better now, Thomas. Get up whenever you want."

He did, the next day, but he was not cured yet. There was too much unspoken and unsettled. Because of that, he continued to avoid Arianna. Ten days after his return he confronted Guy and Meredith in their private chamber at the top of the tower keep.

"I know the truth of my parentage," he said bluntly. "I wish to speak with you alone, my lord."

"There is no need for that, Thomas." Meredith glanced at her husband's white face and took his arm, moving protectively closer to him. "I know it, too."

"I'll not ask who told you," Guy said. "There is only one person who could have done so. Isabel. You have seen her."

"I was with her when I learned of Selene's death." Thomas told them the story, not leaving out his suspicions about Isabel's influence on Selene, or what Isabel had admitted about arranging their marriage.

"I think there is still more in this tale than we will ever know," he concluded. "But Selene is dead and cannot speak, and Lady Isabel never will. Let it rest there, let Selene rest in peace. She had little enough in life, poor tormented woman. My lord, what we must talk about now is Isabel's claim that you are my father."

"That she should deal you such a blow," Meredith cried, "by telling you when you were already in such deep pain. What cruelty."

"To be cruel when one of her intrigues had failed was always Isabel's way," Guy said. "Thomas, I tell you truthfully I did not know it was Isabel who came to me the night you were conceived. I was not quite fifteen years old. I had never had a woman before, and at first I thought I was dreaming. Then I thought it was one of the kitchen wenches, a girl I fancied, come to lay with me in the dark. Had I known who it really was, I would have run from that woman in horror. Although," he added, "I cannot say I am sorry you were born. You have always been a joy and pride to me, and I loved you well, even before I knew you for my own."

"And you, Meredith," Thomas turned his gaze on her. "You said that you knew."

"Guy told me after Cristin was born. It seemed we could have no more children, and I was distraught that I had not given him an heir of his own body. I told him to set me aside and take another wife."

"That I could never do." Guy put an arm about Meredith's shoulders. "I told her the story, so she would know you were my true heir."

"And what might have distressed another wife," Meredith added, "was comfort to me. I loved you before, Thomas, but all the more dearly once I knew you were Guy's own son."

"But I am a bastard!" Thomas cried. "You should have told me."

"We kept the secret out of love for you," Guy said. "Why hurt you needlessly? The fewer people who know of this the better. I have more than enough land to divide between you and Meredith's son, and still provide dowries for my daughters. No one will be cheated, and no one else need ever know."

"I should have been told," Thomas cried again. "Do you know what I have suffered, believing I was Sir Lionel's child? Even as a page at court, at that young age, I was fully aware of what manner of man my supposed father was, and I lived in terror of becoming like him, cruel and licentious, and overly ambitious. It's one of the reasons I spent two years at Llangwilym Abbey, and thought so seriously of entering the Church. To avoid passing that bad blood down to another generation. But you, I always loved and admired you so much. If I had known you were my father, how relieved I would have been. I would have been glad to be your bastard."

"I'm sorry, Tom. I tried to do the right thing for you."

"You know now, Thomas," Meredith interrupted. "Can't you forgive Guy for hiding it all those years?"

"Forgive?" Thomas exclaimed. "It's my mother who should ask forgiveness, from all of us, for the wicked things she's done. But you, who have given me naught but love and guidance all my life, you who—*father*—"

"Tom, my son."

They were in each other's arms, slapping each other on the back and trying not to weep with joy, and Meredith turned aside to wipe her eyes. It was a long time before the two men let each other go.

"I think," Guy said, "we had best keep this among ourselves. I doubt Isabel will ever tell another soul."

"There is Reynaud," Meredith added.

"Reynaud?" Thomas stared at her. "Reynaud knows?"

"I told him years ago," Guy explained. "He has written it into one of his histories in case the information should ever be needed after we are dead. But that volume is sealed, and Reynaud will never speak. So, just we four will know."

"And one more," Thomas said. "Not yet, but when the time is right, there is another who must know. It's only fair to tell her, and she will keep the secret."

"I'm not sure—" Guy began.

"I am," Thomas insisted. "I've lived too long with untruths. My marriage to Selene was built on them. I'll have no more of that."

"Agreed." Guy put out his hand, and Thomas clasped it. Father and son stood grinning at each other before they embraced once more.

Chapter 20

Late March, A.D., 1121

When her secretary had finished reading Sir Valaire's letter to her, Isabel cried out in dismay.

"He cannot do that to me!"

"I believe you will find, my lady," the secretary
said, "that he can indeed. The agreement between
you and Sir Valaire was contained within a marriage contract, and was in force only so long as the
marriage continued between your son Thomas and
Sir Valaire's daughter Selene. The marriage is
ended by the Lady Selene's death."

"And so Valaire will drive me out of my home
and leave me destitute?"

"As you have heard, my lady, he suggests you
enter a convent. He has been most generous to
allow you a few months' grace."

"Grace? Grace? How dare he?" Isabel picked up
her secretary's inkpot, preparing to throw it at
him. "Go into a convent? That is just what I've
been trying to avoid for the last six years!"

"Please, my lady." The secretary flinched, backing away from the angry woman before him. "I've
done nothing. It's not my fault."

After a moment Isabel lowered the inkpot slowly, thinking, while her secretary breathed a sigh of relief.

Isabel wanted to weep, but she knew only too well that tears would not help her now. What she had to do was see to her own welfare. An idea was forming in her mind.

"A convent," she murmured. "I have heard that King Henry is completely bowed down by grief over his son's death."

"So I have heard, too, my lady," the secretary eagerly affirmed, glad to have Isabel's attention diverted from the inkpot. "They say he sits and stares before him all the day long, weeping, and leaves the business of governing to others."

"But he has roused himself enough to give permission for William Atheling's widow, Alice, to return to her father in Anjou," Isabel added.

"That is true, my lady. She is expected to enter a convent."

"Where? Do you know?"

"I believe it is Fontevrault." The secretary looked at her, his eyes twinkling with humor, for he knew his employer well after many years in her service. And everyone knew about Fontevrault, where a gentle abbess held sway and noble women often went for peaceful retirement from the world of men. Its rule was not strict, its inhabitants were allowed to bring servants with them when they entered, and a fair measure of freedom was accorded to those who lived within its walls. "And which convent will you chose for your retirement, my lady?"

"I will go to her, that poor widow," Isabel said suddenly. "King Henry is too preoccupied to prevent me, and in any case, in Anjou his writ does not run. Alice of Anjou would doubtless appreciate the sincere sympathy of one who has also lost a close family member in that horrible tragedy. We can mourn our losses together. If enter a convent I must, I'll at least do it in good company. You will come with me, of course, master secretary. And all my personal servants. Write to Sir Valaire, tell him I am content to retire from this wicked world, but will need funds, a dowry of some kind to turn over to the Church to assure my good treatment there. Sir Valaire is a religious man, he will not cavil at giving money to the Church."

"And before you are done," the secretary murmured softly, "before you leave this life, you will probably become Mother Abbess yourself."

"Turn punishment to my advantage once more?" Isabel's sharp ears had caught his words. She smiled at him. "Well, I've done it before, have I not? Do you know, master secretary, I had never thought of that kind of advancement until now? But I might do it. Anything is possible."

"So King Henry has married again." Guy frowned. "And she's only eighteen years old to his fifty-three?"

"So Sir Valaire's letter says," Meredith replied, rereading it. "He says, the better to get a new heir to the throne. It's Henry's most pressing need right now. Valaire says Adelicia of Louvain is a gentle young woman who will do her part with kindness toward Henry."

"How sad to be forced to accept pity in one's own bed, from a wife young enough to be a granddaughter." Guy put his arms around his own wife, heedless of the amused glances of squires and servants, not caring one bit that they stood in the inner bailey in full view of everyone. "I'm glad I have you, my love."

Despite her husband's close embrace, Meredith pressed the parchment flat against his chest and continued reading Sir Valaire's letter, for Guy was eager to learn its contents and Reynaud, busy with the new bell tower for the village church, would not be back until nightfall to read it to him.

"Guy, listen to this. Valaire says Henry is coming to Wales later this year. It is expected the Welsh leaders will sign a treaty with him when they meet. It will mean peace, and an end to the raids."

"We may hope so." At the clatter of horses' hooves, Guy momentarily withdrew his attention from his wife to watch two riders passing beneath the castle portcullis, heading through the town and out toward the forest. "There go two more with hope. Thomas is healing at last. I was not happy to see him retreat to Llangwilym Abbey for more than two months. I wanted my son by my side, but I see now he was right to leave us for a while, to finish his mourning for Selene in that way. He told me last night that Father Ambrose, his old teacher at Llangwilym, advised him once more to return to the world. Though from the way he looks at Arianna, I doubt he would have made a very good monk."

Guy had reason to be well content. He believed there would be peace, for a while at least, between England and Wales, and he had had more than enough of raids and border skirmishes. And now nearly all of his family was living at Afoncaer, where he could enjoy them. His three-year-old twins, Oliver and Elise, were healthy youngsters and were growing up rapidly in close company with Thomas's Jocelyn and Deirdre. Thomas himself had come back to Afoncaer from Llangwilym only the day before, and Cristin, whom Guy had missed more than he would admit, would return during the next week, her days of fostering at another castle completed. It was time to find a husband for his older daughter. Thomas had suggested Benet, who, although only the son of a long-dead and impoverished squire, had proven himself as brave and capable as any more nobly born lad. He would make a staunch liege man to Guy, the more so were he bound by family ties. Guy was considering the match, not a little tempted by the thought that Cristin, wed to Benet, would not have to be sent far away from her parents to live. Looking down at his still-beautiful wife and thinking how fortunate they were, Guy chuckled.

"You have told me often enough how much you love children," he said to her. "I have a feeling that this castle will be full of them in years to come."

Arianna's mood as she rode toward the forest with Thomas was an odd mixture of apprehension and intense pleasure at his presence. She had understood his need, just after Selene's death, to remain aloof from her. She had felt the same way. It had taken her weeks to accept the strong emotions of love and guilt that the loss of her kinswoman had evoked. Thomas's decision to retire to Llangwilym Abbey for a time had been perfectly reasonable, but the man who had returned the day before appeared to her much changed. Maturity sat upon Thomas now. He was quiet and sober, self-contained, with occasional sadness in his blue eyes. He had spent much of the previous afternoon and evening alone with Guy, and beyond his first coolly polite greeting, he had not spoken directly to her. Arianna was thrown into confusion and uncertainty by this treatment, and wondered if the monks at Llangwilym had advised him to forswear his guilty love for her as penance, or if perhaps he simply did not love her any more.

And then this morning, as they broke their fast in the great hall, he had asked her to ride with him. Arianna had looked at his serious face and wondered what he planned to say to her. She told herself that if he wanted her to leave Afoncaer she must do so. Whatever the cost to herself, she could not stay and cause him further pain. He had had more than enough to bear in recent years. And so she had come with him, falling into his silent humor, riding beside him without a word.

They had turned off the road and now entered the forest, moving more slowly through trees and underbrush. Arianna temporarily gave up wondering what Thomas's intentions were in her delight at the landscape around them. She loved this forest in every season. Today the first faint greening of spring showed all about them; leaf buds waited to unfurl in the sun's warmth. But they would not yet, for this day was cool, with pale sunlight contending feebly against a thick mist. The tree trunks and branches were black with moisture, and Arianna could hear the constant drip-drop of water in the eerie silence. There were no birds singing, no raucous calling of crows, only the muted sound of their horses' hooves on wet leaves. Arianna felt as though she were in a

365

dream, wandering through a magical forest. They went further and further and the silence grew deeper, and still Thomas said nothing to her.

After a while they came out into a clearing that was bounded on one side by a tumble of heavy, moss-covered boulders, and on the opposite side by one of those tiny streams that in Wales so frequently rise up from springs deep in the rocky hillsides to thread their way over moss and stones until they reach some larger stream or river. Here the mist was thinner, filtering the sun's rays into a soft, pale gold light.

Thomas stopped and dismounted, then helped Arianna to alight. While he looped the horses' reins around a birch sapling so they could not wander away, she walked to the stream, knelt, and drank from it, fresh, clean water, cold with the chill of mountain snow.

"Sit here," Thomas said, taking off his cloak and spreading it upon a flat rock.

Arianna sat, her hands clasped in her lap, watching Thomas toss pebbles into the little stream. He was silent again, frowning, as if he were deciding how to say whatever it was he wanted to tell her. Arianna waited, forcing herself to be patient. But it seemed to her she had been patient all her life, and she wished he would say the words and be done with them—and with her. She was afraid it was her sentence she was waiting for, the order that would send her away from him forever.

At last he came to sit beside her. The rock he had chosen was not very big, and he was crowded against her. The deep blue wool of his sleeve lay against her arm. She looked at his large, strong hands with the tapered fingers.

"Arianna." One of those hands closed over her wrist.

"Yes, my lord." His smoothly shaven face hovered near hers, his eyes darker than his blue cotte.

"My dear friend." Now both of her hands were swallowed up in one of his. She swayed toward him as he lifted her hands and kissed the fingers one by one, but even in her blissful confusion at his closeness and at this sign of tenderness, some portion of her mind noted that he had called her his friend, not his love. She resigned herself to accepting whatever he commanded her to do.

"It's time to tell you the truth," Thomas said. He took a deep breath and began to speak.

She listened in astonishment as he recounted the circumstances of his birth, then went on to speak of the way his marriage to Selene had been planned by Isabel. He left nothing out except the most private details of his nights with Selene. When he had finished, she sat with her hands still clasped in his, staring blindly at the stream as it rushed madly toward its joining with the river.

"So you see," Thomas finished, "I am a bastard, with no rights of inheritance save those my father chooses to give me."

"You said he would keep the secret of your birth," Arianna replied, "and I'll tell no one. It can remain a secret."

"But you do know everything now," Thomas said, "and that knowledge may prejudice your answer. Still, I had to tell you. You have a right to know."

"My answer, my lord?" She was so amazed by what she had just heard that she could not think clearly. She looked at him blankly. "What answer do you want from me? I do not think the less of you, or of Guy, for learning this. He was tricked, and you—you are still Thomas."

"I love you with all my heart, Arianna. Will you marry me?"

"Marry?" She gaped at him. "I cannot marry. I am a penniless orphan. I have no dowry. Guy would not allow it."

"I am an illegitimate son." Thomas laughed, his somber mood breaking, and suddenly there was the old Thomas, smiling warmly at her, teasing her. "There's small difference between us, my love. My father sees no impediment to our marriage. I know, for I have spoken to him. Now all I have to fear is that you will refuse me. Say you'll marry me, Arianna."

"But the dowry," Arianna objected. "It would be unfair to you not to have a dowry."

"You have one," Thomas told her. "Your dowry is love. It's the only true dowry."

This could not be happening. It was a dream, some trick of the magical forest in which they sat. But he had said Guy saw no impediment to their marriage. He had spoken to Guy. Thomas wanted to marry her, and Guy had agreed. Somewhere deep inside her joy began to rise and spread, wiping out all her earlier fears, all doubts, until she could hardly contain her happiness.

"You do still love me, don't you?" Thomas asked anxiously. "I was not mistaken, was I?"

"I love you." She met his eyes and a smile began, lighting up her face with love and happiness. "I'll tell you the truth, as you have just told me. I have loved you since the first moment I saw you at St. Albans. On that day I recognized you at once. You were the man I had seen in my dreams and never hoped to meet, the other half of myself, the only one I could ever love. You are still all of that and more, for I have come to know you, and the reality is finer and more wonderful than any dream I ever had."

"And I was so blind to that love," Thomas said, his bright smile dimming. "And for so long."

"At that time it would have made no difference if you had loved me, too," Arianna told him. "Your course was set. You had no choice but to follow it, to do what had been planned for you, to fulfill the promises made in your name."

"And that course brought me here at last, so late. I'll have no objections raised by you, my lady," he added sternly, though with laughter in his eyes. "There is no time to waste in quibbling over dowries, or who loved whom first. You are twenty-three and like to remain unwed from advanced age unless I do something about your situation, and I am twenty-nine and growing older by the hour. Shall we seize whatever time is left to us, and make what we can of it?"

"What would you like to make, my lord?" she asked demurely.

"Love," he replied, grinning broadly. "Marry me, Arianna."

"At your command, my lord," she whispered.

369

Chapter 21

Arianna had a dowry after all, though a small one. Immediately after she and Thomas returned from their ride and announced their happy news, Guy asked Reynaud to write to Sir Valaire, who was still Arianna's guardian, asking his permission for his ward to marry. Sir Valaire did not respond for so long a time that Arianna began to fear he would refuse to allow her to marry his daughter's widower. She waited with growing tension through all of April and May, until, in the second week of June, Sir Valaire's messenger arrived at last. He came to Afoncaer escorted by a goodly number of Valaire's men-at-arms who were protecting a train of pack horses loaded with furniture, silver plates and cups and trays, a pair of magnificent silver candelabra, and bolts of enough wool and linen fabrics to keep Arianna well clothed for years to come.

"I would not have anyone think that I do not welcome this marriage," Valaire's message explained. "Aloise and I are both fond of Arianna. She will make a good mother to our grandchildren. Let the gifts we send serve as her dowry, and know that we wish her and Thomas a happy life together."

"Well," Guy said, smiling broadly when Reynaud had finished reading the letter, "I see no reason to delay the marriage any longer, do you? Shall we say the middle of next week? Meredith, can you have a suitable feast prepared by then?"

"We've been planning it for more than two months," Meredith responded with some spirit. "Cristin and Blanche and my other ladies have been sewing Arianna's clothes all that time, too. Midweek will be perfect."

For her wedding day Arianna wore a simple gown of palest blue silk. Upon her loosely tumbling brown curls rested a wreath of violets and ferns which Cristin had gathered early that morning and woven with nimble fingers into a delicate coronet more becoming to Arianna than the finest gold circlet would have been.

Since no holdings of land or castles were involved, the marriage contract was brief, but it was read by Reynaud in a voice so full of warmth and affection for the two people standing before him that most of the witnesses in the chapel dabbed at their eyes. After the contract had been signed or sealed by everyone there, Reynaud stepped aside so the village priest could bless the marriage and say the mass. Then it was time to stand upon the topmost step just outside the entrance to the keep, to show themselves to all the folk of castle and village, who were to have their own feast on the village green.

Arianna moved through that warm, early summer day with calm assurance. It was not until evening, when she was in her own small room, with Cristin helping her to undress and Meredith toss-

371

ing sweet-scented herbs into a tub of warm water for her bath while Blanche laid out her night-clothes, that she began to feel a twinge of nervousness.

"There's a surprise for you," Cristin whispered, her pretty face shining with excitement. "I hope you will like it, Arianna. I did all of it. Thomas asked me—oh, dear, I wasn't supposed to tell, was I?"

"It's all right," Meredith assured her, smiling. "Hand me that linen towel, Cristin. Let's dry Arianna off before she catches a chill. It's time to take her to Thomas."

They covered her suddenly trembling form with a sheer, white linen gown embroidered around its wide neckline with little blue flowers and green leaves. They wrapped her into a pale green woolen robe. All three dear friends embraced and kissed her. And then they led her out of her virginal room and took her to the finest guest chamber in the castle, on the level just below the lord's chamber.

"Thomas thought you should begin your new lives in a room neither of you has ever used before," Meredith explained, opening the door. "Thomas's old room will become a guest chamber now."

The double windows in the wall niche faced west, looking out over the place where the stream joined the river. Opposite the windows was a large carved bed hung with cream wool, the coverlet turned back a little to reveal the new linen sheets Meredith had promised Arianna she would provide as a wedding gift. Blanche hastened to draw the cream wool curtains across the windows and light dozens of Meredith's finest wax candles. Their golden glow chased the evening shadows away, so Arianna could see what she had begun to sense with the first breath she had taken within that room.

The room was filled with flowers. Sprays of pink and white roses decked the mantel and sprouted from baskets set into the fireplace opening, where logs would blaze when winter came. Clove-scented gillyflowers and sprigs of sweet woodruff spilled from pitchers. Lavender lay strewn across the floor, while cuttings of pot marigolds, rosemary, and spearmint had been stuffed into small baskets and set on the seats in the window niche, from where their fragrance mingled with the scent of the roses. Other baskets placed about the room held ferns with small white daisies and blue forget-me-nots. And in every corner, on the floor or on tables, there were baskets and pitchers and large crocks filled with roses.

"I've never seen anything so lovely," Arianna whispered, "nor smelled anything so heavenly. Meredith, you must have robbed your gardens to do all this, and taken all the baskets from the still-room, too."

"It was Cristin's doing," Meredith replied. "This is the surprise, her gift to you and Thomas. She rose at dawn to pick the flowers."

Arianna could not speak. Her heart was too full for words, but she put her arms around Cristin, hugging the girl tightly, to express her gratitude. She saw in Cristin's eyes that her feelings were understood.

Thomas appeared at the chamber door, wrapped in a blue woolen robe and surrounded by men, Guy and Geoffrey, who had come from Tynant for the occasion, Kenelm and Benet, and a few of the men-at-arms who were Thomas's closest friends.

The men did not enter the room at first, but simply stood in the doorway looking at the flowers and the bed, their joking laughter stilled into silence by that scene of flowering beauty.

Arianna trembled and blushed, nearly overcome by happiness and a sudden rush of nervousness, until Thomas stepped forward to take her hand. At the loving pressure of his fingers all her nervousness fled so she was able to smile into his blue eyes with complete love and trust.

"When we were wed," Guy spoke softly, "it was winter and there were no flowers."

"There was love," Meredith responded, going toward her husband, her eyes on his still-handsome face. "That was enough."

"We must see them bedded." The voice of the always-practical Blanche effectively broke the tender mood that had momentarily held two couples entranced.

Now the men came in, treading carefully, as if they feared to disturb the fragile blossoms that filled the room. Blanche and Cristin removed Arianna's woolen robe. Meredith helped her onto the high bed, and Arianna sat on top of the coverlet. Shivering a little in her delicate nightdress, she watched Guy and Geoffrey strip Thomas of his robe and push him onto the bed so they sat there together before all the witnesses.

Meredith kissed Arianna one more time, then leaned across her to kiss Thomas. And then suddenly the room was empty and quiet. Thomas got out of bed, quickly covering his nakedness with his blue robe.

"I asked Blanche to leave a pitcher of wine here," he said, pouring a little into a silver goblet. "I noticed you scarcely ate or drank all day."

He sat down beside her on the bed, handing her the goblet. Arianna sipped, tasting the herbs she and Meredith had put into the wine the day before, recognizing each herb, seeing in her mind's eye the bee hives in Meredith's garden from which they had taken the honey.

"You are far away," Thomas accused her with loving tenderness.

"I was gathering honey to sweeten your wine," she replied.

"It needs no honey. It's sweetened enough from the touch of your lips." He took the goblet from her, turning it until he could place his mouth on it where hers had been. His eyes never left her face as he drank.

Arianna raised one hand and lightly touched his face. When her fingers reached his lips he nibbled at them, and before she knew what was happening one of her fingers was inside his mouth and he was sucking on it gently, his tongue stroking around it.

She sat staring at him, immobilized by the sensation of his tongue on her finger, just barely aware that he had put down the wine goblet. Her finger was still in his mouth, and each time he sucked on it something happened to her, some new and exciting heat raced along her veins, turning her bones and muscles to liquid.

"Stand up a moment," Thomas whispered, letting her finger go at last.

"I can't." She knew her knees would never hold her. She felt much too weak to stand, yet at the same time, stronger than the bravest warrior and completely unafraid of him.

Thomas understood. He gathered her into his arms and lifted her off the bed. Holding her up with one arm, he pulled down the coverlet and the linen top sheet.

"Cristin!" He began to laugh. Arianna had been gazing at his beloved face. Now she looked down to see the source of his sudden mirth.

Pink and white rose petals and branches of lavender had been scattered across the lower sheet.

"When I said I'd like a few flowers in our room," Thomas informed her, still laughing, "I didn't mean in our bed, too. Cristin always was overenthusiastic."

"I think it's lovely," Arianna murmured, resting her head on his shoulder. "They smell wonderful."

"But this might scratch you." Thomas pulled out a long piece of lavender, then found another. "We had better remove all the lavender before we get into bed."

"I think you are right." Arianna was out of his embrace, reaching across the bed, picking up the stiff branches. "Cristin did this with love, Thomas."

"I know. You needn't worry; I've no plans to scold her."

By the time they had gathered all the lavender, the coverlet and top sheet had been pushed down to the foot of the bed to reveal the full extent of soft pink rose petals which drifted all across the bed. Thomas took the lavender branches from Arianna's hands and scattered them onto the floor. He let his robe drop to the floor, too, before he turned to face her.

He was so beautiful. He was all she had ever dreamed of or wanted. His tall, firm-muscled body was perfect to her eyes. His golden hair shone in the candlelight, his blue gaze held her a happy prisoner.

He picked her up again, holding her close for a moment before he laid her down upon the new linen sheets and the fragrant petals. He stretched out beside her in the perfumed atmosphere of their marriage bed. And then, at last, he kissed her. His mouth caressed hers gently at first, until Arianna herself deepened the kiss by opening her lips. His tongue plunged into her with a sudden fiery burst of passion. She welcomed him, giving back her own awakening desire.

His hands were on her body. Thomas had never touched her like this before, not in their brief stolen embraces while he still belonged to another, nor later, when he might have done as he wanted because she was promised to him. He had carefully kept his distance during their two months' betrothal, and now she knew why. It was because if he had touched her, if he had put his hands on her breasts as he was doing now, or kissed her throat while her head was thrown back across his arm, or stroked along her back, or caressed her legs in just this way, she would have done what she was doing now. She would have let her legs fall open and moaned while he kissed her knees and thighs. She would have begun to touch him, too, with her hands running through the crisp hair on his wide chest and across his shoulders and then down his back when he leaned over her to kiss her hungry mouth once more.

If he had touched her before this night they would have made love at once. They would not have been able to stop themselves, and then this precious, sacred night could not have happened. But Thomas had known, and had kept himself from her until the time was right for them to come together.

He kissed every inch of her delicately trembling body. He told her over and over again how deeply he loved her. And she responded with all the tenderness and passion she had hidden for so many years.

"I love you," he whispered, nibbling at her fingers again, then slowly working his way across her palm to her wrist and up her arm to her shoulder. She was close to fainting from the exquisite tension he had generated when he stopped—to begin again, on her other arm this time.

"You are my very heart." She could just barely hear his words, for his face was buried between her breasts, and his hands—ah, his hands! And his mouth! She did cry out then, and reached for him, but he had moved away.

"My darling." His mouth was on her cheek, his voice a broken, husky whisper in her ear. "Please stop what you're doing. Take your hands away. I don't want to hurt you, but if you continue I'll lose all control. Arianna, you must stop."

She realized then that all the time he had been touching her, she had been caressing him in return, though she had not been fully aware of what she was doing, and she knew with a deep, feminine instinct that he was poised on the very edge of a wild, loving madness. She knew it because she felt close to madness herself. But she had to reassure him, had to let him know he could do anything and she would accept him with all the love she felt for him.

"You wouldn't hurt me," she whispered, pulling him nearer. "Thomas." His name on her tongue was a sigh of deep longing, a last faint echo of the time when he had not been hers to love.

He heard that echo and knew it in his own heart. He pulled her closer still, pressing himself against her. She yielded, opening to him with a happiness that filled her soul and heart.

Arianna gave a soft, choked gasp. Thomas breathed a deep, long sigh, and they were one. As her instant of slight distress passed, Arianna looked into her husband's eyes and knew they would never be separate again. She knew now what consummation meant. It was this fulfillment, this joyful union with her beloved Thomas, and it was worth everything they had both had to endure in order to reach this moment. And she knew something more: it would never end. Indeed, it would grow deeper and richer with every day, with every year that passed. The singing fire in her veins, the closeness of his warm body, and the spiraling delight she now experienced were all because of Thomas. She cried out his name in a breathy whisper and gave herself up to love.

She wakened far into the night, when the setting full moon was sending streaks of silver light across the bedroom floor. The sheet had been pulled up to her shoulders to ward off any chill. Arianna turned over, opening her eyes. She saw Thomas standing by the windows, pulling back the woolen curtains and opening the shutters. It was the sudden light that had wakened her. She slid out of bed and went to him, treading along a path of moonlight and lavender. His arms enfolded her, and they stood watching the moon and listening to the sounds of woods and stream and the soft footfalls of the guards patrolling the castle walls.

There was no need for words. They had loved each other well and fully opened their hearts to each other, and Arianna knew it would always be so. They stayed together in contented peace, Thomas's arms around her, keeping her warm and safe within the circle of their strength.

"Guy will send us to Kelsey next week," Thomas said after a long, quiet moment.

"Away from Afoncaer?" Arianna drew back a little, the better to see his face in the moonlight. He was laughing down at her.

"It's only for a short time," he said. "The seneschal at Kelsey is old and needs to be replaced. I'm to see to his retirement and the choosing of a new man, while you are to supervise improvements in the domestic arrangements. I think Guy believed we would enjoy a few weeks away from family and close friends, time to ourselves before we take up our usual duties again. We must be back at Afoncaer before King Henry comes to Wales in late summer."

"King Henry," Arianna murmured. "I remember the morning when he knighted you. I thought then that you were the most handsome man I had ever seen. I know now that you are without a doubt the finest knight he ever made. You are all that a knight should be, Thomas."

"Once I wanted to be a perfect knight. I dreamed of it all through my boyhood," Thomas said. He laughed again, ruefully. "I am not perfect, as you will learn, my dear wife, after you have lived with me a bit."

"We shall have sons," Arianna told him, "boys like you. And one or two daughters, like Cristin.

Meredith has told me about you when you were little."

"Lies, every word of it," he teased. Then, "Daughters, with your spirit and gentleness. And your enduring love. We'll make Afoncaer a happy place, Arianna, not just for the Normans, but for the Welsh on our lands, too. For years I've wanted a wife I could love as Guy loves Meredith, and now at last I have one." He kissed her, a long, deep, tender kiss that turned into something more than tenderness.

"You smell of roses," he said when he had caught his breath again.

"So do you, my gentle knight," Arianna murmured as he picked her up and carried her back to their bed.

Those who went about their business in the great hall of Afoncaer that morning noted with knowing, understanding smiles that Thomas and his beloved lady did not leave their chamber until the day was nearly done.

WIVES, LIES AND DOUBLE LIVES

MISTRESSES ($4.50, 17-109)

By Trevor Meldal-Johnsen

Kept women. Pampered females who have everything: designer clothes, jewels, furs, lavish homes. They are the beautiful mistresses of powerful, wealthy men. A mistress is a man's escape from the real world, always at his beck and call. There is only one cardinal rule: *do not fall in love*. Meet three mistresses who live in the fast lane of passion and money, and who know that one wrong move can cost them everything.

ROYAL POINCIANA ($4.50, 17-179)

By Thea Coy Douglass

By day she was Mrs. Madeline Memory, head housekeeper at the fabulous Royal Poinciana. Dressed in black, she was a respectable widow and the picture of virtue. By night she the French speaking "Madame Memphis", dressed in silks and sipping champagne with con man Harrison St. John Loring. She never intended the game to turn into true love . . .

WIVES AND MISTRESSES ($4.95, 17-120)

By Suzanne Morris

Four extraordinary women are locked within the bitterness of a century old rivalry between two prominent Texas families. These heroines struggle against lies and deceptions to unlock the mysteries of the past and free themselves from the dark secrets that threaten to destroy both families.

NON-FICTION FROM PINNACLE BOOKS

ZONE THERAPY   (17-208, $3.95)
by Anika Bergson and Vladimir Tuchak
For the first time, here is a layman's guide that pulls together all the systems of direct-pressure therapy on key parts of the body, including acupuncture, foot-and-hand reflexology, finger message . . . and much more! Zone therapy is simple, easy to learn and use. And anyone can do it!

THE POPCORN PLUS DIET   (17-065, $3.50)
by Joel Herskowitz, M.D.
By sticking to Dr. Herskowitz's painless and nutritious 21-day meal plan and curbing those annoying pangs of hunger with hot, tasty popcorn, you can lose up to two pounds a week. The Popcorn-Plus Diet is doctor-devised, medically tested, and nutritionalist-approved.

THE RELATIVITY OF WRONG   (17-169, $3.95)
by Isaac Asimov
There is no scientific region too remote nor area inaccessible to the probing pen of Isaac Asimov. In this, his remarkable twenty-fourth collection of astonishing real-life wonders, the good doctor carries the reader on a breathtaking rollercoaster ride that races from the center of the human brain to the outer reaches of the universe.

Available wherever paperbacks are sold, or order direct from the Publisher. Send cover price plus 50¢ per copy for mailing and handling to Pinnacle Books, Dept.17-411, 475 Park Avenue South, New York, N.Y. 10016. Residents of New York, New Jersey and Pennsylvania must include sales tax. DO NOT SEND CASH.